BURIED VALUES:

THE TREASURE

JOSHUA ADAM WEISELBERG

To Wil,

Josh Adam Weiselberg

6-24-22

BURIED VALUES: The Treasure
Copyright © 2014 Joshua Adam Weiselberg
ISBN 978-0-9913732-9-1

Published by Buried Values Media Group

Cover painting by Monte Moore, Maverick Arts, www.mavarts.com
Editing by Andrew Wetzel, Stumptown Editorial, www.stumptowneditorial.com/
Interior formatting by Yvonne Betancourt, www.ebook-format.com
Exterior design by Linda Boulanger, http://telltalebookcovers.weebly.com/
Legal representation by Steins & Associates, http://steins-patents.com/
with Special Thanks to Laura Taylor
The Old Town Temecula Gunfighters
The 69th Pennsylvania Infantry re-enactors

This book contains multiple references which are graphically violent, misogynistic, racist, and that disparage common practices of mainstream religions, and reference the dereliction of military duty. While these incidents do not necessarily reflect the views or preferences of the author, *they are meant to be highly offensive or distasteful to the reader*. It is the author's hope that each individual reader will recognize buried values within themselves and develop a better manner in which to view the world and conduct themselves towards others they will encounter in it, than do the characters within the following pages. This is a tale of reprehensible people and *their* true buried values.

www.BuriedValues.com

4

being there, is to assassinate his entire family. However, nothing can go as planned, when entering into this competition will be Arnold Rothstein, Babe Ruth, and Al Capone – while always fighting to stay alive, will be everyone's true buried values. And then the signal's given for the next player on-deck.

BURIED VALUES: The Fall – *The Rookies make the plays in a lot of extra innings that the Cubs were surely never planning on. Now in the middle of their killer 1918 season, Taddeo Villetti is murder on the mound serving up his special kind of cutters and Arlene Masterson will be the mother of all vengeance on the streets. The fire for women's rights has turned into a one-woman vicious crossburn that can run from the cornfields of the Midwest to the corrupt Congress in the capitol. And the Villetti Family with its part in gambling, drug dealing, and Big Jim Colosimo's bordellos is right in its path of devastation. And there's no going back to how things used to be, especially with Arnold Rothstein's agents on hand to practice their particular brand of playing hardball. Dark money is lining all the wrong people's pockets. Now Taddeo is a man who's losing control and can only hope he has enough balls to be that one pitcher who can finish the game. He struggles to form an alliance with Johnny Torrio's enforcer the young Al Capone while his last true love is torn between strengthening her ties to the infamous suffragette Katherine McCormick or The Windy City's favorite Madam, Victoria Moresco, ally of the fledgling Outfit. Blood's being let into the Chicago River from Little Italy to Rogers Park and in its backwards flow it is painting everyone's true buried values in red. And now it is the new players' turn to witness some strikes up close. But all it will take is one now-veteran man to be called off the bench, for he to become the real game-changer.*

BURIED VALUES: The Library – *In 2016, several young women's futures will hang on the choices these rivals make in a deadly hunt for Civil War treasure so valuable, that as evidence, it's powerful enough to end a government insider conspiracy to take over control of Homeland Security – or see to it that the plot succeeds! Entering the adventure, are over a half-dozen men with special skills ranging from officers of the law, politicians, gangsters, the daring archaeologist Dr. Darren Hughes, and LSU freshman, Tony Porter, who's just smitten with the ladies. At stake is the highly profitable fast and furious flow of guns going south and drugs flowing north, and one woman's mission to*

5

foil the restructuring of a new Villetti crime family that's forming some very dangerous alliances south of the U.S. border. Going down amidst all the sex trafficking, prohibited weapons exchanges, illegal immigration, and the ever-present corruption in the failed war with the Mexican drug cartels – and with the shootings of police officers, clashes between the races, and the U.S. Presidential Election all in the mix – is a nail-biting mystery who the triumphant femme fatale really is, and how Naomi or Davina will react when in the aftermath of the Gulf's catastrophic flooding, the survivor's tempted with an unexpected and irresistible opportunity to take full control over everything! Now the past continues to haunt not just the true heirs of the bounty – but instead, its influence runs full circle back into the swirling winds of just one more very real hurricane that's bearing down, in tandem with one political maelstrom that no one foresaw – to join forces so as to blow the entire cover off of our whole country's true buried values – in our present.

BURIED VALUES: The Recovery – *In the shocking sequel to Buried Values: The Library, will it be Naomi or Davina who has survived to now have to attempt to run the new Louisiana Mafia? The young woman will form the uncomfortable but necessary alliances that might barely keep her afloat in what's left of a sinking criminal empire, trying to rebuild in hurricane devastated flood lands. There's no electricity, no chance to call for any help, not even many roads still above water, and there will be no rescue coming for quite a long time. It is only the worst of the prison gangs – who escaped drowning behind bars – who now rise to surface and seek to satiate their all-consuming thirst for revenge – who can still hold even the slightest grip on any tangible real power. A shaky alliance with the street boss Demetrius Lamont appears to be the only way to push on and complete one thoroughly-soul-consuming quest for a fortune in lost treasure, now the sole currency of any real authority. But who will turn on whom first? One young woman, now ultimately corrupted, will relentlessly compete to capture unimaginable reserves of the real kind of tender she'll need to secure her status as power shifts drastically in America, following the wake of the controversial 2016 Presidential Election. What are the real values which lie beneath the surface, waiting for her to find? And could they save a lot more people from dying? The legacy of Buried Values continues – but only for the last carriers of enough personal fortitude to still remain breathing, when everything else purportedly held dear, seems destined to drown!*

6

Find Buried Values online at **www.BuriedValues.com**
for exclusive story excerpts, book tour news,
and the Buried Values store.
T-shirts, hats, and posters are now available!

Like Buried Values on Facebook:
www.Facebook.com/BuriedValues
for exclusive videos, contests, and up-to-the-minute news
about live battle reenactment shows!

Follow Buried Values on www.Twitter.com/BuriedValues

It's hoped that aspiring storytellers might find useful writing tips
and stimulating debates online at all the official Buried Values
social media sources.

BURIED VALUES:

THE TREASURE

*"We never wanted to fight for the Blue or the Gray.
We fight for our Gold and our Silver!"*

– Captain Daniel Winthrop, USA, May 1862,
Baton Rouge, LA

Chapter 1

Summer 1860 – near Athens, Georgia:

The peacefulness broke with a furious rustling of leaves. Dozens of crows were unsettled by an unseen threat. They burst into the blue sky in every direction, but the large, ugly vultures stayed in their tree to feast on the dead they knew would soon arrive. An intense and eerie silence settled over the green landscape. The only audible sounds that remained were the tearing of paper cartridges, the powder they contained being poured into muskets, and the ramrods making metal scrape against metal, ammunition being packed in tight for a kill. A short distance away a horse snorted. A hand signal was conveyed by one of many armed civilians, and they advanced their long range weapons from well-coordinated forward lines. Assembled in strong tactical positions, hidden by trees and down the slopes of tiny ravines lining either side of the dirt road, the men waited.

The ground seemed to shake from the rumble of dozens of hooves traveling at a full gallop; the scraping noises of metal parts swinging off of other metal hooks grew in strength. As the sounds drew closer, the vultures shifted anxiously in their tree. Then the definitive squeaking of spinning wagon wheels reached the setting for the attack. The hammers on the weapons of the ambush party clicked as their owners cocked the instruments of destruction, ready to release the first barrage.

Over the crest of a slightly inclined, grassy slope, the slouched hats of the first riders appeared, heading straight into the forthcoming field of fire. One of the men in the lead employed hand signals to direct his companion ahead of his position. The second rider charged forward along with several other horsemen, drawing six-shooters as they took in the sight of the forested area on the trail ahead of them. They advanced, well aware that they rapidly approached the perfect site for an ambush. More riders appeared after them until at last two covered wagons had completely crested the slope and started to make their descent.

The leader of the ambush party made a quick chopping motion with his arm and all hell broke loose. Red and yellow bursts of light flashed between the trees, the smoke instantly engulfing the attackers as dozens of long range arms unleashed their loads. A hailstorm of mini-balls flew across the horizon and tore into the oncoming horsemen's ranks. The men under assault returned shots. A crackling like that made by a huge forest fire roared with great intensity while the formation on horseback broke apart and the lead launched from everywhere at once. Men fell from their mounts on either side of their forward-most leader, but the young man steadied himself and jerked his mount ninety degrees to the right and rode straight for the tree line, firing his pistol. Though difficult to see through the gun smoke that hung around the base of the trees, an arm was caught reaching out, firing the weapon it thrust into the sky before its owner collapsed, taking a fatal hit.

Bonnie was shot several times. The round that struck her skull sounded like a walnut being cracked open. The shots she took in her neck and side resembled a side of beef being slapped down on a cutting block as the musket balls displaced tissue and blood. At least death was almost quick for her, but she was hurling forward at a full gallop when she fell.

Christopher Pratt, thrown from his saddle, landed face down on the dirt path in front of his mount. Bonnie's momentum carried her forward onto him. The impact of her bulk slamming into him drove the air from his lungs. She should have crushed him, but Pratt's luck held, and he sank into some soft mud beneath the trail. A faithful steed to the end, Bonnie's body also provided cover for Pratt as the men from his cavalry unit took heavy fire. As more and more were hit, men screamed all around him. But Bonnie had also effectively trapped Pratt. He could do nothing to help his comrades between inhaling the dust of the road, drowning in the groundwater, tasting horse-sweat from the air, and slowly becoming soaked in the animal's blood. He strained just to give his nose and mouth the access needed to breathe.

Concerned for his men, a panicked Pratt continued struggling to free himself. Seconds later, his anxiety heightened as Captain Lennox was gunned down right before his eyes. His superior was shaken off his own mount, as the steed tripped over Bonnie's carcass. Ordinarily, he'd have been thankful to be spared listening to Bonnie's wheezing final breaths, but the deafening gunfire erupted all around him, stung his ears and left them ringing as if someone had clobbered him on both sides of his head. Pratt's men and their horses continued to fall, corralled into the kill zone by constant weapons fire coming in from every angle.

Clutching at the dark red stain under his white shirt and brown vest with his left hand, Captain Lennox used his right arm to drag himself through the dirt, closing on Pratt's side. In his mid-twenties and not much older than Pratt, Lennox looked deathly pale, almost ancient, as he collapsed near his subordinate officer. He was dying. "Lieutenant…," he gasped.

"Sir?"

"Do you hear that? They're not local militia or there'd be some pause in their fire while they reload. But now they're pouring it on from revolving chamber weapons – they're armed professional soldiers! It's an ambush and they don't mean to leave any survivors." Pain glazed his eyes, but he continued, "I'm hit bad. You're going to have to take command. Can you move?"

Bullets flew past them. The sickening sound of slapping meat came to their ears as Bonnie's carcass took additional hits from low flying rounds. Her blood splattered Pratt's face and decorated Lennox's neatly trimmed beard.

"I don't know." Shell-shocked and frightened, it hadn't occurred to Pratt to attempt to get up, let alone stand in the path of a hailstorm of bullets. But that wasn't his immediate concern. After an attempt to shift free of Bonnie, he knew the truth. "Sir, I'm pinned under my horse."

"Get your ass free, Lieutenant. That's an order! Just survive three more days and you'll reach Montgomery. Buchannan's men could persuade the South against seceding, then we'd stop the real war before it's even started."

A musket ball slammed into the center of Lennox's back. His body violently jerked forward, causing him to spit blood onto

13

Pratt's tanned hide jacket and drool over a flintlock pistol attached to his belt. It came loose as Lennox clawed at the dirt, trying to pull himself forward so that his body could shield Pratt's from incoming fire. "Lieutenant...,"

"We're running out of ammunition!" someone shouted.

"Too late! They got the ambassadors," another man cried.

Lieutenant Pratt heard a sergeant trying to rally the men to dismount and charge a single position of the ambush to claim the attackers' cover in the trees for their own. The answering volley of shots fired suggested that the tactic had been deployed, but Pratt already knew the inevitable outcome in this new age of warfare with modern revolver weapons.

"It sounds like the Rebel spies did their job. We were betrayed, and they're outfitted for a slaughter," Lennox remarked, eyes half-closed and his voice replete with sadness and regret. Making one final attempt to protect Pratt, the Captain managed to cover his lieutenant just as another musket ball smacked into the back of his skull, splattering brain tissue out around the edges of the wound. Something sharp cut into Pratt's cheek just beneath his eye, and the sour taste of iron filled his mouth. Lennox never uttered another word.

It ended not long after it had begun. Lt. Pratt heard the footsteps and approaching voices of his enemies as he lay pinned between his dead horse and the still warm body of his dead commanding officer. He couldn't make out most of his attackers' words, his ears still ringing from the gunfire, but the glances he risked confirmed that some of them held rifled muskets, while many others carried revolvers. None wore uniforms. They wore instead civilian work clothes, like farmers' coveralls. An illusion. Pratt could tell by their discipline and armaments that his enemies were indeed professional soldiers.

At first glance the remains of his own cavalry unit could have also been mistaken for civilians. A little less than a fifth of a regular company, barely twenty men, they were also out of uniform. They'd been escorting a two-wagon train occupied by several gentlemen, and the entire group resembled plantation owners who were accompanied by their work hands. But upon closer inspection, their boots and sidearms matched those of the Federal Cavalry. The gentlemen were President Buchanan's ambassadors, each man now with a bullet in his head.

Their aggressors had known what they were doing. Some players at the table really wanted a war, and there was plenty of maneuvering going on in secrecy to see to it that they'd get one. The enemy stalked through the bodies of the fallen, one taking a musket with a bayonet from one of his comrades and systematically driving it deep into each of the dead to confirm their kills. A soldier periodically cried out as his body was pierced, to be followed by a shot fired into his skull. Pratt held his breath, wishing he hadn't lost his gun as a pair of boots circled the corpses of his horse and Captain Lennox. Pratt prayed he wouldn't be discovered by his enemy.

The bayonet came down hard, slicing through his commanding officer's back. It penetrated Lennox's shoulder blade and poked out through the dead man's chest, just nicking Pratt through his shirt. Fortunately, the blade wasn't driven deeply enough to significantly pierce a second body. Pratt couldn't help but wince, but he also couldn't be spotted from the angle at which his enemy stood. Pratt kept as quiet as possible. His bored tormentor never noticed him. The other man moved on, glancing at what remained of Bonnie, a "Guess you can't really beat a dead horse," remark thrown over his shoulder. The action completed, the aggressors began to descend from the adrenaline rush of battle.

"Should we look after the bodies of our own, Sir?" a man asked as Pratt's hearing began to improve. A few of the attackers had been killed in the ambush, but the impact on their force had been minimal as the Northerners were less able shots on horseback than their Southern counterparts. "Give 'em a Christian burial?"

"No," an older, sunburned man with a thin beard answered. "Let whoever finds the remains of this think it was an attack by bandits and robbers, or other less-than-principled men. Sometimes, we must do the despicable in order to serve a higher cause. We've completed our mission here. Time to move out."

The man in command approached Pratt's hidden position. Pratt felt unnerved when he lost sight of his enemy's leader, only able to focus on his boots, *a curiously pricey pair at that*, he realized.

"Collect ammunition from the dead and commandeer any rideable mount. God knows they owe us more than that. Take their weapons too. Then to your horses." Their captain continued, "Lieutenant, collect any officers' swords, search the wagons for their papers, and take their money holders. Bring everything forward."

From his very limited field of vision, Pratt saw another pair of boots running towards the enemy commander's position. "Hold on right there, Captain! I didn't know you were going to smoke everyone."

"I told you I'd take you along to show you just how I was going to use that little bit of information you provided me," the Rebel officer calmly responded.

The other man fell quiet, as if pausing to collect his thoughts for a moment. He then found his comeback. "Well, I need to be paid extra for *this*. Ten dollars more. I'll give it to Masterson to assure his silence."

"Go to hell. No more deals. When we captured you, you seemed an enterprising man from whom I could acquire information. Then I granted your wish and allowed your man to survive your President's last ill-fated mission. As far as I'm concerned, that was generous enough, and a serious breach of security for my mission. Now you want to be paid more? Take a good look around you, Lieutenant. All I need to do is give the order, and my men will cut you down where you stand."

"Any of them who try chance going with me *wherever* I may be headed," the newcomer shot back. "Your offer's still not good enough for all of this." He spoke in a very bold and confident voice as he adjusted his stance for a better tactical position.

So that is the traitorous officer who sold us out and caused this travesty, Pratt thought. If he lived, he knew least one name: Masterson. He now wished he could see the face of the other man!

"You're not getting any more money off of me," the enemy captain retorted.

"How about those boots of yours? For my pain and suffering?" the traitor countered, his tone conveying the pretense of humor. Pratt imagined the traitor pointing at the captain's expensive footwear.

"My alligator hide boots are worth far more than ten dollars, Lieutenant. Are you going to give them to your man Masterson?" He laughed.

"What I do with them is my business. For now, it will be your boots or your life, *Sir*," he said, a nasty edge to his voice. Pratt assumed the newcomer was armed, his hand resting on his holstered revolver. "Your men will shoot me before I can leave, we both know that. But once you go down, what happens after that won't really matter much now, will it? Take off the boots, Captain. I have a new pair that will fit you."

The senior officer sighed with resignation as he kicked off his boots and they landed with a thud at the newcomer's feet. "Thank you, Captain. A pleasure doing business with you."

Pratt watched a hand reach down and grab the boots. They disappeared in one quick motion. The resulting shadow spinning about, shrinking from view.

Soon Lt. Pratt heard the fading footfalls of his enemies, their steps scraping against the dirt as they marched away from the ambush carnage to retrieve their own horses. He remained perfectly still, the hot Georgia summer sun beating down on him. Sweat and blood caused his shirt to cling to his battered body. Trying to distract himself, he studied a patch of grass that had rooted itself in the center of the trail. He forced himself to ignore the blood that slowly seeped from Lennox's body, which still covered part of him, and the crushing force of Bonnie's weight.

Pratt was too scared to move for some time. He worried he'd be found still alive by his enemies. He also couldn't be sure he didn't have one or more broken bones. When buzzards started to circle overhead, he knew it wouldn't be long before they descended on the fresh kills. He didn't want to be around to make a live meal for them. Pratt tried to move again.

After he rolled his captain's lifeless body aside, Pratt found he couldn't extract himself from beneath his dead horse. He exhaled in anguish as he made yet another effort to work himself free. He experienced a shaft of pain in his back as he tried to use his free arm to shift his weight. Pratt clenched his teeth as bit by bit he clawed his way out from under Bonnie. The soil, soft and giving way to his efforts, had previously given way just enough to leave him mostly uninjured. Otherwise, his horse's weight would have crushed him. A huge buzzard landed on Bonnie, the wicked carrion bird burying its beak in one of the many bullet holes that felled her. Its full head resurfaced with a piece of bloody flesh in its beak. Pratt became even more anxious, kept struggling, and finally freed the upper part of his body. He rested, breathing heavily. Turning his head he spent the time staring down the ugly bird. As well, he reflected on his current situation which was also just plain ugly and would only become more so. Anger fueled his ability to ignore his pain as he pulled himself the rest of the way out from under Bonnie.

Pratt could tell by the position of the sun that it was late afternoon. His shadow seemed to unsettle the bird as he cautiously stood up. If the cruel bird was startled, it was only for a moment. Not terribly intimidated, the scavenging creature seemed faintly disappointed that the human wouldn't be sticking around to become the carrion bird's dessert. If Pratt had a loaded gun, he'd have shot the damned thing he reflected, even if the action alerted his adversaries that he'd survived the ambush.

Pratt's survival was foremost in his mind as he began to search the bodies of his slain comrades. He began with Captain Lennox. He knew the boys had all been stripped of their six-shooters, but he remembered that the captain also favored carrying that old-style flintlock pistol that he'd bragged had been in his family for over one hundred years. Lennox had thought it brought him good luck. His assailants had taken the rounds for the weapon, but they'd missed it where both the weapon and its ramrod had fallen off the captain's belt. The man who'd searched the fallen command officer must have either never seen it beneath his crumpled body, or considered the pistol too outdated to be of any use and had no appreciation for the value of an antique. For now it would have to do. Pratt needed protection, although an unloaded gun wouldn't be of much help.

He closed his eyes shuddering at the thought of what he needed to do next. He examined his commanding officer's body, now sprawled on his back. Pratt drew his utility knife with one hand, slid the other one beneath Lennox, to the fatal entry wound in his back, and approximated where that same region of the dead man was located on the other side of his body. Pratt plunged his knife into his fallen leader's chest, widening the wound. Blood bubbled inside the cavity as he hit the heart. Ripping open the flesh even more, he buried his hands in the man's insides until he found a chunk of metal amongst soft tissue. He jerked his hands free, completely soaked in blood, and frowned as he tossed aside a spent cartridge bullet. Rolling Lennox over on his left side, Pratt repeated his excavation procedure on the captain's shoulder wound. This time he hit bone and found nothing he could use.

Rising, Pratt began to search the other bodies of his fallen comrades in the same gruesome manner. He didn't particularly relish fighting the buzzards for the horse remains, which must have been more attractive for the birds due to the animals' stench and size. Plus, Pratt knew the rounds could be deeply buried and, therefore, much harder to locate in the animals' dense flesh. Still in a state of shock, his hearing intermittently impaired, his body hurting him smartly, and feeling pressed for time in vacating the morbid site, the young lieutenant made haste.

He kicked a stubborn buzzard off of Sgt. Cush. It departed with the sergeant's eyeball. Beneath the grotesque hole in the man's face, Pratt picked at another hole in his chest, found a conical .44 caliber slug, and wiped the blood off of it as best as he could before depositing it into his utility pouch on his belt. This round, perhaps expanded some by having been fired, nevertheless possessed an almost perfect form. It should prove reusable in a larger caliber weapon like Lennox's old flintlock, Pratt hoped. He continued his excavation of the dead, sometimes requiring a greater longitudinal cut so that he could crack apart their ribs and reach the fatal round left inside the soft insides of each of the fallen. They all had names and faces. Pratt knew and had served with many of them for at least the past year, and a little longer in several cases. He accumulated thirteen rounds from the bodies, but that was no guarantee that Pratt would even be able to fire that many with the spilled gunpowder from wasted cartridges that had been left behind. He scraped up the powder, tucking it back into the paper he resealed. Then Pratt, in a state of shock over what he had done, took one final, mournful glance at Bonnie before he lunged away from the grisly scene. He ran across the field towards the banks of some nameless river. He needed to flee from the horror of the last several hours.

Reaching the water's edge, he tore off his bloody plantation hand's disguise, dove into the clear, clean water, and tried to wash away the evil that had stained him. His athletic body lost its vile filth from combat, as did his light brown hair. His clothing was another matter entirely. The blood of man and beast resulted in a permanent stain and there was really nothing Pratt could do. Naked, he washed and then spread out his soaked clothing on the river bank to dry in the afternoon sun. Alone for the first time since the ambush and exhausted, Christopher Pratt savored the quiet. He fell asleep as his clothing dried nearby.

Chapter 2

Fifteen year-old Abigail Hutchinson had never seen a full-grown, naked man before. At least that's what she wanted her father the minister to believe. While she was not an innocent, this sleeping fellow was a magnificent example of manliness, and he provoked her most private emotions. Curiosity competed with lust. Abigail probed the creek's shoreline for a spot where the natural lay of the rocks would allow her to cross.

Presently, she found a path. Removing her sandals and hiking up her blue dress to keep it dry, Abigail started across. Halfway there, she slipped, yelled out, and tumbled into the water.

On the opposite embankment, the young man awoke with a start and jumped to his feet, his utility knife held at the ready. He suddenly remembered where he was and that he was naked. Upon realizing a young woman had fallen into the water, he hesitated due to his embarrassment at being caught nude and out in the open. He didn't seem to know if he should rush into the creek to save her or get dressed first.

Abigail righted herself almost immediately, and she began reaching to climb back up on the rocks. The object of her fascination grabbed his now nearly-dry underdrawers and pulled them on, thankful at achieving some semblance of modesty.

It only took that long for the young woman to complete her crossing of the creek. She straightened her blonde curls, smoothed down her drenched dress in an effort to feign some amount of dignity, and approached the man directly. Having already been seen, she saw no reason to either hide or downplay her presence.

"It's a nice day for a swim, isn't it?" she offered with a cautious smile and a deep Southern accent as she approached the young man, who held out a wicked-looking knife. He lowered it as Abigail drew closer.

"Yeah. A nice day, Miss." His words seemed to imply that he felt the exact opposite way, although he seemed to see the humor in the

21

young lady's fall and her attempt to regain her composure. It took a few seconds, but he smiled in spite of himself. "But I think we each prefer to experience the water in our own unique way."

"Would you have preferred it if *I* swam naked?" she teased. "I've heard some like it better that way."

"You've heard? Uh...right." The man glanced behind him at his blood-soaked clothing on the embankment. He reconsidered his situation, an expression of hard resolve on his face. "Look, you do what you want. I have some things I need to take care of."

"Like hiding those bloody clothes and getting yourself out of whatever trouble you've obviously gotten yourself into?"

"Oh, you heard?"

"Five hundred gunshots in an isolated area along a Georgia road kind of echoes a bit in the wind, you know?"

"Right. You shouldn't be here Miss," the man began.

"I'm Abigail."

"You shouldn't be here, Miss Abigail. It might still be dangerous."

"Any more dangerous than you running around in your underdrawers or your blood soaked clothing after escaping a lynching or heck-knows what?"

"I was riding with the law."

"If you say so. Anyway, we can stand here and debate that or you can follow me and I'll find you some clean clothes back at the house. And if you're very lucky, maybe even a meal. Then you can go back to your secret mission."

"You like playing with danger, don't you, Miss?"

"Abigail."

"Right. I'm Christopher Pratt."

"Hello, Christopher Pratt. I'll just call you Christopher though. If I wasn't a proper young woman, I'd make a bet that everyone else calls you 'Corporal,' or 'Deputy,' right?"

Christopher still seemed guarded and his answer only deflected her question about his rank and affiliation. "A proper young woman. All right, Abigail. Give me a moment to put my clothes back on and then please lead the way," he said.

Abigail couldn't tell whether there was a touch of sarcasm to his tone or not.

Chapter 3

Christopher kept pace with Abigail as she led him away from the highway and across a spacious pasture. The heat rippling in the humidity was visible in the air above the lush green landscape. In the distance a plantation came into view. The size of the main residence house helped it stand out beyond planted trees that lined a long pathway which led up into the estate. Other buildings also occupied the property. Pratt assessed them as the farmhands' bunk houses, the main barn, grain silo and millhouse, and the slave quarters. He also saw horse stables, hog pens, and other out buildings. A low wooden fence divided the field. It transitioned into plowed lanes of cotton as they navigated the terrain, the plants obscuring them from view. This was fortunate considering Christopher's bloody attire and that it was not at all acceptable in Southern society for a young lady of Abigail's age to be found alone in the company of a strange man.

"I'll bring you as close to the main house as I can, but then I'll leave you for a short while. I must make certain my brothers and sisters won't see you and report you to my father," Abigail said. "If I can't take you inside unnoticed, I'll bring a fresh change of clothes out to you as swiftly as possible."

They quickly ducked down in the cotton as a big man on a white horse suddenly appeared and nearly ran them down. He didn't spot them, however, his attention focused on the slaves he supervised and who toiled in an adjacent row of cotton. Some of the dark-skinned men wore bell collars. As Christopher drew closer to their location, he could hear the unfortunate souls' presence before he even caught sporadic glimpses of them. They were harder to see, hunched over and working as they were. The foreman was always visible though, a solid, broad-shouldered man in a blue shirt with a mustache who wore a wide-brimmed hat to shield his narrowed eyes from the sun. Almost twice Pratt's age, he made an intimidating impression, especially on his horse. Christopher hoped he'd never have to fight him. The big man sported a bullwhip and a revolver on his utility belt. Pratt absently checked his own weapon, Lennox's slug shooter, while longingly eyeing the other man's sidearm. If he was found now, in his current condition, people would quickly figure that he was, at the very least, in a lot of trouble, or maybe involved in something far worse. Christopher didn't need a formal declaration of war between the states for this land to represent a huge threat to him.

"That's John Davis." Abigail nodded towards the big man astride the horse. "He oversees my Papa's entire work crew. It's best you stay out here and hidden from his view. He's been in a bad mood for the past several years," she flashed Christopher a quick, nervous smile.

"I'll get into the house and bring you out a fresh change of clothes. Just keep out of sight!" And with that cautioning remark, Abigail disappeared into the rows of cotton in the general direction of the estate's main residence.

Chapter 4

"Mother's been looking for you," Rachael called out after spotting Abigail from where she sat, sewing a dress for a doll on the spacious veranda of the plantation home. "She expects you to read Rebecca's Bible lesson to her like you're supposed to."

"I may not get to it until after supper. I'm busy right this minute!"

Rachael, the middle sister in a family of five children was a younger version of Abigail, wearing a pink dress. She'd become more precocious as her sensibilities were tugged from both sides: Rebecca, the baby of the family, always doted upon, and Abigail, the oldest, always left in charge, though her brothers rarely heeded her. If Rachael wasn't going to be a problem for Abigail, then Mark and Luke would be. Fortunately, they were nowhere to be seen. They'd probably been told by their mother to wash up before the evening meal as, no doubt, they'd been out by the stable all afternoon breaking in a new pony. Mr. Davis usually found work for the boys to do, as their father wanted them to learn responsibility. In turn, the boys always found a way to play more industriously than they worked. Their knack for finding ways to test and undermine authority worried Abigail, especially if they were currently spying on her. Those two would dearly love to get her in trouble.

So she hurried, racing up a long, gracefully curving staircase, and looking in both directions to make sure she was unobserved as she hurried to the end of the white-walled hallway and entered her parents' bedroom suite. In her father's tan oak armoire she found a fresh pair of gray pants which appeared to be the right length to fit Christopher. From the closet, she selected a white shirt that would likely fit him. Finally, she grabbed a pair of walking shoes. She wrapped the pants and shoes in the shirt, stuffing them into a knapsack she found in another armoire. Abigail cautiously exited the room, easing the door closed behind her.

She jumped as Mark demanded, "Does Pa know you're playing in his room?"

"I'm not playing!" Abigail spoke with more harshness than she intended to the blonde, twelve year-old boy. "Mother asked me if I'd sew something for her."

Her brother seemed briefly satisfied. After pausing to collect his thoughts, he pointed to the front of his trousers. "I just need to find wherever I lost the button, and then I've got something for you to sew right here."

Abigail rolled her eyes. Little brothers were most annoying. She was interested in real men who undertook real adventures in the larger world. She felt that Christopher Pratt might just be the man she needed to help her escape the life her father had planned for her. She would surrender her family loyalty and her heart, not to mention her father's clothing, to the man who could free her. No longer a child, she refused to be treated like one.

Abigail hurried down the back stairs of the house. She needed to locate Christopher before the sun would set and her mother called the family in for supper.

Chapter 5

"Hurry and dress," Abigail said, handing the knapsack to Christopher. "Mister Davis has already taken in the slaves and he's probably washing up for supper. He dines with us ever since his wife died in childbirth. The Lord also took his son with her. Now, once I'm back in the house, I want you to pay us a call. You'll tell my father that you're road-weary and you'll ask if you can impose upon his hospitality. He can be a good man and will certainly agree. However you and I must pretend we've never met before. You'll be invited to join us for supper."

Hungry, Christopher began to strip off his bloody clothing, and then remembered he was not alone. He sighed, arching an eyebrow at Abigail. "Oh, all right," she huffed as she turned around. "I've seen everything already so it's a little late for modesty."

"You have no idea what sort of situation you're playing with, girl," Christopher replied curtly, pulling on the new clothes and securing them with suspenders and his own belt. Then he softened. "But thank you for your kindness."

Then he frowned. "No fresh socks? I hate wet socks. Ah well…" He didn't bother to complain that the shoes were an inch too long. He hid the slug shooter, bloody ammo pouch, and the cartridges of gunpowder he'd collected as well as his utility knife in the knapsack, in order to appear dressed like any Southern gentleman.

"Alright," said Abigail, turning back to face him. "Wait about ten minutes and then head up to the house. Our maid Emma will answer the door and then call for her master, my father. Good luck!" Much to Christopher Pratt's surprise she kissed him on the cheek, smiled, and hurried back to the plantation house.

Chapter 6

Reminding himself that he was the traveling civilian Christopher Pratt and not a soldier felt odd. He'd been in training or military school for the last six years of his life. He tried to walk with a casual slouch, instead of marching up to the great plantation house. Along his way, he hid the knapsack under some shrubbery by a large magnolia tree. Then he journeyed deeper onto the property. Several slave children in the yard took notice of his approach, but they quickly returned to their game of chase. A heavyset black woman clad in drab-colored clothing eyed him warily as she labored to hang bright, freshly-cleaned laundry on a clothesline fastened between two trees near the slave quarters. Christopher remained unchallenged as he mounted the steps to the front veranda of the main house.

He knocked audibly, but unenthusiastically. A large and middle-aged, black woman in a fashionable red dress opened the door. She had short, dark hair with a hint of gray, but a round, youthful looking face that displayed exuberance as she addressed the young man. "Yessir?"

Christopher cleared his throat. "I've traveled a great distance today, but now the sky darkens and I'm far from my destination. I'd like to call upon the hospitality of your master."

The woman's bright eyes flashed with kindness. "Oh, please come in, Sir. I'll find the mastah directly." The large woman Abigail described as the house servant Emma disappeared down the hallway while Christopher waited patiently. He noted the costly chandelier hanging above the front entry room archway and a collection of portraits he assumed depicted the family's lineage.

Soon after, a slim, middle-aged man with a thin mustache, eyeglasses, and short, brown hair, appeared in the entryway. He had a kind smile about him and was dressed for dinner in a rather formal manner. "Emma says you're a stranger traveling through our country. Welcome to my home. I'm David Hutchinson." He

28

extended his hand, offering a firm and sincere greeting.

"Pleased to meet you, Sir, and I'm very sorry to intrude at the dinner hour. My name is Christopher Pratt, and I am indeed a weary traveler. I'd like to inquire if I may put upon you for a night, Sir. I journey by foot and can go no further."

"Why, certainly, Mister Pratt. You may join us for supper. I'm sure you must be very hungry and thirsty. You carry no canteen?"

"I was robbed on the Georgia road, and I'm afraid I lost almost everything."

"Well we must both be grateful that they at least left you with the clothes on your back. I own a shirt just like that myself," Hutchinson smiled, as he started down the hallway. Christopher followed his lead. "Where were you headed?"

"Atlanta. I'm to become an apprentice to my cousin, a blacksmith."

"I see. You don't talk like you're from the South, you know."

"I went to school up North for a bit. I was studying to be an accountant, but I ran out of funds," Christopher responded, hoping he sounded believable.

"Well applying yourself as a craftsman is working an honest trade. Jesus was a carpenter, of course. Besides owning this plantation, I have devoted myself to the Holy Scripture, and I'm privileged to serve as the minister of a fine congregation. If you find yourself ever journeying back this way close to the Sabbath, you're more than welcome to enjoy the fellowship of our services."

"Thank you, Sir."

They arrived in the dining room, where Mr. Hutchinson pulled out a chair for Christopher and bade him to sit down. "We'll be having a guest at our table tonight," he announced to his family as Emma refilled everyone's water glasses. "This is Christopher Pratt." Davis, the overseer, made no effort to change the sour expression he always wore. He simply nodded in Pratt's direction.

By contrast, Mrs. Hutchinson flashed Christopher a wide, welcoming smile. "I'm so glad you could join us, Mister Pratt."

"This is my wife, Missus Hutchinson."

"Pleased to meet you, Ma'am. Thank you for allowing me to dine at your table," Christopher said to the auburn-haired, distinguished-looking woman clad in a white dress.

"These are our children. Abigail, the eldest; Rachael; our boys Mark and Luke; and our baby, Rebecca."

"I'm not a baby anymore," Rebecca squeaked out, much to the amusement of those gathered at the table.

Christopher tried not to make eye-contact with Abigail or give any indication that he already knew her. However, during the introductions, his casual glances around the table revealed her struggle to suppress her urge to send smiles in his direction. He dismissed any interest he might have developed for Abigail. She'd obviously lived a privileged and sheltered life, and she was exactly as she appeared: young and naïve. Christopher knew he didn't belong here and that he would not be staying.

"Mister Davis is a great help to me, one that I cannot do without, as well as my dear friend," David Hutchinson continued, acknowledging the man seated immediately to Christopher's left.

"Mister Davis." Christopher nodded politely. In return, he received only a second, silent nod from Davis.

"Now that we're all acquainted, we must join hands and thank our Good Lord who has blessed us with this meal." As he joined with the rough hands of Jonathon Davis on his one side and his host David Hutchinson on the other, Christopher suddenly felt as if the rest of the family had been shielded from the presence of a stranger at their table and he wondered if they always sat to dine in this manner. As if reading his thoughts, David Hutchinson added, "Because she's such a lovely, little girl, my daughter Rebecca gets to dine at my right hand side." Mrs. Hutchinson sat at the opposite end of the table from her husband. Meanwhile, the seven year old girl smiled at Christopher as they bowed their heads and then her father began.

"Heavenly Father, we thank Thee for the food Your kindness has blessed us with and we pray that You will forgive us our trespasses, as we will strive to forgive those who trespass against us. Please lead us away from temptation and all evil so that we may walk in the shadow of Your greatness, Oh Lord. Your Will shall be done here on earth, as in Heaven. Amen."

The family appropriately acknowledged their prayer. Christopher began to withdraw his hands from the grasps of Mr. Hutchinson and the strong grip of Mr. Davis when the former continued on. "It is the Will of God that I must speak of now. I have had a vision from the Lord that there will be war, terrible fighting, and the land will be stained with the blood of our American brothers." This change in subject matter by Hutchinson surprised Christopher and he paid close attention.

"Thus, we may not be able to stay here," the patriarch continued. Everything is going to change soon when the Northerners invade our land and bring the evil that comes with the kind of freedoms from the natural order of things that they promise."

Christopher risked interrupting. "The natural order?"

Mr. Hutchinson suddenly seemed to recall his guest seated to his left. "Yes. The order of our traditional society. Surely you can't think that it would be a better world for there to be thousands of freed Negroes running about the countryside with no one to guide them? They're inferior creatures, and they're brought discipline in their service to us. In our benevolence, we look after them like they were our own children." Hutchinson seemed oblivious to the presence of the servant Emma, who stood dutifully in one corner of the dining chamber waiting until she was needed. Her input on the matter would never be needed.

"Perhaps you've seen the younger males in the fields that we have to keep bells on?" Hutchinson went on. "They don't know how good their lives are here, so when they try to run the bells make it much easier for the dogs to track them."

"You're very kind," Christopher said, wishing he could release the man's hand.

Hutchinson continued, "Our role in this matter is written for us in the Bible, in Leviticus: *'And as for your male and female slaves whom you may have from the nations that are around you, from them you may buy male and female slaves. Moreover, you may buy the children of the strangers who dwell among you, and their families who are with you, which they beget in your land; and they shall become your property. And you may take them as an inheritance for your children after you, to inherit them as a possession; they shall be your permanent slaves'.*

31

"We are all taught the words of Our Lord, and yet the Northerners seek to distort the teachings of the Good Book in order to propagate their evil. And I'll tell you what that evil is. This plantation ships bale after bale of cotton north by wagon, and then by rail or by boat. The South also grows much of the vegetables and grains needed in the North. But how do the bankers in New York, and Boston, and Chicago reward us? They extend us credit for our tools and building materials at extortionist interest rates, so no matter how well we seem to be doing here, we're always indebted to them. And this goes a step further because they utilize their advantage in manufacturing to gouge us for their woven or forged-metal goods, when they paid only a pittance for the raw materials, which we supplied them with in the first place. All this is occurring while their servants who hold the majority vote in Washington tax the heck out of cheaper imports until it strangles foreign trade, profits from exports dry up, and operating a plantation starts becoming unaffordable. It is so bad that Jonathon here has all but given up on his dream to start a farm of his own, and many a man my age can now only envision working for another rather than for himself. I ask you what is happening to the American dream?"

Mr. Davis silently looked down at his empty plate.

"David, the children are hungry and all this talk of politics and war is not becoming for their suppertime sermon," Mrs. Hutchinson intervened.

"Yes, of course you're right, My Love. I just was getting to my point that everyone should be prepared for this family to be leaving."

"We'll be doing what?" Abigail blurted out, looking startled.

"Well, it's nothing you should concern yourself with now, girl. But should shots be fired, and I think it is likely they will be, I intend to close the plantation and move our church. No matter that we are on the side of our Lord and justice, if it comes to war, I fear our state is ill-prepared. The bankers can fund more arms which the northern factories can readily forge. And the enemy, ever encouraging of more and more foreign immigration," he said, contempt in his voice, "will have many more men at their disposal. They'll next promote their cause as some kind of misguided crusade against our traditional way of life, recruiting the zealots along with the mercenaries. And then all will not end well.

"So I must look to the safety of my family and our community first," Hutchinson said, glancing at his sons. "I won't hear of us betraying God and needlessly taking our brothers' lives in vain as we fight a war we would very likely lose. No, we shall head out West. There is still new land and a wide new frontier largely untouched by all this political turmoil. The times are changing and our family must adapt. But now it is time for our family to eat."

"Yeah. I was getting really hungry, Pa," Luke remarked.

His father smiled indulgently at him and nodded towards his plate. "Go on then and enjoy your supper, Son."

Emma had prepared for them a delicious meal of roasted lamb.

Chapter 7

After dinner, Christopher longed to excuse himself of his host's company. He needed privacy in order to plan out just how he'd be able to fulfill his duty, return to his regiment, and report the ambush and deaths of the President's ambassadors as soon as possible. His superiors needed to know that the war had actually begun. And while it was now being fought in secret, in the shadows, the tinderbox had been ignited and was poised to explode. The military should be put on a readiness alert and warned that they could count on there being units disloyal to Washington at any given time now. However he still had to maintain a false identity, concealing his anxiety for as long as he remained alone and stranded in the South. So Christopher acted as if he was in no hurry, and offered David Hutchinson his contributing a hand on the plantation for a day in exchange for his food and lodging. It was the right thing to do. Besides, he needed to figure out how he would travel north without any food or a horse.

As everyone was rising from the dinner table following the evening meal, the conversation brought Christopher back from those anxieties he hoped to keep internal to only himself. "It's not dark yet, Father. Can we show him around the farm?" the older boy Mark asked, his younger brother Luke echoing his enthusiasm.

Abigail quickly interjected, "I'll go with them and I'll make sure the boys return to the house and clean up for bed on time."

Mr. Davis eyed the girl, catching her quick glance at Christopher as she tried to conceal another smile from breaking across her face.

Christopher thought he saw the man's expression darken with disapproval.

"Would that be alright with you?" Hutchinson asked Christopher. "Then Abigail will show you to your room. You'll be our guest in the house tonight. I just couldn't ask you to bunk with our workhands after it was so pleasant sharing our table with you, young man. In the morning, Mister Davis will educate you on how you may contribute to our efforts to make this a prosperous plantation once more, and I'll thank you now for your future work."

"You will join me for breakfast with the men at five o'clock," Mr. Davis said curtly. "Then we will see what kind of work you're cut out for, Mister Pratt."

Christopher thought it might have been the only words the man spoke all evening.

Mr. Hutchinson added more gently, "I have breakfast with my family later in the morning, but I join the work crew for mid-day meal and prayer. I look forward to seeing you then."

"C'mon," said young Mark, pulling at Christopher's left arm as he shook hands with the boy's father.

As twilight fell, Pratt followed his three guides outdoors and they began an exploration of the plantation's grounds.

"Father says there's going to be a war," the elder brother said "Are you going to enlist and fight for Georgia?"

"If I need to, I'm going to be fighting for all the states," Christopher offered, not necessarily revealing anything.

"I'm going to sign up and be a war hero!" Mark announced.

"Me, too!" Luke exclaimed.

"You're too young," Mark retorted.

"I'm only two years younger than you," Luke snapped back.

"You're both too young and Father has forbidden you both from discussing the subject any further," Abigail interjected. "Fighting is terrible. A lot of people get hurt."

"I agree," Christopher said softly. He also saw his opportunity to change the course of the conversation. As they walked into the mill house, he viewed large metal gears with interlocking teeth connected to a wooden roller that moved piles of wheat strands down a heavy cloth conveyance which sorted the grain into bales. A donkey was still tethered to a harness connected to the tow bar, which moved the whole of the machinery. "Do you expect your father will abandon everything your family has built here to move you west?"

Abigail sighed. "Yes," she said reluctantly, glancing past her brothers to the donkey. Anger flashed on her smooth face. "You two were supposed to un-tether Yokezie, put him in his stable for the night, and feed him!"

"Sorry. We forgot," Mark said dejectedly.

"Well do it. Now," Abigail ordered.

"C'mon," he said as he motioned to his little brother. He and Luke began to unhitch the weary-looking animal, the younger boy petting his nose.

As they led the donkey out, Abigail's eyes followed them. After she assured herself of their departure, she said to Christopher, "Here, I want to show you something. Help me." She began pushing straw away from the wood floor boards that the grain bundler was connected to and a large trap door was revealed at her feet. Abigail took a torch handle from a bucket that contained at least a dozen, picked up a cloth from a nearby stack, dipped it into a liquid-filled pail, and wrapped it around the wooden handle. Placing it on a stone worktable, she struck it with a rock and a spark ignited the soaked cloth. Abigail now had a useable torch. She nodded to Christopher, who found a metal hand grip attached to the cover of the hatchway built into the floor. His muscles ached as he lifted the heavy door, swung it upward on hinges, the top of the door winding up high above his head. The light shining from Abigail's torch allowed him to see the stairs that led down beneath the mill house. Abigail began to descend the stairs, waving Christopher to follow after her.

The torchlight illuminated scores of shiny objects in a large cellar that contained silver coffers, porcelain plates, and neatly arranged pieces of costly women's jewels, the necklaces hung from miniature coat trees.

"The valuables from my own family and many of our neighbors" Abigail offered quietly. "Father accumulated everything the congregation could offer in hopes of selling it off and starting a distillery operation that would be owned and operated by the church. He believes that collectively we can build and operate an inn on our land, thus earning enough money to retire everyone's debt. He promised everyone that their property would be safer if it were hidden here and trusted to God, rather than remain where it might be found and pillaged by Northern invaders if war comes."

"The North wouldn't go to war to pillage and plunder the South," Christopher offered before thinking better of the comment. "The federal government just wants to preserve the union and keep the peace."

"You heard my Father. He thinks they want to take away our freedom and force us to change our way of life. That's why I believe he really *will* sell all of these items and relocate everyone someplace else to live the way he says God intends for us to live." Abigail moved close to Christopher and held his arm. In the torchlight, the highlights in her irises seemed to be in motion as she searched Christopher's eyes in an effort to find hope. "I don't want things to change."

Christopher knew that everything had already changed. He'd experienced the change first hand. All of this collected wealth gave him the idea that he might be able to stay on an extra day if he worked hard once he persuaded Hutchinson to allow him to earn some pay for a second day's work. Then, he could afford to quietly hire transportation back to his unit's camp in the North, arriving there much faster than he would have on foot.

He hadn't failed to notice the way in which Abigail looked at him. He needed to move quickly, not only to deliver his report to his superiors but to avoid becoming entangled with this girl. She was pretty, he'd give her that, and very smart for her age. Persistent too, but Christopher knew that their destiny was not linked. Abigail was nothing more than another complication he didn't need. Christopher was a soldier; doing his duty was his sole mission.

Chapter 8

"The safety and prosperity of the men under my command is my mission. As it is, I've got no time or interest in fighting for ideals or vague notions about almost anyone *else's* rights." The speaker's animated brown eyes fell to his new alligator boots, a smile turned up on the corner of his mouth. "But you'll turn him loose, or I'll fight *you* right now," he said as his voice changed to a darker tone, and he stared straight through the other man with whom he spoke. The determined young man's hand moved to hover barely an inch above his holstered revolver. His clean-shaven, handsome features were focused with intensity, especially those eyes of his, and locked on the slightly older man with the dark brown beard who stood before him. Droplets of perspiration formed on the other man's forehead beneath his slouched hat as he began to realize the agitator confronting him meant business. Meanwhile, the stranger watched as many of the others in the room as he possibly could with his peripheral vision, already sure this situation was about to explode.

"C'mon. Do something already," he taunted, just to ensure it. "Some men just like to fight. I'm betting you brag to your boys how you're one of them." The challenger flashed a disarming smile. "And you tell your men that you're good at it, too. It gets you respect. Well, then, here's your chance to prove you've earned it." He smiled, sure that his seemingly-innocent expression and the insight he offered of the other man's character would provoke him beyond caution.

Dozens of glasses slammed down on the bar and surrounding tables, all attention upon the newly brewing conflict. Not another sound could be heard in the dark, smoky tavern. Sunlight streaked into the watering hole through several windows along the front wall, but dusk would soon fall. More brightly burned the intensity of the stranger under his Stetson hat, who had just arrived among them.

Another larger man, visibly muscular beneath the white undershirt he wore tucked into dark gray trousers, was taking three other men to restrain him by the bar. One of his captors wrapped his arm around the prisoner's neck. The other two held his arms, his biceps locked in the curves of their elbows. They all strained to keep him from breaking free. His eyes betrayed his anger, but once in a while a flicker of fear entered them and they sought out the stranger with a silent plea for a rescue.

"My captain will send word as to what he wants done with our prisoner. There's no way he would have sent you here alone," the bearded man countered.

"He didn't." The stranger held up a throw-over saddle bag with a new bullet hole in it. "But this was the last I heard of him. He must have fallen behind somewhere on the road back from Georgia." Another satisfied smirk reflected on the newcomer's features, his saddlebag dropping to the wooden floor. He could tell the older man with the beard was getting even angrier.

"And I should just take your word for that? How do I know my captain's even still alive?"

"And here I thought it was the custom to take people at their word in South Carolina."

"You're not from southern anywhere," the bearded man retorted. "But if you don't stand down, we'll put you down south, for sure. We'll put you way down south," he threatened.

"Yeah. Alright. No need to get riled up. We're just having a conversation," the stranger said as he carefully raised his hands away from his gunbelt and slowly stepped closer to the other man. Then, with unexpected speed he decked the other fellow, hitting him hard with a sudden straight thrust of his right fist. This man fell back into another man behind him as one of the other three restraining the prisoner reacted instinctively to catch the second one.

The prisoner used the opportunity to break one of his arms free thanks to his raw strength, then delivered a swing across his chest with a left hook to land a blow on the man holding his right arm. Then he threw himself forward, using used both arms to hurl his last captor, who formerly held him in the headlock, right over his front side. He slammed the man onto the plank floor of the tavern, the heel of one booted foot landing on his former captor's neck with an audible crunching sound.

39

At the same time, the stranger grabbed the pistol carried by the bearded man, who doubled over into him when he got hit, and tossed the weapon to his comrade, while smoothly bringing to bear his own sidearm with his left hand in spite of the awkwardness of a reverse cross-draw.

The prisoner fired a shot into the ceiling, both men drawing back the hammers of their revolvers before anyone else could react. Silence ensued again. For a few moments, sawdust streamed down from the hole the former prisoner had put into the ceiling. Then the stranger spoke, "We're riding out of here and I don't recommend any of you boys following us in the dark. Sleep on that, why don't you? And thank you for sharing the fine hospitality of South Carolina."

Chapter 9

Christopher rested uneasily during his first night at the Hutchinson home. Unable to fall into a deep sleep, even when offered a comfortable bed, he remained semi-awake. Twice he thought he heard soft footsteps stop outside his door, but after a pause the person quietly slipped away. A little more tired than he would have liked at dawn, Christopher felt eager to start the day early to pay his host for his hospitality, thus enabling him to return to his unit sooner than later. Mr. Davis unwittingly encouraged that desire even more by deciding to lean on Christopher rather hard that morning.

Christopher dressed in borrowed work clothes and was only halfway through his breakfast, with nary a sip from his coffee, when Mr. Davis summoned him. Davis didn't conceal his opinion that Christopher needed discipline and training. "If you can't make it doing soft desk work like accounting, you won't amount to anything as a blacksmith. You're going to learn to buckle down doing hard work and I'm going to teach you."

Great, Christopher thought, aware of how Mr. Davis supervised the plantation's slaves. Now, he'd apparently volunteered to become one.

They started with easy work. At least it was easy for Davis, who watched Christopher milk the cows and offered a stream of criticism. "Mister Hutchinson likes fresh milk for his family every morning so I don't take chances that the slaves might add something extra to the boss' breakfast. I make sure a ranch hand fetches it. Squat down more and don't sit on that bucket. You'll hurt your back if you lean all the way into it, and injuries don't get you out of doing your work around here."

Of course not. Christopher bit back his retort. He wondered who actually did get out of their work today so he could have the honor of being trained by Mr. Davis. But Christopher wasn't unfamiliar with this kind of labor, having helped his own family back in

Michigan before he was sent off to the military academy at age sixteen. His parents had hoped for a better life for him, so his father had signed over the family's land, to assure an education for his only son. Christopher hoped he'd live long enough to honor his father's sacrifice.

After gathering up other ingredients for the Hutchinsons' breakfast, including fresh eggs from the chicken coop, Christopher delivered them to Emma. Then Mr. Davis had decided that Christopher might hone some skills he would use as a blacksmith by working in the tool house, fixing some of the equipment that would periodically get broken on the plantation. "Unbend these longer nails from this pile first. When you've finished straightening them I'll point you towards the next bucket which won't be so easy to work with," Davis grumbled out. "That ought to wake you up enough before I put you to some real work."

Christopher started a fire beneath a work stove, heated water in a pail, and then used a set of tongs to dip each nail into the boiling liquid. Then, he placed each nail out on the metallic work counter top, using a small hammer to pound each one to straightness. Left alone for a while to focus on his task, Davis stalked off to give others in his charge their marching orders for the morning.

Pratt mused on how the past two days had brought him to the extreme opposites of human existence. Yesterday, he'd been shot at and frightened out of his own skin; today, he was safe, hidden away, and doing the most mundane of tasks in a dark barn. *Isn't there some kind of middle ground one can find to walk their path in life on?* Christopher wondered.

He wasn't always alone as he worked. A shadow would fall just beyond the door, elongated by the light of the sunrise. The first time its source revealed itself to be one of the family's dogs, a young and curious golden retriever. Twenty minutes later, the quick flash of long blonde hair and the glimpse of a white day gown, hinted at the identity of his secret observer. However, Abigail never initiated contact with him while he labored.

Once he completed straightening both buckets of nails, Mr. Davis returned promptly, almost as if he knew exactly how long the task would take Christopher. Looking over his work, Mr. Davis seemed disappointed that he saw nothing about which to complain. He told Christopher, "Those are needed in the millhouse for other work that'll be done later. Put 'em over there where the mule won't kick 'em and then meet me back here for your next job. Quickly."

As a soldier, Christopher was used to taking orders, so he didn't hesitate to follow the foreman's instructions. He jogged out of the tool house, heading in the direction of the mill.

As he placed the buckets of nails on a worktable inside, Christopher involuntarily scanned the floor, his gaze settling on the location of the trapdoor to the cellar that Abigail had shown him the night before. Now, strewn straw concealed any evidence of their prior trespass and the trapdoor to the secret chamber. Silently, Christopher apologized to the Lord for even considering theft in order to hurry him back to his regiment without further delay. It would be too dishonorable a thing to do to a family that had offered him their hospitality, or to their daughter, who'd likely saved his life. They weren't the people who had slaughtered his men, but they could still be dangerous if Christopher aroused their suspicion by hurrying off all too soon.

Once again, he felt Abigail watching him. When Christopher turned around, she didn't flee this time. Instead, she held her ground in the millhouse doorway, blocking Christopher's exit.

"I won't say anything if you want to steal something that will help you get on your way. I know what happened to you, but you must promise to take me with you. I'll even help you to fetch something right now," she offered. "Then I'll go with you to Atlanta, or further north, whatever direction you're really headed."

"I can't take you with me," Christopher quietly said. "Why are you asking this of me?"

"I can't tell you right now, but I'll explain everything soon. Isn't Mister Davis expecting you?" she said, deliberately cutting short their conversation.

Christopher nodded, not at all eager for another one of the man's lectures. "Yeah."

"Then we'll talk later," Abigail replied.

Great, Christopher thought as he headed back to meet him, *more farm chores*. He'd once thought that a military career had offered him an escape from a life no different than his own father's. He'd craved excitement and the chance to earn honor and glory with his service. However, recent events had given him good cause to rethink this. Boredom still loomed as an occupational hazard that came with farming, but it was a lot safer life. Christopher reminded himself that if he'd stayed at home in Michigan, he'd be taking orders from his own father and not Jonathon Davis, but it would amount to the same thing. *At least I had a choice*, he thought as he caught a glimpse of the slave shacks. He'd wanted independence. *But there must be something else.* Christopher could not put his finger on exactly what, but he felt certain he was destined to play a role in something larger than himself, and even larger than the whole looming war.

After he returned to Mr. Davis, Christopher received his next assignment. Apparently, the majority of his tasks involved skilled metalwork. Behind his gruffness and his purposeful toughness on Christopher, as though he determined the younger man to be a slacker, Mr. Davis possessed a simple pragmatism.

Christopher thought about Abigail as he labored. He wouldn't suspect the girl of testing his honesty. She'd already figured out that he rode for the North, and supported the interests of Washington. She was young, but very quick and well aware of the larger world about her and the extremely tense state of the nation. Though he empathized with her resentment of being controlled by her father, he couldn't imagine why she wanted to run away from her life here. It seemed privileged and relatively simple. He guessed he wouldn't be surprised by her story whenever he was destined to hear it, but it would make no difference. Yes he owed Abigail for hiding him, clothing him, and then involving her father with feeding and lodging him, but bringing her along with him when he left was simply impossible. The girl was attractive but too young, and she couldn't return with Christopher to his regiment in Massachusetts. What would Major Fuller say when he arrived with a young Southern girl in tow? What would his superiors think he'd been doing when no one else from his company returned alive? And, no doubt, Abigail's family would object. Even if he even dared to entertain the idea of leaving with Abigail, Christopher suspected that Mr. Davis would organize a posse, hunt him down, and hang him. And if he reached his regiment's camp, he would be violating his late captain's orders and jeopardize the secrecy of his unit's original mission were he to be followed.

Rebel intelligence had obviously been tipped off to the nature of Lennox's expedition for the Army's enemies to have planned that deadly ambush in the first place. But their adversaries didn't know Christopher survived. That fact might provide the Union an advantage if the South planned on a betrayal of the North taking them by surprise. And Christopher, determined to learn the identity of the traitor whenever it became possible, had a score that needed to be settled with that man.

Christopher put his strategizing on hold when it was time for lunch with the plantation's hired labor crew. He casually socialized with some of the others while he ate, being careful about what he said if anyone asked him any questions. Of course the men were curious about him. Mr. Hutchinson arrived to listen in when he joined his crew for their midday meal and then read selections from the Bible. Predictably, Hutchinson read from the Book of Job, preaching about loyalty, hard work, and honesty. Christopher marveled at the irony of how his past and present experiences with Bible sermons frequently demonstrated their relevance. However, that coincidence annoyed him now, given his current company and set of circumstances.

Following lunch, Mr. Davis kept Christopher busy until the sun sank low in the sky and it was time to wash up and change for supper. Christopher dined with the Hutchinson family once again. During the course of the evening, he cautiously broached the subject of working another day to earn a little pay, which might afford him the ability to hire a ride off the plantation and complete his journey to his final destination.

David Hutchinson said, "After our midday meal today I'd been considering that, too." He displayed a timepiece he'd removed from his pocket before he passed it to Christopher. "The value of the states' various printed currency is in something of a dispute right now, but you can use this timepiece to barter for services and catch yourself a ride. I'm sure its value will get you where you need to go and provide provisions for your journey as well. You need not stay and labor tomorrow. Mister Davis offered his compliments on the excellent work you did today. I thought you should know."

Christopher glanced at Davis, who sat next to him at the table, but the older man never made eye contact. He secretly appreciated the compliment, though. Supper was a quieter affair than the previous night. When everyone finished, they all retired to their respective rooms while Mr. Hutchinson chose to read from his Bible by the fireplace. Emma, ever dutiful, cleared the dining room table after the meal concluded.

Chapter 10

It was well past midnight when Abigail stirred in her bed and coaxed herself awake. She had a bedroom to herself, as did the other children, save for Rebecca, who refused to sleep alone because of monsters that visited her dreams at night. Rachael had inherited the duty of monster-patrol once little Rebecca relented on her demand that she sleep in her parents' room.

Now Abigail needed to be extra cautious not to be mistaken for a monster. She cautiously lifted herself out of bed, cracked open the door to her room, and peered into the long hallway. All of the upstairs bedroom doors were closed. As her eyes adjusted to the dark, she made out the form of a large man lying across one of the sitting benches near the middle of the family level. Mr. Davis. With no family of his own anymore, he kept a room upstairs with the rest of Abigail's family at the invitation of her father. Obviously, he'd taken it upon himself to protect her family.

Abigail tip-toed down the upstairs hallway, heading away from the children's wing. She winced as the floor creaked and Mr. Davis' mouth twitched as he stirred slightly in his sleep. She noted the revolver tucked under one arm, its metal catching the faint starlight that came through one of the plantation home's tall, front windows. He didn't look too comfortable and he'd probably awaken in the morning in an even worse mood than usual, if that was possible.

Abigail made it past Mr. Davis without incident and drew nearer to her parents' master bedroom. To her left was the guest room that Christopher had been provided for the night. The door had no lock. Abigail quietly pushed it open, stepped inside, and silently closed it behind her.

Christopher slept deeply. Abigail, sensing he'd awaken with quite a start, crept up close to his bedside and cupped her hand over his mouth. Christopher nearly jumped out of bed, his hands on Abigail's throat in an instant. He quickly removed one to feel at his waist for his knife, but his memory started to catch up with his sudden consciousness and he remembered where he was and that he was not carrying arms of any nature.

With some effort, Abigail managed to whisper, "Christopher, it's me, Abigail! You're choking me."

He immediately relaxed. "Sorry, but you surprised me," he admitted.

"I'd never have guessed," Abigail whispered. "Move over." She climbed into Christopher's bed.

"What are you doing?"

"Using my last chance to spend some time alone with you," she responded.

"They didn't tell me the South would be like *this*," Christopher half-muttered to himself.

"There you go again, giving hints you're not from around here," Abigail said. "Are you a soldier? Or are you a spy? Is that why the men you rode with were being shot at? You escaped, didn't you?"

"If you're so convinced, why don't you call for your Pa and Mister Davis? If they caught me with you, I'm sure they'd love to hang me."

"Yeah, they would gladly do so if they caught you in *my* room, but I came to you. Remember?"

"Right... So, why *are* you here? If not to pump me for information?"

"Since I first saw you by the river, you knew I wanted you," Abigail playfully replied. "Would you deny a girl her pleasures? Would you deny yourself the same, especially when you're facing such danger?" Abigail rolled over atop Christopher, smiled as she sat up and straddled him. Then she pulled her nightshirt over her head as she mounted him, naked in the darkness save for the faintest of light that came from the starlight outside the window. "Once again, I may be your last chance."

Just barely being able to view her perky, young breasts aroused Christopher. Abigail quickly stripped him of his underdrawers and manipulated his hard shaft inside of her welcoming, warm body.

He shuddered at fate's touch of mercy. Surprised by how quickly everything happened, he managed to say, "You're not new to this."

"I've never married if that's what you mean, but I have been able to satisfy my curiosity about men," She grinned at him. "And I've enjoyed the pleasuring they've provided."

Christopher gripped her hips and held her still, despite the hunger he felt to complete the act she had initiated. "Why me, Abigail?" he asked.

"Why not?" she countered.

"Tell me."

She studied him in a thoughtful manner. "Since you want the truth, I'll tell you. My father is considering wedding me to Mister Davis."

Christopher frowned. "But he is too old for you. Surely there are younger men in the area who'd be better choices for your husband."

"Father doesn't agree, and his word is the same as God's law in our home. I'll be forced to wed Mister Davis, but thus far I'm refusing to cooperate. I used to go out into the fields and spy on the young slave boys for fun. Sometimes Rachael would go with me. Many times I saw them pulling on themselves and it looked they were having quite a good time. They'd moan, shudder, and fall down. It looked very pleasurable. I made a bet with Rachael that they'd let me help them out with that and sooner than later, I was meeting two of them almost every day out in the field. No one can see what's happening beneath the corn. It was so nice and private. So once I learned to rub myself, I let them rub me. Finally, I couldn't stand it any longer and I let them enter my body.

"I was always with the same two boys who were about my age. Well, one – the more cautious one – might have been slightly older. Anyway, I never learned their names. I couldn't pronounce them anyway. But we made like we saw the dogs and pigs doing – beastly things. It hurt at first, though soon it felt much better.

"Father would preach on about sin, and I'd get hot with passion during every sermon just thinking about how later I'd be able to slip out into the fields and recreate Sodom and Gomorrah just like it was described in the Bible. I originally got the idea for it in church. After that, his droning sermons were never so boring.

"Well, I didn't know it at the time that father was planning to promise me to Mister Davis. Remember I told you that he'd lost his own family? Well, the other year I became pregnant by one of my friends in the fields, and for whatever reason, Mister Davis felt compelled to help me conceal it. He said it would break my father's heart. So Daddy preached on about virtue and almost no one was aware I was with child. I chose clothing that would help me hide my condition. Plus, my parents hardly notice me anyway, except to order me around.

"So the baby came last winter. Mister Davis was making a long trip to Charlotte to bargain on behalf of my father for the plantation's latest yield and he said he'd take me into town with him to set up a cover-story. Father felt it would be good for us to get to know each other better anyway. So, we left when I felt the baby was coming but instead of going into the city, Mister Davis had provisions for us for an extra week and I gave birth out in the fields at night. There wasn't much light but when he saw the child, he only said, 'So brown…,' his voice trailed off, and then he took the baby, it was a boy, and carried it away from me for good. I think he drowned it in the river.

"After that, unbeknownst to me, Mister Davis followed me out into the fields for one of my secret rendezvous with my slave friends. He caught me with the older one in my mouth and he took the boy by the throat and then strung him up in front of our property by his neck. I was told that the unfortunate slave boy had led me into evil and he was to die for it. He told my father that the slave had been caught stealing from the farm, but I knew the real truth. He was hung because he was caught with me. After that, all our young male slaves had the bell-collars affixed to them so Mister Davis could hear them wherever they were or whatever they were doing. Ironically, I know it was the younger of the two slaves who was actually the father of my baby, but you see, after what happened to his friend, he was afraid to see me any more.

"I've been so lonely for almost half a season, until you came along," Abigail finished. She leaned forward to kiss him.

"I didn't come along to wind up hanging from a tree," Christopher responded, his eyes betraying that he was half-shocked by this young girl's story. He clearly had not expected this.

"Oh, stop worrying about yourself. Mister Davis likes to think he's being vigilant by sleeping in the hall with a handgun."

Christopher's eyes widened as he pictured that image. "But once he's out for the night, nothing wakes the old man," Abigail said hoping to relax Christopher.

"I am very worried for myself," Christopher countered. "You've taken advantage of my situation."

"This may be *my* last chance," Abigail said. "I must leave here and I must do it soon."

Christopher finally understood. "And you'll accuse me of intimacy with you if I don't help you escape your father. You know that your father will force a marriage between us or have Mister Davis hang me. Either way, I'm now also trapped."

She nodded. Then Abigail said, "I'd rather just leave with you, Christopher, but it's up to you what happens." Before he could speak she settled forcefully against his loins, drawing his sex even more deeply into her body.

Christopher was relenting. "Somehow, I will find a way to help you, Abigail."

"Then don't make too much noise." She laughed softly, then fused her mouth to his and rode his erection into mutual oblivion.

For his part, Christopher surrendered to physical need, which Abigail repeatedly satisfied until just before dawn.

Chapter 11

The morning saw a weary Christopher Pratt awake at the crack of dawn to assist with the farm chores in order to further demonstrate reciprocity for the timepiece, his meals, and lodging. Although exhausted, he wouldn't have traded his time with Abigail for all the sleep in the world.

Mr. Davis' only comment that morning was "Let's keep our cows over their buckets, Mister Pratt."

Around seven o'clock, Emma served breakfast to the workhands. Christopher ate with the other men and he did not see Abigail until several hours later when he bade farewell to Mr. and Mrs. Hutchinson and thanked them for their hospitality. Abigail offered to escort him to the edge of their property where he would find the road.

The young pair left the property unobserved. They made their way along the pathway that led to the main road, pausing when they reached a large magnolia tree. Christopher nervously looked around before he stepped into the shrubbery beneath the tree and retrieved the knapsack containing his weapons. Everything was just as he'd left it two nights before.

"Here," said Abigail.

"Hmm?"

"This is where I'll instruct the post rider to leave the letters you'll send to me, and where I'll leave my letters to you for him to carry."

"Doesn't he bring all of your mail up to the main house?" Christopher asked.

"I think I can come to a new arrangement with him. You *will* write, won't you? Let me know you're alright? And that you are keeping *our* new arrangement."

Christopher nodded. He at least owed Abigail that, although he wouldn't speculate on anything more. But he'd been raised to keep his word, protecting his honor. Now he would have to demonstrate that with the girl.

Abigail continued, "Once you return to your normal life, you can send for me. I can trade things I have for transportation so that I can come and join you. I have no desire to endure my father's eternal Sunday sermons until he succeeds in marrying me off to Mister Davis or moving us to God only knows where."

"I thought you said that Mister Davis was no longer interested in marrying you."

"Well, my father doesn't know that." She looked up at him. "Don't forget about me, Christopher," Abigail said as she leaned in to passionately kiss him. "Please don't forget."

Chapter 12

"Daniel Winthrop." The well-dressed stranger did not forget to write his name in a legible fashion onto the passenger list of the three masted schooner departing Charleston early that morning. Beneath the moniker, Robert Masterson added his own signature. Then the stranger in the neatly kept, dark suit of a gentleman paid the chief of the boat in silver coins so as to avert any difficulty finding another acceptable currency. The burly man with unkempt sideburns and a sweaty, hairy chest exposed beneath his half-buttoned and soiled shirt smiled wide as he received the payment. Then he turned to find the dock master to provide him with the final cargo and passenger list before his ship would depart.

The early sun shone bright in the sky, the air was still cool down at the waterfront a few hours after dawn broke over South Carolina. The former prisoner breathed a sigh of relief as his rescuer nodded that their business was concluded. Peaceful waves lapped against the docks where dozens of large and small ships were tethered up, the white from their rolled up sails contrasting against the clear blue summer sky. Seagulls called out as they drifted lazily above those engaged in the usual early morning activity in the harbor. Appreciative of the serenity, Masterson began to relax after his ordeal as a prisoner in a Southern military stockade where he'd been kept over the past month.

Then instead of walking down the dock to their waiting ship, his benefactor said, "I think we now have time to go across the street to that bakery over there and get ourselves some coffee."

"When does our ship leave, Lieutenant?"

"Soon. In less than an hour, I hope, but it doesn't matter. We won't be on it," Winthrop answered.

"What do you mean, we won't be on it? You just paid good money out of your own reward to book us passage north," Masterson said, sounding surprised.

"Yes, I did, and it's fortunate for us that I thought of the tactic.

Your pursuers will be here soon. They've been tracking us, and the first thing they'll do is check the passenger lists of all the departing vessels. With any luck, they'll trace us to that tall mast over there, which will have hopefully departed well before the posse arrives. Then, they'll move directly to catch up to us at sea, which is why we're going north over land." Daniel Winthrop smiled and Masterson grinned back at him, the latter grasping Winthrop's clever ruse as they walked.

"Now, as much as I'm touched by how you worry about my money, you shouldn't bother yourself about that either. I'll bet I can get Mister Secretary to reimburse me, and I'll also pay you your share. I know we can reason with him, since he can't afford a public scandal. How would that look in the papers? The United States Secretary of the War Department guilty of high treason; member of the President's Cabinet responsible for the deaths of Federal soldiers. They'll try and kill us now to keep it all nice and quiet, but I doubt Floyd will risk challenging us if we make it back to Washington. Plus, there's two of us for them to contend with now. We'll watch each other's back," Winthrop explained as his sharp eyes looked out the window of the small café in which they'd signaled the proprietor that they wished to order drinks.

Abruptly, Winthrop said, "Over there." He pointed at about a dozen men who'd just ridden into town at a gallop. The bearded man from the tavern led them, and they all wore blue Army uniforms now. The horses' footfalls from a quarter of a cavalry troop and the rattling of metal canteens against the cartridge containers worn by the riders sounded audibly as the troops made their entrance into town. Curtains parted in the windows of apartments above the shops on the street, and curious citizens began to poke their heads from windows to take in the view. The leader of the posse ordered his men to dismount and hitch their horses outside a hotel across the street and east of Winthrop and Masterson's current location.

A glance back at the dock revealed the empty mooring berth where the ship on which Winthrop had booked passage had been. Its masts with partial sails already deployed were visible at the mouth of the harbor, about to head out to the open ocean and its trip north up the coast.

The bearded lieutenant saw the ship, too. Masterson heard his voice, but he couldn't make out the man's shouted words. His men immediately dispersed, running in pairs to search every building in town. The soldier in charge took one of his men with him and cornered the dock master who had been conferring with the captain of another tall ship when he approached and started gesturing excitedly at a very fast looking, double-mast clipper ship. Then the three men started walking away from them and further down the landing towards that ship.

The fugitives couldn't watch any more as several of the blue-coated soldiers were now spotted rushing across the street towards the café Masterson and Winthrop sat in. The heavyset baker, a man with thinning hair under his white cooking cap, had also been watching the activity. After having served Winthrop and Masterson their coffee, he moved into the door frame of his establishment, looking at the soldiers rapidly approaching his business. He squinted while he dusted flour from his hands, glanced at the soldiers again, and spat on the ground just beyond his door. Without turning his head, his gaze shifted to Masterson and Winthrop. He nodded ever so slightly.

The men, who'd seen the baker's signal, got up from the table and immediately headed to the back of the bakery and into the kitchen, drawing their pistols and checking them. Masterson saw the baker step aside and welcome the armed pursuers without the courtesy of a handshake. Their guns were drawn as well.

"I have orders to search this establishment," one of the men told the baker.

That was all Masterson heard as Winthrop silently tugged on his sleeve and motioned for them to make their exit through a back door into the alleyway behind the bakery. With a last glance back, Masterson's eyes opened wider as he looked back to where he and his companion had been sitting, their rolls and coffee still set out, half enjoyed at their table with the street front view.

The two men ducked out the back door, flattened themselves against the back of the building, and drew back the hammers of their guns. Both caught the sight of the rear door of a neighboring building as it swung open, a head topped by a slouched hat turning to look up and down the alley. Masterson and Winthrop pushed back into the shadow of the bakery's rear door. Fortunately, they remained unseen. When the blue coated shoulders and the slouch hat disappeared from sight, Winthrop burst out of his hiding place and pulled Masterson after him down the alleyway in the same direction their enemy had disappeared. He suddenly motioned for Masterson to double-up with him in that doorway just as the bakery's back door swung open, another soldier glancing up and down the alley.

Once the man disappeared, Winthrop holstered his weapon and tapped Masterson to follow him back in through the rear of the bakery. They quietly opened the door and listened for a few moments. Hearing nothing, they re-entered the bakery through the kitchen, again looking and listening for any signs of the men searching for them before they re-emerged into the front of the café. The owner had commandeered their table and sipped Winthrop's coffee, watching the soldiers out on the street.

"I told them I was eating breakfast with my daughter and had just sent her to borrow some Scotch from a neighbor when they arrived. If there's one thing I can't stand, it's the Federals always poking their noses into other people's private business down here. They didn't figure I'd seen you two."

Winthrop nodded in gratitude and exchanged amused smiles with Masterson, who couldn't believe the baker had mistaken the two of them for local Southerners out of disdain for the federal uniforms of the soldiers who'd pursued them – the same men who'd come up from South Carolina in the first place.

The men watched out the front window as one of the troops signaled by bugle for the men to reassemble before the officer with the dark beard. He then ordered them to march after him in two columns down to the docks where the men could file aboard the same clipper ship he'd inquired about a short while ago.

"Let's enjoy some fresh cups of coffee while we watch them cast off, shall we?" Winthrop raised his old cup in a salute to the baker, who smiled back at him. The larger schooner on which they had booked passage had already sailed out of view. It would take a while for even the faster clipper ship the troops boarded to catch up.

But by the time they could board the other vessel and search her, Winthrop and Masterson would be long gone leaving Charleston back on the road behind them.

Chapter 13

The first stagecoach on the road out of Georgia that Christopher encountered was under a New York bank's employ. The lieutenant recollected what Mr. Hutchinson had told him two nights before about mercantilist Northern banking practices, and he wondered whose pawn in whose game he'd become an unwitting participant in. *No*, he thought, *it wasn't ever a game*. People were dying and others endured a lifetime under debtors' liens. Those with the capital controlled everything.

However, Christopher found the driver, Paul White, and his guard, Travis Ollinger, to be honest employees who would take his watch that Hutchinson had given him as a worthy bribe for a ride and a share of their provisions. "Very fine craftsmanship," White had said when he'd first inspected the timepiece and agreed to the exchange.

After a few days' journey, they arrived in Charleston and White said he knew a place where they could unload the watch for some good coins. They made their way through town, with Ollinger following a short distance behind them to make sure that Christopher didn't run, not that he ever entertained the idea; the man had already displayed his skills with his carbine when they encountered a bear stalking them during their trip north. The port city was bustling when their stagecoach arrived, Christopher wary of the Army troops he saw everywhere he looked in the town. He decided against checking in at one of several Army forts that protected South Carolina's major seaport entry. Trust no longer existed between Northern and Southern troops. Instead, he asked White to purchase passage for him on any ship bound up the coast to Virginia, offering his companions two-thirds of the funds garnered from the timepiece.

Once he registered as a passenger on a large frigate still loading cargo, Christopher used his time before the ship's departure to mentally note the activity in the port. The Army was unloading tons of their own supplies, among them small arms, munitions, and, surprisingly, a lot of heavy artillery. *Incredible*, Christopher realized, since he'd heard President Buchanan had ordered the downsizing of the federal military in order to promote peace. Nevertheless, flat bed wagons were being loaded at the docks, as well as cargo skiffs that could sail across the bay to deliver the armaments to other coastal defense stations that guarded Charleston and elsewhere.

Dressed as a civilian, Christopher acted the part of just a curious citizen when he approached a soldier, who introduced himself as artillery officer Daniel Hough. "Major Anderson has orders to receive a lot of arms today. We got plans from Washington to reinforce every fort covering the harbor. I'm seeing this load outbounded for Sumter," he explained. "Some contractor's making a lot of money."

This was all very distasteful to Christopher, who had been trained to believe that the military's mission was to protect and serve the country. However it was obvious to Pratt that South Carolina was arming for war, and he filed away this information as he hurried to board his ship before she left port.

Christopher felt unsteady on his feet as the big ship was rocked by the waves as she headed out into an ocean that reminded the Army officer that they were all just specks on the great sea. He felt insignificant – a small part in a vast conspiracy to ignite a full scale civil war between the North and the South. What he'd seen convinced him that it was inevitably coming.

As he mulled over reporting what he'd discovered to Major Fuller, or if he should bypass the battalion and go up the ladder to more senior officers, the almost deafening sounds of exploding ordinance echoed across the water. Christopher had been on the port side, top deck, leaning over the rail and vaguely noting the eastern U.S. shoreline while he vomited, so he ran over to the starboard side of the ship to discover the source of the explosions. A clipper ship running with full sails and flying U.S. colors closed fast on his larger and slower frigate. The captain of Christopher's ship immediately ordered their sails down and his ship slowed toward a full stop. The clipper came up fast and bore its broadside to them, her twelve guns trained on the passenger ship. Men in Navy uniforms lowered boarding launches over her port side and the Marines scrambled down netting that hung over her rails. The rocking of the boat added to the churning of Christopher's stomach some more as he watched them – or maybe it was his mounting anxiety.

When the troops had rowed over to Christopher's ship, sailors on board the frigate helped the Marines to tie up before they climbed over. Christopher felt nervous but told himself that he shouldn't be. By all accounts, his enemies in the Army units defecting to the South should believe him dead, and the Navy would have even less reason to be looking for him. Nevertheless, the Marines searched the cargo and interviewed every passenger, including Christopher. He gathered they were looking for someone else – two individuals, he learned. Fugitives from the military who might have boarded a vessel bound north out of Charleston. Times were getting crazy, he thought.

When their search yielded nothing, the troops disembarked and returned in their boarding vessels towards the revenue cutter from which they'd launched. The captain of the frigate ordered her sails raised and they were on their way again.

Nervous and seasick, Christopher welcomed going ashore once they reached Virginia. He planned to travel by land the rest of the way around the Chesapeake, aware that he still had enough money to buy him passage on a coach headed to Washington. From there he would check in with his regiment's command, thus bypassing the question about whether he could trust his superior back at battalion headquarters.

Reflecting on the bigger picture, he also wondered just what in the hell he was doing. He could have stayed in Georgia, defecting to the South, taking work, and establishing a residence near Abigail. He'd never had a real girlfriend and besides, everyone else believed him to be dead. But he dismissed that idea quickly. If he reported in, he'd be sent straight back into the fight as soon as the war began, yet he knew he'd fare no better in the South. The state's militia would be undermanned, young white men his age quickly drafted into their rebel army. So he'd serve after all, but with the loss of his rank and the privileges he'd earned in becoming a Union officer. His father had sacrificed too much for him. Not only that, but Abigail would find herself being relocated by her father as Hutchinson would very likely move his family at the start of the war. As well, Christopher could not imagine himself being disloyal to the unit to whom he owed his service, especially not after the betrayal and slaughter of the men he was charged with looking after. No: he must identify the traitor and avenge his fallen friends. He'd never switch sides now.

As he'd become conscious of a world he found treacherous, dishonest, and very disappointing, Christopher decided to set a counter-example. He reasoned the best way to keep his promise to Abigail and pass the time of his sea voyage would be to write his first letter to her. She'd placed her trust in him and he actually did care for her. No longer lacking anything interesting to write about, he described his adventure on the way out of Charleston, which he thought she would find exciting. Also, now that he was almost free and clear of the South, he could reveal his true rank and affiliation because he needed to send her an address that he could be reached at through the War Department. There was no telling what assignment the Army would order him into next.

After the frigate docked in Norfolk, Christopher debarked and purchased passage by stagecoach through Richmond. Arriving there after some time spent enduring the bumpy roads, Christopher located a post office from which to mail his letter to Abigail. Exchanging small talk with the middle-aged and mustached clerk, he tried to establish a report with him so he'd be referred to the next, least expensive coach headed out of Richmond, or to learn if the best option would be to go by train. His head and stomach certainly favored the latter but Christopher needed to be frugal until he reached the Army to which he belonged.

"You know, during my travels, Norfolk was very quiet and relaxed compared to Charleston. The port in South Carolina was busy as a hornet's nest with all kinds of munitions and other Army supplies being ferried through, the exact opposite of what Buchanan originally said he was going to do. I don't know if the rest of the country knows that this is what's going on now."

"Some do. A fellow passing through here just the other day seemed like he were allocating his belongings, and he had me packing up a crate to ship these alligator boots of his all the way to Wisconsin! I guess some relative will enjoy them, as this guy seemed as troubled as a man heading to his own funeral."

Christopher was immediately intrigued with the mention of the alligator boots. "That sure sounds like a friend of mine," he lied. "A buddy I know from the Army."

"You in the military, too, boy? You're out of uniform."

"I'm on leave."

"Oh."

"Say, did you catch this fellow's name?" Christopher asked trying to sound casual.

"Hmm, I should have it in my records. Easy to find. He was here just the other day," the postmaster said. He searched through papers in a file drawer with his right hand, while he scratched his salt-and-pepper head with his left. "Here it is," he answered, thrilled that his file system proved effective. "Robert Masterson."

Pratt involuntarily coughed. He'd just missed both of the traitors! They'd been right here. Had they been the same men whom the troops on the revenue cutter had been searching for? They must have traveled northbound over land, and just ahead of him. This settled things. Christopher requested directions from the post master as to where he could board the train. If they journeyed by horseback, he reasoned, he could get ahead of them.

Christopher bought passage by railway heading to Washington, D.C. After a long journey with very little to view aside from Pennsylvania's endless wheat fields, Christopher debarked the train at a stop near the docks on the Potomac where he could cross by ferry. After one last journey by water, he arrived in the nation's capital under gray skies. Asking locals for directions, Christopher made his way straight to the location of the brick building that housed the United States military's high command. He needed help. Once he was in sight of the large three-story, red structure, however, Christopher hesitated. He surprised himself when he decided to turn around and search for an eating house in the near vicinity to mull things over once more. He enjoyed a much needed meal with the last of his funds. His trust eroded, he concluded that he needed to make his next move very carefully.

Chapter 14

Winthrop still had some money left. "After this, I'd say we are long overdue to head into New York City for some fun. Don't you think?" He and Masterson walked on the corner of Pennsylvania Avenue and 17th Street outside the headquarters of the United States Army. The day to day business operations of the War Department were conducted here, adjacent to the grounds belonging to the White House.

Winthrop evaluated his companion's appearance. They made an odd pair. Winthrop sported a refined pair of trousers and an unbuttoned jacket over a near-new white shirt. His gun was in his brown leather holster on his left hip, mostly concealed by his jacket. Though he now wore standard issue Army boots, his gray trousers hung over them to the point that they could be mistaken for dress shoes. Masterson's shirt was torn, and his pants filthy and raggedy, courtesy of his prison term. His hair was dirty, and he needed a shave.

"I don't think they're going to let you in there," Winthrop finally said after assessing Masterson. "But don't worry. I know some Irish girls in the Points who aren't so particular." Winthrop removed a few coins from his jacket pocket and flipped one of them to Masterson. The two exchanged conspiring smiles.

The sergeant of the guard they'd just spoken to came out of the brick building they were waiting at and marched up to meet them. "Major Venable's a busy man, Sirs. You have no way of proving you are who you say you are?"

"I paid you. Now you go back inside and insist we speak with Secretary Floyd. You tell him I'm Lieutenant Daniel Winthrop, serving under Captain William Brewster. This is Sergeant Bob Masterson and we're reporting back from our mission. Never mind what Major Venable thinks. Secretary Floyd will understand the message, so you go back and tell Secretary Floyd just what I told you."

The guard looked them both over with obvious skepticism and then departed once more as another Army enlisted man remained in his place to protect the entrance to the War Department Building. Winthrop sighed and wished for a cool breeze off the Potomac as he was getting hot under the collar and could only imagine what Masterson felt concerning his ordeal.

Secretary of War John Buchanan Floyd was a pale complected man in his mid-fifties with sunken cheeks and dark, graying wavy hair. He wore a stern, no-nonsense expression on his face, suitable for a man who had previously held the title of Governor of Virginia. A vest and business jacket with a bowtie finished off his refined look. He was clearly a civilian with authority over Major Venable, who wore the blue coat of an Army soldier, tied with a red cummerbund to denote a high ranking officer. Younger than Floyd, and sturdier, Venable didn't laugh or express emotion of any kind when Floyd repeated the same questions, "They say they're from Captain Brewster's company from Major Fuller's battalion? And one of them is in rags and the other looks like some kind of gentleman-cardplayer?"

"Yes, Sir. The sergeant of the guard said they told him you'd want to see them immediately. I told him to report that you were very busy, but they insist on waiting. I could arrest them, Sir."

"No. That won't be necessary, Major. Bring them in to see me."

Winthrop and Masterson were escorted into the wide oak-trimmed office of Secretary Floyd, who was now prepared for their appearance. The secretary still sat behind his desk, papers in four neat stacks arranged atop it. A painting on one wall depicted George Washington. A United States flag hung from a pole on one side of a large window, and the flag of the State of Virginia on the opposite side. "Major, would you wait outside?" he asked Venable. In spite of being in civilian clothes, his two visitors stood at attention in the center of the room.

When the door was shut he stood up from his desk and walked in a circle around Winthrop and Masterson. "So you two survived the last mission of Captain Brewster?" He eyed them warily, noting both men were obviously armed, the Colt Army pistol stuffed into the front of the big, raggedy-looking man's pants.

"Lieutenant Winthrop, Sir."

"Sergeant Masterson."

"I see. I can understand if you're angry. I would be, too."

"Mad, Sir? Why would we be?" Winthrop asked in a deceptively innocent tone. "The way I see it, Sir, we're rich men."

"Oh? So you've gotten yourself out of the fire and now you have a chip in the big game? You've been holding onto that piece, and now you're ready to cash it in?"

"Let me tell you about cash, Mister Secretary, Sir," Winthrop said angrily as he stepped forward to stand toe to toe with the head of the President's War Department. "We spent all of ours just getting out of there. You set us up in the Carolinas just like you had me help set up Captain Lennox in Georgia. You said the company would be captured like most of the men in mine were, but this time they killed everyone – *every single one*." Winthrop emphasized. "You knew what would happen, and Major Fuller knew. But this isn't about the men. It's about your friends back in Virginia.

"Well, here are two of my friends," Winthrop held up his hands and Masterson rested one of his on his gun heel. "And now my friends are going into *your* billfold."

Floyd nodded. "You came here for money," he stated matter-of-factly. "I'll pay you, re-supply you, and get you back into uniform, but it ends there. If I get caught up in some scandal, so do the two of you. There's blood on everyone's hands. Do you understand?"

Winthrop laughed as he shot a sidelong glance at Masterson. He continued to press Floyd, "You're helping your allies in Virginia and their neighbors prepare for war. I've no intention of fighting your battles for you so you and your contractor patrons can make money in the arms trade at my life's expense. Do *you* understand?"

"Do what you want. I'll have Major Fuller re-assign you to a new company in his battalion and promote you to captain. It will be your outfit and you can command the missions as you see fit." Floyd saw the interest in Winthrop's eyes. "But I don't want to see the two of you here ever again. Is that clear?" Floyd aimed some strength in his voice at Winthrop.

"I want my promotion in writing, new horses, new uniforms, and one hundred dollars for each of us, and reimbursement of all of my expenses. And I'll also take that new bottle of whiskey you have sitting on top of your file cabinet."

"Just tell me something, Winthrop. How did *you* come to learn so much about our operations?" Floyd asked.

"Why? Because I'm just a company officer? And you wouldn't think I'd know about such things?" Winthrop fired back at him. "Well, I'm a card player too. You don't become a winner at my games unless you learn how to bluff," he said with a smirk. "I didn't know a thing about what was happening to me and my men when we first rode down south escorting President Buchanan's original emissaries. We were just sent down there out of uniform, without any documents or any authority whatsoever. Then we were surrounded by Federal troops or troops who thought they answered to the elected assembly of South Carolina. The emissaries in actuality turned out to be some of your contractors, returning to their families in the South whilst they went reported as missing in the North. Very clever. They separated the officers and I never learned what happened to Captain Brewster. But he had previously told me that Fuller briefed him for this mission, and I told our enemy captain as much. Then I lied and said Fuller sent me down there with that unit to ensure nothing went wrong and that Brewster's men didn't start firing back. We weren't looking for bloodshed. The Rebel captain saw that I had it all figured out, and he thought I was part of the plan. He released me on the condition I did something for him. I agreed if he'd free Masterson, which took some real persuasion." Winthrop tapped his holstered gun with his right hand. "Major Fuller's bragged how he sits in favor with you, and I knew he was also from Virginia. I thought he just might be telling the truth, so I took a chance that he was playing on your side and I came here. You cost me."

"And you just conned me! Get out of my sight!" Floyd shouted.

Chapter 15

After giving it a lot of thought, Christopher resettled himself upon his original course of action. He was in Washington, D.C., and he had sworn to do his duty to the Constitution of the United States. He was supposed to report, and so he would report.

Pratt wasn't sure what kind of impression he would make as he walked up 17th Street dressed both for dinner and like he was going off to war, perhaps a century earlier. Lennox's flintlock pistol was once more secured in his holster at his side, and the ammunition cartridge case on his belt really didn't fit with his civilian clothes. But he gathered the War Department was welcoming of all kinds of visitors today as he approached the building's main entry and passed by two departing men. Pratt didn't really notice the first man, because he was too focused on the second. Hard to miss, he was a large, bulky fellow and he looked capable of doing any kind of hard physical work, but he was dressed in tatters. *Well, everyone's got a story today*, Pratt thought.

He was about to see how far he'd get with just the truth to comprise his own tale.

The sergeant of the guard sighed as Christopher tried to talk his way into the War Department building just as Winthrop had done an hour earlier. Pratt didn't know it, but he was only the second visitor out of uniform to claim a higher rank than the tiring man stationed at the guard post. This time the caller insisted on speaking with the regimental command. If the last man had pulled some display of stubbornness, Christopher unknowingly topped that by pulling a knife – if only to send a message. The utility blade that he withdrew from his belt was engraved with his military academy insignia. "Here, take this to the Colonel, then see what he says," Pratt suggested, extending the blade so that its handle could be easily taken by the guard. The man ran his eyes up and down the length of Christopher fixing on the flintlock pistol secured at his waist. Then, he rolled his eyes and sighed again before heading back inside the building to ask Major Venable what he should do with this one. It was turning into one busy day.

Minutes later, Christopher was escorted into the office being used by Colonel Thomas Cahill. About twelve years older than Pratt, Cahill was still a young man in his early-thirties with a neatly trimmed beard. He smiled while he extended a hand to welcome Pratt.

Christopher liked him immediately. He stepped back and saluted the colonel even though he wore civilian attire. "Lieutenant Christopher Pratt, Sir." To his pleasure, the colonel saluted back – at the very least, a gesture of friendship even though he had not yet proven his identity.

"I trained in New York myself not that long ago, Lieutenant," Cahill recollected.

"That's why I'm here, Sir," Christopher said. "I learned my duty well. It's my responsibility to report. But you're not going to like what you hear, Sir."

Cahill looked concerned as he sat down.

"I didn't know who I could trust with this," Christopher went on, memories of his men, Captain Lennox, Sergeant Cush, and his beloved horse Bonnie all coming back to him in a flood. Emotion stung his eyes and he started involuntarily blinking a lot.

"Take your time, young man," Cahill gently said. "What do you want to tell me?"

"I was with Captain Lennox, Sir. From Major Fuller's battalion. Our mission for the President…" Christopher got out.

"I'm aware of that mission," Cahill softly interrupted.

"I am the only one who survived, Sir," Christopher sobbed, unable to contain his emotions any longer. He realized now that he'd been blaming himself. *If I'd only been able to get free, I would have fought all of them off and helped save my men and my captain!* Then, he thought of Abigail, and he felt so very conflicted.

"It's alright now. Why don't you tell me what happened?"

"He sold us out."

"Who?"

"Some lieutenant. I'm not sure who, Sir. I didn't get his name but rather that of one of his subordinates. A man named Masterson.

But the lieutenant had to be from our battalion. No other group was training for this mission. I'd only served with Captain Lennox, Sir. There were a lot of men in other units I didn't know. But it's now apparent that Major Fuller secretly ordered a backup squadron to be formed from out of another company and readied just in case they were needed. Things were being kept real quiet. Yet we all know that cavalry doesn't operate east of the Mississippi, and now I've learned there was a mission before the one I rode with Captain Lennox. *Mine* was the backup squadron. And for Christ's sake, we have trains to get the Army around out here – where there's civilization. So, who else knew the cavalry was coming?

"We were ambushed, Sir. Everyone was lost – the men, the President's emissaries. There was nothing I could do." Christopher's voice cracked as he tried to hold back more tears and stand up straight before his senior officer.

"It's a good leader who cares about the men under his command, Mister Pratt."

"I care about my country too, Sir. And there's still more you need to know. I came back by way of the port in Charleston. And I saw them. They're stockpiling ordinance down there and preparing for war. There is no doubt in my mind, Sir."

"That's not right," Cahill mused. "The President is trying to reduce the size of the military presence in the east, hoping it will preserve the peace. The questions about the rights of slave states have been wrestled with since the birth of this nation. John Brown's violent revolt by radical abolitionists was recently put down permanently by Colonel Lee at Harper's Ferry. Why would things suddenly erupt into armed conflict again, right now, of all times? The health of our country is strong and we are enjoying the fruits of victory with its expansion after the Mexican War. And there's the admission for statehood of rich territories like California. Our nation is growing and prospering."

"It's not about the question of slavery, Sir – or even greater rights for the states with regards to self-determination." Christopher swallowed fear in this throat before suggesting to the colonel what he'd long began to suspect. "It's all about exactly who it is that's prospering."

70

The colonel frowned then looked down at his desk. Christopher couldn't tell what he was thinking. However, he didn't seem surprised by Pratt's statement, and he even acted as if he was expecting it.

"Major Venable," Cahill called out.

The major opened the door to the office. "Yes Sir?"

"Could you ask Secretary Floyd to join me, Major? Tell him it's very important that he comes over here immediately."

"Would you like me to wait outside?" Christopher inquired.

"No. I want you to give your report again to the Secretary of the War Department. I want to see his reaction."

Moments later, John Floyd came through the doorway. "What is it, Colonel? I'm very busy today. And how is it you figure you can summon *me* to your office?"

Lieutenant Pratt gave his report.

"Well, that's some story," Secretary Floyd responded after hearing Christopher's testimony.

"Is it true, Mister Secretary?" Cahill interjected. Then his eyes moved quickly from Floyd to Christopher and then back to the cabinet secretary. "If so, we could finally get this over with. My men are ready for a fight. But if the South wants to go, then personally, as a private citizen, I say let them go. I want my country to prosper and for that we need a strong government, not one constantly tied down by obstructionists trying to maneuver things for the benefit of Virginia."

"Excuse me, Sir, but Virginia will stay strong for the sake of Virginia, so help me!" Floyd exclaimed. Pratt suddenly realized that Cahill wanted to provoke the older man.

"I have no problem with that, Sir," Cahill explained, "but I've sworn to serve and protect a strong national union. My union's based on freedom. If Virginia doesn't want to be a part of that, then my private opinion is that she should be free to leave our union of the states. I just don't feel that the rest of my nation has to continue to pay for her protection. But as an officer, I will obey the President's orders. In the meantime, we have to do something about this." Cahill nodded in Pratt's direction, but Floyd didn't notice him quickly let a wink and a grin quickly escape his features that he guided towards the young man.

The Secretary shook a dismissive glance at Pratt. "He's your man. You do what you will within your own ranks," Floyd responded, sounding like better sense and caution had caught up with him. "Only I want Fuller brought back here as soon as possible," the cabinet secretary said, anger entering his voice again. "I'll find you a suitable replacement to lead his battalion."

"I'll select my own commanders, Mister Secretary," Cahill responded. "You just said I can do what I need to within my own ranks."

"Quit trying to manipulate me!" Floyd hissed. "For years I was a practicing attorney, so I recognize what you're up to."

"What I'm up to is for the good of my country, and you yourself have already agreed that it's also for the good of Virginia. I can keep this information about your little maneuvers quiet. It doesn't change things. I'm promoting Pratt here to captain, effective immediately. I'll sign the letter he'll take back with him to battalion and personally inform the man I choose to be his new commander. I think that should wrap things up nice and tidy."

Floyd growled, "I don't like you holding things over my head, Colonel."

"My state is the union, Sir. And like you, I'm just looking out for my state's best interest."

Secretary Floyd muttered under his breath, turned, and quickly exited Cahill's office, slamming the door behind him.

Pratt looked at his senior officer, unspoken questions reflected in his eyes.

"I'll tell him that I'm ordering you somewhere nice and dangerous, thereby tying up his loose ends," Cahill replied to the newly promoted Captain Pratt's unvoiced concerns. "I'm actually drafting new orders for you that will accomplish exactly the opposite.

"You liked it in New York before this chaos broke out." It wasn't a question, and Christopher kept silent as the colonel continued. "You've also now got real combat experience. I'm sending you back to the academy to train our new recruits. The Irish are flooding into the country and enlisting by the hundreds. We need good officers to set an example for them. Not only that, I need you where it's safe and I can find you if I need you. You're a living witness to that man's treason. Floyd's people and their scheming has gone on for longer than I can stand – and I only just found out a few minutes ago. We may not ever know how many have died because of their maneuverings. But I've suspected that, eventually, something like this would occur. I must be very careful about how I proceed against a superior, and a member of the Commander-In-Chief's cabinet."

Christopher nodded.

"Now, I don't think the two of us will succeed in stopping this thing," Cahill said, referencing the looming war between the states, "but we can survive to testify against those who started it for their own selfish reasons."

"Yes, Sir." Christopher came to attention and saluted.

"Stay out of trouble, Captain Pratt. Your country is going to need you."

Chapter 16

From Washington, D.C., Winthrop and Masterson navigated a course back to Massachusetts so that it led them through all the Irish whorehouses in New York. They finally arrived at their base camp in fresh crisp blue uniforms after taking their new horses with them on the ferry from Long Island to Boston Harbor. They looked clean and sharp as they rode into camp to report to Major Fuller.

Major Fuller, they were told, had been transferred. "Well, who's in command?" Winthrop demanded of a Lieutenant Remick at battalion headquarters.

"Captain Hunter, Sir. He assumed that responsibility since the Secretary of the War Department personally recalled Major Fuller. I've been working as the aide de camp for the battalion. Since Hunter doesn't outrank you, perhaps you should head over to C-Company command to sort this thing out. You'll find him there now, Sir."

"On that note, I've made a list of NCOs I want as squad leaders in my unit. I've served with them before," Winthrop stated. "They know how I like things done." He handed Remick the written list of names. The junior officer saluted Winthrop, who smirked. He was enjoying his new rank and privileges. "I'll send Lieutenant Talbot to you later to make sure you don't have any problems."

As they left the wood framed structure that served as the battalion command post at the fort, the men crossed the dirt grounds of the base camp site to look for Captain Hunter. Winthrop suddenly stopped short as soon as they were away from the command building. "This is just great." His sarcasm lacked subtlety. "Fuller's gone, and so's our money!"

"You didn't know for sure that you'd get anything more from the major after you emptied the pockets of Secretary Floyd back in Washington," Masterson said. "Is Floyd not telling Fuller that he promised you any money?"

"Floyd could be too embarrassed about that to bring up

74

the subject in the first place. But the way he's spending the government's funds on his military contracts, he's not very likely to worry about small payout requisitions down at the battalion level. Personally, I think Major Fuller owes us and then some. He could have drawn the pay for all the vanished men from our last mission, since no one's officially been declared dead. They aren't yet even listed as missing."

"But those men have families who expect money to be sent home. I can't see your plan working for more than a month."

"Then next month, I'll think up something else," Winthrop said as he grinned.

"You'd be well served to consider how your family would feel if the checks stopped coming and they hadn't received word as to whether you were alive or dead."

"I doubt Daniel's father would care," said a new voice as another man in a blue uniform approached and invited himself into the conversation. "Good to see you in one piece, Bob," he said, gripping the big man's forearm, despite Masterson's sour expression. "Captain," the newcomer said saluting.

"Lieutenant Talbot," Winthrop smiled, then returned his salute. "Have you been keeping things together?"

"I have, indeed. I had Corporal Crawford transferred to my platoon out from under Lieutenant Holloway. I couldn't get the lieutenant drunk so I just bothered him enough until that worked."

"Good. I wrote out a transfer list for this Lieutenant Remick that Washington sent us. I want you to follow up with him."

"Yes, Sir."

"It looks like Major Fuller got himself transferred. He'll no longer be here to protect us, and I don't think we've got any friends left in Washington. Floyd might have pulled the plug on him just to get after us. We'll see who high command sends next to lead at the battalion level, but we'll need to be careful of whomever it is. I think we're on our own for now."

"I'll make sure that Corporal Ritter knows I'm back and who's in charge now," Masterson said. "Captain," saluting Winthrop, before briefly glaring at Talbot. Then he strode off.

"You were quite right before, Jack," Winthrop addressed Talbot.

"My father doesn't give a damn if I send money home. He thinks I still earn enlisted pay, and he just wanted someone else to feed me and put clothes on my back. He taught me self-sufficiency. The other soldiers' families might learn a bit of that for themselves. We're the ones going out there under fire, risking our lives for other people's agendas. I'm just following their example and serving my own needs. We have to use our next best opportunity to come up with something big, take the money, and get the hell out of here while we're all still alive. The war is starting. And of course there's always the danger that someone outranking us could figure out who we really are."

"That was some stunt we pulled after enlisting to fight on the frontier," Talbot grinned. "Back then, I should have figured you'd never go soft, Dan. The way you outmaneuvered our officers, took their uniforms, and blamed it on the partisans. We left Wisconsin for the West as first-time enlisted men, and returned to the East as full lieutenants. And now you made captain!" Talbot chuckled. "You need to stop with all your schemes, Sir. You're making me laugh."

"They robbed the indigenous peoples of their lands and killed their women and children, then tried both expanding and abolishing slavery by force versus democracy. I just saw to it that the hypocrites reaped what they sowed, and a few of us prospered along the way, didn't we, Lieutenant?" Winthrop flashed a wide smile towards Talbot.

"They say ingenuity and perseverance reward themselves, and I'm always in favor of being rewarded!"

Chapter 17

"Captain Winthrop will receive his just rewards, Benjamin. That insolent son-of-a-bitch has earned what's coming to him. Of that you can be sure," Secretary Floyd told Major Fuller, who sat in his office and across the desk from him. "In the meantime, I'm re-assigning you to Washington where I can keep an eye on you. You'll replace Major Venable and serve on my recommendation. Colonel Cahill will soon find himself deploying with his regiment, so he won't be around to interfere with any additional personnel changes I want made around here." Floyd shifted back in his chair. "He might think he's protecting Pratt for the short-term, but no one's watching over Winthrop, and I haven't even begun to think up all the hellholes I could send him to. But first I'm sending him a loyal son of the South to personally convey new and immediate orders for our captain. Christopher Pratt must be eliminated. There must be no witnesses, Major. I'm sure Winthrop will stay obedient for just a brief while longer – it's in his best interest to cooperate anyway. At least while he waits for his money he thinks I'm paying him. Business will go on, Benjamin. Thanks to you, in spite of a few setbacks, but business will go on."

Chapter 18

The day to day business on the plantation never seemed to
change so when the post rider brought the newspaper, the appeal of
the larger world captivated Abigail and more than ever, she longed
for life beyond her parents' farm. She thought often of Christopher,
jealous of him and the adventures she imagined him having.

Abigail wrote to him frequently at first and prepared a letter
maybe twice a week. The mail carrier was a blond-haired French
man, young and slight-of-build, who told her that everyone
referred to as Bonaparte. He obviously liked Abigail and used the
secret hiding place by the magnolia tree for her mail, eager to do
everything he could to win her favor. Annoyed by his affections,
Abigail nevertheless needed the letter-carrier, so she led him on.
Christopher wrote Abigail back with about half as much frequency,
yet it didn't matter. She presumed him to be busy. However, Abigail
was not. Plantation life bored her enough that by the time the first
month had passed, she too wrote less often. There being nothing
left to say, she described her fantasies to Christopher. They always
involved him. Beyond that, to entertain herself, she would wait until
after her father read the newspaper, then snatch it before Mr. Davis
got his hands on it while her father set it down to read from the
Bible. Everything new intrigued Abigail and that certainly ringed
true about the turmoil in the country during a critical presidential
campaign.

October already, the election of 1860 only a month away,
fighting words championing Georgia's right to self-determination.
A man named John C. Breckinridge was the favored son of the
South and winner of the support of the Democratic Party. A new
Constitutional Union Party nominated John Bell for President.
But the Northern Democrats said Breckinridge's candidacy stood
invalid and Stephen Douglas won the nomination. The Yankee states
didn't even acknowledge Bell. However, contention caused by the
issue didn't even compare to the fear the Southerners had that a

man named Abraham Lincoln from the newly formed Republican Party would win, with South Carolina threatening to secede from the Union. Lincoln's backers were known to count both the pious abolitionists and Wall Street's big money class amongst them, the latter the chief holders of Southern debt. Lincoln's election would signal to the Southerners that the federal government could be open to using force to confiscate property and free the slaves as many of Lincoln's backers surely hoped their candidate would do, thereby drastically punishing the Southern dissidence. That would lead to open rebellion and civil war.

One day a mounted party brought back Mr. McGraw and Mr. Henry, along with other members of their party, to pay a visit to Abigail's father. When she caught sight of them this second time, the changes they evoked in her father during their last trip to see him did not make her feel comfortable with another encounter with these men at all. Following that first contact, Abigail had been kept awake all night by a loud, anger-fuelled discussion between David Hutchinson and Jonathon Davis and the jarring sound of their empty bottle of the church's wine being smashed into a thousand pieces against the dining room wall. She overheard heated words about 'changing one's religion' and 'having to pay the God-damned niggers unless they hired Irish.' For the next several weeks, Emma couldn't clean away the dark red stain the wine had made and Father threatened to whip her if it couldn't be washed off. Not wanting to disfigure his chief house servant, he ordered Davis to instead whip her friend Helena, a kitchen slave Emma always kept company with. He told them both in no uncertain terms how God frowned on laziness and that Hutchinson was ensuring that the slave women did good before their Lord. Abigail remembered watching as thin, light-skinned Helena, stripped of her shirt and bound chest against a tree, received the punishment while Emma stood there, forced to watch by Abigail's father. Abigail wondered if Mr. Davis thought he did good before the Lord. He certainly drew enough blood. The young girl quickly learned to hate these Northerners because of this injustice Hutchinson had told his daughter that the Northerners had brought on, which had spoiled the happiness and tranquility on the farm.

Now McGraw and Henry were back and they brought four more men with them.

Abigail decided to accompany her father and Mr. Davis when they walked down the plantation's long, tree-lined approach way to meet the visitors. She slipped in amongst Mr. Beehan, Mr. Hudgeons, Mr. Bailey, and Mr. Rawlings who walked out to take positions standing behind Hutchinson. The other men had been working, and some visiting, when the newcomers suddenly arrived. The Southern men were unarmed save for Mr. Davis, who was strapped with the gunbelt he always wore. Abigail pushed through the tall men and came up between Davis and Hutchinson, taking her father's hand. He quickly regarded her for only a second, gripped his daughter's hand tighter, but did not dismiss her, the gentlemen's conversation having already begun.

Mr. McGraw was a short, broadly-built man with thick graying hair and a bushy gray mustache. He proudly wore a gold timepiece on a chain across his puffed out chest and an even more distended stomach that he displayed under his black suit. He dismounted from his horse and stood toe to toe with Abigail's father.

"Not smart enough to reconsider, eh? Not smart at all, Mister Hutchinson," he said in a rough voice with a thick Irish accent. To her left, Mr. Davis spat on the ground. The men with Mr. McGraw moved their hands towards their gun holsters, but another large man who sat much taller on his brown horse turned toward their direction, behind him, and shook his head to indicate he meant for the other pedestrian-clothed men to take no action. Abigail felt his eyes turn to rest on her, a scrutinized focus above his dark mustache. She'd seen Mr. Henry once before with his sharp nose and black curls grown out, protruding under his brown Stetson the last time he and McGraw visited her father.

McGraw carefully touched Hutchinson's arm and boldly guided him between the plantation's men as Abigail, still holding her father's hand, kept close pace with them. Jonathon Davis stayed where he was, staring at Mr. Henry on his horse. Accorded the respect becoming a young lady, Abigail was aware that the more restless-growing strangers desired to reach for their guns, but those they looked to for leadership did not want to fire upon mostly unarmed men, especially amidst the presence of one of their children.

"You have to see it," McGraw continued. "Lincoln is going to be elected and South Carolina will start a war. Your plantation is heavily burdened by debt and the ensuing conflict will completely disrupt trade. How will you sell your cotton? You'll have no means with which to make your payments, which have been quite paltry I might add, serving the interest charged only. I know," he nodded. "The people I work for are connected in Tammany and they oversee many... banking concerns," McGraw coughed. "But I also know it is a very long, hot, and uncomfortable trip to come down here and discuss unpleasant matters with you, Mister Hutchinson. Just so that I'll never have to make this journey again, I will not take no for an answer this time. You have to sell the plantation. And I'm certain I'm your best, as well as *only*, offer." McGraw might have laughed out his last statement.

Hutchinson reached for his pocket and removed a flask he'd been carrying with him. Abigail caught the bitter-sweet smell of the wine she tasted when she took Communion. Her father sipped at present, then paused in stride and abruptly turned into Mr. McGraw. Anger supplied Hutchinson with power that he gathered into the words he hissed out with surprising force from his usually unimposing form. "I'm certain that things are the way we like it down here and you and your Catholic papist pigs are not going to wash up out of a boat onto my land and dictate my business to me! Tammany Hall and its corruption does not reach down here Mister McGraw, and so help me, I'll be damned if I'm the one who allows that to ever change!"

"You're making a very large mistake, Mister Hutchinson. A very large mistake. It's my observation that the farming business has gotten too expensive for you." McGraw's features hardened and he made the full turn to hunker down and barrel forward, reversing the distance they'd walked, and stomp right back through the Hutchinson workhands who parted to let him pass. He gathered the reigns to his horse and swung himself up into the saddle. With a glance at his men that they made no mistake interpreting, they parted their rides to either side and turned around, heading back the way they'd come.

Chapter 19

As darkness began to fall that evening, the white men on the farm occupied the sitting room in the main plantation house and loaded their rifles and guns. Abigail and Rachael observed them from the doorway. Rebecca wasn't interested, and Mark and Luke sat on the floor by their pa and watched the men, offering to help. Some seemed nervous, others angry. Their wives and the girlfriends that several of them had been courting, were also on hand, voicing their concerns.

Screaming over one another, their voices so loud that no one could hear the screaming from the slaves' quarters which came through an open window from a room adjacent to where the girls stood. Abigail and her sister ran in the direction they heard the noises coming from and saw the dark silhouettes of men running from the farm, one seeming to carry a white dress or being encumbered by someone wearing one. Looking to her left, Abigail saw why she could see anything on the dark farm in the first place. Several large crosses had been erected and lit aflame in the northwest corner of the front yard. She screamed for her father and Hutchinson came running to the window and then followed by his men they turned back down the hall and burst out the front doors into the yard. Abigail and Rachael followed her brothers outside after them.

The women slaves were in an uproar and came rushing out of the domicile where they were quartered in to run up on the white men. A few of the more distinguished-appearing black men appeared behind the Negro ladies, their bell collars ringing with their agitation, but they stayed back with explicit caution as Helena ran crying to Abigail's father and pounded her fists on his chest, collapsing against him within seconds. "They took my daughter! They took my Lilly!" She yelled aloud. Everyone looked at her, even the men who had drawn buckets of water from the well and were preparing to throw their contents to put out the burning crosses. "She be yours,"

Helena carried on. "You know this! You have to save her!"

Abigail sensed Rachael's look of curiosity fall upon her, but when she turned towards her sister and confirmed it, she impatiently motioned for the younger girl to look away and return her attention to the scene unfolding before them. She didn't have patience for her sister's questions right now as she felt her own emotions stir.

Hutchinson hesitated, uncertain what he should do and caught off guard by his slave's public and passionate insubordination. At last he closed his arms around her cautiously, gently rubbing the scar a whipping had left on her cheek. The pastor's eyes betrayed worry and he said in low tones, "It's alright. It's alright, Helena. We'll search for her."

"She be only twelve!" gasped out the slave mother. "My Lilly be only twelve!"

"Would someone kindly escort Helena back to her quarters and calm her there?" David Hutchinson then asked in an authoritative tone.

"Go back to your beds! All of you. Now!" Jonathon Davis commanded. The black men moved to reign back their women. Emma led Helena gently off Mr. Hutchinson by the arm.

"David, we're not going after them in the dark. That's what McGraw wants," Jonathon Davis said out of almost everyone else's earshot.

Hutchinson nodded in agreement. "So this is their move." He paused thoughtfully, just then noticing that his wife and the other women that had been inside the plantation home had appeared, outlined in the front doorframe before stepping out onto the veranda. Hutchinson immediately motioned them to return back inside, but his wife wouldn't move and even in the dark he paused, not needing to see her to be able to feel her stare steel daggers into him. "Margaret, for The Lord, take the women back inside, now. I want everyone but my men staying indoors tonight." To Davis he said, "We'll organize round-the-clock watches just in case they return."

"C'mon." Turning her gaze away from her parents, Abigail hoped her sister wouldn't notice the single tear that escaped her eyes, in their involuntary motion. She forced her features to harden, then addressed Rachael. "We spent all our lives playing about in this

country. We can find out where the men who took Lilly have gone.
The bad men will be watching for our own men to come on horses.
They won't ever notice us sneaking up on them on foot. No one
usually notices us." The girls ran through the home and out the back
door.

Two hours later the girls were filing through tall grass, walking
in silence for much of their travel, too weary to talk. Rachael
finally broached the silence. "Why do you think they headed in this
direction?"

"Water. This way leads down to Morgan's Stream." Abigail
pointed to the horizon ahead of them, indicating where the dark
shade of the night skyline separated from the still darker shade of
the landscape that the girls could just see over all the vegetation.
"As long as we keep focused on the higher ground, we know we're
heading north. Those men probably stayed on the fixed trail that
would take them either east or west when they came to Borland's
Crossroads. I'm guessing they turned west if they'd been down here
before and father had told them where to find water. They can't keep
riding back to threaten him if they turn east and head all the way
back towards Charleston. They don't like it down here. Besides,
they now have Lilly to mind to."

"I wonder what they'll do to her," Rachael said.

"Everything!" Abigail smiled to her sister in the dark. "I can
imagine all those big men all over her. A little black girl, she's just
property to them."

"Stolen property that belongs to our father," Rachael offered.

"Yes," Abigail said, her voiced distant as she mused, "our father."
Rachael could have no idea what her sister thought about.

The soil began feeling softer under the girls' feet, a clear
indication that the terrain changed. They were nearing the descent
to the creek bed. "Careful how you step," Abigail said. "It becomes
easy to lose your footing here."

Their voices became abruptly silent as they heard soft
whimpering and a man's angry voice garble something, then the
sound of flesh striking flesh. A girl cried out and her voice was lost
in the sound of male laughter until Abigail and Rachael overhead

her scream. The girls moved towards the sounds, parting the tall grass before them and watching the movement of large shapes that revealed themselves to be horses as they drew nearer to the commotion. One of the animals snorted as another very audible slap reached them, followed by repeated screams and more men's laughter.

Rachael stopped Abigail abruptly and silently pulled her arm, motioning her to look towards a tree just past the horses and before the water. A man with a satisfied smile on his face slept against the trunk, his red shirt barely visible by the moonlight, contrasting with the dark wood bark. His rifle rested against the tree behind him. But Abigail could not conceal the fact that she wanted to hurry up to see what went on inside a large tent the girls spotted, one end of it tied against another tree, and lit by a lamp from its interior. They proceeded on the tips of their toes around the sleeping man, nearly tripping over bedrolls that had been scattered out around the cooling embers of a fire ring assembled from river stones in the center of the circle of sleeping bundles. More of the laughter of the men reached their ears and Rachael started breathing faster. Abigail put her hand over her sister's mouth and pulled her back. "Do you want to give us away? Be quiet!" she commanded.

But both girls were too frightened to dare be the first to advance directly towards that lone tent that gave off the only light as the darkness of night settled in. Succeeding in having kept silent, they instead made their way around the encampment's perimeter through the brush that surrounded it, stopping behind a lone supply wagon. Abigail and Rachael were too scared to move again and could only listen and watched the shadows projected inside the tent reveal the outlines of a larger body thrusting itself upon a smaller form, and overheard the repeated screams with every collision. Other shadows, topped by the shapes of slouched hats, surrounded the subjects of their focus. The girls could see them shake in concert with the sound of male laughter. The scene unfolding being exciting for Abigail, her emotions were slow to adapt to the fear she should have felt at once when a man burst out from underneath the far side of the tent and came right toward the wagon. His foot landed hard on a boot-step and the girls felt his bulk swing into the wagon and its weight shift as the man fumbled around in the dark. In fear they listened to the sound of something heavy scraping the flooring, accompanied by the creak of hinges, and the sound of glass scraping against dry straw. Seconds later appeared the outline of the man stepping back out of the wagon with a liquor bottle in his hand. He disappeared back into the tent, where the screaming had resigned to the soft sounds of a girl sobbing.

It took a while longer, but eventually the shapes of five men emerged from the tent, lifting its rear side to each make a stumbling emergence out from underneath the cloth. The lantern that had illuminated it had begun to burn low. The shelter had been set up so that the side with its door flap had been tied up against the tree. Now the men all collapsed around their bed rolls, conversing and boasting loudly. Abigail motioned Rachael to follow her and the girls made their way from the cover provided by the wagon, around its edge, and scrambled for the tent. They moved behind it, out of the view of the men who were restoring their fire and falling asleep for the night. Arriving at a depression in the earth made by the roots of the tree to which the tent was affixed, the smell of urine and feces reached the young ladies' senses. Rachael furrowed her features. "Do we have to look?"

"Well we ought to find out what kind of shape they left Lilly in so we know if she's even worth returning to our father. Besides, I want to see," Abigail told her. She turned away just in case her sister could see her smirk in spite of the dark.

The girls parted the cloth from one of the entry flaps and found themselves staring at eye-level directly at Lilly's bludgeoned face. Puffed out from being repeatedly struck, her eyes were swollen shut and she slept from being overwhelmed and exhausted by her terrible ordeal. But she was still alive. The twelve year old girl tied up in a manner so she was restrained bent over, face against the tree, naked and standing in her own excrement. Blood had ran down and dried to her bare legs. Rachael moved to test the ropes with which the Northerners had bound her, but Abigail brushed her sister's hands away. "No," she whispered. "We can't rescue her. We don't even know if she can walk and it'll take us half the night to make it back to the plantation on foot from here."

"Then Father will get Lilly away from here?" Rachael asked.

"Yes. Father will get her," Abigail said dryly.

When they'd turned to regard each other in their discussion, one of the men burst into the tent from beneath its far side and the girls instantly released the door flap which they'd held. Abigail thought she saw one of Lilly's eyes open a crack and spot them as the girls left, but doubted she recognized whom she'd seen. Her glimmer of hope for a rescue died with the arrival of terror as the little black girl tried to scream again through the bandana that the man had just gagged her mouth with. The newcomer took her from behind. His thrusts were banging the wind out of her limp little body, repeatedly slammed into the tree.

"C'mon!" Rachael whispered, anxious not to get caught.

"No. I want to watch," Abigail stated with quiet discreetness, inserting a finger into her mouth and no longer bothering to hide the fact that she was aroused by what she was witnessing.

As Rachael tried to pull her older sister away, both girls were started by the sharp crack of gunfire as a new group of men on horses stormed into the camp, firing their carbines and six-shooters. White pillow coverings concealed their heads, punctuated by eyeholes cut into them so their wearers could see. The Northern men in their bedrolls scrambled to get to their feet and find their own firearms. Abigail had a second to take account of the charging four horsemen as they drove their steeds right through the still occupied bedrolls the Northerners had strewn on the ground. The campfire was scattered about, with burning timber exploding out of the fire ring, setting one bedroll aflame, its occupant making a panicked dance to free himself. Shots flew wild. The smell of sulfur permeated the air as the whistling noise of streaming bullets sliced through the sky. A shotgun erupted with the sound of thunder. The burst hit the tent and Abigail saw the large splatter of a bloody outline appear from the inside. The brown arm of a child hung through the doorflap and remained still. Crashing noises of something large moving through the underbrush behind them discouraged the girls from trying to make an escape in that direction and instead they turned and sprinted for the far side of the wagon. It would surely provide better cover than the tent.

As Abigail watched Mr. McGraw run from the tent stumbling while trying to pull up his belt and pants from off the ground to unholster his gun, she felt strong arms snatch her up from behind to be yanked off her feet and onto a moving horse. A masked rider sat her down in front of him. With an instinct she never knew she had, she reached over and grabbed his six-shooter he carried for quick access from a custom holster in his saddle, the man's concentration divided between balancing her on his horse and steering the jolting animal. Distracted at that moment, he actually didn't notice. "It's me, John Leahy," he proclaimed from beneath his disguise. "We've been searching all over Creation for you. Hold on! We've got to get you and your sister out of here while your father and Mister Davis distracts them."

Abigail caught a sight of Rachael on another horse, seated in front of another masked rider, as that mount and the animal she and Mr. Leahy rode on rushed for the cover of the underbrush. "We're to lead them back to the farm," Mr. Leahy informed her. "There's a surprise waiting for them. The slave's dead?"

"Yes. She's dead," Abigail solemnly told him.

Chapter 20

Mr. Leahy's horse threatened to jolt Abigail right out of the saddle as they galloped towards the tree-lined pathway onto their plantation manor's grounds. He brought his mount to a jerking halt as did his companion rider who'd carried Rachael. The women and the slaves alike all came running out into the front courtyard to meet them, Abigail's mother gathering Rachael in her arms as soon as she slid down from the horse. Her sister closed her eyes as she was taken in her mother's embrace.

"Oh my dear girl," Margaret Hutchinson wept. "You had us all so frightened that something terrible had befallen you."

The rest of the masked men made their rapid approach. One jumped down and removed his head wrap and Abigail recognized her father rushing forth to also embrace her sister. Helena pushed her way through the crowd behind several men who acted as wranglers. Her eyes desperately searched the new arrivals as the handlers made the horses their priority.

"Quickly! Get our families hid in the cellar. Use the stables and the pens to hide the slaves before the Yankees arrive here. They're right behind us!" Mr. Davis took command even while he dismounted and unmasked.

"Where is my Lilly? *Where is my Lilly?*" Helena rushed forward demanding of David Hutchinson.

Mr. Beehan grabbed her and pushed her back, but Hutchinson looked up, regarding her. "I'm sorry, Helena."

He shook his head and she fell to her knees crying, "No! My baby!" She'd let herself go limp, so Mr. Beehan grabbed her by one arm and began dragging her back towards the stables, her dress tracking through the dirt.

Abigail watching this scene unfold, got caught off guard when her mother's right hand smacked her across the face. "What were you thinking?" she exclaimed. "Taking Rachael with you and running off like that over a slave child of all things! You frightened the hell out of me and your father. And now you've forced this confrontation. The blood will be on your hands, Daughter. I hope you're mature enough to live with that," her mother spat.

Then Abigail's father grabbed her from behind. She nearly dropped the gun she'd taken and now tried to conceal in the folds of her dress. Her parents didn't notice anything in her hands. Typical. "We love our children and could not stand to lose two of you, let alone even one," Hutchinson said.

"What about Lilly?" Abigail asked. Her mother's reddened face reflected surprise at Abigail's question, but her jaw clenched with anger.

Noting their exchange, her father said, "There's no time for that. You must take shelter with the rest of the women."

Mr. Leahy rushed upon them at that moment. "I…I don't have my gun," he exclaimed. "I must have dropped it. Are there still extra rifles in the house?"

Then the muzzle flashes of the now-mounted Northerners' carbines sparkled like embers jumping about in the wind and their thunder called out their owners' intentions.

"There's no time!" Hutchinson exclaimed. "Take my family! No wait. I'm armed. I'll accompany you to the cellar…to protect them."

The property owners, farm workers, and the slaves all alike, scattered to their hideaways as powder flashes lit up the night, streaks of red lines cutting through the black. The majority of the armed men amongst the Hutchinson's plantation hands and the neighboring farm owners with their workmen dispersed to take cover behind the trees lining the main pathway, while Davis, Hudgeons, Bailey, and Rawlings rushed to overturn a large transport cart in the dirt drive and use it for cover as they returned fire over it. Mr. Beehan barked orders as the men took positions amongst the trees.

McGraw's men concentrated their fire on Davis' group behind the cart and were riding right into the hastily assembled ambush.

Apparently working, Abigail thought that her people's plan had to have been rehearsed as she stopped short of the barn's entrance that led to the storm cellar and spun around to watch the fight ensue. Better prudence lost to anger, McGraw and the unmistakable form of Mr. Henry drove their attack. His tan duster reflecting starlight, Rawlings stood distinguished in the battle when he rose to fell McGraw with his shotgun. Black spray emanated from the man as he launched backwards off his horse straight into the path of Henry who never paused to regard him, trampling the fresh corpse with his own steed.

The Southern men behind the trees opened up as the Irish horde passed them. The yellow and red flashes of ignited sulfur paralleled these men falling over their horses and being trampled upon even before the crackling of the gunfire reached Abigail's ears. A shot smacked into the wood beam just above her head and splinters exploded out in every direction. The girl gasped but couldn't move or avert her eyes from watching it all play out.

Suddenly, Davis emerged from behind his cover and walked in plain sight of Mr. Henry, who slid his horse to a standstill while he balanced on his toes inside the stirrups and released one round and then another at the foreman. "Fucking Protestant heretic! Acting all high and righteous while you think you can default on your debts and steal from us! From us!" Henry's shots scattered the dirt at Jonathon Davis' feet as the commander of Hutchinson's work crew scattered Henry's brain matter out the back side of his head with a shot from his Walker Colt right between the Yankee thug's eyes.

"Not a smart move, Mister Henry. Not smart at all," Mr. Davis said.

Chapter 21

Now prudence required getting the dead bodies off the front drive as quickly as possible. With dawn breaking the daylight could bring any manner of passerby. Hutchinson organized his slaves into a burial detail and six fresh graves were dug out along the path to the main house, yet deliberately as far away from the residence as possible. The excavations were made nearest where the Northerners had fallen for expedience. The slaves could always be ordered to relocate them later. The minister of the plantation as well as the master, David Hutchinson informed the Negroes that the actions of his men and the resulting deaths occurred in the course of him defending the slaves, as he loved all the black folks on the plantation like they were members of his own family. They were all the children of the Lord of his church in whose name he had done his solemn duty. Hutchinson could be a captivating speaker. It certainly motivated the slaves.

Hutchinson also informed them that they would be dismissed from their work for the rest of the morning, and that Mr. Davis and some of the plantation hands would escort the slaves down to Morgan's Stream so that they might take care of their own kind's remains afterward, according to their customs. A wolf howled in the distance, another one answering it, and Abigail wondered how Helena would react when she found what was left of her young Lilly, and what condition the girl's body would be found in.

As she wandered about on the path that approached her home, the clapping noises of falling hooves claimed her immediate attention. Daylight had just broken and the slaves were not done hiding even the first of the bodies of the Irish men. Abigail checked the weight of the satchel she now carried, just like Christopher's. Reassured by feeling the now familiar mass of the gun she's swiped off Mr. Leahy, she headed back down the path, away from her residence and the grave diggers, to intercept the plantation's visitor, Abigail being the closest to the road.

But the road didn't rest far enough away from the site of the previous night's carnage, and Bonaparte had already drank in the scene. "Abigail…," he stammered. "I don't…I'll go for help. Your family will need a magistrate to sort this out. I can't…"

"You can do nothing," Abigail interrupted. "You will say nothing. You don't understand what happened here."

"I understand I care for you," the blonde Frenchman said in accented English. His blue eyes revealed his concern for her. "If your family be in trouble with bad men…" Bonaparte really didn't know how he would complete his sentence in any language.

Abigail sighed. For his part, Bonaparte looked legitimately scared. "The mail." Abigail called to remind him as he started to trot his horse away from the Hutchinson farm.

In that instant, Abigail knew he would run, yet he couldn't be allowed to report anything to the authorities. As a letter carrier, when the county sheriff and the attorneys questioned him they'd requisition the Hutchinson's mail to look for evidence. Correspondence from Christopher might be found, and the identities of these corrupt agents from New York that her family was burying would surely be exposed. Everyone would know how and why the Northern men failed to return from Georgia. Then, not only would the Hutchinsons be accused of bringing Tammany Hall down upon their neighbors, but everyone would be put in further danger from the criminal institution's giant grasp for vengeance. That meant Christopher could quickly be exposed and also put in that danger, his being much closer to these thugs' base of operations. Then Abigail's whole scheme to run away to him would be put in jeopardy.

She reached into her knapsack and withdrew Leahy's pistol. It was suddenly heavier than she remembered and she had to use both hands to draw back the hammer. Abigail fired. The recoil jerked her back so hard that she nearly fell down. Her own shot being the loudest she'd ever heard, especially at that range, it really scared her. The bullet went wide and Bonaparte startled, still not far away, stopped his horse and turned in disbelief that Abigail had actually shot at him. Less than twelve yards away from her, an easy target for even an inexperienced shooter, he'd be taken by her second bullet, mouth open, still in a state of surprise that Abigail made the move to kill him.

The slaves will just have to dig one more grave, the girl thought as she anxiously looked to her right, up the long path to the plantation. Her father, Mr. Davis, and Mr. Rawlings were running down the driveway, responding to the shots fired and rushing to see what had now just happened.

Abigail ran to the dead letter carrier and quickly searched his mailbags, spilling the letters out everywhere. Her intuition proved correct, and she did find one letter from Christopher which she immediately stuffed down the neckline of her dress, safe inside the tightness formed by the ties of her corset. She dumped the rest of the spilled mail back into the dead post-rider's carry bags, her actions obscured by the fact that before he died, Bonaparte had moved his horse beyond the trees, not allowing for a clear view for the men running down the plantation's main pathway.

Abigail looked at Leahy's still-smoking gun, lying in the dirt next to the body. Bonaparte had instantly fallen off his horse. The animal stopped only half a dozen yards away and had paced around and sniffed its former rider for a moment while Abigail had been re-packing all the mail.

She had only seconds to stand back up and reflect upon the scene she'd painted in front of her until her father and his men arrived. Abigail had already seen slaves beaten, a child lose her life, and six men taken down so her reaction to death was now quite desensitized. And she felt rather detached and distant from whatever her father was shouting at her.

Mr. Davis examined Bonaparte's body and found the gun. He held it up for Hutchinson to view. It had been Leahy's pistol.

"What were you doing with a gun?" Hutchinson demanded of his daughter. "What were you thinking?"

Abigail suddenly turned around and pushed her small face into her father's, hissing, "At least *some* Hutchinson needs to fire a weapon and defend this family!"

"But I–," her father stammered, crunched up his features as he looked away from his daughter, then turned and reached for his flask he'd filled to carry in the pocket of his gray vest he now wore.

"I'm so glad you could keep everyone safe in the wine cellar last night," came his daughter's retort.

"Storm cellar," Hutchinson corrected her.

"Uh-huh." But Abigail thought that this time she smelled whiskey in the flask and on her father's breath. Mr. Davis and Mr. Rawlings were staring at her. "He was going to report what happened here to the authorities," Abigail nodded towards Bonaparte's cooling body. "I made the choice I was supposed to."

Chapter 22

Privately, Abigail did not stand so sure that she'd done the right thing. Her parents didn't talk to her much, but they never had. Yet she could feel her sisters distance themselves from her, though Mark and Luke showed a bit more respect for their oldest sister. Now the previously ever-friendly Emma seemed to limit the time she'd spend listening to Abigail. Her attitude towards white people in general had changed since the death of her best friend's daughter. With no one on the plantation with whom she could talk to about Bonaparte's killing, Abigail finally decided to write about her doubts to Christopher. She figured that while the government couldn't decide complicated things like the questions of states' rights and the status of slavery, they could at least figure out that the mail no longer got through. She'd come to another arrangement with the new letter carrier. Someone had to send somebody to replace Bonaparte soon.

November now, the Hutchinsons had been collecting their supplies for the winter in Atlanta. Though they preferred to do their business in Charleston, many were avoiding the ruckus developing there since Abraham Lincoln's election. So they came by the first newspaper they could get their hands on after the election by way of their own state's largest marketplace. They timed the trip for when the voting members of the white male population with property needed to report to the capitol anyhow. The growing defiance in South Carolina put pressure on Georgia for the state to make up its mind about secession as well.

In the city, Abigail pleaded with strangers for coins. Her charms worked and she mailed off her letter to Christopher. She hoped that by describing the events that had occurred the past month on the plantation, he would not think that she and her family were a bunch of monsters, but Abigail couldn't possibly know what kinds of lies the Northern capitalists were spreading through *their* newspapers that Christopher might be taken in by.

November 11, 1860
My Dearest Christopher…

Abigail had begun, first inquiring about his welfare and whether he'd had the opportunity for any contact with his parents and the well-being of his family. She used 'family' as a segue into discussing her deteriorating relationships with her own kin, and then described to him the horrible incident on the farm. Abigail related the start of her father's new drinking habit, and the nervousness also shown by the other plantation owners like Mr. Bailey and Mr. Hudgeons, their previous violent contact with the Northern Catholics, and its effect on all their future planning.

It was Abigail's opinion that though her father talked a lot and often brought up relocating everyone and restarting his own *real* Christian values church congregation somewhere out west, she was the only one amongst her immediate family who had actually taken any real action. She'd re-evaluated things once more and now took pride in her behavior. Though the results had been unintentional, she had known how to find the slave child and making her move had forced the other men into doing something about the corrupt Northern tyrants that plagued them. And then she'd made the decision that one immigrant postal carrier's life wasn't worth bringing down any further wrath upon them from New York's most powerful criminal gang. Christopher would have to see it her way.

Chapter 23

"Major Fuller doesn't see it that way," Richard Wythe said. "As long as Christopher Pratt is still breathing, the major's not paying."

"Really," Daniel Winthrop said, his voice dry.

An average-sized young Virginian wearing a United States Army sergeant's blue uniform, Wythe's narrow eyes and tight square features seemed chiseled out of stone. He looked much older than his age, and there was something dangerous lurking behind his unassuming physique. Expressionless, the man continued speaking privately to Winthrop and Jonathon Talbot in the company headquarters tent, as Sgt. Masterson stood outside and blocked the entry door.

"Not long after you left Washington, he learned that Pratt was a living witness to his treason. He suspended the deal you and Sergeant Masterson made with Secretary Floyd indefinitely."

Winthrop turned slightly to direct his comments to Talbot, "I'm sure Floyd's still shipping arms south and he's afraid that sooner or later he's going to get caught. And Fuller's hands are dirty. That's why Floyd had him relieved. Probably sent to a desk in the War Department where Floyd can keep an eye on him. But I see Fuller's still enjoying any opportunity to mess with us, and he wants something to hold over Floyd so he has a chair when the music stops. Yet it's been, what, four months gone by now? I haven't heard of any specific problems with this coming out of Washington. Have you?" Winthrop asked Talbot.

"No. No problems. Why?" Jack responded, eyebrows arched, trying to look as disarming and innocent as possible, his extended length of light brown hair moving with the shrugging of his shoulders.

Winthrop turned back towards Wythe. "So who is this Christopher Pratt and what's he got to do with it? What does he think he knows?"

"He knows your sloppy work, *Sir*," Wythe said, still almost expressionless, save for that slight hint of disrespect afforded to his tone while he addressed his superior officer. "Pratt survived when Captain Morris attacked Buchanan's convoy in Georgia."

"That's bullshit, Sergeant." Winthrop shook his head. "I was there. I saw what remained of Alpha Company when the smoke cleared. Morris made sure that no one walked out of there."

"At least not in the same boots they rode in on," Talbot said under his breath. Winthrop laughed but waved his friend to be quiet anyway.

Wythe continued. "Secretary Floyd found someone who'd beg to differ with that assessment standing not three feet in front of him in Colonel Cahill's office four months ago. Floyd's been obstructing his enemies from making their move against him and has held out thus far, especially motivated to keep the Democrats from becoming involved in another scandal before the election. But his friends that were protecting him no longer have any interest in doing so, now that Lincoln has won the vote. Floyd's business rivals are already prepared to make their move against him – and all his cohorts. Floyd tied himself to Breckinridge and lost, but Tammany Hall also slipped their dirty money behind Douglas. Even with two candidates they couldn't win the election, but they still have a lot to lose – notably their interest in the arms shipping business if their intermediaries are exposed and forced to give up their suppliers. Now there will be a war and that's the truth. Christopher Pratt can testify on behalf of that version. Since you have your own version of the truth concerning your role in the arms trade, if I were you I'd see to it that's the only version that becomes known." Wythe's voice betrayed no emotion.

"Then I get paid?" Winthrop asked, his tone now more serious.

"Then you get paid."

Winthrop's smooth features scowled and his hand rubbed his chin while he thought. "Where is this Pratt now? Still in the service? Is he some private or corporal? Stationed where?"

"*Captain* Pratt is in New York at the Academy."

Winthrop and Talbot exchanged quick, nervous eye contact. "I can't believe this. I'm supposed to just drop everything, take off, and ride down to New York to take care of another errand for Major

Fuller?" Daniel Winthrop asked, his attitude inflected in his voice. "Neither of us can ever set foot in the Academy. Fuller knows that. I don't suppose you know anyone who's good at this sort of work, do you?" he asked Wythe, his suspicion aroused.

"I can give you some names."

"It figures. There's just one man, right? Then we should only need one shooter," Winthrop reasoned. "One who could get the job done."

"These Sharps come as a team. As of only this year they were hand-picked by Hiram Berden for special training in New York, to exemplify the potential of organizing elite units to the president. Just in case there's a war." Wythe's mouth twitched as if he'd tried to smile.

"And I'd bet that paying whatever they cost to hire would cost us almost as much as Floyd promised that Fuller would pay me. Right?" Winthrop asked, no longer looking amused. Talbot's expression had grown as cold as stone, too.

"Can either of you two, or Masterson, get into the Academy? And have you the kind of skill with a firearm that's necessary for a job like this? The men I work for don't want a running firefight – especially not on campus at West Point. This has to be executed perfectly. At the right opportunity. A single, clean shot."

"Then why pay four shooters?" Jonathon Talbot interjected.

"There could be one second chance," Wythe replied matter-of-factly.

Winthrop rolled his eyes. "This is just great," Winthrop said aloud. "You know, I wasn't even part of the original ambush. I just supplied information and got coerced into coming along." Winthrop gestured towards the front of the tent where Masterson stood guard outside. "So Pratt's not my responsibility. Why doesn't Fuller get Morris to handle this? It oughta be his job."

"Secretary Floyd has you," Wythe coolly reminded him.

Chapter 24

"So we're going to New York for Christmas?" Corporal Ritter asked the rhetorical question with a half-hearted smile. The three top commanders of what was formerly Bravo Company stood around in the headquarters tent rubbing their arms to fend off the winter's cold during this meeting with three of their enlisted subordinates. None of them looked happy.

"I'm sorry about this Will." Winthrop addressed Ritter, while Masterson would periodically peel open the tent flap and keep his eyes trained on Richard Wythe, making sure the man's tracks led him across the snow and far out of earshot. "Fuller's given me no choice. So I have to deal with this and I'll need my best men with me if I'm going to finish my business with these fellows."

"Oh, he already knows that you and the *lieutenant* here aren't cut out to handle this kind of thing," Masterson stated contemptuously.

"Not now," Talbot sternly rebuked him.

"Masterson's right, Jack. Fuller really underestimates me and what I'm capable of. That will be his undoing." Then Winthrop ignored his officers in favor of continuing to address Corporal Ritter, who could have easily been mistaken for Winthrop's younger brother, if the captain had one. The men looked alike. Putting his hands on Ritter's shoulders, he looked into the young man's eyes as he continued informing the corporal of his plan. "They'll expect me and your First Sergeant here to try and pull something out of our hats. And they'll probably figure on that being me having Lieutenant Talbot follow us. So this is where you boys fit in. Are you ready to make a little money in this?"

The large, tough soldier Jonathon Hill pressed his index finger into the tip of his field knife that he'd been examining, testing its sharpness until it drew blood and responded for Ritter. "Christopher Pratt *and* Richard Wythe are as good as dead, Sir."

A short while later in the company headquarters tent, Jonathon

101

Talbot vigorously rubbed his arms again. The officers' subordinates had departed. "I'm sure glad we at least got to spend some nights in the barracks. Sleeping on the trail in the wintertime when we shouldn't have to is not my idea of fun."

"We'll have fun in New York City, Jack." Winthrop answered him, but his face reflected no nonsense. "After Wythe and his team make their move to kill us."

Talbot's eyes reflected his concern at Daniel. Masterson rotated the cylinder on his gun by rolling the half-cocked weapon down his arm. Resetting the hammer in the rest position, he spun and holstered the revolver. "We were expecting this," the sergeant said. "Albeit a lot sooner than now."

"It's a set-up. Get rid of the witnesses, and then eliminate the rest of us, framing us as the assassins, I'd bet. But you can just relax," Daniel finally smiled again. "I already have a plan."

Chapter 25

"The plan for you is to stay where you are, young man," Colonel Robert E. Lee addressed Captain Pratt, who stood at attention in West Point's Superintendent's office.

Pratt felt in awe of Colonel Lee, decorated veteran of the Mexican War, and the man rumored to be the first recommendation of the new Secretary of War Edwin Stanton, for becoming the next commanding General of the whole United States Army – pending the seventy-four year old Winfield Scott's expected resignation, of course.

"Colonel Cahill spoke to me personally about you," Colonel Lee continued, his hand stroking his short, white beard.

Though respectful of such a renowned officer, Abigail's recent correspondence about the attack on the plantation had heightened Christopher's desire for permission to take his leave off campus to a state of urgency. Prepared to even offer his resignation as a training officer at the academy, he'd been considering running down to Georgia and eloping with Abigail. He'd have done so before but rumors that former Secretary Floyd would finally come under criminal investigation, caused Christopher to feel obliged to do his duty and keep his promise he made to Colonel Cahill. So he waited, disappointed that Floyd's treason had still gone unpunished by the government he'd been taught to revere. He owed Cahill for protecting him. But he also had thought Abigail remained safe where she was so long as she stayed on her father's plantation. The violent events of late demonstrated that was not to be the case. Abigail had wanted to be with him and Christopher had owed a debt to her first, and he'd promised her that she would be with him. Once in the past, he thought his best option was to lie to the girl and tell her what she wanted to hear just so she would not complicate his departure from her family's farm. That being his original intent, it hadn't taken long for the temptation she offered him to take root in his very soul. Now, so as long as danger stalked her anyway, he might as well be the one ensuring her protection, and they'd survive or die together if the reach of Tammany Hall could ever catch up with them.

"Now I understand you love this girl, but you must let Our Lord and the local authorities help defend her and her family's situation," the white-haired colonel continued. "There's little you could do and South Carolina is putting our Army in a very difficult position. Georgia, preparing to vote on whether or not to organize its own secession committee, is not the place for you to be right now, young man. Your life may be endangered by Southern rebel partisans, as well as those in the arms business. Let us not forget, your betrothed and her family are targeted by a powerful Northern criminal organization holding considerable political clout both north and south of the Mason-Dixon. You see that there's nowhere the two of you can go, Captain. On top of that, we may still catch my old friend James Floyd. Now he's a very influential man. But if a Congressional tribunal could find he's acted dishonorably in office, as a very important witness, your very life would be in immediate danger – from him and those he's doing business with. I know Floyd to be a man of conviction, and his loyalty to our home state of Virginia allows for there to be no compromise with this man. He believes in the cause, but he won't go as far as to become a martyr. It will be others that he'll make pay for his transgressions. You my son, must stay safe. Now I thank you for bringing this to my attention, but you will have to entrust this to God's hands," Colonel Lee said. "It's all in God's hands now."

Christopher felt amazed and very grateful that he could be so comfortable talking openly to this great and most experienced commander before him. The empathy the colonel offered astounded him. Nevertheless, he'd predetermined his course, and Christopher's next tendered his resignation.

"Your offer has been duly noted, Captain, but I cannot accept it at this time," Colonel Lee informed him. "We are soldiers in this great Army and our duty binds us, just like Mr. Floyd's knows that his own binds him in the service of Virginia. I trust that you will fulfill your obligation to your country in the honorable manner of an officer and gentleman graduated from this institution."

"I see, Sir," Christopher responded. Disappointed and shifting in his uniform with frustration, he found a way to keep the conversation going so Lee couldn't dismiss him, all the while panicking on the inside as he searched for another approach to winning his freedom. His curiosity and the casual climate fostered by the colonel inspired him to ask, "Do you think the other Southern States will follow South Carolina in secession? What will that mean for the Army, Sir?"

"South Carolina was poised to make up her mind before Christmas." Colonel Lee spoke thoughtfully, his expression troubled. "These are most precarious times. It's expected that the cotton states will follow them into the rebellion." Lee paused, then solemnly offered, "I too must abide by the wishes of the legislature in my home state of Virginia."

Christopher's disappointment became fully realized as the knowledge of who he spoke with truly settled in.

Chapter 26

"I first wish you to know that Cabinet Member Floyd just resigned from his post," Richard Wythe said, as Daniel Winthrop and Robert Masterson took their seats with him one evening in a brick tavern located on the corner where three of many nearly anonymous streets converged in downtown New York City. "I had to read it in the paper myself on December 29th."

"Like that wasn't expected," Daniel Winthrop commented dryly.

"Happy New Year. But it changes nothing," Wythe said.

"That's right." Winthrop agreed, his voice turning nasty.

"Then understand me," the representative for the assassins said. "The men that you wish to hire don't work for free. It's not our way to work for nothing up front, but I understand the circumstance you're in. Nevertheless, we better get paid when the job is done." Wythe's exhale, as icy as his tone, appeared as clearly as his meaning in the cold drinking establishment, the busy room not warmed in the slightest by all the patrons and the oil lamps and fireplaces lit to welcome them. In spite of their quest for anonymity in the bustling establishment, Winthrop knew that there were eyes watching him. Nevertheless, there wouldn't likely be any hostilities exchanged here.

"Or else?" Winthrop coolly asked.

"Or else, the Sharps come after you," Wythe responded to him.

"Of course. I have to run your fee by Major Fuller," Winthrop said to him. "There might be some further delay because of Floyd's change in career plans. But I still want my money those two owe me. Upon receipt of the funds, I offer to pay the Sharps the bounty of sixty-five dollars after I've seen that Pratt is dead for certain. That's fifteen dollars per man, plus five for your role in arranging it." Winthrop tested Wythe.

"Two hundred. That's non-negotiable," the sergeant countered.

"Two hundred?"

"Yes. The men each spent over three months of their own pay

for their own state-of-the-art firearms. Then trained hard with them – a lot on their own time. They need to cover our expenses. I also happen to know exactly how much Floyd promised you. But you didn't get the job done the first time around."

He said 'our expenses,' Winthrop thought, *Wythe's not an intermediary. He's the leader of the fire team.* Daniel had suspected this. Wythe had given off many tells in their conversation already. He might be a good shot but the man was a lousy liar, while Daniel was a pretty experienced gambler. Winthrop had already been planning just how to aggravate him so Wythe would make a mistake. Out loud he responded, "I wasn't in command. Captain Morris ran the whole show. I was practically his prisoner. I told you that when we first met," Winthrop said, anger accompanying his explanation.

"Are you whining to me?" Wythe glared at the captain.

Winthrop's eyes danced around the bar. "I'll show you what I can do to you," he said. Suddenly he moved to draw his revolver. But Wythe was quicker and his pistol stood aimed at Winthrop's chest before Daniel's own gun came up. Both men had locked the hammers back into firing positions, when Masterson made his move to draw. Instantly, four other guns were trained on the cavalry officers. Curiously, Daniel Winthrop never blinked. Masterson watched his boss. Winthrop smiled instead.

"I thought it was time to make you introduce us to the men we'd be hiring," Winthrop said. "Him first." Daniel nodded to one of the gunmen, a large fellow with a pistol directed straight at Winthrop's face, and Jonathon Talbot's tall form emerged from the crowd by the bar behind this man, his cocked gun stuck behind the big fellow's left ear.

"This is Private Luther Ladd," Wythe said, introducing him while never taking his eyes off Winthrop, nor lowering his gun. Ladd made no acknowledgement of his introduction and kept his gun trained on the cavalry captain as he approached Winthrop's table. Dressed in civilian clothes so he blended in, Talbot now moved with Ladd, his own pistol kept flush against the big man's skull. Right handed with his revolver, Winthrop noted that Ladd also carried a new breach-loading rifle in his left hand. "He's pleased to make your introduction. And behind you are Corporal Sumner Needham, Privates Addison Whitney and Charles Taylor," Wythe smirked, obviously pleased with the men's covert tactical positions. He removed a small box from a satchel he wore over the tunic of his blue extended winter uniform and plucked a cigar from it, biting the tip and spitting the wad off on the floor beside him.

The other patrons at the ale house didn't seem too concerned about the military officers drawing weapons on each other. Some handled their own instruments of destruction that they carried with them, various stabbing weapons, a few revolvers, and an occasional axe or tomahawk as they observed, eager for someone to escalate the confrontation. *A rough joint*, Winthrop noted with approval. Most soldiers wouldn't be stupid enough to open a ball in a place like this. To all other eyes, these men in uniform represented the government, and the bar's patrons appeared none too appreciative of the law. There even existed talk of secession in New York that he'd come to know of. The men who lived amongst the streets here made up their own rules. But so did Winthrop.

"You can lower your weapons, Captain. Neither one of us wants to start a firing contest here," Wythe said, sure that at least on this issue, he stood in agreement with the other man.

"I love New York," Daniel grinned. "You go on and holster Sam Colt first – as a gesture of good will towards your fellow men, perhaps." Winthrop smiled at Wythe. Their sergeant nodded and the Sharps recovered their arms. Winthrop took a mental inventory of the breach-loaders that even counted new Spencers, and Henry Rifles amongst them. He licked his lips. He still kept his pistol trained on Wythe who never gave any indication of his being the least bit troubled about it. "Next tell me why should I believe that you and your men won't kill *us* when you're done with Pratt? You don't need me or my boys for this. Fuller could then pay you our money he's stealing. Or does he find *me* completing the transaction with you to be amusing?"

"Major Fuller must feel you're still of some use to him. You have rank, command more men then I can, and you work a lot cheaper. Quite a bargain for him, I'd say. Yeah?" It was the first time Wythe genuinely smiled, as he lit the cigar with a match he struck on their table.

Winthrop's feigned laughter at his own expense with a glance aside and a sniff. He caught some air fouled by the stench of Wythe's cigar. His own expression settled into something unreadable, and hardened like stone, his eyes narrowed and trained like daggers on Wythe.

"So your team's fee buys our lives, and then we're through?"

"Your cavalry and the Sharps' business is through. So is Christopher Pratt when we set out to do our job. Beyond that, me and my men have nothing to do with your relationship with the major and our disgraced cabinet secretary. That's all between you and them."

"Alright. I don't see that we have much of a choice," Winthrop said dryly, leaning back in his chair and finally lowering his weapon. "We'll keep in touch and look for opportunities. You can locate Pratt and then keep your eyes on him if your unit's not otherwise occupied."

"My men are being added to Lieutenant Holloway's platoon and it's being transferred to serve under your command, *Captain Winthrop*." Sergeant Wythe sneered when he stated Daniel's rank. Winthrop figured that Major Fuller must have informed the sergeant that he and Lieutenant Talbot were only freshly enlisted recruits when they'd achieved nearly impossible self-promotions by involving themselves with this arms-dealing scandal.

"Well, it seems I'm to plan some holiday travel back to Washington. It's the season to call upon your friends, and I need to make sure that my friend Major Fuller has a good present for me." Daniel glanced at his right hand and it folded into a fist. "And I have a present for him. Then once we have our funds, we'll settle up over Pratt's cooling body and I won't owe you anything further, *Sergeant*. I hope we're clear." Winthrop forced himself to speak with authority in spite of everyone in their present company's knowledge of his unearned rank. But he felt assertive, angry he dealt with Wythe and not the major.

"We're clear, Sir," the man revealed to be the Sharps' leader replied, for the first time being respectful of Captain Winthrop's official status, a profitable deal for Wythe's team now secured by their meeting's conclusion.

"You should have blasted that smart-ass. I thought you were always a quicker draw than that," Masterson said when the other gunmen had left them.

"I am. It's to my advantage not to let Wythe know that, until the second comes for him to learn it the hard way," a reflecting Winthrop stated, glaring after the closing door where Wythe and his men had exited. Another glance around the crowd revealed the locations of Ritter, Crawford, and Hill, dressed as civilians, blending in with the other patrons of the bar, nevertheless ready to back their boss up in the event of some action.

Immediate action on their plans did not happen though. On January 27, 1861, Floyd was indicted by Congress on charges that his office coordinated running guns to arm the southern states preparing for secession. President Abraham Lincoln would be sworn into office on March 4 and his Justice Department wasted no time. By March 7th, the case would be closed and Major Fuller had taken the blame for the weapons shipment scandal and stood imprisoned, while all charges against Floyd were dropped and he returned home to Virginia. Colonel Cahill had been dispatched to contain increasing threats of violence in Missouri, and Christopher Pratt had never been called to testify what he'd witnessed the previous summer. However, Fuller got an appeals hearing for his sentence, and still had access to considerable funds through Floyd. The latter clearly didn't want his role in the case to be further investigated, and demonstrated his appreciation of Major Fuller's taking the fall for him by keeping funds for the defense of the officer on the table. The money that had originally been Winthrop's. Since Fuller planned to be acquitted of the charges against him, Daniel learned the bounty on Pratt remained valid.

The Lincoln Administration moved slowly on this while Major Fuller remained behind bars, awaiting his appeal trial, no bail being set for treason. South Carolina had claimed possession of all federal forts on her lands and Major Anderson lay under siege in Fort Sumter. When the President ordered the resupplying of the

Charleston Harbor installation, tragically low on provisions, South Carolina's soldiers fired upon the *Star of the West* and the *Brooklyn*. The warning shots were enough to turn the supplies away. As Anderson, under orders, heroically refused to surrender, the Rebel General P.G.T. Beauregard began a huge bombardment of the island installation on April 12th. Civil war had finally begun.

Chapter 27

War creates opportunities and the first opportunity to eliminate Captain Pratt came one week after the shelling on Fort Sumter. Baltimore began rioting.

On April 17, 1861, Virginia did indeed vote in favor of secession. Popular opinion predicted that with the only Southern industrial state's departure from the Union, the other slave states would vote to form a confederacy and join her and South Carolina in rebellion. Maryland struggled tremendously with delivering its decision.

President Lincoln called for thousands of men to sign ninety-day volunteer papers and began to form brigades from the state militias and move them south to defend Washington and position themselves for action on the northern border of Virginia. The ranks swelled. These new troops, often comprised of immigrant soldiers, had to pass through Maryland, and the anti-Unionists joined together in what began as a hostile protest that blocked the transfer of railway troop and supply cars. The transports had to be towed by teamsters since the railroad tracks bound down south from Washington were not connected to the northern rail lines that ran back to Massachusetts. Not allowing themselves to be delayed by the unruly civilians, the Army ordered the soldiers to debark their first rail trip's cars and march through Baltimore to their next connection. The cavalry's horses were temporarily being put into use for the teamsters, and the dismounted troops marched in columns along with the infantry.

Many supplies had to be left behind. Captain Daniel Winthrop, who curiously looked a lot like Corporal Will Ritter wearing his commander's uniform, made sure Fox Company assumed guard duty over the armory cars. The majority of the hostile crowd, now hell-bent on taking more aggressive action against the Union soldiers, followed the larger body of marching troops through the narrow cobblestone streets of the city. The civilians were pressed against the white-washed buildings by the marching columns, until they forced the violent acquisition of more room. Fruit being thrown, quickly got substituted with far more injury-threatening rocks. Then the guns made their appearance.

Many guns also disappeared, special weapons, brought out of the abandoned railway cars, by the members of Fox Company under Ritter's supervision.

Daniel Winthrop, Robert Masterson, and trailing a ways behind them, Jonathon Talbot, all moved through the riotous crowd with civilian coats and dusters concealing their weapons and uniforms. They had spotted and started to follow Richard Wythe and his team, whom Daniel had previously ordered Lt. Holloway to separate from Fox Company for special duty. The lieutenant had been befuddled, as few actually knew Wythe and his men had completed Sharps training. It only took Winthrop winning a few rounds in card games with his fellow officers to make sure Wythe's Sharps hadn't been outed and reassigned to a real Sharps Corps. They'd been serving anonymously in Fox Company, wearing standard cavalry uniforms, no companies of the regimental unit having been transferred west, as should have been done if all involved were playing honestly. But it would have been problematic to put the Sharps under Lieutenant Talbot's command, made so by Richard Wythe's insubordinate protestations, so first Winthrop had to deal with Holloway, and all the while Wythe and his men were acting autonomously anyway.

As if the Baltimore Riots weren't enough to deal with, the deadlier situation actually existed within Fox Company. As they walked amongst the unruly crowd following the soldiers onto the ironically named Pratt Street, Winthrop's eyes were in constant motion, assessing the tactical situation while keeping an eye on Wythe, also dressed in civilian clothing. He kept moving, weaving in and out amongst the crowd, following the troop formation with the protesters into the town marketplace. Wythe glanced about cautiously, reaching into his pocket. He produced a tomato. Suddenly, Wythe hurled it high into the air above the blue-uniformed body of the troops.

Winthrop knew the sergeant's action was designed to play for the crowd, as he could've tossed the fruit directly at the Army, but he meant to make sure the crowd saw it. As no doubt Wythe predicted, the rest of the civilians suddenly availed themselves of more fruit to hurl at the soldiers, at the expense of Baltimore's hapless farmers. They watched their produce get ransacked before their eyes as protesters grabbed everything they could to throw at the troops. So the farmers also began grabbing weapons.

Christopher Pratt felt the sticky juice of a tomato run down the side of his jaw where it hurt when it impacted, the flow streaming down his neck under his shirt collar. He had finally been transferred out of West Point and assigned command of Ghost Company which, upon his arrival from New York, immediately received orders to move out from Massachusetts by railway on into Maryland when the war began. Colonel Lee had granted the young captain his freedom after all, as Lee confided in the junior officer and revealed that with Virginia's secession, the colonel had written two letters of resignation for delivery to Winfield Scott and Edwin Stanton. His last words to Pratt had been to encourage him to not throw away a promising military career. Christopher could smell the sour aroma of the very next reward he'd earned with that career as it stained the white shirt Abigail had given him which he wore under his uniform.

Then rocks started being substituted for fruit and vegetables and Ghost Company's columns collapsed when civilians broke into the soldiers' lines and started spitting on them, punching and kicking them. The men fought back and the streets quickly became the site of one large melee.

Shoved off his feet, Christopher saw that the man who collided with him also wore the blue uniform, just as he heard the gunshots fired simultaneously. "Second Lieutenant Travers, Sir. That was close! They're shooting at us. They are actually shooting at us!" The report came from an excited young man with dark blonde hair and intense yet friendly eyes. They matched the smile he offered Christopher as he pulled him back up on his feet, seemingly confused. The man started to salute and then started turning around every which way trying to find his forage cap that he'd lost when he dove to the captain's rescue. "I apologize for being out of uniform, Sir," he said while ducking a punch thrown by an enraged farmer, spinning and slamming his fist into the bearded man's face. "I didn't steal your tomato!" Travers hollered at him as he continued to twist looking for his cap.

With fruit, rocks, and the whistling sound the air made, more bullets flew past them from gunshots that crackled like fire, amplified in echoes between the city's buildings. Plaster exploded out of the walls at impact points. "Nevermind your hat!" Christopher shouted at him. "Let's just get the men out of here." It took only the first shot for the vivid recollection of the ambush that nearly claimed his life in Georgia to come back to haunt him.

"I got separated from my unit!" Travers informed him.

"Now you're with me. Reform First Platoon, I'll take Second. Ghost Company is moving, now!" the unit's commander shouted.

Just as he'd lined up his shot and took it, something blue slammed into his target and smashed the captain onto the blood-spattered cobblestone. Wythe thought he'd been unobserved in light of his civilian clothes and the ruckus on the street when he'd moved ahead of the Army column he'd been shadowing. He'd burst into a deserted warehouse the soldiers were just about to pass, and took his most careful aim at the company officer with the fine and expensive Spencer rifle he'd been concealing. Wythe had thought he'd be alone.

The second shot fired came from Daniel Winthrop's Remington .44 and though the powder ignition in the cylinder it fired from rang out loud, Wythe remembered the bone cracking sound his spine made as the bullet passed through it. A thought tried to form in his mind that became dislodged by the second shot of Winthrop's going through his skull, and splattering the raised window Wythe had spun around from with a clump of the Sharps assassin's scalp, brains, and blood.

Daniel kicked Wythe's body out of his way so he could watch out the warehouse's window. Wythe's crimson discharge left behind on the raised window, the only part of him still remaining in motion, dripped on Winthrop's disguise hat and coat shoulders while he re-identified the other Sharps on the street and tracked their position. The crowd in a frenzy didn't take notice of heavy winter coats falling away from men who wore the blue uniform beneath them. They hastened to come up fast on two men that had hit the ground for cover when the first shot fired. These officers, and Daniel had good cause to assume one of them would be Captain Pratt, would not suspect men wearing their own colors of attempting to assassinate them.

Talbot and Masterson were already on it. Drawing his own weapon, Masterson rushed both Corporal Sumner Needham and Private Addison Whitney. Hitting Whitney in the jaw on his left side from behind the assassin with a right hammer blow as he forced his target to turn into his strike, Masterson then shoved past him, spinning and firing at point blank into Corporal Needham. The latter grabbed Masterson on his way down, pulling the sergeant with him, where blood, bile, and fruit juices were intermingling in the crevices between each cobblestone. Fortunate for his fall, Masterson inadvertently dodged the bullets that Capt. Pratt and Lt. Travers fired in response to the gunshot they saw fly from a civilian-garbed Masterson, mistakenly thinking they ought to rush to the defense of the uniformed Corporal Needham. Whitney, recovered from Masterson's blow, whirled to fire back but unintentional friendly fire from Captain Pratt downed him.

Lost from sight while the panicking crowd scrambled all around them, Masterson stayed low and quickly relieved both Needham and Whitney's bodies of their fire arms, including a Sharp's breach-loader and a Spencer rifle. He crawled beneath the frenzied crowd, evading Pratt and his man's regaining sight of him.

As everything degenerated into chaos around him, Luther Ladd's quick eyes had scanned the action and he instantly came to the only reasonable conclusion that Winthrop had betrayed his team and their Baltimore mission. He spotted Masterson looting Needham and Whitney, and barreled through the crowd toward him, the giant man shoving aside any of the other rioters who crossed his path. Masterson didn't see him. Winthrop, having relieved the dead Sergeant Wythe of all his valuables and weapons, started to climb out the warehouse window, sat on its ledge, and tried to take aim at Ladd with the Spencer rifle to help Masterson. But Baltimore's population gone mad kept interfering with Daniel lining up a clear shot at him.

Also unable to be targeted, Charles Taylor hurriedly parted the crowd to back up Ladd, drawing a pistol to fire at Masterson. He holstered it when he ducked under the swing of a farmer who turned a shovel on him, and came up punching the laborer with the thrust of his right fist, grabbing the man's coat collar as he fell backward, to change his course and pull him into Masterson's left jab. Now both Masterson's hands grabbed at the clothing of the farmer and threw him backward into the masses. As he turned around to relocate Ladd and Taylor, Christopher Pratt had come up alongside of Taylor, brushing past him, having already spotted the two other fighting men. Taylor drew his gun again, seeing his opportunity to take out Pratt, when a lieutenant, impaired by the crowd, shouted from behind him, "Look out, Captain!"

Pratt whirled, his weapon already in hand, and shot Taylor through the heart, felling him. Then Christopher dove after the fallen man. He shouted to the lieutenant, "You take those two! I need to find out what's going on!" He grabbed Taylor, bleeding out from his chest wound. "Who hired you?" Pratt demanded of the already-dead Taylor, obviously not responding.

Meanwhile, throwing two of the rioters out of his way at the same time, Ladd burst through the crowd to press his attack on Masterson. He grabbed Robert from behind, pinning Fox Company's 1st Sergeant's arms and throwing him further in front of him. But Masterson didn't lose his footing and recovered his balance quickly, spinning his momentum into Ladd and punching him with a right while he delivered a knee into the groin of the larger man. Ladd's face contracted in agony, his forage hat fell off, and he hunkered down, his hands reflexively reaching too late to protect the targeted location. Swinging up with his right leg, Masterson kicked him in the abdomen as the just arriving-on-the-scene Talbot walked over and shot Ladd in the chest. Without expression, Masterson just stared at the lieutenant, who said, "C'mon. Let's get out of here." The two officers from Fox Company blended back into the crowd as Lt. Travers finally broke through the protestors to rush upon Luther Ladd's location.

As Travers searched the crowd for another glimpse of the long-haired man who he thought had fired upon the trooper before him, he didn't have an eye on the dying Ladd who still held his revolver and brought it up to shoot Travers.

The left side of Ladd's head broke apart like the flight of rose petals in a storm as Christopher Pratt shot him. Turning to thank the captain, Travers' jaw dropped as he saw another protesting farmer swing a pitchfork at Pratt's head and the lieutenant brought his own firearm to bear. Travers' shot wounded the man in the riot-soiled tan coveralls, adding the largest bloodstain to the laborer's shoulder and violently reversing the man's momentum. The shot jerked him backward away from Pratt and he dropped his farming tool he used for a weapon.

"Thanks again," came the gratitude from Christopher. He turned to examine the second man he'd just killed on the streets, instantly saddened when he regarded him. Though he didn't even know Luther Ladd's name, the man still wore the blue uniform and Christopher Pratt had just shot him. *What are things coming to?* Christopher wondered.

Chapter 28

With the crowd in Baltimore frightened by the start of real shooting, the riot started breaking up, the town calming. Protesters were fleeing and this made it all the easier for Captain Winthrop to hop from the warehouse window and move through the calamity, its participants more interested in abandoning the street than picking fights with any more soldiers or other civilians. Daniel ran amongst the citizens, catching a brief glimpse of Pratt as he passed him and tapping Talbot and Masterson to follow him. They ran up on Hill and Crawford, pulling them with their civilian disguised officers as they ducked into another abandoned building, an eatery deserted for the time being.

Winthrop motioned for his men to guard the entry way and stay indoors out of view but at the front of the building. He invited himself into the back kitchen area and grabbed a handful of baked breads and rolls, hurrying back to his men's location. He dropped his loot on a table, along with several rifles and holstered guns attached to utility belts that held their ammunition. Drawing a knife, he started slicing bread and passing out the pieces to Hill, Crawford, Masterson, and Talbot. Taking one for himself, chewing a piece along with a swig from his canteen, Daniel started addressing his men with his mouth full.

"Alright," he said as he chewed. "Let's see what we got. Spread out those guns! This here's a beauty," he said, holding up the Spencer. "I think Fuller's option to use the Sharps isn't going to pan out for him," Daniel stated with a smirk in spite of a full mouth. "Too bad, huh? Bringing a man bad news like that while he's lamenting in prison. But the good news is that two hundred dollars, and some interest now, pays his way out. I love it." Daniel, walking around the room, reached into his haversack and pulled out one of Wythe's cigars. He lit it, took one puff, started coughing, then threw it on the ground and stomped it out. Grabbing the rest of the smokes from his satchel, he studied the handful of them, frowned, then threw them to the floor of the restaurant.

Then he walked back to the table with all the rifles and ran his fingers over an almost-new Henry rifle, admiring it. "Sergeant," he addressed Masterson.

"Yes, Sir?"

"Who ensures the following of regulations by the men?"

"In Fox Company, I do, Sir."

"And he reports to me," Talbot said, purposely reminding him.

Winthrop smiled at him. "And in the Federal Army, we don't carry non-regulation weapons on our persons," Daniel said, projecting his voice for all four of the men. "But our missions are not going to have anything to do with regulations."

Muffled laughter sounded amongst the group of them.

Winthrop continued giving orders. "Lieutenant, Sergeant: see to it that Fox Company is armed according to the needs of our special situation. By now Corporal Ritter has secured the armory cars and the appropriate part of their contents to let the men pass *my* inspection." Daniel's formality broke with an even more enthusiastic expression of his now infamous and gleaming smile. This was promptly returned by all of his assembled men.

"May I ask what we're going to do now since we didn't allow Wythe to complete his mission?" Talbot asked.

"Christopher Pratt is the ace up my sleeve when I visit Major Fuller in prison. Our heroic captain doesn't even know we were the ones who rescued him. I think it's time I got acquainted with Mister Pratt. The Army now seems to need everyone in the war and those hiding the good captain at West Point obviously released him. I mean Floyd got away clean – and with everything *he* did. If they already locked up Fuller, they don't need Captain Pratt to testify. Do they? The government's case is closed so far as they're concerned. But Fuller must still be afraid the prosecution will use Pratt to defeat any appeal he can arrange, else he could've kept our money and called off Wythe's mission. Fuller's next move will be to give us up in exchange for leniency. We'll make the major think twice about double-crossing us and protect Pratt so he can still be used as a witness against our dear friend Major Fuller. Meanwhile, I'll manipulate things so that we can all eventually return to

Massachusetts after the defeat of the rebellion, and Captain Pratt and I will become friends, as should every loyal officer of the Union." Winthrop sniffed as he finished the briefing of his men. "Then I'll find a way to make use of *him*."

Fox Company had a new plan in motion.

Chapter 29

July 27, 1861

My Dearest Christopher,

I pray in these troubled times that my letters continue to reach you and that my words will carry my hopes to you by the wings of an angel. More than a month has passed and there is still no word from you. I cannot help but put a voice to my fears: I do not know whether you are alive or dead, My Beloved. At night, I try to tell myself that you are just unable to send letters out; that you are deep in your duties as a soldier, and that you will write to me when you can. But these are troubled times and there is little solace to be found by those who are faced with war.

But I must write you now. I'm sure you know my country's army has reveled in our victory at Manassas. Perhaps you were there? Father still fears that the Union will regroup and defeat our young nation, and we will all be sent to internment camps – or I do not dare say what's worse. So he constantly listens for news, and he talks of moving us more than ever – of moving the entire congregation as a good shepherd moves his flock away from danger – and heading west. He still does not know I've stayed in touch with you. If he'd ever known who you really are, he'd have definitely viewed you as that danger. He drinks more and more now, and is more restless than I've ever seen him. There's so much pain and anger in his preaching. I couldn't bear to hurt him more by letting him know anything about us.

The new young post rider seems to feel affection for me, and he does his best to meet with me each day he brings the mail. Do not worry, I can only think of you in that way. But Father is usually at the church when the post rider calls, so he's never had reason to be suspicious of your letters. I arranged for this latest boy to use the same hiding place for your mail if you do send word to me. When Father is home to receive the mail, I steal away after supper and run out to that old tree to see if there's been a letter left there for me. But

I secretly dream that, instead of a letter, I find you. Then, I climb up on your horse and, together, we run far away – away out west and miles and miles away from this insanity that tears apart our nations.

I pray that you are alive and well and that no tragedy has befallen you. Please know I needed to write to you now in case it is the last of my letters for a while. If you should ever stop hearing from me, never give up hope. If Father moves us, I will find you. After the war, if it ends soon. And in the meanwhile, I'll search for a new way to write you and let you know how you can reach me. And if this fight goes on forever, I will still find you. I am sixteen, no longer a child. I cannot stay here forever. I will be so ever frightened, but I will find you, My Beloved. Please do not ever lose hope.

I love you dearly,
Abigail

Captain Christopher Pratt re-read the letter again, despair welling up inside his chest as a tear snuck out of the corner of his eye. He wiped it away before any of the other men in his tent could notice it glisten in the candlelight. Nothing had gone the way he'd originally envisioned it. Now he lay stretched out upon his cot keeping his back off the cold, moist dirt beneath it with only his wool blanket between him and the chill of the night's elements. He could see through the flap door to his shelter that it was still in the dark before dawn. But none of the three other men in his tent slept either. He did not really know them, nor did he want to confide in them. Most of the men Christopher had first served with since his days in the Academy were assigned with him to his first troop. And they were dead now. The men here were strangers – and survivors. They too had lost everyone they'd served with, and now they were just stuck together because of circumstances. Christopher had barely met several of his bunkmates, who were as fresh as he was to this new battalion command, but no one was the slightest bit sociable. Everyone expected what was coming: the North had been humiliated at Bull Run, which meant the politicians would soon call for the weary soldiers to form up and re-engage the enemy. The circumstances demanded it, thus warranting a forced march at a brisk pace to catch the Confederate Army and fatally punish them. Thousands had already died. It was going on the fourth month of the war to decide if there would be one American nation or two. There was no quick resolution in sight.

Christopher knew that if his parents had not sent him off to the military academy he'd have never left Michigan or met his darling Abigail. The otherwise tragic situation in Georgia had led to their chance meeting, which had worked out for the better in the end for him, hadn't it? Abigail's attentions had sprung hope in Christopher, causing him to hold tightly to them in order to get him through the war. He carefully folded up her letter and placed it atop his haversack. He'd put it inside later when he could see better with the light.

Then Christopher thought about War Department Secretary Floyd again. There'd been no call for him to testify against the cabinet member. Floyd resigned, went unpunished, and predictably turned up serving the Confederate States government. Meanwhile, Christopher had long since concluded that the government he served was corrupt, poisoned from the inside. Abigail became all he had left. She meant the world to him. He collected her correspondence, holding on to it like treasure.

"A letter from your girl back home?" a fellow officer asked.

Christopher had briefly met him earlier. A handsome, trimly built young man with short, dark hair and intense and alert brown eyes, his blue uniform denoted that he was also a fellow cavalry troop captain in Christopher's battalion.

"Sort of," Christopher responded suspiciously. It wasn't wise to advertise to the men that he was corresponding with someone who lived in the Confederacy, although it was a common enough event given the nature of a civil war.

"If it's not too personal, may I read it? I don't get much news from home," the other man said.

Christopher stared at him wondering, *Who was this guy wanting to read my mail?*

"It's personal," Christopher finally said. He couldn't explain his relationship with Abigail and he didn't intend to try with a total stranger. He didn't want to get to know him either. In his experience, one of them would end up dead soon enough, so beyond reunions with those men he'd trained with in New York he didn't especially want to make new friends.

Christopher still remembered the vulture that had flown off with Sgt. Cush's eyeball. That man had been invaluable in guiding Christopher as a young lieutenant in establishing his first mounted command. He still felt he had a penance to pay for desecrating the man's body when he'd dug into it for any still-useable ammunition. He had his doubts that his present companion had experienced any war trials so traumatic. Christopher's personal trials began even before there was a formal declaration of war to begin with.

"Well if we're going to be camping together, I think we should get acquainted. I'm Daniel Winthrop." The other offered Pratt a bright smile.

"Christopher Pratt."

"I'm from Wisconsin. You?"

"Michigan, originally. I've been moved around a lot."

"Yeah, the Army will do that – especially to us cavalry officers. But a fellow Westerner? That'll do."

"We're not from the West any longer," Christopher observed. "Not since California was admitted to the Union."

"Yeah. I reckon that's as far west as you can go unless you can swim. Have you ever seen the ocean?" Winthrop asked.

"The Atlantic. I trained in New York. Did you go to an academy?"

"No. Field commission. All the other officers were dead." Winthrop grinned.

"I see. Alright Winthrop, I'm going to try and get another half an hour of sleep. I'm sure Command's got some hellacious orders for us today."

"Mmm-hmm. Rest well, Captain."

Although Christopher tried, sleep was not forthcoming.

Chapter 30

Daniel Winthrop had grown up on the frontier back when Wisconsin *was* the frontier, and he'd fought hard along with the rest of his family to make a better life for themselves. He was of German stock on his mother's side of the family; she'd been lucky to marry a poor but hard-working Englishman who stayed deeply devoted to his wife and their small family. In his opinion, that was Winthrop's father's mistake, and the son never passed on a chance to seek out any new opportunity that would improve his position.

Not really able to see Pratt in the dark, Winthrop nevertheless studied his bunkmate. The neatly kept young officer behaved in a manner far beyond his age. Had he not known better, he would have thought he'd just conversed with an elderly man in that darkened camp tent. He briefly wondered what of the war Pratt had experienced that had left him almost a shell of a man, just filling out his blue uniform. Winthrop didn't really care. He'd fought at Bull Run, and he'd seen his fellow soldiers slain right before his eyes. His ingenuity and covert insubordination saved most of his men. Still, he was lucky to have survived the places the Army ordered him.

Rather than allowing the experience to leave him devoid of passion, Winthrop chose to gain strength from his anger and bitterness. Captain Pratt, a total stranger, meant nothing to him. In fact this whole war and the madness it brought didn't mean anything to him either. Being a soldier was just a job that earned income. His parents lacked enough children to properly work a farm and they couldn't afford to hire help. So they hired themselves out and often let their own land lay fallow. Understandably, the Winthrop children would have to leave the nest to find their own way in the world. Daniel stood as one very inspired individual at that.

Although Winthrop could barely make out Pratt in the dark, he saw him shift, adjusting his position on his sleep cot. Reinitializing conversation, he asked, "Still awake there, Captain?"

"Umm-hum."

"Nervous about our future?" Winthrop asked with a derisive laugh.

"I don't know," Pratt mumbled.

"Well, don't lose any sleep worrying about that. I can tell you that we haven't got any future. The geniuses they've got running the show at headquarters are going to march us right into the enemy's bayonet. Then it will be all over and you'll get your sleep. For a long time, you'll get your sleep."

"You sound resigned to your death during this conflict," Pratt commented, sounding a little more alert.

"I guess we'll wait and see about that. Have you got something or someone special you're living for, Captain?"

"Call me Christopher. We're the same rank, for heaven's sake."

"My friends call me Daniel. But you didn't answer my question, Christopher."

"I just stay focused on my duty. It's my job to keep the men under my command alive."

"You could try to sound confident that you'll succeed and keep your own life in the process. Then you can collect that girl of yours and leave all of this," Winthrop commented, making a sweeping gesture that probably couldn't be seen in the dark.

"Huh. It's more likely I'm never going to see her again. Give her a little bit more time and I'm sure she'll be long gone, completely forgetting about me. It would be for her best too. Her family lives far too close to this war for anybody's taste," Christopher observed, "and it's a good bet they'll be packing up their farm and moving west soon enough. That's what she had to say in her letter."

"It will be expensive to start up another farm someplace else – even for a small operation. How do they expect to do that in the middle of a war?" inquired Winthrop.

"Oh, don't worry about them. Her father's some kind of preacher and his flock will follow him anywhere. He's got the whole lot of them donating every valuable they own to his collection in their cellar. When Abigail's family moves, her father's entire congregation will move with them. They've got the ideals and the money to afford them," noted Christopher.

"But what makes them think they can afford to move in the middle of all the fighting? Overland civilian caravans make..... for really fat targets..." Winthrop mused, his voice trailing off while he thought.

"Stubborn people, used to their way of life," Christopher responded.

Daniel emerged from his private thoughts to inquire, "So how much would you say all that stuff is worth?"

"It's got to be thousands, I'd guess. I'm no expert. But I saw jewelry, china, cutlery, art."

"I bet you wished you could add a wedding ring to that." Daniel Winthrop smiled in the dark. "There's not many other ways a cavalry captain could ever acquire that kind of wealth."

"Who needs it? There are more important things."

"Really?" Winthrop asked. He mused that he'd wait for Pratt to fall back asleep and then take a look at the man's personal mail after all.

After a little more conversation about the war and their family backgrounds, Pratt drifted back asleep. Quietly, Daniel stood, picked up Pratt's letter from his girlfriend, and read portions of it by match light. Before Christopher awakened, Winthrop had copied Abigail's address and replaced the letter back among Pratt's things.

He'd also learned a very interesting fact. Pratt's lady friend lived behind the enemy's lines in the Deep South, something he'd suspected from the outset of his conversation with the officer. Abigail had earned Winthrop's intense interest, igniting a creative but very dangerous spark of inspiration within him. *This could be my way out of all this madness,* Winthrop thought. *Floyd is out of my life for good and Fuller no longer has any control over me. Now only I have influence over my destiny. What an opportunity! What have I got to lose by singularly pursuing my own best interests now?*

Chapter 31

My father and his father before him would turn over in their graves if they knew what I'd sold their plantation's land for, David Hutchinson thought as he signed the paperwork ceding the ownership of his lands to the bank and handed over the documents to its representative. The man in the black suit nodded and his armed assistant, who looked more like a bodyguard, brought forward several cases over-filled with Confederate cash vouchers and handed them to Mr. Hutchinson.

"This concludes our business here," said the banker. "You may have until the end of the week to remove yourselves and your property from the land. I wish you luck in whatever shall be your new endeavor."

With that, the banker climbed back inside his coach and the guard hopped onto the driver's station and coaxed their horses forward. Their wagon moved counter to the half-dozen other wagons arriving at the farm.

Everyone was busy packing things from their secret storage place under the mill house and toting the bundles out to the staging area for the other wagons. China, silverware, gold, and jewelry were all carefully wrapped and protected by linen, then stored inside deep holds beneath the seating in the wagons. The neighbors who formed the Hutchinsons' collective congregation were doing likewise. Every hour or so, a new wagon or two would arrive ready to follow their pastor's lead. Inside the plantation house, Mrs. Hutchinson looked up with regret at having to leave behind the beautiful chandelier from the front hallway, but there was just no way to bring such an item with them.

The chickens and smallest hogs would be contained in cages in specially designed wagons. Most of the larger animals would be herded along by work hands on horseback, so there would always be fresh milk until such time that the beasts were needed for food.

During all the commotion, Abigail managed to slip away and

return to her bedroom. There, beside the now empty-frame of her bed, she hastily wrote a letter to Christopher. She knew it would take a while for him to receive her note. Civilian-Through-the-Lines Mail had to be routed through Richmond, Virginia and then taken by Flag of Truce through Old Point Comfort to a Federal mail station, one of the many inconveniences that came with the war. It usually took less than a month but it could also take much longer. Abigail hoped her words would find their intended recipient before too long as it pained her to imagine Christopher writing letters to an unoccupied home.

Chapter 32

Mail-call was a popular time in the Union forces camp. It was the only contact most of the troops had with life outside of the war. Sometimes it was the sole source of information *about the war* many of them received out in the field, except when a newspaper was found in a nearby town by troops dispatched for reconnaissance or a supply run.

Ever since learning about the migrating Confederate girlfriend of his campmate, Daniel Winthrop made it his priority in life to make the mail call before everyone else, especially Christopher Pratt, who'd always attended to his duties before collecting his personal mail. Pulling rank, Winthrop advanced to the head of the line. That day, several privates and a corporal who could read labored over sorting the letters.

"Name?" they'd call when the next person in queue advanced.

"Captain Christopher Pratt," Winthrop replied.

A sharp private said, "Sir, I've met Pratt. I'm sorry but that's not you."

"Pratt was wounded in the last engagement. Our friendship goes back quite a long ways to basic training in New York. So I'm picking up his mail for him and bringing it to the hospital tent. Would you complicate that, Private?"

The young man glanced at Winthrop's rank on his blue uniform. "N-no, no, Sir. Here you go." He handed over a letter stamped with the extra postage necessary to clear it from Georgia into the United States.

Instead of returning to his tent, Winthrop made his way to the edge of camp. When he was sure he was alone, he sat down against a tree to read. When he finished, he took out some paper he'd carried with him along with a pen and a small container of ink and using his canteen as a writing surface, he began to scribe a response. Time was of the essence if his plan was to work, and everything would go south if he were to be caught at his newest game.

He addressed his letter to Miss Hutchinson in Georgia and he hoped she'd still be there to receive it. His scheme was a shot in the dark, he knew, but considering how dark his future looked, he took it. He didn't have anything to lose, and fate just might have just handed him a once-in-a-lifetime opportunity.

Chapter 33

August 18, 1861
Dear Abigail,
I must apologize for this letter arriving in the hand of another besides your beloved Christopher. Indeed he is a dear friend of mine as well, but I regret to inform you that he has been seriously wounded and has lost the use of his right arm. It was his request that I help him write to you before he is to be taken to the surgeon. He wishes me to tell you how much your correspondence has meant to him and that his love for you has grown so strong, he'll credit it for seeing him through this difficult procedure. He wishes for you to please continue going on so that at least one of you will know peace and serenity. Christopher fears this war has forever crippled him, but he does not regret doing his duty for his country. He doesn't want you to worry over him. If fate intends you to be reunited, then it shall be. For now, I, his comrade-in-arms, Daniel Winthrop, will continue to advise you of his health and recovery.
"With all my love sent your way,"
Christopher

Winthrop inserted the letter into its envelope and addressed it. He then headed off to request permission to leave camp so he could head into a nearby town and navigate the complex purchase of postage in order to send his note through Old Point Comfort and then on to Richmond. He also volunteered to take the other soldiers' mail with him, which facilitated his departure from base-camp.

Some post offices offered limited hours on Sunday mornings, a fact greatly appreciated by the troops. Winthrop didn't doubt that his letter would be opened by the military censors assigned to both nations since the recipient lived behind enemy lines, but no one would know or care about personal correspondence concerning the welfare of some random Captain Christopher Pratt. Winthrop hoped someone would be sympathetic and that the additional three cents he enclosed would be used to purchase the Confederate postage required in Richmond to send his letter on to Georgia. The United States, ignoring the claim of Confederate independence, refused to sell the would-be nation's stamps. Winthrop also hoped that his letter would arrive in time before Abigail's father closed their home and moved their family. But it was a thrill to make the gamble and it wasn't like Daniel Winthrop had anything better to do on a Sunday morning.

Chapter 34

Dale Tippen had been driving the mail for several months now. Each time he rode past the old Hutchinson estate, he gathered any mail he might encounter for the long-since-departed former residents and set it aside in his returned-letters pouch. However, when he saw the letter addressed to young Miss Abigail, he recalled the promise he'd made to her.

He wasn't sure if it still applied now that she and her family had moved, or if she would ever return for her mail in the forgotten-letters-store. However Tippen decided it would be best if he followed instructions exactly this time. The young Confederate volunteer had lost his leg from the knee down at Philippi, because he had been inattentive to his duty and celebrating when an expected attack failed to materialize. Only it did materialize later, once the Union forces determined their position.

Now Tippen was considered something of a miraculous recovery case, courtesy of the resilience of youth, and he quickly became popular on his mail route. Dismounting from his horse, the fair-haired fellow used a crutch along with his one good leg to maneuver himself under the large, old magnolia tree. He carefully lowered himself to the ground to dig under the stone in the center of the bordering shrubbery. He unearthed the small box buried there and he concealed Abigail's letter inside. It would be protected and only she would know its location.

Tippen doubted he would ever see the pretty young girl again, but he took comfort in knowing that he'd finally learned to fulfill his duty. And he would never waiver in that resolve again.

Chapter 35

It took nearly two months before Abigail's letter reached the Federal camp where Winthrop and Pratt were stationed.

Of course, Winthrop intercepted the letter intended for Christopher Pratt. That particular piece of mail arrived the day before Winthrop was scheduled to move his troop out to Missouri to relieve forces under General Grant, who was engaged in securing the northern Mississippi River near the site of his victory at Belmont.

Daniel Winthrop, deployed in the western theater of the war, escaped a second line of fire as Christopher Pratt became increasingly distraught. The letters he'd received from Abigail had given him hope for a life of happiness after the war. Looking forward eased the endless drilling and training of the new men that were continuously brought in to complement their growing force. Deeply concerned that she'd stopped corresponding, he interrogated every private and corporal who sorted the mail, finally learning from a soldier that his 'friend' Daniel Winthrop had collected Abigail's letters while he was supposedly in recovery from being wounded. Of course, he'd never been wounded. Because of his experience training men, he'd barely seen any more action. When he finally did receive a letter from Abigail, only because Winthrop was out on deployment, Christopher confirmed that the man had lied to her too. *Why would that officer possibly be writing to my lady friend?*

Christopher felt enraged by Winthrop's duplicity, but the man was nowhere around to confront. On top of that, a new battalion commander, Major Kenneth Tithing, had taken charge over their unit and was rumored to be above and beyond dedicated to discipline. The man couldn't see beyond his own uniform. He was just the type that their regiment commander Colonel Thomas Cahill liked having around to sharpen his men into the tip of the Union's sword.

Christopher didn't want to press Tithing for a favor at the outset of their relationship, but he was a decorated soldier and well-respected in his own right. Surely he could take some personal leave, if only for a week? He needed to find and reconnect with Abigail. Her most recent return address indicated she'd sent her letter through Biloxi, Mississippi, but nothing she'd written that Pratt had received had indicated she'd left the plantation. Knowing there was a fifty-fifty chance his trip could turn out to be for naught, Christopher still felt compelled to race down to Georgia and find Abigail. He'd see if he could covertly book passage on the trains bound south for himself and his horse, and otherwise ride his mount day and night on the occasions when this wouldn't prove possible. He'd find out what had become of Abigail, pick up her trail, and most importantly, warn her about Daniel Winthrop. Perhaps together they could figure out that conniving man's motive.

Christopher could never have predicted that he would come to need and care that deeply for Abigail, but it had happened. He only hoped he could travel the distance for her – and fast!

Chapter 36

Somewhere in Ohio on his way to Kentucky, Captain Daniel Winthrop took the time to read the most recent letter he'd stolen from Christopher Pratt prior to his troop's deployment.

November 29, 1861
My Dearest Christopher,
To keep hope alive, I continue to write to you. Nearly four months have come and gone without any contact between us, and in these times I no longer remain optimistic.

Things have become desperate for us. By this season Father had hoped to have resettled us, perhaps permanently in California, or at least in Arizona or New Mexico territories, to say nothing of leaving for Old Mexico as a last resort. But events conspired against all his planning.

The money he was paid for our plantation, for all our property, has not held out. Many are not eager to accept Confederate currency. We were forced to sell all of the slaves – at least the males sold first and it was so sad to see them being broken away from their families. But Father just complained to Mr. Davis that he was only getting three-fourths of what they were worth. We figured them to be taken off to plantations near to Biloxi (close by to where we're staying right now in Gulfport), but I know there will be some that the merchants will try and smuggle out through the Yankee naval blockade to be sent to work in the sugar islands. But Father said they weren't working for us, and it did neither us nor them any good to feed them, thus rewarding them for being idle. He said it taught them to expect handouts and he wasn't going to have any of that. We simply couldn't afford it, anyway.

That led to the horror I was forced to witness next with the solution Father and Mr. Davis found for the women and children. I personally had to see this and will never forget it as long as I live. Father even asked me to gather the children and promise them food

*or toys, whatever it took to get them all together. Then, they shot
them! Mr. Davis had assembled his own work crew and some of the
men from our church, and when we were in the wilderness outside of
Biloxi and Gulfport, they just shot them all!*

*Father said it was the Christian thing to do so they would
not wander lost and starving in the countryside. He would not
free slaves in our nation, on our people's land. He said that last
August your President Lincoln sealed their doom by issuing the
Confiscation Act. He venomously complained about losing maybe
even one-hundred dollars per Negro-head, and then some change
for the women that he did sell as breeders. But he'd be damned if
he was going to just let the Yankees take them away from him for no
compensation at all.*

*I begged and pleaded for him to spare Emma. He did so, but he
made her my responsibility to feed her from my own rations. I can
feel him looking at me with contempt now, but I don't care. Emma
is alive, safe for the moment, and that's all that matters. Even my
mother has no influence with the man, and I feel ashamed to call
him my father. He and Mr. Davis drink together constantly it seems.
I know he's lost everything and I guess a tiny part of me forgives him
because he's so affected by that.*

*But I feel things are still getting more dangerous. I have to
get out of here. Please come and rescue me, Christopher! We're
in Gulfport and will be so for a while. We didn't feel welcome in
Biloxi. It's a military town and we felt the people there directing
their resentment towards us and others that have been migrating out
of the Deep South. They believe we should have stayed in Georgia
and that my Father, Mr. Davis, and all of the other men should have
signed on to fight. But Father got us out of there quickly. Mark will
soon turn fourteen, and the Confederacy is now drafting boys that
young. I don't think Father could bear to lose him to this war. I
sense he feels that he's failed our family as it is.*

*We do hang on to some hope that this war will soon be over.
Father said your country just made a critical error in the seizure
of the Trent out at sea. He said that Britain and France won't take
kindly to their appointed Commissioners being held as captives.
Whereas they previously refused to take a side, they won't stand to*

lose the revenue from their trade business with the South. 'Just wait'
he says, 'and these two countries will enter the war to protect their
own interests and the Union won't be able to resist the combined
might of all three of our nations.'

I know that you have no weight on your President's decisions,
but I pray you will see their futility and run away from this madness.
Come find me and together we can head West and make a new life
for ourselves. Let the rest of the world destroy their lives over this
nonsense, and you and I can just live the way we want to live. But
please stay safe and let me know you are alright.

Father has chosen to keep us in Gulfport for the time being to
wait out this Trent Affair. None of us want to leave our country if
we don't have to. Send word down to me through Biloxi, and I'll see
that I get there or have someone bring me your letters to me here. I
trust we'll be staying in Mississippi for a while. Please write!

With all my love,
Abigail

Winthrop closed the letter and snorted in contempt. Why did
this girl think she was entitled to anything, especially considering
the *wholesome* family she came from? She was even encouraging a
Union officer to desert? He felt even more justified in undertaking
his own little enterprise at their expense. Now he needed to re-
establish contact with her and then find some way to get down to
Gulfport to conduct some reconnaissance of the situation.

And so he re-wrote a version of his previous letter to her, now
that it was apparent to him that Abigail Hutchinson had never
received the original.

December 14, 1861
Dear Abigail,
I must apologize for this letter arriving in the hand of another
besides your beloved Christopher. Indeed he is a dear friend of
mine. I regret to inform you that he has been seriously wounded and
has lost the use of his right arm. It was his request that I help him
to write to you before he is to be taken to the surgeon. He wishes for

me to tell you how much your correspondence has meant to him and that his love for you has grown so strong, he'll credit it for seeing him through this difficult procedure. He wishes for you to please continue enduring, so that at least one of you will know peace and serenity. Christopher fears this war has forever crippled him but he does not regret doing his duty for his country. He doesn't want you to worry over him. If fate intends you to be reunited, then it shall be. For now, I, his comrade-in-arms, Daniel Winthrop, will continue to advise you of his health and recovery.

As this letter might reach you in time for Christmas, please allow me to extend my hope for the coming New Year.
"With all my love sent your way,"
Christopher

Chapter 37

Oh my God! How cruel the world can be, Abigail thought as she read Christopher's letter penned by Daniel Winthrop. Were she to stop and objectively study the situation, her concerns were really for herself. She'd been counting on Christopher to rescue her from life as a refugee. Her first thoughts were always for herself, not that Christopher lived in constant danger and had to make sacrifices because he was a soldier at war. Now, she worried about how his becoming a cripple would affect her. This thought weighed heavily on her as she penned a response.

January 5, 1862
Dearest Christopher,
I have just received word of your injuries, and I cannot express how concerned I am for you. I so wish that I might be there for you, my love. Know in your heart that I am constantly thinking about you, and I wish for your swift and complete recovery.
Unfortunately, we are now trapped because of the war. Father says we'll move on when we can. But your Lincoln and Seward's apologies to England and France seemed to come at just the right time to placate them. Now, going it alone, will drag this war on for the Confederacy. As the fighting continues, there is no resolution to this mess in sight, so it just endlessly progresses.
I really wish to write to you of something more jovial, but you'll just have to imagine what that might be. Perhaps when it becomes possible, we'll both go swimming naked! Let the military censors read about that. I am so tired of this, Christopher. Please tell me you've come through your surgery and that you're being discharged from your service. Let me know that everything will be alright and that I'll see you soon.
Love always,
Abigail

As Captain Winthrop was now deployed in the western theater of the war, he didn't intercept Abigail's letter. But four days after writing his forged correspondence from Christopher Pratt, he penned a second letter, this time representing himself.

December 19, 1861
Dear Abigail,
There are no words to adequately express my regret at having to inform you of the death of our friend, Christopher Pratt. Unfortunately, he did not survive surgery. I don't think he was in too much pain. The medics did everything they could for him, but he was going to have to lose an arm. Instead, we all lost a great man's life. I am so sorry.
There may be some personal effects of his that he might wish for you to have. I'll see what I can do to get them down to you in Mississippi. This is a terrible tragedy for us both. If you so desire, please feel free to correspond with me. I spent much time with Christopher in his last days and I recall how highly he spoke of you. But it is too soon and painful for me to relate any of that to you now. So I'll just close with wishing you well.
Sincerely,
Daniel Winthrop

Abigail wrote back to Daniel Winthrop:

January 10, 1862
Dear Mr. Winthrop,
It is with the greatest difficulty that I put my pen to paper. I am still in shock from the news of the death of my dear Christopher. It is so unfair!
I am unable to write much, but I needed to let you know how grateful I am for your informing me of the fate of my beloved.
If you have chance to contact his family during all of this, I have enclosed a letter to his parents, whom I've never met. If you can, it would be a great favor to me for you to forward my correspondence to them, for I know not how to contact them myself.
As to your offer to bring me any of Christopher's personal

affects, while I can't imagine how that is possible as there is a war going on, there are three items I should like to have. They might seem strange to you or unseemly for a lady to request these items, but I have no idea what use they'd be for his family, and I have no use for anyone else's opinion on the matter, anyway. I should like Christopher's service knife, and should you find it, an old-style, outmoded slug shooter weapon and its accoutrements. Perhaps most oddly, I should like a pair of Chris' shorts he will not be needing for his burial.

Broaching the subject of burial, I am truly regretful that circumstances will make it utterly impossible for me to attend his being laid to rest. Amongst Christopher's items, you might find a tailored, white, buttoned shirt. This was a gift to him from me and I request that those preparing his body for burial to dress him in this particular shirt, under his coat or uniform, before he is placed in his casket. It is all I have left to offer him.

It appears my family and I will be staying in Gulfport for a while, and there will be those in Biloxi who will know how to contact us. I shall hope to hear from you again.

Thank you for your assistance and God bless you for your kindness.

Sincerely,
Abigail Hutchinson

Chapter 38

A young officer with intense eyes and long wavy brown hair presented himself in his blue uniform in front of his commanding officer as the latter man finished reading a personal letter. They stood in a field not far from the tents of their base camp in Kentucky. Winthrop returned his salute as the two exchanged appropriate formalities.

"Lieutenant Jonathon Talbot reporting as ordered, Sir."

"Lieutenant, do you want to die?"

"Sir?"

"Jack, what I mean is, is this what you signed up for? Did you have this overwhelming desire to commit suicide by riding your horse into Rebel muskets?"

"Are we dropping the formalities here, Dan?"

Winthrop sighed, mostly because he long since wearied of dealing with all the military discipline. "Yeah, Jack, you can speak freely."

"I signed on with you back in Wisconsin so as to avoid being called a coward. We were supposed to be actually taking responsibility for ourselves after that first big fiasco. I thought I could take the pay you promised that our original plan would make us, remake myself into a hero, and then return home to marry any girl I wanted."

"That's great. A man with truly far reaching motives and ambitions."

Talbot caught the other's cynicism. "Alright, Dan. What are you in this for?"

"Opportunities. Wars create opportunities, and I think I've been nurturing the greatest one."

"What do you mean?" Jack stroked his light down beard that had just started filling in.

"I've been secretly corresponding with Pratt's Confederate girlfriend."

"He's sending letters behind the lines? You're going to blackmail him, aren't you? Then bypass him up to make 'major' before he gets a chance to blink at Tithing's back. Sir, if you're looking for someone to replace you as troop captain, we've served together since training in Wisconsin and-"

"You want to die with another bar on your shoulder patch? That's what the system's done to you, Jack. You can't see beyond the military any more and the extent of your imagination is restrained by its discipline. Well, fortunately for both of us, I can see well beyond my uniform," Winthrop snorted.

"I've been corresponding with this girl for more than a month now and I've convinced her that Pratt is dead. Now she wants to meet with me."

"Where is she?"

"Gulfport, Mississippi right now."

"Mississippi? You're not thinking of doing anything stupid, Dan?"

"You wanted command a minute ago. I'm going to give you your big opportunity while I'm away. I'll count on you to hold this troop together and give Tithing no cause to give us a reviewing. I'll only be gone a short while. You see, this Miss Hutchinson and her family are originally from Georgia. They're traveling with a whole wagon convoy of wealthy plantation owners turned into war refugees, and they've temporarily holed up in Gulfport. The whole lot of them are carrying everything they own."

"If you're thinking what I think you're thinking, Dan, I'm sure they're armed."

"Of course. But who are we? The Union's drum line? After I first lead our troop on a little mission detour, our boys will be more than well-armed and prepared. For now, you'll take them on to catch up with Grant in the Cumberland while I scout out the situation in Mississippi. This is why I handpicked all my NCOs. Now, you're to recruit everyone whom you think will go along with a little unauthorized excursion I have planned. They've already been expecting this."

Talbot turned suddenly pale. "You're asking the men to risk a firing squad if they get caught now. This is war time! It's desertion."

146

"No. It's actually the most sensible way to *not* wind up getting shot. If I'm right, the men won't face anything other than a wealthy retirement in Old Mexico, well beyond Lincoln's jurisdiction. Think about it Jack. The biggest score ever is just waiting, packed up for us, like a treasure already hitched to horses, and we know exactly where it's going. It's almost free money! It doesn't get any prettier than this. Or do you want to stick around here with General Grant, chasing "Dixie" every time it's played up and down these bloody rivers? Haven't you seen enough of this war?"

Jack Talbot nodded, staring off into the distance, a thoughtful, unfocused expression on his face.

"Don't think there aren't those who are profiting by this war back in New York. From the arms makers, who love their military contracts, right down to the carpenters pounding out pine boxes. And if the war goes on forever, so does their business – fueled by an endless supply of displaced immigrants looking for their next potato. All I'm proposing is that we make our own profit and fill our own trunks, instead of their pine boxes."

It all made sense to the lieutenant. If he didn't take control, his own future looked dark indeed. "I'll handle the men," Talbot finally said in a voice barely above a whisper.

Chapter 39

January 19, 1862 arrived with cannon balls roaring. Tennessee Congressman turned Confederate General Felix Zollicoffer had made a critical mistake. He trapped his men east of Somerset, Kentucky, their backs to the Cumberland River. Zollicoffer had been a thorn in the Union's side as he and his men rode through Tennessee, hanging pro-Union sympathizers from railroad bridges that the guerillas were trying to destroy to prevent the South from re-supplying their lines. The unburied, rotting bodies, vultures feeding on them, marked his passage.

Now the western Union Army's General George Thomas had the opportunity to stop Zollicoffer and reap revenge on him once and for all. Zollicoffer planned to evacuate his position by a rear-wheeler and flatboats across the half-frozen Cumberland. General Thomas, once joined by General Albin Schoepf and his infantry reinforcements, intended to pin down the Rebels under the Union's cannonade. Speed was of the essence if the Federals were going to crush Zollicoffer before he could escape. Colonel Cahill ordered Major Tithing to authorize the loan of Winthrop's cavalry troop to assist in the attack, Winthrop's company having established a history of taking the really tough assignments.

Rain hammered the countryside. The haphazard positioning of both the defenders and those attacking them caused excessive battlefield confusion. Lt. Talbot quietly assumed temporary command of Winthrop's company, holding the cavalry in line formation, awaiting his orders to charge. He tried to pull his cap down more tightly to help shield his eyes from the heavy rain.

Private Virgil Walker gulped back his fear as he watched from his position in the line. Just over a low, grassy ridge lay the river, quite visible and lined with Rebel cannons positioned along its nearest bank. Flashes of red flame erupted from the defenders' artillery shooting off to cover the Confederacy's retreat to Rebel flatboats just behind their formation. Smoke filled the air. Clods of dirt were flipped up within range of shrapnel and musket balls, stopping just shy of where the Federal Cavalry was assembled. The rain tamped down the dust but caused its own problems.

The sensible way to conduct the affairs of this battle were as obvious to the private as they must have been to his general. Schoepf's infantry would arrive and be positioned just off center, while Winthrop's cavalry and another unit from Kentucky would be used to seal off the opposite flanks. Federal long-range artillery would then be moved forward to sink the Rebel flatboats and the rear-wheeler. Zollicoffer would be finished.

However, problems existed with this plan. The Confederates, armed with barely anything better than flintlocks would nevertheless defiantly fight to the bitter end. They knew they would likely die but they would take as many Federals with them as possible. The rain turned the grasslands slick. Soldiers slipped and fell while musket balls filled the air with their eerie whistling sound, which was augmented by the thunderclap blasts of cannon balls crashing to the earth, tearing off men's legs and heads and dumping their bodies into the red-dyed mud.

Talbot flinched every time he witnessed another brutal death on the battlefield. The cannon blasts and sounds of gunfire remained constant. Having to shout even when the intended recipient of his words was right next to him, Talbot informed Sergeant Masterson that he was moving out to the side of the engagement toward a clump of trees to the south in order to better observe the situation. He would signal by flag if he were delayed when the time came for a cavalry charge. Winthrop's words echoed in Talbot's mind and he asked himself if any of this conflict between the North and South was worth dying for?

The sergeant stared daggers into Talbot's back as he rode off of the battlefield, leaving Masterson in the first position to charge along with his men. The meaty man would do his duty to the last full measure if that's what it took, but he resented what he viewed as Talbot's cowardliness. On the other hand, Private Walker envied his commanding officer and thought that, if he'd earned the privileges of rank, he'd prefer to be on the sidelines of this particularly bloody scrimmage.

General Thomas had an altogether different style. He stood on the battlefield in the torrent of rain and bullets, commanding the Union artillery line to assemble forward in order to be in range of the Confederate batteries. In only minutes, the tactic proved successful as Federal cannonballs pounded down the Rebels' big guns, with more and more of that whistling sound screaming through the air and followed by thunderclaps that announced the impacts. As forged iron cracked, the spoked wooden wheels beneath were reduced to splinters which flew in every direction as the Rebel artillery was pounded and smashed.

Talbot saw the flag signals through the smoke and he heard the bugle call for his men to go into action. From his position on the extreme sideline he signaled Masterson, who spurred his horse and charged the company forward into the hail of lead that awaited them. Still mounted on his horse and under the canopy of the trees that shielded him somewhat from the rain, Talbot watched Masterson race forward into the breaking and retreating Rebel lines, swinging his sword through the backs of the necks of fleeing infantrymen. The men who were being routed tried to run and reload their old muskets at the same time, packing powder often too wet to fire anyway. These men would turn wildly and when they did get off shots they missed their targets or failed to significantly wound a running horse continuing to carry its rider into battle. Often the pursuing men didn't know when they were hit, rain mixed with hail pelting them along with the bullets. They ignored it all as they raced into the fray to do their duty, very often to bleed to their death while still in the saddle. But they determinedly returned fire with six-shooters, cutting down more Rebels as the combat raged on.

Had Lt. Talbot actually been acquainted with the some of the new men under his command, he still would not have felt any compassion for Private Walker, who took a musket ball right in the mouth. It cut down at an angle into the poor bastard's face, shattering his jaw and plunging into his throat. The deadly projectile ripped his larynx apart so quickly, he couldn't even scream. He fell backward, bouncing off his horse and getting kicked by the animal on his way down into the blood-soaked mud. The first sensation of pain he recognized accrued in his teeth and gums, and then in his back and shoulder as he landed hard and broke his collarbone. By that time, he was beginning to spasm from the lack of oxygen since his windpipe was clogged with blood. He lay awkwardly posed to die in all that mud as he awaited for the Reaper to find him. Talbot never noticed him. All the action was moving forward on the battlefield, pressing the Rebels back towards the river. The lieutenant watched from his shelter in the trees, anticipating this event becoming his first great victory.

Talbot's flag was down. He rested, watching everything unfold when a man with the rank of a commanding general rode up with a major in tow, obviously his aide de camp. "No! No! No! Tell your captain that I said to turn those men around! The first row will turn and fire while the next line forward will cross from in front of them, shooting, while the former front line reloads, to keep up steady fire. We must show good form. Never let them see us run!"

Talbot was confused. He first feared he would be reprimanded for not charging with his men into battle. Now this general was giving him orders intended for the Rebel lines? With far too many still wearing the blue uniform in this conflict, he'd heard of huge mistakes being made on the battlefield. This was his first time to personally experience one of them.

The Confederate major came to the same conclusion just seconds after Talbot, but the general hadn't yet realized his case of mistaken identity. "Did you hear what I said, Lieutenant?" he demanded as he and his aide dismounted and approached Talbot who in his shock had yet forgotten to dismount and salute the higher ranking officers. "What unit are you with? Under whose command? Wait a minute–."

But the major didn't wait. As he started to warn his general, he fast-drew his six-shooter. But he only winged the still-mounted Talbot, whose horse, wary of the cannon fire just beyond their position, had shifted restlessly right in the nick of time. Talbot drew at the same moment, only with slightly more care. The Federal lieutenant blasted his opponent, his weapon falling from his hand, as the shocked commander whirled around from his view of the battlefield and reached for his own pistol. Talbot shot him through the heart. The man fell back, killed instantly. Then Talbot finished off the Confederate major with two more quick shots into the already-downed man's chest.

Several Union officers raced up to Talbot's position on their horses, weapons drawn, but stopped suddenly and assessed the surprising situation. Talbot recognized one man as a full colonel. The higher ranking officer took in the bodies at the lieutenant's horse's feet.

The colonel asked Talbot, "Do you know who you just killed? This was General Zollicoffer, a former Member of Congress."

Talbot thought he'd done well for himself. "He thought I was one of his men, Sir," he reported, his amusement revealed by a beaming smile as he dismounted from his ride.

"We capture enemy officers whenever possible, Lieutenant. We wanted Zollicoffer and we needed him stopped, but he was a politician and he might have been someone we could procure a surrender from. Now, we'll have to deal with their General Crittenden, and he will never surrender, not even with his back to the river.

"And you're with the cavalry, Lieutenant? I see you're not with Kentucky's loyalists, so you must be part of Cahill's group that his Major Tithing loaned us for this action. You wouldn't be serving with Captain Winthrop now, would you?" The colonel nodded to himself. "Of course you would. Well, I've got news for you. Your captain is going to be put up against a wall and shot for desertion as soon as Tithing gets ahold of him. He's nowhere on this battlefield and, if I had to guess, I'd say he's no longer even in Kentucky. Desertion is a capital crime in a time of war, Lieutenant!"

Talbot didn't know how to respond to the colonel, who obviously knew Tithing. They were in big trouble now. At least, Winthrop was. Talbot hadn't actually done anything wrong except for not making the charge with his men. However, as the next highest ranking officer, he could also envision being named as Winthrop's accomplice. But where the action here was concerned, officers would often take observers' positions if good sense warranted it. In the rain and poor visibility, he had an excuse for himself, but not for Winthrop.

But perhaps Daniel Winthrop had bestowed some of his wild luck upon Jack Talbot, along with his command. General Schoepf rode up just then to confer with his officers. Dismounting immediately upon his arrival at the clump of trees, he took in Zollicoffer's body and his officers who surrounded the fallen enemy general. "Colonel Fry, report!"

The colonel whirled from his position of redressing Talbot, and he announced Zollicoffer's obvious identity and death. He risked a sidelong glance at Talbot, and then reported that he himself had killed the Confederate and said there'd been no other choice. He recounted Talbot's story of how the man's death had happened, taking the credit for the kill. This seemed to satisfy the general. While Schoepf turned away and made use of their position to reconnoiter the battle that raged on towards the shores of the Cumberland, Colonel Fry seized Talbot by his arm. "One word of this, and you and your Captain Winthrop won't even have time to wonder if you've found real trouble! You keep your mouth shut, Lieutenant. Understand soldier?"

"Yes, Sir," responded a relieved Jack Talbot, who knew that this trouble he'd supposedly find himself in would never actually materialize now since Colonel Fry had bonded himself to a lie with his false report about how an enemy commander died. Fry had inadvertently given him the means to keep his own company's command secrets. Talbot might miss getting commended for heroism under fire, but he'd miss getting shot for supporting Daniel's insubordination even less. Yes, he was learning how things were really done behind the Federal lines.

Chapter 40

Before he raced behind the Confederacy's border, Daniel Winthrop took measures to protect himself from discovery. First he needed to shed his Federal uniform and locate appropriate civilian attire. Riding through Union-aligned southern Kentucky, he came upon a farm in good repair, but without any visible work crew. Clean clothes drying on a line attracted his attention and the promise of fresh horses in the stable cemented his interest in the property.

Winthrop selected clothing from the wash-line. As he stuffed the garments into his saddlebag, he caught sight of his horse's US Cavalry brand. He couldn't ride south with that insignia on his horse's rump. Eyeing a dark mare in the farm's stable, Winthrop appropriated a rope from the barn and fashioned a lasso. He was unlatching the gate when the farm's resident found him.

"Officer, what do you think you're doing?" asked a large man clad in coveralls, his dark hair and beard unkempt.

"My horse is spent. Everything she's got's been run out of her. I'm afraid I must commandeer yours on official government business."

"Now, wait a minute! I'm a patriot and I support my country. But do you have documents or anything else to prove to me that I'll be compensated? I'm just a poor farmer and my animals are all I have."

"Certainly, Sir." Winthrop put down his lasso, hung the rope on a fence post, and pretended to search his utility belt pouches while he scanned the farm to be certain they were alone. "When I came upon your farm, I didn't spot anyone at home." He looked around one final time as he approached the farmer, his eyes displaying an odd combination of apprehension and avarice.

"Money's tight. I can't afford to hire any help this season. Everyone runs off to work the fields that won the contracts to feed the troops. I guess I didn't make friends with the right politicians."

"I understand." Winthrop's hand came up with his pistol and he fired at nearly point-blank range. The farmer fell away, instantly killed. "Now you won't have to worry about that. And let me personally thank you for the horse," Winthrop muttered under his breath as he kicked the farmer's corpse for good measure.

He briefly reflected on how he'd created those conditions in his life that had made it easy for him to become a killer, as well as to rationalize his actions, at least to himself. He'd never owned a farm, nor was he likely to since the bank would probably foreclose on his father's land before he or his little sister ever saw any inheritance. And the land the small Winthrop family did hold back in Wisconsin didn't amount to anything close to the value of even this very modest farm. Now at least he had his own horse.

Winthrop roped the dark mare he'd selected earlier. She was gentle and obedient as he led her to the barn where he helped himself to the late farmer's saddle. Mounted, he galloped off, stopping to lasso his Army mount to take her with him. The less evidence Winthrop left at the scene, the better, aside from the dead farmer's body of course.

Winthrop donned the civilian garb he'd stolen in Middlesborough and secreted his Army issued possessions beneath a fallen tree trunk near the edge of a forest in southeastern Kentucky along the Tennessee border. Mounting the stolen horse and freeing his cavalry steed to run wild, he set out for Biloxi. He had long moved beyond the point of no return. He was a deserter, a thief, and a murderer. He'd chosen the way of the outlaw. Or as he rationalized it, his environment and circumstances had chosen for him. Winthrop rarely pondered the watershed moments of his life. Instead, he allowed his self-interest to guide him forward.

His journey would take him by horse and rail through Tennessee, part of northern Alabama, and down through the heart of Mississippi. He'd actually never been this far south before, and Winthrop remained unimpressed. The North was fighting to keep these lands? He knew it wasn't for the climate, but rather for the resources and the money – which made the profit that he now sought all the more worth his fighting for. He owned almost nothing in this world, and an officer's pay was paltry. Let the North exploit the hell out of the clod-diggers who lived here, building large plantation houses as monuments to their own sense of self-importance. It didn't matter whether they felt themselves above their ethnic servile class or not. They all still dug in the muddy ground to find their own illusions of an honest living that they could praise the virtues of every Sunday morning.

Meanwhile, Winthrop didn't figure the North to give him even that much opportunity. He could stay in the service with dreams of becoming a general someday like Talbot probably hoped for, or he could be hired on to be some kind of manager or something for somebody else's business that they were the absentee owner of – always serving at another's pleasure. That wasn't for him either. The big lie was that this war was about freedom. Sure, both sides had different ideas they espoused about exactly what that meant. However, Winthrop knew that only with his plan would he ever truly find freedom. In an insane world, his way hardly seemed the craziest path.

Winthrop's journey was halted several times: in Tennessee, once in Alabama, and then several times in Mississippi. Each time he rode into a checkpoint established at a crossroads, and each time the situation felt more daunting than the last. But sticking to the watched roads and bluffing his way through them seemed smarter than being caught well off the main highways and shot because he appeared to be evasive. The first time he reached a checkpoint, Winthrop learned that the militia was checking for Federal spies and horse thieves. Some poor soul hanging from a tree suggested they weren't bothering with the right to a trial either. He hoped the men wouldn't discern his inner-panic when they informed him of their intention to examine his horse for a brand. He'd checked for one himself when he'd made off with his new mount, but these moments were when he second guessed himself. Words could not describe his relief when no such mark was found on his steed. After feeding a lie about being a Confederate scout, they let him ride on.

Pushing his horse hard, Winthrop relentlessly rode south.

Chapter 41

Mr. Leahy drove one of the stripped-down wagons from Gulfport into Biloxi for fresh supplies, Mr. Davis and several of his men acting as escort. Insisting that she could help with the provisioning, Abigail traveled in another wagon with Old Man Hart, who was well beyond the days when he could ride a horse.

By going into town, Abigail accomplished two goals. She escaped her father's contempt after she'd pleaded with him to spare Emma's life, and she re-established her line of communication with the larger world. For now, she held fast on to her new fantasy that Daniel Winthrop would travel to the South, search until he found her, and then rescue her from her life of indignity as a war refugee. It was just a fantasy though. She'd never met the man and she knew nothing about him or his character. But she knew him to be a friend of Christopher's.

Arriving in Biloxi, they found the general store and set about filling their grocery order while some of the other men in their party went to the feed store for their animals. Abigail assured herself that along with a store clerk's assistance, Mr. Hart could handle their shopping tasks himself. Then she excused herself to walk to the post office to inform a new postman that their group had relocated to Gulfport. The postman could notify Georgia to forward their mail to them in Mississippi.

Only one person worked in the small house that served as a post office, a teenager with reddish hair by the name of Shawn Haney. He introduced himself a little too enthusiastically when Abigail entered his store unescorted. While he wasn't unpleasant on the eyes, Abigail wasn't particularly interested in boys any longer, her true fascination now lay with soldiers. Men needed to be brave and capable of committing themselves to causes larger than themselves. Yet although still a young boy, Haney could be useful, and it wasn't in Abigail's nature to be impolite.

"You're one of them vagabonders, aren't ya?" Haney inquired.

"If you mean we're traveling west, then yes," Abigail replied. "But for now we're going to be staying a while in Mississippi, and I'd like to make sure that the families in our group receive their mail."

"I can personally help with that," Haney volunteered. "Where are you flopping at?"

"Gulfport, at the moment. My father wants us to wait things out before we head west again. We may even choose to settle here and purchase property."

"Good luck with that. I've heard about you folks. Rumor is, your money is running out. You had something back wherevers y'all came from, but your men wouldn't fight, and you ran out on that, our nation, and whatever else you had going for you."

"You should talk to my father if you want to question his decisions," Abigail said evenly.

"Maybe I'll do that, but I'd much rather be talking to his daughter," Haney said, now openly leering at Abigail. She resisted the urge to lift the plunging neckline on her blouse. If Haney wanted a look, she'd give it to him so long as she got what she wanted.

"So do you work here all alone? Why aren't you serving in the war?" she asked.

"Our postmaster was called out for cheating at cards, and the man he was gambling with shot him dead as a mangy dog in the streets. I was working with him for a year already, since I'd turned fourteen, and I knew all the ropes that came with the job. Plus, I can read. Still, I was supposed to leave and serve the greater good of Mississippi, but there's no one else stepping up to do this job right now. Even the old men want to join up and fight. So sure, I'll go. Give me a gun instead of a mailbag, and I'll send Billy Yank runnin' home. This war would be over if they let Haney into it."

"You're very brave," Abigail said, hoping she didn't sound as disgusted with Haney's egotistical ignorance as she actually felt. Talking to this kid was like having a conversation with one of her brothers, who were almost the same age.

"So what does a man of your skill cost to brave the ride west once a week in order to deliver our mail?"

Haney couldn't seem to take his eyes off of Abigail's chest as he walked out from behind the store's counter. They were the only occupants of the little post office. "I'm sure we can work something out."

Inwardly, Abigail sighed as she nodded to Haney, who wasted no time in loosening her blouse, inserting his hands inside her top, and cupping her breasts in his palms. He pushed his groin against her. She felt him stiffening as he pinched her nipples. Then his teenage body shuddered, his leer shifting to an open smile of satisfaction.

Gently, she eased back from him. "That's all for right now. I will give myself to a man who proves himself reliable. Will you be that man, Shawn?"

"You'll be able to count on me, Sugar," he proclaimed while slapping her on her ass.

She resisted her impulse to slap him across his face. Somehow, this situation didn't inspire Abigail's confidence, but relying on the services of Shawn Haney looked to be the best she could do at the moment. Younger than Abigail, she hoped she could control him for as long as they stayed in Mississippi, and she prayed that her father wouldn't wind up permanently settling them anywhere within a two-day ride of this kid. For her own security, should he grow too bold with her, she could always introduce him to Mr. Davis, she reflected. Haney took her smile to mean she enjoyed his touching her. Of course he wouldn't know any better.

Chapter 42

Daniel Winthrop arrived in Biloxi on January 21, a Tuesday.
A newcomer, he received too much unwanted attention as he
dismounted and tied up his horse in front of a local tavern. Most
of the elderly residents sat out on benches in front of shops and
eateries, smoking tobacco-stuffed pipes if they had them, as they
observed the comings and goings in town with judging eyes. No
doubt, they wondered why a man of his age wasn't off in the service
of his state, fighting the war.

Winthrop entered the establishment and sat himself down at a
stool he'd pulled up to the bar. The other patrons nodded at him, as
one middle-aged man with several day's beard growth sharpened
his knife and looked over the newcomer. *This might very well be
another rough joint*, Winthrop thought to himself as he tried to
appear innocent. A tavern, he knew, was the best place in town from
which to pick up new information.

Shortly after his arrival, a red-haired, teenaged boy charged into
the watering hole, beaming from ear-to-ear. "I may not be no fighter
yet, but I'm a man today!" he proclaimed to everyone.

Winthrop decided the locals must all know him, since drawing
attention to himself in a place like this would otherwise be too bold
for a boy his age.

"What's got you running without a saddle, Master Haney?" one
old man sitting with his pals at a central table inquired.

"The vagabond's daughter. You know, the preacher? She let me
get inside her shirt today and, whoa, were those titties nice!"

"First time handling a woman, eh?" Another man laughed from
his position at a different table.

"Nah. I've touched a lot of women before her, but she was
different. She was amazing!" Haney insisted.

From his position at the bar, Winthrop cocked an eyebrow. *Was
this the kind of useful information I can expect to pick up in this
place?* "You're making that up," he suddenly interjected in the

conversation. Very bold for a newcomer to question a known local, even a boy, Winthrop nevertheless wanted to entertain a suspicion.

"I am not!" responded Haney to the stranger's accusation.

"If she let you touch her, what was her name?"

"Miss Abigail. Yes it was."

Inwardly, Winthrop smiled to himself. "And she just rode into town to let you touch her?"

"Well, no. See it wasn't like that. I negotiated the deal, but it also wasn't like she could resist me."

"I see. Where was she from? What did she want that she just happened to cross paths with you and discover your irresistible charm?"

"Her old man is Hutchinson. They're running out on Georgia. All of their men are a bunch of yella vagabonds. She just has to go wherever her family goes right now. They're staying in the next town west of here, in Gulfport. I'm to be bringing them their mail."

"Really? Maybe you'll want to take me with you the next time you're making the ride out there."

"I don't think so, Mister. She's my girlfriend now."

"Oh, I see. Well, I'm not interested in interfering with the good intentions of such a loyal and protective friend such as yourself. She just sounds like an old acquaintance of mine. If so, I think that once she knows I'm here, your Abigail will be very grateful to you for helping her catch up with me."

"Well," Haney said, considering the situation for a moment. "I'll let Abigail decide 'bout that. If you write her a letter, I'll take it to her on my run the day after tomorrow."

"You'll do that for me?"

"I'll do that for Abigail. Besides, it's my job and I'm the best there is."

"I'll bet you are," Winthrop replied.

Chapter 43

The term "going without" didn't exactly apply to Abigail's immediate family's living conditions in Gulfport. When their wagon caravan first arrived near town, no one in the group expected that they'd just park their wagons, check into a local hotel, and board their animals. They risked running out of money way too fast with that sort of behavior.

David Hutchinson opted for an alternate plan. The majority of the migrants would camp outside of town, squatting on unmarked land, while several families would reside in civilization for a week at a time, living in comfort before trading places with another group of families. The tactic left an ample number of people to guard the congregation's animals and property. David Hutchinson said it would be necessary for his own family to reside in the hotel longer than the others so that he could be closer to the resources he needed to conduct the church's business. He promised to rotate himself, his wife, and his children out as soon as the opportunity presented itself. Then they would also serve their term guarding the camp.

This turnover hadn't happened yet when Shawn Haney rode into town from Biloxi carrying a note for Abigail. He was excited to meet her out behind the hotel in which her family stayed but the location lacked privacy, much to his disappointment. For Abigail it was perfect though. She suggested that after she'd read her mail, they could find a more secluded location. An eager Haney obviously anticipated a reward for his service.

A moment later, Abigail suddenly grew anxious as she read the letter. It was very brief and to the point: Daniel Winthrop had come to the South and was now in Biloxi. Abigail said, "Shawn, I'm sorry. I won't be able to visit with you today."

"When?" he whined.

"Soon. I'll be coming to Biloxi as soon as possible. When you return, would you find Mister Winthrop and you tell him that please." She paused, then smiled at him. "I'll be very grateful."

"How grateful?" Haney inquired.

"Very grateful," Abigail answered him, her tone and demeanor suggestive.

The excited boy released her hand, stepped back, and bowed to her. "I told you that you could count on me." And with that, Haney turned and marched back around the hotel to untie his horse.

Meanwhile, Abigail entered the hotel from its back door, making her way past the kitchen and management office and through the hallway that led to the downstairs sitting room, which received the main staircase to the guest quarters. Climbing the stairs, she went up to the top level of the only three story building in Gulfport. However, she didn't go to the quarters where she, her sisters, and Emma slept. Instead, she entered the room in which her parents were lodged.

Both of her parents slept soundly even though it was the early afternoon. Her father now started to drink earlier and earlier each new day and then he usually napped at midday. Her mother often joined him in her effort to rekindle the dying flames of their marriage, which had become as strained as the southern man's plight in this reality that was the new America.

They never heard their daughter as she pushed aside her father's coat and shirt, which he'd previously tossed across the dresser top. Beneath it lay his pocket Colt revolver, a six-cylinder weapon with an extra short barrel. When he wielded it, he called it his personal extension of the hand of God. Abigail also found one of his money clips with the remaining currency he'd set aside for his drinking habit. The money probably came from the church's collective funds. In her opinion, wherever he got it, he didn't need it. Abigail hesitated as she caught sight of her mother's diamond brooch. She loved her mother, but she didn't think she'd actually have to pawn the brooch or even reveal she had it anyway. Since her father's weapon would be gone, as well as his money, she reasoned that no true thief would overlook the most valuable item her parents carried. Abigail quickly made up her mind and took the brooch *– just to keep up with the illusion,* she told herself. She actually planned to eventually return everything she'd taken, but she intended to travel with resources, if only as a precaution.

Her mother stirred in her sleep. Abigail froze. Then she placed the jewel, the money, and the gun into the pockets in her dress. After taking her father's riding jacket, she silently slipped out of the room.

Heading back down the dark, narrow, and rickety staircase in the hotel, Abigail glided through the sitting room, passed the reception desk in the main atrium, and stepped outside. She stood on the wooden porch searching out her father's favorite riding horse, a sable brown mare. Already saddled and tied to a hitch in front of Gulfport's general hotel, Abigail released the mare, put a foot into her saddle stirrup, and swung herself up onto the beast. She wasted no time in guiding it around the other animals tethered there and then set the horse into a gallop as she headed for the edge of town.

Chapter 44

News of what the Southerners called The Battle of Fishing
Creek reached Daniel Winthrop as he sat in the same tavern he'd
frequented during the previous two evenings. He smoked a tobacco
pipe another gentlemen had offered him in appreciation for his
service as a scout for the Confederacy. He claimed he'd reported to
the fort and then taken some leave time. His identity hadn't been
questioned since his arrival in Biloxi, unlike his experiences on the
trail south from the fighting in Kentucky. Down here, a man was
as good as his word until proven otherwise. Winthrop enjoyed the
naivety he saw in that philosophy.

Now Winthrop heard about General Crittenden's defeat at
the Cumberland for the first time. His true commander, General
Thomas, hadn't actually beaten Crittenden, however, and the Rebels
had managed to escape even across the half-frozen river. It was
sloppy work, he thought to himself, but just the same Winthrop was
glad he hadn't been part of the battle. He wondered how Talbot
and his men had fared and if his absence had ever been discovered
by Major Tithing. He'd been gone almost five days now and he
knew he was pushing his luck. *This Abigail Hutchinson had better
show up quickly*, he thought. Otherwise, he might not only miss
this opportunity in Gulfport, but also lose his chance to sneak
back to his troop, if enough of them had survived to still be called
a troop. But the engagement would work to his advantage, as he
could say that during the battle he'd been knocked unconscious
for an indeterminate amount of time and awakened to find himself
separated from his men. In all the confusion of battle it was, in fact,
a very plausible story.

Meanwhile, it was reported that Colonel Fry had killed General
Zollicoffer. In order to fit in at the tavern, Winthrop joined in with
a toast to the fallen Southern hero, although he probably would
have hung the man from a railroad trestle himself if he'd had the
opportunity. Then he reminded himself that he really didn't care one

way or the other. He wasn't a partisan to either side, no matter what uniform he wore. No, Daniel Winthrop would survive by playing only on his own side.

That thought refreshed his own sense of purpose just as he noticed an extremely attractive young woman who'd entered the tavern. She wore a white dress that had obviously been soiled by the trail, indicating she might have recently ridden in to Biloxi and hadn't had time to freshen up her clothes. But the dust didn't have a chance to cling to her as she entered the bar with a purpose, her blue eyes searching the faces of the patrons. Her gaze quickly settled on Winthrop as he was, by far, the youngest man in the establishment. She tossed her long, blonde curls away from her neck and down the back of her brown leather riding jacket, wasting no time as she headed directly towards him.

As she drank in the sight of him in, Abigail couldn't hide her smile, in spite of her best efforts to conceal her emotions. "You bring news about the war?" she began, trying her best to sound all-business. Anyone observing closely would notice the swaying of her long dress, which suggested her legs were anxiously twitching, anticipating beneath it.

"I trade information here and there," Daniel said, not hiding his smile or the genuine attraction for the girl that shown brightly in his eyes. "I'm Daniel Winthrop."

"I know. I'm Abigail Hutchinson, and I'm very pleased to meet you."

Damn! he thought. *Why did she have to turn out to be so pretty?* Aloud he said, "May I suggest that we discuss matters of importance some place that's a little more private? I have a room at the lodge down the street," he said quietly.

"That sounds perfect."

The two could feel the press of the other patrons' eyes upon them as they left the tavern. They gathered their horses for the short journey down the street. It had begun to scare Daniel that he could all too easily fall for this girl and, when the time came, he might not be able to kill her.

Chapter 45

Young Shawn Haney approached the tavern from the opposite direction in time to see Abigail and Winthrop depart. He'd already decided that he could not just let Abigail Hutchinson go. Even in the cold January air, his face flamed to almost the same red as his hair. He burned with jealousy as he clenched his hands into fists and watched them leave together. He knew what was probably going on between Abigail and Winthrop since they were headed for the inn without even a moment's pause to converse at the tavern. And it was the middle of the afternoon. *Damn Winthrop*, he thought in total frustration. Perhaps no one else cared enough to be more vigilant, because those most concerned with security were off in training or fighting the war, but Haney intended to do his part and watch out for trouble. But what could he do about it once trouble found him?

Chapter 46

David Hutchinson awakened in his hotel room bed and extracted himself from his wife's embrace with care so as to not wake her. Dressed already since he'd fallen asleep in his clothes again, that suited her husband just fine. He'd just grab some money and head down to the inn's bar for a late afternoon nip before meeting with the heads of the other families who'd stayed in town to discuss the immediate future. It was long past time that they all dealt with the reality of their situation.

To his shock, he discovered that his money clip with all his cash was missing, as was his gun. Margaret Hutchinson stirred from sleep as the preacher cursed God and stormed out of their suite, slamming the door.

Mr. Hutchinson barreled down the hallway and pounded on the third door to the west of his room. John Davis immediately answered his door. "David. What's going on?"

"I've been robbed! The church's money is gone, and my gun is also missing!"

"Shit. I'll organize the men we have in town, and we'll question them and everyone else in Gulfport."

"For all the good that will do," Hutchinson muttered. "Do you think the thief would be stupid enough to stay here in town?"

"Well, it's a place to start. Then I guess we'll ride for Biloxi. They won't get far."

"They'd damn well better not!"

Daniel Winthrop was getting inside of Abigail Hutchinson in any and every way he could imagine. They hadn't even removed all of their clothing. As soon as they were alone in Daniel's room, he drew his bowie knife, cut through every lace on her corset, and then ripped the frustrating garment away from her amidst her protests.

"That's a very expensive piece of lady's fashion!" she exclaimed despite her instant arousal.

"I'll buy you a new one if you really think you're going to need to dress for Paris for the ride west on the back of a wagon."

Abigail didn't even catch her breath before she began to shudder with passion as Daniel took a freed nipple into his mouth and caressed her feminine form with his strong, calloused hands. She had yearned for a man's touch so badly, she'd even entertained the idea of bedding Shawn Haney. But Daniel Winthrop had turned out to be more desirable than she could have ever hoped. It had happened so quickly. They were all over each other.

Abigail felt him enter her body, again and again, repeating his thrusts, and the pair spent several hours enjoying hot lusty sex.

Chapter 47

Gulfport was a small town and the migrants' camp was situated to the northwest. No one there had seen travelers pass that afternoon. The ocean was to the south, so unless a thief departed by boat, which was highly unlikely, there were only two possible directions in which to hunt down the culprit – to the north and to the east.

It would make sense for a thief to flee east, since to the north one would encounter many picket patrols and the war of course. Thus, Biloxi seemed the most probable destination of the quarry now being pursued by Jonathon Davis' posse.

David Hutchinson would not accompany them. In the sitting room at the hotel, he'd assembled all of the men of his congregation. Then Hutchinson discovered the theft of his horse, which enraged him and his followers even more. With no weapon and no mount, the pastor felt completely impotent, opting to imbibe with a drink on credit and to wait for the capture of the thief.

It was past sunset when everyone in Gulfport that Davis could find had been questioned twice, and Mr. Leahy and the men he rode with had returned from the migrant camp. If the thief headed east, he'd have a nice four-hour lead on the group. With any kind of luck, the thief might be fresh in the memory of any witnesses in Biloxi. Mr. Davis directed all of his men to head east.

Upon their arrival in Biloxi at what was still the supper hour, they fanned out to call upon the town's residents in their homes. Mr. Davis sent the eldest among them to cautiously ask questions at the fort, the idea there being that they were the men least likely to be drafted. None of the now very irritable group of men had any qualms about enjoying Southern hospitality, though. The search was lengthened as members of the posse disappeared to take supper at one home or another.

Truth be told, if the Mississippians had felt disdain for the deserting Georgians before, they barely contained their annoyance with them now. Social conventions required them to offer their assistance and comforts to the travelers, but vigilantes looking to root out a thief among their homes would not win them any popularity contests.

Jonathon Davis chose to search for information with a glass of whiskey at the local tavern. Business didn't seem to be slowed by the war, the place filled at this hour with men of Davis' own age or older. Jovial if not drunken voices resounded throughout the establishment as old timers talked of their glory days with tales of their own heroics during the Mexican War. Nothing about the boastful conversations stood out to Davis, but a red-haired, teenaged kid, obviously out of place with this crowd, certainly did. Others appeared to be consoling the boy who'd apparently been entrusted with too much liquor already.

Davis approached them, listening as the youth went on about this girl who'd fascinated him. Now broken-hearted, he explained that she'd spurned his interest in favor of another man, a stranger just arrived in town. Davis continued to listen, and the pieces of a puzzle began to assemble in his mind – a puzzle that made him think of Abigail.

Davis knew Abigail kept her secrets from her family, just as he knew she was untrustworthy. Hutchinson could only see the good in his daughter because that was all he wanted to see. But Davis knew better.

"I'm sure the day will come when you meet a young lady who is right for you, young Shawn," an older man with white hair and a matching white beard said. He wore a gray suit with a badge of office pinned above his heart.

Must be the local law enforcement, Davis thought. He slowed down his movements, and approached the older man's table in the most non-threatening way he could manage while wearing a Walker Colt on one hip and a bullwhip on the other, his broad-rimmed hat pulled low on his face, partially obscuring his identity.

"Are you the man who keeps the law and order in these parts?" Davis asked in a gruff voice.

"I'm Bill Harris, Biloxi's town marshal. How can I be of service to you?"

"I'm Davis. I need to report a crime. Money was stolen, and a good horse. I think a gun is missing too. I can only presume the thief is armed and dangerous."

"When did this happen?" Marshal Harris inquired.

"Only about four hours ago, over in Gulfport," Davis responded.

"Well I haven't got any jurisdiction in Gulfport. This is Biloxi, you know."

"I'm well aware of that, Marshal. My men and I represent our church and we swear to God we've searched through and through Gulfport. The thief must have headed east and Biloxi would be the most likely place he'd first stop."

Harris sighed, clearly ready to be disappointed if he couldn't finish his drink. "So you want me to turn this town upside down and shake out a man who may or may not be here. Do I understand you right?"

"My men and I have already done most of that. I just don't have the authority to request the livery being re-opened at this hour or that the hotel's guest rooms be searched, but you do, Sir. It can't be very easy to hide a horse."

"It isn't. I know where they're at. It's a man and a woman you're looking for, Mister," the red haired boy suddenly piped up. "He's checked in at the hotel." Shawn Haney intended to show both Abigail and Winthrop, whom he imagined were surely laughing at him, just who they'd messed with. Whether the object of the law's interest or not, Winthrop wouldn't get to enjoy his time with Abigail – time that he'd stolen away from Shawn.

"Well then I'd best start by going over and having a talk with them. These two are the same man and lady you were lamenting on about before, Shawn?" Marshal Harris asked, suspicious.

"Yessir."

"Well you do a fine job with the mail and I'd hate to think you'd taint your good service to this town by wasting my valuable time if there's a thief about. But I'm inclined to give you the benefit of the doubt," Harris said.

"You're going alone?" the large middle-aged stranger with the mustache and the Walker Colt questioned the elder lawman.

"In all likelihood, they're just an eloping couple or something of that nature. Relative of yours, perhaps?" the marshal asked with a conspiratorial smile. "From what I've heard from Shawn here, I'd venture to guess the new boy's a scout for our side and he's taken his leave time after that near disaster at Fishing Creek. Now I bet you he's just as scared as we are and he wants to run off and marry his girl. I'm sure he's a good boy. All I have to do is remind him that he's already married to Mississippi and he has a duty to do for the time being. But I only have three other men that work with me and I'd reckon they're all seated at their supper tables with their wives and children right now. I don't really think I need to disturb them over this. You and some of your men can accompany me if you'd like to, Mister."

"Thank you, I would. Rawlings, Beehan, you'll come with us." Two men in workhand clothes slid between patrons and tables in the smoky bar to flank the newcomer who seemed to be in charge.

"I'm coming too, right?" Shawn Haney inquired.

"No," said Davis and the marshal, both at the same time.

Chapter 48

From the collected journal entries of Abigail Hutchinson:

Friday, January 24, 1862
Dear Journal,
I am only able to turn here and record my darkest memoirs for it is otherwise too dangerous to bring the truth to light.

Yesterday began as the best day of my life, but then everything around me fell apart, causing the day to end in a nightmare that would make the date I learned of Christopher's death struggle to be worthy of comparison.

I arrived in Biloxi at approximately three o'clock in the afternoon. I'd ridden father's horse hard and non-stop from Gulfport as soon as I'd received word that Daniel Winthrop was in town. I met him at a local tavern – and when you're in love, sometimes you just know it! In person he was more than I hoped for and even more attractive than I'd pictured in my dreams. I'm quite positive that I didn't disappoint him either, as the two of us left together almost as soon as we set eyes on each other. It seemed like God was making up for everything that had happened to me . I felt like I'd found paradise, and Daniel and I made love to one another for what must have been hours.

But our moment was not meant to last. There came the clanking of the heel of gun handle on our hotel room door and the announcement of the local law enforcement. A man's voice said he wanted to question Daniel about his horse and verify his identity. This set Daniel off into a frenzied panic. Their verbal exchange through the door was cordial enough, but inside our hotel room Daniel urged me to get down behind the side of the bed and pull all the pillows and mattress on top of me for cover. All the while, he dressed quickly and checked his gun. I found my father's pocket Colt and hid it in the folds of my dress. Daniel saw this and nodded his approval – or at least that's what I think he meant. He was ready for

174

the actions he would take next. I can't say the same for myself.

When the lawman once again called out from the other side of the door, Daniel opened fire. A total of five shots went right through the door at chest level, the sound of their blasts echoing over and over again in my ears. Right before my hearing seemed to fade away, I caught the voices of others outside the door shouting "Get back!" and "Take cover!" and I heard a body hit the floor.

Then there was no noise at all, and everything seemed to happen without so much as a whisper: Daniel opened the window to our hotel room and clambered out, saying something to me, but I could not discern what. Then he was gone, disappearing into the dark. Did he jump from the second story? Was he hurt? I was too scared to move from my hiding spot and find out.

That was for the best. Gun blast after gun blast tore splinters from the front wall, and the door quickly broke apart, taking shots until it fell in on itself. When the smoke cleared, who should come stalking in but Jonathon Davis, his hawk-eyes scanning the room. I didn't think he saw me at first. Noting the open window, he ordered Mr. Beehan and Mr. Rawlings to gather up the men and reassemble their posse. As they left, Davis suddenly turned and grabbed me by my hair from where I'd hidden under the blankets and pillows I'd thrown on the floor. He'd seen me after all, but he hadn't let his men know.

He told me I'd taken things too far again. Now, it had gotten a good white man killed. He nearly threw me onto the body of the dead town marshal I was later to learn was Bill Harris, a family man and grandparent. He now lay on the floor just outside my room, spattered with blood, his eyes just staring up at the ceiling. I had no idea why Daniel had killed this man, but I couldn't be concerned with that right then.

Mr. Davis started tossing everything about in the room. In the pockets of my father's riding jacket he found the money I'd taken and the diamond brooch that belonged to my mother. He called me an ungrateful bitch and a whore, and he smacked me hard across my face, knocking me back onto the bed.

I challenged him that if he injured me, he'd have to answer to my father. That just angered him more. He grabbed me by the throat and punched me in the face several times. I'd never really been hit before and my first thought was that it was the strangest sensation. After the first hit landed and I felt the initial sting, my face seemed to go numb. I could see Davis winding up his arm for another strike, but it felt like I was outside of my own body when the punch landed. I saw my own blood splatter across the bedding. Curiously, I didn't feel anything from the blows. Boy, does it hurt something smart today, though! Anyway, somewhere in the course of this, I lost my own gun in the bedding. Mr. Davis never saw it and I tell you, had I found it right then, it would have been the last thing he saw!

But instead, that old bastard raped me! Taking the sight of me in lying there on the bed, half dressed, bleeding from cuts to my face, he actually got aroused. He said he was going to return my parents' stolen property and report that I'd been taken hostage by the thief. That would explain my wounds. If I ever said anything about what he did, he'd tell all the truth there was about me, going all the way back to my pregnancy several years ago, which he'd helped me to cover up. He said there'd be no calming my father then, and he'd take it out on me for dishonoring him by shooting Emma. He couldn't stand that I'd spared a Negro as it was. All I could do was think of her and how much she was even more of a mother to me than my own mother, while Mr. Davis tore up my insides and violated me in every way possible. When I was bleeding down my legs, he swore he'd knock all my teeth out with his gun if I didn't take him in my mouth and not dare to bite him. Then, he punched me again for his own good measure.

Telling me I'd finally given him what I'd gave to everyone else, and what he even felt I'd always owed him, the bitter, old sadist told me he'd leave me in Biloxi and I would have to find my own way back to Gulfport. He said he was sure I'd developed the set of skills I'd need to arrange it. Later I found out that he'd left with father's horse, so I had no transportation.

Alone, I cried for the longest time. I was in terrible pain and hurt just about everywhere. I had to go down to the horse trough to clean up, and who did I see down there, waiting outside the hotel on a sidewalk bench? Shawn Haney sat there with a cruel and satisfied smirk on his face. I just knew it was he who sold out Daniel and me, but there was no way I could ever prove it. So there was little point to bringing that up.

Instead, the little tallywhacker suggested that if I kept up my original bargain with him, he'd give me a ride back to Gulfport in the morning. What nerve! At any rate, I'd implied I'd be very grateful, but I'd never bargained away anything specifically sexual with this boy. Nevertheless, it wasn't actually until the early afternoon today that he was satisfied enough to keep his promise to carry me back to my family.

Upon my return, my father actually paid Haney a small reward for seeing to my safety. He and Mother put on a great show of family solidarity, all hugs and tears over my miraculous return. Father even used the occasion to ride out to the campgrounds in the wild to preach about God looking out for us once again, going on and on about the return of the church's money, to my mother's heirloom, right up to the rescue of his daughter. Of course, since I would need to recover from my ordeal in relative comfort, our immediate family would once again postpone rotating out of the hotel in Gulfport, thus forcing another family from the congregation to delay their turn.

While I was fine with having the creature comforts of the city continue for a longer while, the past few days certainly made me question whether God was ever there looking out for me.

Chapter 49

Firing five of six shots he had in his revolver, Daniel thought better than to empty his last round or to lose any time stopping to reload. He'd climbed out the hotel's second story window, crouched down, and lowered himself into a hanging position, holding on to the splintery wood that signaled the start of the first floor level. Then, he dropped down onto the hotel's porch below. Still not delaying long enough to reload or even catch his breath, he took off at a run to free his stolen horse from the livery, which he'd blasted open with his last bullet, and then rode like the wind out of Biloxi. He started his hard drive north.

He hoped Abigail had stayed down and remained safe during all the shooting. He'd write to her as soon as he could, and he hoped she'd respond. Daniel knew that those who'd come after him would now paint a very poor portrait of his character to Abigail and, no doubt, question her all about him. He couldn't count on her not exposing his true identity either. But for all he knew, she might be dead. Then everything he hoped for would really be over, if he wasn't caught and killed first.

His mission to catch up with Abigail's family and their church-clan was a bust. If she lived, he might be able to straighten things out and try again. He'd missed the opportunity to have her escort him to Gulfport so that he could scout out the situation. But he had no idea how the girl would handle their sexual encounter being followed up by him running, putting them both under fire, and making them suspects in the murder of a law officer on top of that. And on that topic, Daniel didn't know how it was even possible for the law to track him down for a killing in Kentucky in the first place, but he wasn't going to be able to figure that one out.

Right now, his priority was just to stay alive. Winthrop's mind raced ahead to how he could run the picket-watches going back to Kentucky with a lynch mob posse on his heels, as he expected would be the case for sure. He'd heard a body hit the floor and in all likelihood one of the shots that he'd fired in the hotel killed Biloxi's town marshal. They'd come after him for that.

Unfortunately for Winthrop, every checkpoint he crossed delayed him and could bring any man hunters following him that much closer. He planned to retrace the exact route he'd taken through northern Alabama on his way to Tennessee. If the same men were on duty at the checkpoints, they might recollect him and let a now familiar man pass. He'd say he'd been ordered to rendezvous with General Crittenden, carrying top secret dispatches from Montgomery, and he hoped no one would demand to see them.

Winthrop still moved too slowly, and he rode well past the point that was healthy for man and horse. He finally concluded that he had no choice but to stray from his course and find a shorter route.

When his stolen horse finally couldn't run any longer, Winthrop dismounted and relieved the animal of its saddle, letting her roam. Attempting to ride again was still an option, but he also had to face the fact that he was lost. He considered shooting his horse and eating her meat like an Apache would. If it came to that, he could do it. Perhaps he could carry enough meat on him to sustain him until he was able to walk to the next town. But there was a good chance that the posse would catch up to him before that, especially if they were on horseback, and he was moving on foot which would be as good as if he were standing still.

Winthrop didn't have very long to worry about that however. A shot whizzed by him, just an inch from his face while he sat on a log to reload his gun while he pondered his options. The mob from Biloxi had found him. They now spread out to quickly surround him.

"What the hell do you think you're doing? We're not in position yet!" Robert Beehan hollered.

"He's just one guy and he's no longer even mounted. There are eleven of us! Why are we even wasting our time with this?" Bill Rawlings demanded.

"We'd waste a whole lot less time if I had anyone with me that was a half-decent shot!

"Bailey, Hudgeons, move out over there to the right, get around behind him, and let's finish this!" Beehan ordered. "And for the record as to 'why?' Why is because that man stole our church money and by that way endangered the well-being of our families. God protects us, and sometimes He will call on us to serve justice across His Creation. We'll kill this bastard to demonstrate our love. So please don't you go thinking I give a damn about Hutchinson's horse. I don't. But since the fugitive shot Marshal Harris, the townspeople of Biloxi might be grateful for our support and the day may come when we rely on their charity. I have a wife and two children to think about. I am showing God I am His servant and will do His work, and hope that the Good Lord will then answer my prayers to help me do mine."

Return-fire suddenly rang out like thunder, and one of the men circling around to the right cried out in pain.

Daniel moved immediately. He knew the posse would surround and encircle the area where the man he'd just cut down had fallen, trying to get a fix on his location. So he wouldn't let them box him in. It was a smart Indian way of fighting. As soon as he saw the other man trying to flank him become distracted with his fatally injured comrade, Winthrop weaved in and out of the shadows of the trees. These men were not modern professional soldiers, up to date with their training, and they weren't looking for this move to be made by him. And Daniel was long since desensitized to losing comrades. In war, it happened to him all the time.

Getting around Bailey or Hudgeons, he didn't know which one he'd killed and he didn't care either, Winthrop climbed a large, dense magnolia tree with lots of foliage for cover. The posse didn't seem imaginative enough to look to the trees for the next assault. The height would allow Winthrop the best vantage point to scout out what he was up against. He could even stay hidden if they didn't spot him and let the whole posse lose his trail if he got really lucky. But he doubted that. The County Sheriff now led the manhunt for the town marshal's killer. The others were obviously all deputized under him, though they seemed to look to the one called Beehan for leadership. Winthrop made it a priority to watch the lawman's movements instead and, if at all possible, kill him next.

Bob Masterson was the first to react to hearing a shot fired. In one fluid motion he dismounted from his horse and drew his revolver. His men caught his hand motions, and they did likewise. Several more shots rang out, and they used the noise to locate its source, a ravine just up ahead of where they rode. Lieutenant Talbot appeared by his side.

"It's coming from over yonder, Sir," Masterson reported.

"Alright, let's check it out. Keep the troop on the ground and order a flanking maneuver, but stay in the cover. I don't want anyone engaging until I give the order."

Daniel Winthrop thought he had a good shot lined up on the County Sheriff's head from his perch in the old magnolia tree. He wished for a rifle, but knew that being hidden, he had the opportunity to achieve the steadiest hand with his pistol. He was about to plug a bullet into the other man's face when the back of the man's head exploded and his nose blew off with a bloody spray from the inside out.

Winthrop saw the other men from the posse jump and wildly turn every which way about. The other man with the comrade Daniel had already felled was taken by a shot through the heart and he was out for the count.

The crack of igniting gunpowder and quick flashes of smoke and fire from within the trees beyond Winthrop's location showed the posse had now gotten itself surrounded by a new contender on the battlefield. More bullets flew by, making their now-familiar whistling sound as they punched holes through bark and leaves.

"Jesus Christ! They're Union soldiers, Beehan!" he heard another man cry out. Then the gun shots intensified. Winthrop's former hunters had suddenly become the prey, and they fought as if they already knew there'd be no surrender.

Corporal Crawford rushed up to Talbot and Masterson's position, saluted, and then tried to catch his breath.

"What is it, Corporal? Report!"

"It's the Captain, Sir. I recognized him with my spyglass. He's in the tree over-yonder. "It looks like these men are hunting him."

"You're sure, Soldier?"

Crawford nodded.

"Very well. Kill everyone else. We'll get the Captain back and sort things out later."

The exchange of gunfire remained intense. Only eight men from the posse still lived, but they fought hard against the four dozen men under Lt. Talbot's temporary command. Masterson only had to put in three squads to catch the Southern posse in a crossfire and finish them. Any more men and the sergeant risked his own soldiers being hit by friendly fire. The rest of the troop hung back as Crawford and Ritter's squads finished the action, with Hill's people in covering positions.

Winthrop watched from the trees, growing excited as he recognized familiar faces in the blue uniform maneuvering to his rescue. What crazy luck!

On the other side, Mr. Beehan shook off the surprise and fear that momentarily paralyzed him when he first realized his men were now engaging Union soldiers, and his military training from the Mexican War came back to him. He didn't know how many men he was up against, but he knew he had only two choices: order them to split and run, or try to hold a retreating formation until they reached better ground to signal their surrender from a relatively safer position.

Beehan, too accustomed to order and the preservation of authority, took the second option. He thought about the irony that the men he rode with had left Georgia all those months ago so as not to be mixed up in the war, causing death and destruction, and now they would probably die fighting the Yankee tyrants anyway.

Corporal Ritter dove and rolled through the dirt and a light dusting of snow, not quite melted. He came up behind a tree and fired four shots in close proximity to the muzzle flashes of the man-hunters. As shots from across the small clearing briefly halted while the enemy took cover, Private Gamble rushed up to join Ritter behind the large tree. The corporal hand-signaled him to climb the tree's trunk as their captain had apparently done. The limber young soldier obeyed immediately while Ritter provided cover fire with his remaining two bullets and a quick re-load from his reserve cylinder.

No one noticed Gamble's move. From his position in the tree, he gained a clear view over some shrubbery that had obscured his line-of-sight from the ground. An older man with dark hair and a mustache, and a younger one with light hair and wearing a long duster, hunkered down and traded shots with Ritter. Gamble's first shot put a bullet right through the dark-haired man's forehead, but the recoil from his shot nearly knocked Gamble from his precarious perch in the tree.

"Beehan?" the other suddenly cried, and then turned his attention and answering shots upward towards Gamble's position. "Yankee bastard!" he heard the lighter-haired man-hunter say.

Rawlings' sudden spray of bullets caused Gamble to shake and lose his grip but not before he got several shots off. He thought his aim was good, but he couldn't verify it as then he did fall out of the tree. Landing on his back in the mud and ice with a hard thud, he was close enough to Ritter that his squad leader pulled him back under cover.

Eager to kill someone – anyone – Masterson moved up next to several of Crawford's men, firing and fell another. Then he saw a man take off running, trying to simultaneously reload his six-shooter, but losing his bullets on the ground as his nerves got the better of him. His weapon useless unless it could be reloaded, he threw it away from his body as he continued to flee. Older, he was no longer fit enough to evade Masterson's sturdy body as he barreled down on him. The sergeant drew his knife as he tackled the Southerner, plunging the blade into his chest and ripping it upward from the man's heart to his collar bone. Blood sprayed over Masterson and he felt it like it like a warm rain. The killing satisfied him. He felt some steam blow off as he took another man's life, ripping through flesh and soft tissue like a meat carver, then feeling the hard impact from his knife jamming into the other man's bones.

Someone else tried to get past Hill at his position in reserve.

Bored up until now, he hadn't seen any action. At the time he noticed his fleeing enemy, his gun still remained holstered, as he gripped his carbine in anticipation of a long range shot. Adapting tactics to use the weapon he could most quickly deploy, he swung the butt of the longer weapon around and nailed the other man in the face as he ran past. His enemy fell, and Hill proceeded to use his rifle butt to repeatedly pound into the man's face breaking his nose and jaw, the latter cracked, hanging askew. His assault collapsed one of the man's eye sockets with a killing blow that drove bone into his brain. A larger patch of snow that remained where he'd fallen now resembled red, crushed ice.

The remaining three members of the posse were shot, silence descending on the ravine in the aftermath. Darkness approached as another day ended. Captain Daniel Winthrop scrambled down from the tree from which he'd watched all the action, feeling exultant with the unexpected turn of events.

The men recognized him, smiled broadly, and offered him their salutes. Daniel spotted his lieutenant rapidly approaching. Winthrop abandoned all military protocol. Instead of saluting, the two men embraced each other in a firm grip, and then stepped back to regard one another.

Talbot started first, "Glad to see you made it, Boss."

"Yeah. I had some doubts about whether I should return to this outfit, but I figured I'd give you all a second chance. I even provided the men with some opportunity for target practice." Winthrop nodded towards some fallen bodies that were still smoking from powder burns and offered his sarcasm with some inflated bluster.

"While I was gone, I heard about your sloppy work at Fishing Creek."

"Fishing Creek? You mean by the Cumberland? We called it Mill Springs. And if I do say so myself, I do brilliant work, Dan! I killed that bastard Zollicoffer myself," Talbot bragged.

"I heard it was Colonel Fry," Winthrop remarked.

"That's what we let General Schoepf think, and that's what got reported back to Thomas, but I made that deal for you, Dan. I lose the credit for the kill, but Tithing never hears about you going missing – from Fry or anyone. Not ever. No one above Fry in the chain-of-command has any knowledge about what really happened anyway."

"Well then, I salute you, 'Colonel' Talbot." Winthrop offered him a wink, a handshake, and a smile. "You should consider yourself as having earned that promotion you so covet, in whatever command we end up serving." Winthrop's voice trailed away with that last sentence.

"So tell me how your mission went. Is all 'a go' Boss?" Talbot asked, bracing himself for bad news since he'd noticed his captain's change in disposition.

"Well, I actually took a demotion, to be honest," Winthrop said, letting his eyes drift away from Talbot to once again survey the cooling bodies of the dead posse.

The lieutenant looked confused.

Winthrop turned back to him. "I was only a lowly scout, you see – in the Reb Army," he announced with a forced laugh. "The fools believed I was working for Crittenden all the way through Mississippi. I guess they never heard of lying down there."

"But as you might have guessed," Winthrop said as he gestured with his gun, "I ran into a little trouble anyway."

"Did you find the girl?"

Daniel laughed. "Yeah, I found the girl. That wasn't the problem. C'mon," he indicated that they should walk back towards the rest of the troop. They repeatedly stopped to liberate weapons, ammunition, and any money and valuables from the corpses as they worked their way back up the ravine. The other men who'd fought with Masterson, in Crawford's and Ritter's squads followed their example. Hill's men claimed the Southerners' horses. Winthrop approved of their efficiency. "I'll tell you all about it Jack – once we're riding out of here. Oh, where are we anyway?"

"Tennessee, Captain. You made it as far as Tennessee."

"And what have I got left?"

"You're down to forty-eight from one hundred," Talbot gloomily reported.

"What about my little moonlighting proposition? Who's on board? Do we have Lieutenant Holloway?"

"He's dead. He died at the Cumberland," Talbot reported. "With you gone, and neither one of us outranking the other, he never really accepted that you'd given me any more authority. So we drew straws to see who's platoon would charge Crittenden first, and who would fill in the reserve. Holloway drew the shorter straw."

Winthrop did still have some interest in his officers after all. "So he went down with his men?"

"No. I think he was hit by – something – before they all went in. Yeah. It was loud, noisy, and a very confusing engagement. It was really too bad," Talbot said looking away from his commander.

"I'll need to promote someone to replace him. Who would you recommend? Should we field-commission Masterson?"

"We don't need to do anything at this time, Captain. I can handle the work, at least until we get more men. I think we're best off just keeping the unit we've got. And I've got experience doing that."

Chapter 50

Christopher Pratt drove his current horse Gracie harder than she'd ever been ridden. He'd had to suggest a family emergency to get any leave-time from Major Tithing, and he credited his success with his still being a good witness against former Secretary of War Floyd, whom he felt that the United States would bring to trial once the ex-Cabinet Member was apprehended. He'd counted on that making it still seem worthwhile to the Army, to keep Pratt happy. Tithing begrudgingly offered Christopher slightly more than a week away from his duties drill training. He was into his fourth travel day in his desperate run to central Georgia, a fact that absolutely no one could be allowed to discover.

His greatest difficulty involved evading the militia patrols along the border. Christopher, though out of uniform, knew he couldn't always keep his riding blanket covering Gracie's United States Cavalry brand on her hind quarter out of view as he endeavored to reach Abigail during the time he'd been allotted. On train rides, he even insisted he stay in the animal's cart using the need to calm his nerve-racked personal transportation as an excuse. That wasn't far from the truth. But he did enjoy his privacy away from the inquiries of other passengers. Of conscription age, if Christopher wasn't caught and hung as an enemy spy, he might find himself suddenly drafted into the Confederate Army.

Christopher knew Tithing's impatience with him reflected his superiors' impatience with the major, which made Christopher feel even more distressed when he finally reached the Hutchinson Plantation in Georgia. He worried constantly about his men during his absence, so his priorities – Abigail and his men – caused him never ending, internal conflict.

The condition of the plantation as he approached told him the land had been abandoned and the main house the object of break-ins by squatters. Christopher felt the frightened eyes of runaway slaves as he dismounted and ran into the deteriorating house. The great chandelier in the front hallway had been taken down and, no doubt, sold off – as clear as sign as any that the Hutchinsons didn't plan to return. None of the dark faces who observed him from the shadows dared to step out from their perceived security to challenge him.

Christopher ran up the winding stairs, dashed from room to room, and found only squatters' blankets on the floors. Each door he opened sent a sharp pain through his heart beginning from the moment he looked in to the room that he and Abigail once shared. He whispered her name, then shouted it aloud, not caring who might hear his anguish.

He raced downstairs, suddenly worried about his horse and the loss of his possessions, including the blanket that covered Gracie's U.S. brand. No one had disturbed her. She waited for him, tethered to the porch just as he'd left her. A quick survey of the workhands' bunkhouse and the slave quarters confirmed the plantation's abandonment by its previous occupants.

In despair, Christopher made his way down the pathway that led back to the road, walking, with Gracie in tow. Then he remembered something and stopped at the clump of brush by the old magnolia tree, closed his eyes, and said a silent prayer. Unconcerned about those who watched him, Christopher dug into the dirt beneath the aged tree and unearthed the little treasure box Abigail had left there.

His emotions shifted from the self-pity he'd been feeling when he left the plantation house to a gripping rage when he found and read Daniel Winthrop's letter.

After scanning Winthrop's words, including his false account of Christopher's wound, mutilation, and pending surgery, which had never happened, he read the letter he'd sent Abigail so many months ago:

August 17, 1861
Dear Abigail,
I too miss you so much, but I pray you will never witness the horrors that I have seen. I must admit they left me speechless and, for a while, unable to put pen to paper. There is no other reason for my silence, and nothing can excuse it. I have seen far too much of this war already.

188

You have been my anchor to another reality, a far better world filled with happier times. And it is because of you that I have been able to go on

I wish I could leave and quit this whole business, but I am an officer and my country and my men need me. I am bound by my duty, which I must fulfill.

Please stay close to your family. This way I know you will be safe. I cannot believe our forces would ever knowingly attack civilians. And one day we will be together again, I promise you.

And if your family does ever leave Georgia, please write and tell me where to look. I will find you. You have my word.

I love you,

Christopher

His own words very nearly immobilized him. With Winthrop's duplicity, Christopher couldn't fathom what Abigail now believed about his health or their relationship. And faced with the abandoned Hutchinson home, he saw no hope in ever seeing Abigail again. He thought to search for her in Biloxi because of the post-mark on the letter from Abigail to Christopher that had fortunately missed being intercepted by Daniel. But that would be equally as dangerous though it promised one last chance of success. Only how could he ever keep the promise he made to Abigail now, he wondered?

For days he'd ridden in danger behind enemy lines, all for a girl who'd saved his life and with whom he'd fallen deeply in love. Now, he thought his life might have been easier if he'd just gotten himself shot right through the heart. Though he could do nothing in the moment except return to his battalion.

Then it dawned on Christopher that when he did get back *he could look into Daniel Winthrop's mail.* That realization helped him waste no more time dwelling on his disappointment, and gave him a new plan of attack. He packed up the old weathered box, the letters stowed within, and quickly mounted Gracie for the long ride back to his Union troop's encampment.

He resolved to have new information very soon that would help him to locate Abigail and to deal with Daniel Winthrop.

Chapter 51

Upon his return to his battalion, reading Daniel Winthrop's letters offered little comfort to Christopher. He felt livid as he reviewed Abigail's correspondence.

January 26, 1862
Dear Daniel,
I am alive. If you are as well and this letter reaches you, then I trust you'll be relieved to know this.

I have no idea what to make of the events that just occurred. What in hell is going on? All I can tell you is that, for the time being, your secrets are safe. A business associate of my father's found me in Biloxi but for his own reasons, he will never report my involvement with you. I know his darkest secrets, lest he divulge mine.

But I also have a lot of information about you. On that subject, little is publicly known, although Shawn Haney couldn't keep his mouth shut. As soon as he had the opportunity, he reported your real name as he knew it from the letter you had him deliver to me. The county sheriff matched that with the name you used on the hotel registry so that I could find you. But while the progress of the law couldn't establish any culpable connection between us as I refused to talk, the court of public opinion sought to convict our entire congregation for causing all the trouble. If our reputation was bad before, it is intolerable now. Local stores refused to do business with us, and running out of supplies forced us to move on.

Father has his eye on a town called Baton Rouge in Louisiana. It is north of the port of New Orleans, but right on the shores of the Mississippi River, the last great, natural barrier our people need to cross to leave this war behind us. You will look for me there.

All assume I was forced to accompany you from Gulfport to Biloxi as your unwilling prisoner, and my injuries were the result of your forced taking of my innocence. If my father were to ever learn your true identity, he has the men to hunt you like you've never been hunted before. Fortunately for you, our people never saw your face and folks in Biloxi are in no mood to work with them.

However, to avoid any more unpleasantries, I suggest you let me know as soon as it becomes possible, just how you plan to meet up with me again. I can come to you. In fact, that might be much safer. We need to discuss making a fresh start.

My time with you, though brief, was some of the best and most exciting, as well as my most horrible, moments in recent memory. There should be nothing stopping just the good days from continuing though, were we to be reunited.

I will wait a month to hear your answer. Send your response to me through Louisiana. I'll arrange to receive my letters there.

Sincerely,

Abigail

Christopher Pratt angrily crumbled Abigail's letter in his fist. Damn Winthrop! The letter insinuated he'd had intimate relations with her. What else would she be doing in a hotel room with him? On top of that, he had already intercepted several pieces of correspondence that suggested the bastard had falsely reported him crippled or even deceased.

When he'd returned to the battalion and began to intercept Daniel Winthrop's mail, the latter had not yet returned from his Kentucky assignment. That was just as well, for Christopher knew he stood a better chance of surviving desertion and flight to Louisiana than of getting away with the murder of a fellow officer should he ever get the chance. And Daniel Winthrop was begging for far worse!

But events conspired to lead him towards the alternative with the slightly greater probability of achieving some satisfaction. With Christopher's cavalry troop back to full strength, they were ordered to advance into the South – into Arkansas, to be more precise. Finally being sent into the action, he could move with his unit as ordered for the time being, and then flee to neighboring Louisiana when the opportunity arose. He felt he'd done his duty for his men and his country by now, but it had failed him and his troops to concern itself with giving them justice, and he now he had few second thoughts at all about rededicating his loyalty to only Abigail and to himself.

In the meantime, he intended to quench his thirst for revenge against Daniel Winthrop on the Secessionists in Bentonville, Arkansas.

Chapter 52

In February of 1862, Brigadier General Samuel R. Curtis received orders to drive out all of the Confederacy's units operating in Missouri, wiping them out permanently. He'd amassed a great Army of the Southwest for the Union. His orders traveled straight down the chain of command to Colonel Cahill, then to Major Tithing, and finally to land on the shoulders of Captain Pratt. They would pursue the Confederate General Earl Van Dorn into Arkansas and they would destroy him.

On March 7th, Pratt's cavalry troop, now directly commanded by General Curtis, held station with massed infantry on the north side of Sugar Creek in Arkansas. The troop constituted a very small part of the Federals' total of ten thousand, five hundred men with artillery in support. Part of that force was splintered off by Bentonville and the Eagle Hotel, where Curtis' General Franz Sigel retained a limited force to protect the town.

General Van Dorn, neither stupid nor impatient, split his forces. The group led by Missourian Sterling Price moved to the east with Van Dorn, while the Texan Benjamin McCulloch took his command of sixteen thousand men, which included eight hundred Cherokee Indian warriors, and circled around to the west. They intended to get behind Curtis, cut him off from his supplies, and finish him. For once, the Confederates outnumbered the Federals. Everyone would be out for blood.

In fact, Van Dorn assumed that command of such a sizeable force would assure prompt victory, so he left his own supply train behind. His plan, to crush the Union forces, add their supplies to his own, and re-open his path back to Missouri, changed dramatically – as did the weather.

Mounted on his horse, Christopher tightened his scarf over his mouth and ears as the chilling wind whipped at him. He'd traded constant drilling and training for the constant war-time threat of violence and fighting and, this time, the violence of battle would likely occur under blizzard conditions. *Perfect*, he thought in disgust.

He squinted when he first viewed the dark outline of a massive, moving shape that seemed to slide across the snowy landscape. He summoned Lieutenant Travers forward to offer his assessment of what his spyglass had revealed.

"Hmm," was Travers' only reply before he called forward his best pair of eyes, Sergeant Hewitt. "What do you think, Sergeant? We're having trouble seeing a damned thing in all this snow."

"Sir, it looks like the Texans. There was a road under all that drift out there before the weather changed. If they're following it, I think their columns will swing left and take them around that small village over there." Hewitt pointed northwest.

"They're trying to flank us," Travers agreed.

"What's the name of that village over there? Let me see that map," Christopher said as Lieutenant Travers handed over the rolled document. "Here it is. Leetown. They'll march half-starved, some barefoot, all the way down from the Boston Mountains south of Fayetteville. Is that correct, Sergeant?"

Hewitt nodded.

"Well, there won't be much fight left in them. We're faster, so we'll engage them before they can even reach Leetown, surprise their cavalry with our own, and then kill the officers, all before they can get their infantry lined up."

"I thought our standing orders were to capture enemy officers, Sir?" Travers asked.

"That's a good way to become dead officers ourselves, Lieutenant," Captain Pratt remarked dryly. "I've seen too much of that already." He looked up from the map. "Travers, pass my order on to Lieutenants Cutter and Pullman and get the men moving. Tell Pullman I want him in reserve position. When he's set, send him back to report our deployment to Major Tithing with my request for additional troops to back us up. They've got a lot of men, but we're the end of the Federal line, so it looks like we'll have to engage them here."

"Yes, Sir!"

"Hewitt, prepare our squadrons!"

A short time later, Pratt finalized his company's battle-readiness. "Travers, I want you to place sharp-shooters inside and on the roof of that tavern," Pratt ordered, nodding at the building behind him.

"Sergeant Finch!" A non-commissioned officer who looked older than he probably was broke the cavalry line, rode up to his commanding officers' position, and dismounted. He immediately saluted the senior men.

"Sir?"

Captain Pratt looked him over. "Will you be able to identify their officers, Sergeant?"

"Yes, Sir. But Private Willows is an even better shot than I am, and he's never missed."

Christopher glanced at Travers and raised an eyebrow. The younger man nodded.

"Alright, Finch. You're on the rooftop with Willows. As a matter of fact, take two squads and make them fit. When you see the Rebs coming, you don't have to wait for an order to shoot. You just fire and keep firing!" Pratt ordered.

"Travers, you and Cutter are going in hard. You'll surprise their cavalry and knock it down. Travers, take some of Pullman's people to maintain your unit's numbers. When we strike, we're going to leave their infantry blind and confused and without their officers. They won't know what to do and discipline will break down."

"I think the Texans are also using Injuns, Sirs," Hewitt added.

"Even better. Like I said, discipline will break down – but not before this gets really bloody." Christopher continued, "Finch, after you take out the officers, you're to try to take down the natives, alright? They'll be the ones wearing bear skins and carrying tomahawks. Kind of hard to miss. You got that?" Pratt asked him.

Finch nodded. Christopher reflected on just how angry he'd become in recent days – angry enough that he looked forward to all the killing.

Captain Pratt turned his horse around and nudged her forward so that he faced almost his entire company of one hundred men. "These are treasonous Rebels in defiance of the United States! Remember what they did to us!"

Travers joined Pratt. "Bull Run, bull shit!"

"Bull Run, bull shit!" all one hundred men shouted back in unison. They were fired up and ready for a good fight.

"Lieutenant…"

"Advance carbines!" Travers ordered. The other mounted platoon commanders followed suit.

"Advance carbines!" squadron leaders echoed. Every soldier freed his rifled weapon from a sling attached to his horse's saddle. The newest, modern weapons made for a short but wide-ranging clapping sounds of wood slapping onto flesh as the men readied their firearms.

"Pullman! Dismount and take cover positions!" Pratt ordered, in a shout that all could hear. The rear of the formation moved as one unit to comply, hurrying through the snow to dig in where they'd make their stand. One member of each squad pulled their horses off to a remote location where they could be tethered but still be within reach.

"Finch, let me use your spy glass for a moment," Pratt commanded. He focused in on McCulloch's Texans, who began to make the turn in the road that would lead them around to flank Pratt. Satisfied by what he saw, Pratt handed back the glass. "Alright, Travers, deploy your sharp-shooters and then I want you on the line with Cutter."

Just then a new officer Pratt didn't recognize rode up and saluted. "Captain, Major Tithing is deploying Captain Hunter's troop behind you, and Captain Payne's boys will be backing us up! We're going to be all set for this brawl."

Christopher smiled to himself. *We're still outnumbered sixteen to one*, he thought. *One does the duty he's drawn. But not forever.* He hoped his unconventional tactics would give them the edge they needed.

He decided that they were as ready as they were ever going to be.

"For the Union… all units… ATTACK! ATTACK!" Pratt shouted.

Chapter 53

Lieutenant Buck Travers spurred his horse forward, shouting, "First Platoon… attack!" Thirty-five men mounted on horseback plus two squadrons of Pullman's men moved as one. They barreled forward, heading in a western direction from a southerly route. At the same time, Lieutenant Cutter paralleled his movements with the Second Platoon from a northerly tangent.

The Confederate cavalry column had just made the turn in the road to momentarily face east when they were lined up in Private Willow's rifle sight. His first shot seemed to be the loudest of the entire engagement. He hit a major to the left of the Rebel's commanding officer. It was a fluke miss. Then the rifles of his comrades along the rooftop of the tavern also started firing. Willows reloaded and then lined up his next shot with extreme care. He had only seconds to take it since the Texans had begun scrambling out of the line of fire and repositioning into combat formations. The eagle-eyed Willows put his next bullet right through the Rebel cavalry commander James McIntosh's Adam's apple. No matter that he'd actually been aiming for his heart. The shot got the job done and the man hurtled out of his saddle from the force of the blast, falling in the reddening snow.

The Confederates tried to assemble a cavalry charge to fight back against what might have been infantry or even Union-sympathizing militia. They were caught completely off guard as Travers and Cutter came in from their sides, blasting holes into the shocked Rebel formation. It was hard to be certain of anything they were seeing in the blinding snow.

Heavy clouds darkened the sky, in contrast with the reflection off the ice blanketing the ground. The discharges from the carbines were clear and constantly visible, red and yellow fire flashes that resembled lightning in a snowstorm. The thunder-noise that followed those discharges quickly became deafening.

Driven by a hunger for glory, the Cherokee warriors rushed to engage the Union Cavalry charge. They were fast – faster than the white soldiers. Their axes cutting into Pratt's men, they flashed past them, hostiles and friendlies mixing in the melee. Here and there an Indian blade would decapitate a soldier, while other swipes of the weapons severed arms before men could bring their carbines to bear. The Indians were excellent horsemen and just as effective with their own carbines.

The men on the rooftop hesitated and Sgt. Finch reminded them, "Shoot the bear skins!" Their firing resumed with its previous enthusiasm. Once again, the native fighters began to fall in front of the flag of the United States of America.

Unable to just watch his men make a charge without him and reeling with a pent up lust for action, Christopher charged after Lt. Travers. He drew his sword seconds before he entered the cavalry melee and immediately started hacking away at Texans and bear skins.

In the confusion, Pratt spotted Travers and angled his horse towards the other man's position. The glinting metal of a battle axe caught his eye just as Pratt reached Travers. He dove off of Gracie, tackling Travers from his horse as the axe sailed over their heads and buried itself in a Texan. The two men immediately rolled across the ground to avoid being trampled by their own horses. His uniform soaked, Christopher was glad it was the chilled kind of wetness from the fallen snow and not the warm liquid of his own blood.

Travers and Pratt made brief eye-contact. "Thanks!" Pratt's subordinate offered in exasperated-sounding gratitude. Pratt's carbine lay beyond reach beneath too many stomping horse hooves, so he switched to his six-shooter and pulled Travers to his feet.

"We've got to get off the ground," he said, grabbing the stirrup of a passing rider-less horse. Pratt got a foot into the stirrup and swung himself into the saddle while Travers grabbed the reins. Then, Pratt helped Travers swing himself onto the back of the beast and he spurred the animal forward. As luck would have it, he spotted Gracie in spite of all the confusion and galloped to her side, firing shots at the Cherokees as he approached his trusted horse. Travers slid forward after Pratt dismounted to reclaim Gracie. Now the two men had their own steeds once again.

Just moments later, McCulloch's Rebel infantry was moved forward at the double-quick to join in the fight. Pratt and Travers galloped right into them, six-shooters blazing. The Union men, inspired by their commanders, followed suit. Cutter's men and Travers' force swiftly joined them. The Rebels only carried muskets, which had to be reloaded. They were unable to respond quickly enough.

Before he knew it, Christopher had ridden right into the middle of the Southern infantry lines. That fact dawned on him the moment he found himself staring directly into General Benjamin McCulloch's eyes. The other man opened his mouth wider than his eyes as he took in the crazy young Yankee officer charging him right through his own ranks, partly because Christopher had shot a bullet right down the general's throat.

Chapter 54

Corporal Everts returned to Tennessee and Winthrop's troop's hiding ground after two days riding hard from his scouting mission in Missouri. Daniel didn't waste time waiting for the young soldier's report to reach him via the chain of command, but was on hand to hear it straight from the source.

"Major Tithing got orders from the colonel himself and took everyone else south into Arkansas. They're engaged at Pea Ridge by Bentonville!"

Winthrop frowned thoughtfully. "Jack, a word please?"

Talbot approached him. Both men moved out of earshot of the rest of their remaining company.

"If we all go back, someone who knows Cahill, Colonel Fry perhaps, will assign us to train replacements, maybe even in another battalion. Command's always messing with us. On the bright side, you might make captain, but I wouldn't give a bucket of piss for your life expectancy after that."

"Yeah," Talbot said as he nodded, despite feeling torn by the tempting prospect of a possible promotion.

"You know what I say? I don't need my uniform any longer. I think our next move ought to be to return to Mississippi in force, but in disguise. Their pickets are spread thin, anyway. We'll ride right past them and their old men will be none the wiser. We'll claim the Confederacy, even pick up some of their flags along the way. Then we'll look like we're heading in to the fort at Biloxi while most of their soldiers are out and I'll get us some new information in town. And I have a pretty good idea as to exactly who I'd ask."

"Sounds good, but not all of our men have civilian clothing, Dan. We can't take branded horses, either."

"What we don't have we'll make sure the great State of Tennessee will provide us with on our way out," Winthrop said with a crooked grin.

"And won't the townfolk in Biloxi recognize you after your last quiet, little visit?"

"It'll be the last place they'd look for me. Besides, you'll lead the troop. Coming in with all our men, I won't particularly stand out. I'll be just another face in the crowd. Besides, almost anyone who'd recognize me might very well be dead by now. Trust me, I think I can get away with it. Besides, all our men will be right there for backup. What could possibly go wrong this time?"

Shawn Haney's brown eyes widened and his knees knocked with fear as he recognized the man who'd just entered his small post office: Daniel Winthrop in the flesh.

"Y-you're not dead?" the boy stammered. "I watched at least a dozen men take off on your trail after you killed Marshal Harris. None of them ever returned."

"But I've returned, Squirrel. Aren't you glad to see me again?" Winthrop taunted.

Haney ran around the clerk's counter and made it past Winthrop without the other man even trying to stop him. He pulled open the door and stopped short. Another man with longer, wild, dark hair stared at him with a predator's eyes. He effectively blocked the exit door while he rested one hand lightly on the heel of the revolver he wore holstered for a cross draw from his waist.

Shawn shrank back from him, turning back towards Winthrop. The other man had drawn two long and wicked-looking knives.

"I think we are long overdue for another little talk. How about we catch up on our mutual friends? Let me think. Who do we both know? Oh yes, let's talk about Abigail." Winthrop was going to enjoy this.

Outside the little post office in Biloxi, Jack Talbot wondered how far away the screams of the young kid could be heard. A stray dog barked up a storm, but remained just out of reach. It didn't matter too much to Talbot. Ritter was across the street with several of his men, and Crawford and Hill hid on rooftops, just in case. Ironically, Masterson was at the fort in Biloxi with most of the men, resupplying courtesy of the Confederacy via very real requisition papers they'd managed to pick up off some fallen southern officers they'd accidentally come across. Meanwhile, the screams inside continued.

Suddenly, the noise stopped. Daniel emerged from the little office, his right hand stained red. In his hand was a small, bloody object.

"They're in Baton Rouge," he stoically commented

Then he tossed the bloody chunk of something to the dog and made his way back to their hitched horses. Talbot threw a curious sidelong glance at Winthrop, then back at the little post office building.

"At first the boy didn't want to cooperate," Winthrop shrugged. "But I convinced him to put his heart into it."

Talbot laughed, then added, "I reckon I've always wanted to see Louisiana."

Chapter 55

From the collected journals of Abigail Hutchinson:

Sunday, March 28, 1862 – Baton Rouge
Dear Journal,
It feels like it's been so long since I've felt able to come here and retreat within your pages. It's true that, for nearly a month, I have been unable to find the peace with which I need to write.
We spent nearly all of February being quite transitory. No longer welcome in Gulfport, the Congregation had to move west and out of the warring states for good. But it being winter, it was the most terrible time to be forced to travel. It was so cold, my hands would shake and I could not write. And the Mississippi River lay ahead of us, a dangerous affair for the inexperienced to cross in any weather, winter was not the ideal time for that at all.
Father wanted to stay away from the cultural contamination that was New Orleans, not to mention the fact that Louisiana's main port city was a key military objective in the war to control the Mississippi River. So we came in north of New Orleans to the smaller town of Baton Rouge, which also serves as the southern state's seat of government. Father felt that perhaps he'd find interests there that would want to help protect Confederate refugees and we wouldn't encounter the same prejudice that we faced from the people of Mississippi. In short, Father thought that folks in Louisiana might have less clear of a picture of what was happening in the East.
I couldn't testify to any real knowledge about that, but we definitely did find Louisiana far more hospitable. Arriving at a plantation we learned once held the Spanish name of San Carlos, we found the land owners more than willing to take us in. Without our own slaves in transit with us any longer, and taking into account the deaths along the way, the members of our families numbered only fifty-eight in total now. This plantation, just outside of Baton Rouge, had lost its own slaves when they fled seeking freedom,

inspired by rumors of northern military incursions into Louisiana –
which have actually failed to materialize up to this point.

Having no choice but to accept the indignity of taking shelter in
what had been the slaves' quarters, and even taking on the slaves'
work, Father and Mr. Davis had set the congregation to making
improvements to fortify the main plantation compound. It borders
right on the Mississippi. Even the military needing to transport
lots of men and equipment is cautious to cross the river. No one's
bothered us and the former agricultural concern has been adapted
to serve as a small religious sanctuary.

A barn at the far western side of the compound was converted
into the church; pews, an altar, and giant crosses were erected
inside. As many were now ill from being out, forced to travel in the
cold of winter, it was felt we had to be prepared, and a basement
storage beneath "the church" was fashioned into a crypt. We prayed
that we wouldn't need it though, and it became the best location
to hide our valuables we'd traveled with. We quickly felt welcome
and comfortable in Louisiana. Father felt it best to be prepared to
stay for some time. And here, the men could find work and not have
to trade their remaining possessions for the supplies necessary to
survive. He hoped we wouldn't need to ever trade away the rest of
our heirlooms and better wares.

Things were not easy at all, but they did look brighter for us than
they had in a long time.

Across the compound in one of the buildings to the north, beyond
the slave quarters we now occupied, I helped the women convert
a workshop into a school for the children. The land owners had
young ones of their own and thought it was a wonderful idea for
their children to interact with others their age and we fostered
enthusiasm for a learning environment.

And it would be a protected environment. The entire perimeter
of the compound will eventually be defended with a great wall that
surrounds the inhabited areas. An ivy or some kind of moss was
planted to grow over it, creating a more inviting covering and a less
military look to the compound. While our new home needed to be
defendable, it was after all civilian quarters, and we didn't want to
become a target should the war come to the heart of Louisiana.

Meanwhile, there was so much work to do, I was able to bury my own heart, and found I could easily avoid my father and Mr. Davis, who both chose to leave me well enough alone anyway. I spent most of my time with the children in the school, teaching them to read. I almost hadn't noticed, but Rachael had started to become a young woman now. I remember only recently having been jealous of my sisters' innocence and the life of privilege granted them by my father. But after we all endured the harsh flight from Mississippi as a family, and the girls had gotten sick during the travels, I'd found new love for my sisters that I'd never felt before.

I hoped they wouldn't endure what I had gone through with the mistakes I'd made, always surrendering to my temptations. Perhaps their religion would save them. Indeed, I realized it was I who had exploited my own life of privileges before, which allowed me to adventurously explore all the opportunities I took and to use the people I encountered – from the slaves, to poor Christopher, and Daniel.

Recollecting the latter, I have not heard from Daniel, since arriving in Baton Rouge. But we hadn't been here for that long. In my journal I must confess that I am far too tired of all this to take seriously the threat I made to him. If I never hear from him again, so be it. I'm resigned to just surviving my life and looking after my sisters. I don't feel any special desire to adversely complicate Daniel's life – more so than he's already complicated it himself. Yet I confess to being susceptible to being lured into one more adventure with him should he ever actually return for me. With no better explanation for his actions, other than perhaps the natural reaction of an enemy soldier's, the man is a fugitive and a murderer – and I'd gladly give my heart to him in a second.

Oh, Father's managed to apply his usual charm to convince the land owners to allow our immediate family to move into the plantation house "to help bring the Lord's blessing back to their family." I barely considered not going along with the rest of his brood and staying in the slave quarters with our congregation's other families and Emma, but why give up comforts in exchange for the emptiness of principles? In the end, the way I see it, you're only left with better excuses for why you don't actually have real and tangible comforts. So there I was again, staying a few bedrooms down a hallway from Mr. Davis. I don't really care if he can sleep with himself at night after what he did to me. I just care that I can sleep at night and that I feel safe being back with my sisters again. All this time I have still managed to retain father's gun I stole from him in Gulfport and I swear I'll never give that bastard the chance to do what he did to me ever again.

In the meanwhile, I'll always be re-evaluating my opportunities for escape or revenge. I know that someday I'll find some closure to all of this. But I can't even imagine that right now.

Chapter 56

Following their victory at Sugar Creek, Christopher and his lieutenants, his peers, and their immediate superior officers were all summoned to Bentonville where General Curtis had set up headquarters. They met in shelter from the winter cold inside the warm brick walls of the Eagle Hotel and were debriefed on the battle well past sunset. The plan to conquer and hold Arkansas was the main order of business. Following that, the men were dismissed. Many of them were so glad to have liberty time, they pushed off in groups to explore whatever recreation they could find in the Southern town – that was hopefully being poured near a hot fireplace.

It was evening, and darkness had fallen over Arkansas when Christopher realized that he didn't want to share anyone else's company. He bundled up, added gloves, and wrapped his face in a warm, woolen scarf. Then he trudged out into the snow to take a good, long walk away from everyone. Now he had the luxury of being able to organize his thoughts without interruption.

Buck Travers saw Pratt depart the hotel and go out into the cold alone. He elbowed Lieutenant Cutter, who stood with him and Lieutenant Pullman following their dismissal after the meeting. Pullman's eyes tracked where Cutter had turned to look when Travers nodded in their captain's direction. "I'm going to talk to him," Travers said as he crossed the room and followed Pratt outside.

Christopher shuffled through the snow at a lethargic pace caused by his downtrodden spirit. Buck Travers soon caught up to him, his smooth face still pink from the warm fire that heated the hotel. Crystals of ice had already begun to sparkle across his blue uniform.

"Travers?" Pratt said, his surprise evident.

"I just wanted to…Well, you saved my life back there at Sugar Creek, Sir."

"I did my duty, Lieutenant. Now we're even."

"Well, I needed to thank you anyway, Sir." Travers studied Christopher, with a concerned expression. "Sir, you have both my loyalty and my confidence. Is there anything…?"

"No. I just want to be left alone for a while, Lieutenant."

"Yes, Sir." Travers looked down, turned, and took a few steps back towards the direction he had come when Christopher changed his mind.

"Travers, wait."

The lieutenant stopped and turned to face Pratt again, admiration and hope for his commanding officer's approval readable in his round, blue eyes.

Christopher needed to talk things out with someone. Protocol demanded that officers vent their concerns up the chain of command but Pratt didn't think he had a choice. In the event he didn't survive the next engagement, or some fight after that, he decided he could trust his subordinate officer. They'd been through a lot together afterall.

"I've got to get something off my chest." He sighed. "We're in the middle of some very bad business, Travers. I think I owe you and the other officers an explanation. About eighteen months ago I was enlisted for a secret mission out of Washington. Part of our company was to be the military escort of a peace envoy sent by our former President to Montgomery, Alabama. There, they were to meet with the then would-be founders of the Confederacy to negotiate the terms to avoid armed conflict, but we were betrayed and the enemy knew our route. Everyone was killed. I alone escaped.

"This is only part of the little known history of our company and its regiment. Before our mission, there were no cavalry units organized east of the Mississippi River. I thought my unit was the first, but I was mistaken. There was another man who led a company before the one formed under Captain Lennox whom I served with in my first assignment. But, several of the officers back then betrayed our unit and only served themselves. A lot of our boys died."

As he and Travers walked through the snow, their course took them down the main street away from the hotel on the opposite side of the street, until they crossed the throughway and wound up heading back to their domicile. From a distance, Christopher saw Lieutenants Cutter and Pullman step out onto the porch of the hotel. Pratt waved them over. When everyone was closely gathered, he recapped and continued with his story.

"I owe you gentlemen an apology. If you'd been serving under another officer, you might have seen more action and already received promotions. But I personally want you to know that you acquitted yourselves well in the battle we fought here today.

"However, you should also know the reason why when we were reorganized as G-Company the unit barely saw any action in '61 when most everyone else was fully flung right into this maelstrom. The colonel was protecting me. I was a Federal witness against none other than our former Secretary of War, John Floyd." The men exchanged quick glances, as if to confirm that each man had correctly heard this new bit of information.

"I'm pretty sure that my report was the reason Major Fuller was relieved from this battalion and eventually replaced by Tithing. But, in the end, this was as far as the investigations and punishments went. The Army probably decided it couldn't afford any more scandals or further shake-up of its higher commands. Someone had to take the fall for this treason – that's what it really is – and then things needed to get back to functioning as normally as possible during a time of war.

"But I was there and I learned what was really going on. The colonel used me as a training officer and that kept me close to battalion headquarters so I'd be safe until it was time to produce me as the star witness, when it fit best with the political design of the time. I want you to know what I know, in case I'm killed. I was witness to a traitorous officer being paid off by the southern commander who led the slaughter of a fourth of the original troops that comprised our company. Though I didn't see his face, I learned the name of one of his accomplices, Masterson. Then, a young Southern belle saved my life by getting me out of there and hiding me until I was in a position to safely travel home."

"Awww, I know where this is going. I can just imagine where she hid you." Lieutenant Pullman grinned.

Pratt didn't smile, but he wasn't upset with his young subordinate either. "I corresponded with her for some time," Christopher admitted, "and then I discovered that Fox Company's commander Daniel Winthrop had misled her into believing I'd been killed so that he could involve himself in an affair with her."

"That bastard!"

"Of course I'd feel that way about anyone courting my girl, but there was more to it than that. My involvement with a Secessionist citizen right after I lost all of the men under my command would discredit me as a witness, and it would paint me as being no better than one of the traitors who'd served under Captain Brewster, the man who preceded Lennox in commanding the original mission of our outfit. Brewster disappeared, either because someone sold him out, or bought him out. For a very young battalion, this unit has a terrible history of corruption and of losing good officers. But the traitor I saw traded the lives of many a loyal man for twenty dollars and a pair of alligator boots, though he'd also bargained for the life of one of his men, the one called Masterson."

"Sergeant Bob Masterson," Lieutenant Cutter interrupted, abandoning military protocol. "I'd considered promoting him when he was a corporal to serve as my senior NCO, but he was just too darn mean. I held out for someone still training whom I knew I could work with. Masterson has been with Winthrop for about eighteen months, and this time frame matches up perfectly with your story, Sir. I thought you should know."

"With Winthrop? This is all starting to make sense. If you're sure, it ties up a lot of evidence, Lieutenant," Pratt said. "Masterson signed a shipping order in Virginia just before the war in order to mail one pair of alligator hide boots to a family in Wisconsin, which is where Captain Winthrop hails from. It can't be a coincidence. Those two are as thick as thieves.

"I'd been wondering why Winthrop would want to secure my lady friend's cooperation, if he needed it – and why it would even be so important to him after the government's closed the investigation. It occurred to me that I'd mentioned the Secessionist families would be departing Georgia, fleeing the war with all the wealth they could carry. Winthrop seems to be raising the price he'll sell himself out for. Meanwhile, he must have handpicked his lieutenants and NCOs he'd already trained in order to assemble a rogue outlaw gang to attack targets of opportunity. I suspect he controls them with the threat of charging them with treason if they don't cooperate.

"The Army won't hear any more about this. They've rotated us back into circulation both out of necessity and because the powers that be hope we'll be killed on the battlefield. Then, knowledge of this whole incident will just be buried away with us," Pratt concluded.

"I've heard former Secretary Floyd was due to stand trial. Powerful friends with business interests in the South probably ran interference for him, and now he's turned up serving as a Confederate general," Cutter added.

"Do you think Major Tithing is in on this conspiracy? Or Colonel Cahill?" Travers asked.

"I don't know how far up the chain of command this goes, but I was an eyewitness to Secretary Floyd's involvement. As the former Governor of Virginia, his sympathies clearly lay with his state, so we know this scandal reached as far as the Buchannan White House," Christopher mused. "Whoever else might be involved, they left men like Floyd and Fuller to take the fall, but apparently Winthrop was smart and looked out for his own people.

"But now he's put the woman I love in immediate danger, and I know beyond any doubt that he's responsible for the deaths of men from our unit whom I swore to protect. If the Army won't listen and act, then it's my duty to bring Winthrop to justice. This I have to do myself."

Pratt's lieutenants were moved by this story. Travers spoke. "Sir, you don't need to do this alone. You've proven yourself and saved all of our lives by your leadership. Our NCOs love you, too. Our troop will follow wherever you decide to go."

Cutter added, "And when the enemy attacks the legacy of Alpha Company, no matter what we're designated as now, it's our job to respond in kind. It seems that Ghost Company would be completely justified in doing our solemn duty and closing down that twisted Winthrop's treasonous business. And permanently!"

Pratt studied his junior officers. "I'm grateful for your loyalty, gentlemen. However, you should not make this decision without one piece of critical information. Winthrop and his men are heading into Louisiana by now. I've stayed with our unit this far because Arkansas happened to be on my way. I'll be guilty of desertion when I cross that state line, but I've got no choice. I'm going."

"I don't know about you two," Pullman said, his gaze falling briefly on Travers and Cutter, "but if anyone in authority asks, I'll just say I was following my commander in order to secure a deserter's capture." He grinned at Pratt. Christopher actually laughed and extended his arm to shake the man's hand.

"The men of Ghost Company await your orders, Sir," Lieutenant Travers said, saluting crisply.

Chapter 57

On Saturday, the 26th of April, 1862, Colonel Thomas W. Cahill received confirmation that the Confederate forces were abandoning Baton Rouge. New Orleans had just fallen to United States Navy Admiral David Farragut, and the Rebels were retreating to Shreveport, having decided that they couldn't hold Baton Rouge at this time.

Monday the 28th the sky grew dark with smoke as the cotton fields were burned down to their last fibers by Louisiana's Secessionists, who were determined to never again allow the Union to profit from the Southern state's misfortune. Brigadier General Williams intended for the Federals to take Baton Rouge. Cahill was ordered to send some of his men through the smoke and fire to join up with United States Navy Commander James Palmer of the *Iroquois* and support them. They were to hold the wharf and the Pentagon Barracks as new bases of operations in order to establish control over the Rebel state.

The assignment would not be an easy one. The river was aflame as the locals loaded cotton and whiskey onto barges and deliberately set them afire. The town's main wharf burned as well. If Louisiana fell, she'd leave the Northern mercantilists no prize. The Army's assignment to occupy Baton Rouge would hopefully restore order so that the Navy could hold the river and deploy the Marines.

The advance force's command duty would fall on one of Cahill's subordinates, one of his best, handpicked junior officers, Major Kenneth Tithing. Cahill summoned him at once. The militant Scotsman reported immediately but he appeared to be distressed as he faced Cahill. "Report, Major," ordered Cahill.

"I understand my orders, Sir, but my cavalry unit is not at full strength."

"Our scouts reported the Rebels have regrouped at Opelousas and are making for Shreveport. You won't encounter any resistance except for disorganized civilians. We need to get into Baton Rouge, keep the peace, and support the Navy in holding her," Cahill explained.

"With all due respect, Sir, that's not the problem."

"Well, please fill me in."

"Yes, Sir," Tithing continued. "Two of my mounted troops are missing, and I fear they are operating with impunity. I have no idea where they're at now."

"You've lost track of nearly two hundred men!" exclaimed Cahill in disbelief.

"It's possible they encountered difficulties making the rendezvous with the rest of the battalion, Sir," Tithing admitted, feeling flustered.

"I see. Major, you have nearly two weeks to get your house in order and your men entrenched in support of the fleet before Palmer arrives. But the sooner you re-establish order in town, the less the Navy can lay blame on the Army, on *my* Army, for the condition of the city, and the happier I'll be. I hope I've made myself clear?"

"Yes, Sir."

"Send out scouts to find your lost cavalry if you have to. It looks like the duty you've drawn just amounts to maintaining security, so you'll have the luxury of time. I'm sure the South wants Louisiana back. We'll have to dig in here, but the wake of destruction they left when they retreated indicates to me that they won't be coming back here any time soon. Settle the issues with your battalion."

"Yes, Sir."

The Pentagon Barracks was a five-sided brick station for housing troops, abandoned by the Confederacy when they retreated to Shreveport only days ago. Federal troops had moved in and found the facility to be quite to their liking.

Real barracks were fine, but the breakdown of efficiency with his link in the chain of command displeased Major Tithing. The disgruntled man ordered the assembly of his troop captains on the parade grounds. At least, the troop captains still present with their units who held the positions they'd been ordered to. *Where in the hell were Pratt and Winthrop?* he wondered, not for the first time.

During his Army service, Tithing had heard of units botching their navigation, getting lost in detail, or running off on unauthorized missions due to misconstrued orders. But his orders to his men had been precise and clear. So how had he lost not one but *two* entire cavalry troops? If he did not have his duty to focus on, he might have developed a persecution complex from the whole affair. As it stood, he'd been ordered to reinstate order in a town of thousands with a battalion command reduced to half strength thanks to nearly two hundred men missing in action.

Tithing began to address the small group of senior officers who were present. "Gentlemen, you're here because we have two crises. But dealing with crises is what you've been trained to do. On one hand, we've got the plantation owners burning their fields and setting fire to the barges and harvests they carry. Negroes are running around the streets setting everything ablaze – on their masters' orders, no less. The wharf has collapsed so the Navy will come ashore in landing craft, making their Marines more vulnerable to small arms fire from the shores, instead of benefitting from the protection of disembarking directly from their ships. We need to contain the population and institute a curfew.

"Our second crisis is that we're operating at half strength. Pratt and Winthrop are missing in action. I need their men, but I cannot spare a single mounted platoon to find them. We have a mission to fulfill here, of which they should be a part. Captain Hunter!" he barked.

"Yes, Sir?" The rather non-descript, light brown haired man stepped forward in military fashion. He stared straight ahead, his unyielding discipline as stiff as his blue uniform and only the pink in his cheeks revealing his youthfulness.

"Release one squad to be divided as ten scouts. Deploy them to find Pratt and Winthrop, and have them report back here at once when they do. I want all the men in Baton Rouge as soon as possible! We must get this battalion up to its full strength. Even if Pratt hasn't left Arkansas yet, he should be able to move cavalry across this country with enough speed to be concurrent with Commander Palmer's arrival. By then, we need the town secured, the wharf reconstructed, and the situation stable so that the Navy can land and maintain control over the southern stretch of the

Mississippi. We're to act as the lightning battalion. Are there any questions about our mission?"

"Will we have to surrender these quarters when the rest of our forces arrive?" another officer asked. Some of the men coughed to stifle any inappropriate laughter.

"Captain, the only reason you're this comfortable right now is because the bricks didn't burn. War is not meant to be comfortable, gentlemen. Our assignment in Baton Rouge is not about camping by a fireplace. You're inside the crucible, men. You'll learn that as you hit the streets and this town shows you its hospitality – or rather, its lack thereof. Captain Hunter, tend to the task I've given you."

"Yes, Sir!"

By May 9th, there was still no sign of or word from Pratt or Winthrop, but Commander Palmer arrived on schedule. The good citizens of the town were not taking it so well, however.

Marches and assemblies to protest the Union military's occupation of Baton Rouge seemed to spontaneously blossom and the verbal assaults from the townsfolk were the very least the Federal soldiers and sailors had to worry about. Greater threats were rumored and the Union officers in command warned that if any of their troops were injured, the entire town would be punished by a thorough barrage from the warships.

It came as a pleasant surprise to the citizens under occupation that, for the most part, the Union troops behaved admirably. In time, the residents began to show them the same courtesy, although they still exercised their rights to assemble and protest. The populace remained calm, but nearly everything of export value had already been destroyed.

Major Tithing had achieved his mission objective, but he took little comfort in it. He still had to report to Colonel Cahill that he was missing some two hundred men, and word of the situation had spread through the Navy's chain of command. Thus, Cahill could be certain that Admiral Farragut knew, as Commander Palmer would have surely had to include that bit of embarrassing information in his report.

Where in the hell were Pratt and Winthrop? he continued to wonder.

216

Chapter 58

It was nearly a week and a half later, a little after an evening
church service on Sunday the 18th of May, when Daniel Winthrop
arrived on the plantation-turned-fortified-grounds – *in Rebel hands*.
Unmistakable in his blue Federal uniform, along with wrist chains
and leg irons, he was jerked down from his horse and shoved
forward by non-uniformed militia when Abigail first spotted him.
One of his captors carried a thick, corded rope, the end of it tied into
a noose. They all had a cruel air about them.

Abigail wished she could immediately run to Daniel. They
caught each other's eyes, but she perceived the slight turning of his
head, warning her back. This was not the time to reveal that she
knew him. Abigail was deeply saddened, but she understood. He
was being presented as an enemy soldier, and he was to be treated as
such. Abigail realized that Daniel was missing any and all military
insignia usually accorded to the uniform of an officer of his rank.
His captors must have stripped it from him to add another insult to
his dignity.

Next, a young man with intense eyes and unkempt brown hair
introduced himself as Jack Talbot. He dismounted and asked
those cautiously greeting the new visitors to guide him to the
land owner. Mr. Hutchinson stepped forward, explaining that he
didn't own the land, but that he spoke for his church congregation
which had settled on the plantation temporarily before journeying
west. Hutchinson informed the newcomers that his party found
themselves cut off by the Union lines upon reaching the Mississippi.
He stated they'd been permitted shelter there by the authority of
God and that the people he led were biding their time until it was
safe to move on or otherwise became too dangerous to stay. To
Abigail's surprise, Mr. Talbot did not appear to pass judgment on
her father or his people. He let the matter rest, asking instead about
a secure location in which he could confine their captured Union
scout in until they decided what to do with him. Talbot was directed

to use the converted school. Meanwhile, Winthrop drew hard looks from both Hutchinson and Davis, whose struggles had solidified their perception of any Northerner as an enemy, especially one in the Federal uniform. Though he had never seen Daniel Winthrop before, Mr. Davis already knew with absolute clarity what this Union soldier represented.

"We've been trying to get him to talk," Talbot explained, "but so far he ain't said nothing. I'd have shot him myself, but we still might get something out of him, so I reckon we'll wait until we make contact with Louisiana's Army regulars and see what they have to say about it."

"Word is they pulled out and regrouped in Shreveport. It's not the safest ride from here," Davis said. "And there's the Mississippi to contend with."

"This man stays alive and in our custody for as long as there's even a remote chance he could wind up being useful," Talbot said. "That is unless he *really* finds a way to get on my nerves. But what we'd like to know is the strength of the Union occupation and their plans to reinforce their position in Baton Rouge and on the River."

"Give me a few minutes with him," Mr. Davis said, his hand straying to the bullwhip hanging from his belt while he stared daggers at the prisoner.

"Indeed, it might come to that," Talbot said, throwing a glance back at Winthrop.

Abigail was suddenly seized by terrible fear for Daniel. However, her father calmed everyone when he interceded. "Sometimes violence is not necessary amongst civilized whites, gentlemen. One thing this war has proved is that the North doesn't understand this yet, but their time to receive divine revelation is coming, I assure you. Though, for now, please allow me to serve as a mediator between this young man and God. There's often much a soldier may wish to confess to his Lord. Perhaps I can help."

"I'd appreciate whatever you think you can do in that capacity," Talbot responded. "You have a building you've been using as your chapel?"

Hutchinson hesitated, appearing apprehensive for a moment, then he nodded towards the north end of the plantation-fort's compound.

Talbot turned to his men, "Take the prisoner to church instead, boys. That sounds like the perfect place to me – for his confession or his funeral."

Abigail watched helplessly as several members of Talbot's Rebel posse marched her beloved Daniel away from her.

Chapter 59

Having ridden hard all through the night with minimal stops to rest their horses, Captain Christopher Pratt's troops were now only an hour out of Baton Rouge. And in stolen clothing – they were presumably under orders to be out of uniform.

Lieutenant Travers approached Pratt, who stood thigh deep in the Louisiana bayou under gray skies.

"Our scouts have returned, Sir. They didn't make contact with our own military, but they report Tithing is in town and entrenched at the local barracks there. There were no signs of a firefight. But we have conflicting reports from our other troopers of what might be Rebel militia settled in at a plantation directly south of the city and west of our current position. No way of knowing who they are though, Sir."

"Winthrop?"

"We cannot confirm that, Sir. Wouldn't it be best if we got back into uniform, reported in to Major Tithing, and then went in with crushing numbers? We haven't replaced the men we lost at Bentonville."

"I'm sure Cahill ordered Tithing to hold the city here in Louisiana. Controlling the Mississippi is too important to our overall campaign strategy. Tithing won't interpret orders. He'll follow them exactly. He'll never dilute his force once we've reported, and we've been missing in action for three weeks. None of you had to follow me here and make this into your mission, but if you're going to be loyal, then *stay* loyal and trust me.

"I won't trust that Tithing will let us report in and then release us to investigate the plantation. We have no evidence, but I have to trust my gut feeling. Letters I've intercepted describe such a location. It sure sounds like Winthrop, up to no good again. I need to make certain."

Another man stumbled up, using a branch to hastily gauge the depth of the swamp in an effort not to plunge into the water or wet his gun powder. Awkwardly, he made his way to his commanding officer. "Sir, Sergeant Hewitt reporting."

Travers answered him, "Yes, Sergeant?"

"We have a visitor. He's also out of uniform, but he got close enough that I could read a Federal Cavalry brand on his horse with my spyglass. He looks like someone Tithing sent out, and he's headed straight for us."

"Well it would be too much of a coincidence for him to be out for a ride in this swamp wouldn't it?" Pratt kept watch on a log that floated not too far off in the water. An eye blinked, revealing itself to be a gator. "Let's make contact." He turned and waded back to his horse. Pratt and several of his men mounted up, driving their horses ahead, splashing water in every direction as they headed for the lone scout. The alligator quickly darted under the water, the predator's role suddenly reversed to being the one in danger should the horse hooves trample it.

The scout continued to ride toward Pratt and his men, his arms raised, showing his hands visibly empty – until he seized his horse's reins to stop the animal. "Corporal Vaughn, Sir. Is one of you Captain Winthrop?"

"I'm Captain Pratt."

"That's a relief, Sir. This is wild country out here and with everyone out of uniform, I can't tell friendlies apart from those who might fire on me. I'm from Captain Hunter's cavalry in Major Tithing's battalion. My mission is to relay your new orders to you. You are to follow me back to Baton Rouge where you and your men will join the Army lines to support the Marines who are holding the town until the Navy can report to President Lincoln that the river is secure."

"Your message is understood, but we've got other plans, Corporal."

The young man blinked in surprise. "Sir?"

"I take it that the battalion is not under fire?"

"No, Sir," Vaughn responded. "The Rebels left without a fight before we even got there. We're trying to enforce a curfew and uphold order with the civilians now."

"I'm glad to hear that's the mission. You are to report to Major

Tithing that due south of the city is a converted plantation-turned-fort which is occupied by a rogue Federal unit under the command of the Daniel Winthrop you've been looking for. They're bound to stir up real trouble. So that's where we'll be and that is where Tithing will find us, Corporal. When my job is done there – and not until – this troop will rejoin the battalion in town. Do you understand?"

"Sir," Vaughn began, prepared to speak his words carefully. "This is war. I don't outrank you, but I understand the Code of Military Justice and its rules for insubordination to an extent such as this. You risk being shot for mutiny, Captain."

Pratt sighed. "I'm well aware of my how my duty binds me, Corporal. You give Major Tithing my response."

"Yes Sir!" With that, Corporal Vaughn turned his horse and charged back the way he'd come through the swamp.

"Sergeant Finch!" Captain Pratt shouted.

The non-com rode up to bring his horse alongside the Captain and the Lieutenant. "Yes, Sir?"

"Your sniper rifle, please."

"Private Willows!" Another very young soldier rode up to join them. Finch motioned him to hand over his scoped musket, which Sgt. Finch then passed to his Captain.

Pratt looked down, regretful for a moment. Then, he said, "I can't ask any of you to do this." With that, he aimed and sighted the man now riding some distance away from them. He fired. The shot hit the center of Vaughn's back. He fell from his horse, disappearing into the dark waters of the bayou.

"Captain?" Willows asked.

Lieutenant Travers responded for his superior. "The man rode out into the middle of the bayou to find us, out of any uniform. And we're also out of uniform. So he mistook us for a Confederate company and that particular soldier was serving as some advance scout. We're in no position to take prisoners out here, Private."

"Yes, Sir."

It sounded plausible and Christopher reminded himself to thank his lieutenant later. However, Pratt felt like he'd just shot himself. He glanced down toward his boots, but hesitated less than a minute.

As captain, he couldn't let the men see him reveal any uncertainty about their new mission. Then Christopher Pratt felt all his resolve harden into stone. "Let's get the rest of the men moving," he ordered. There was only going forward with his plan now.

Chapter 60

Daniel Winthrop took special care to note everything about his surroundings as Jack Talbot and several men with whom he rode pushed him into a storage house at the north end of the compound which had been converted into a primitive cathedral of sorts. David Hutchinson and his thug-of-a-friend John Davis accompanied them.

There were rows of newly cut church pews. Two huge wooden crosses had been mounted on the furthest front walls, one on each side of a make-shift altar. Apparently, the congregation had settled in here with semi-permanent intent. The floor was swept clean and the room brightly lit by candles under glass positioned in place-holders along each of the walls. Daniel could tell that there had had been time and effort invested in the make-shift church.

"I think you can leave us alone now, gentlemen," Hutchinson said.

"David?" Jonathon Davis questioned. Talbot looked ready to speak, but he bit his tongue just then.

"We're just going to talk," Hutchinson said softly.

"Then I'll be right outside," the large man said, eyeing the noose one of Talbot's men still carried.

"I've got nothing to say to you." Winthrop defiantly faced the preacher. "I'm Corporal Harrison Kent of the 4th Wisconsin," he said. "My loyalty is to the United States of America."

"Your loyalty is to yourself," Talbot said over his shoulder as he stepped outside.

"Ain't that the truth," retorted another member of the posse. They returned to the company of their own men who led their horses into the compound and guided them to the troughs and the shelter of the compound's fortified walls. They didn't rate the fortified structure as secure enough though to house all the men and beasts. Roughly half of the men were stationed outside the compound, keeping ever vigilant eyes on the perimeter.

Davis remained near the door to the converted chapel.

Approaching the church, Abigail ignored Mr. Davis who called after her, "Your father doesn't want to be disturbed while he's with the prisoner!" But he so rarely spoke to her any more, she disregarded him. Everyone else might seem threatened by the distempered man, but he would never touch her again. Otherwise Abigail's father would hear of it and never forgive him. She just didn't like the idea of a confrontation with Davis just yet, since he might be turned into a useful ally if it ever became convenient for her.

Abigail poked her head inside the doors of the make-shift church, listening as her father tried to begin some kind of dialogue with Daniel.

"Well, young man, I know your name now. Let me tell you about myself. I'm David Hutchinson. I serve as the pastor of this here church. I owned a plantation in Georgia, but I gathered the Lord's followers from our lands and left our country before the calamity of this war overtook it. I suspect that I may never be able to return to see my land again. I truly lost everything – everything but the love of God, who saw us safely to this place.

"You mentioned that you were from Wisconsin, or at least you served with the Federal Army's forces that were organized there. Why can't you see that we are of mind to let you live as you would wish in Wisconsin, but we are fighting for the right to live as we would wish in our own states of origin? That's all my people ever tried to do... live. But we can't because the North exploits us at every turn and forces us to be forever indebted to your banks. And that will only get worse if you rob us of our workforce. Our new nation with its strong states' rights will free us from this sort of exploitation, so that then our governments can represent *us* rather than sell out to what's in New York's better interests. Besides, I can't believe you'd want millions of Negroes unleashed upon the land to live as savages when we just fought so hard to subdue all the heathens. Presumably they'd be free to migrate to your lands and disrupt your life and civilized culture as much as they'll disrupt ours."

"Oh, I think you're right actually. You're making a lot of sense to me now," Winthrop encouraged Hutchinson, who Abigail thought probably reminded the former of the worst kind of religious buffoon. Daniel sat on a pew in the front row of the church, his back to the door, so he didn't notice Abigail's entrance. But her father did.

Yet Mr. Hutchinson felt he was steering the conversation in the precise direction he wanted it going, so he didn't acknowledge his eldest daughter but rather pressed on with his attempt to reach Winthrop. "So you should see *that* as your highest duty as a soldier – to defend civilization – yours especially. Otherwise, President Lincoln will be the undoing of us all. Do you understand? We must know what your General Williams and Admiral Farragut have planned. If all the citizens of Louisiana answer the call to arms, perhaps the Lord will see us out-maneuver the Federals, perhaps even prevent a fight and save lives. Don't you want to serve God and save lives?" Then, after a brief pause, Hutchinson said, "I am trying to save *your* life. Think on that for a moment – Abigail come inside. Corporal, this is my daughter, Abigail. My Dearest, allow me to introduce to you Corporal Harrison Kent."

"How do you do?" she said, playing her part in the charade.

"I'm thirsty," Daniel replied.

"Daughter, please fetch some water for Mister Kent." Hutchinson said.

Abigail sighed, turned, and made her way outside to the well.

"I need to step outside *myself* for a minute, if you'll excuse me."

"Yes, of course." Daniel watched him depart, secretly disappointed that he hadn't had a chance to maneuver the dialogue. He just needed a little more time alone with David Hutchinson to obtain the information he wanted. But perhaps Abigail would oblige him instead.

Outside the church walls, Jack Talbot watched the young lady emerge. A few moments later, her father followed her and paused near his foreman. Talbot started to meander in their direction and he overheard some of their conversation.

"How's it going in there?" Davis asked as Hutchinson approached him.

"I think he's sympathetic to our cause. He likes this war no more than we do, but I think you'll have better luck getting through to him."

"Me?"

"Yes. Our prisoner is a soldier, through and through. He might understand what our side fights for, but he realizes I'm no warrior. But if I read him right, his honor is partly defined by his loyalty to his side. You've served and fought, John. He might relate to you."

"I would not relate to him! He has no honor. I did not have the opportunity to tell you this before, but he resembles the suspect Leahy reported being pursued by the sheriff out of Biloxi – the same man accused of stealing your horse and other effects in Gulfport, murdering Biloxi's town marshal, and kidnapping Abigail! The rest of our men I sent after him never returned. He seems to have gotten himself into a uniform now. Don't know what he's up to, but I'll tell you something else. Your daughter knows this man and for reasons only known to herself, she's covering up for him. I'm sure it may break your heart to hear it, but you must listen. This man is likely a criminal, and maybe even a Yankee deserter. Let me question him *my way*, and I *will* have the truth out of him!" Davis insisted.

"No. He'll expect harsh treatment from you, John. Instead, be his friend and just tell him your story. Begin with that. I believe you'll discover a man in him who will understand you, rather than an enemy who's fighting to exploit you. He's young, John – half our age. Whatever he's done, we must forgive him. It is the Christian thing to do. God will be his judge. If you ask me, this young man is also being exploited and sooner than later that kid is going to wind up with a rope around his neck or on the wrong side of a musket ball."

"I'll think on that tonight," Davis said reluctantly.

Hutchinson adopted an approving expression. "Good man."

The men grew quieter as Jack Talbot approached. Then they abruptly ended their conversation.

"I don't know what experience you two have, and I am grateful for your hospitality, but I don't want my prisoner left alone," Talbot said in a hard voice. "You'll excuse me, but my duty requires me to check on him."

Chapter 61

As soon as she was assured she and Daniel shared some privacy, Abigail ran to her lover and embraced him, dropping the pail of water she'd collected for him. Daniel's wrists remained bound, and he could not return the affection shown to him, but he could clasp her hands as their kindred spirits also made contact by their anxious, animated eyes. Then Abigail's flashed from hope to anger.

"What in God's name are you doing here, Daniel?" Abigail demanded as she recovered the water bucket and handed over a ladle of water she filled for the prisoner and he drank eagerly. She had barely been able to wait to ask him. Now they were alone in the church for the moment, and she finally had her chance.

"I had to come back and find you," Daniel said between gulps.

"Well you found me, and they'll hang you for your trouble," Abigail said, sounding angry. Then her voice softened. "I'm sorry. I'm not mad at you, especially when you're so devoted to me. But I thought I sent word that I'd find *you*."

"What? When?"

"My letter. Didn't you receive it?"

Daniel frowned, considering. "I've heard nothing from you since I saw you last January. Then our forces began their push south, and my troop was reassigned to Louisiana. I wanted to send word to you, but things kept getting in my way. When word of a resettlement by refugees from Mississippi reached us at our new base camp, I slipped away to search for you here. It wasn't likely but I hoped. At the very least I would discover if there was indeed Rebels south of our position and whether they'd be a threat to my men. It looks like I found out."

"But *Corporal Kent?*"

"It will be worse for me if anyone learns I'm a Union officer. Don't look so worried. I've got a plan."

"Wonderful," Abigail said with sarcasm. "I can't wait to see how our situation is going to get any better."

At that point, Jack Talbot entered the church building and strode up the center aisle. "Had enough time with the lady, Mister Kent? That's as much Southern comfort as you're going to get. Give me this!" he seized the empty ladle from Winthrop and pressed it into Abigail's hand. "Take this away, please. I don't think the rest of our talk is for the ears of any lady. You'll excuse us, Miss."

Abigail sighed as she looked at Daniel one last time. He saw the worry in her eyes, and one corner of his mouth turned up in a grin as he winked at her. She took her time making her exit.

Once they were alone, Daniel Winthrop and Jack Talbot shared a great laugh.

"This is working out perfectly. They're completely buying it!" Winthrop said.

"I really had them going when they thought I wanted to give you a good whipping."

"You had me going, too. I wasn't sure you were just pretending. And Masterson? Talk about a man with a chip on his shoulder."

Talbot said, "Some business back at Mill Springs probably. But no matter. We'll soon be able to pay him to forget. So what's the plan, Boss?"

"Keep playing along like you've been doing," Winthrop responded. "Our timing and their location couldn't be better. With the real Rebels in Shreveport and the Union Army and the Navy between us and them, it won't arouse any suspicion if you order the men to dig in here for a while. It's not like there's going to be any communications with this compound and the actual Confederacy. Tell the men they should shoot anyone trying to approach this position. Double the watch. Meanwhile, I'll play the nice prisoner for a little while longer," Winthrop continued. "I'll see what I can get voluntarily out of the good Reverend Hutchinson. I think the loot's here or close by. They've only gotten this far since leaving Georgia, and I doubt they left their valuables in Mississippi." Winthrop snorted derisively. "When I find out what we need to know, we'll make short work of these people, change back into uniform, and ride out of here, through with this charade."

"We won't be challenged by Tithing? He's got Cahill with

General Williams coming in, you know?" Talbot nervously reminded Winthrop.

"We'll avoid them. I'll send out scouts and flankers in tandem, and they'll be quietly sacrificed, if necessary. We'll head north, then around Williams, and cross the Mississippi *from Mississippi* if we have to. In Federal uniform again, the Navy will provide us transport. How would they know any better? Besides, with wagons full of valuables, I think we'll have the right cargo to help us persuade certain officers, don't you?

"Remember, keep a clear eye on our goal. We never wanted to fight for the Blue or the Gray. We fight for our gold and our silver! In the end, we fight for ourselves."

Talbot grinned. The plan was finally coming together.

Chapter 62

Through his spyglass, Captain Christopher Pratt counted about twenty men and their horses lingering near the walls of a large compound while a light rain fell on Monday morning. Pratt's men occupied an unused field that had not been burned like so many others they'd encountered. As it was, this field offered Pratt and his men some cover. He kept up his observation, spotting ten additional men moving around the perimeter. There could easily be more men around the other side of the structure as well, which would have been the prudent tactical position. He could counter that though. What Pratt needed to know was the identity of those inside the compound.

"Captain, I think you better have a look at this," Travers called out to Pratt, who was paying close attention to Sergeant Hewitt. The non-com had been sketching the layout of the Secessionist's compound in the dirt at his commanding officer's feet when the lieutenant approached. Two days had passed while Pratt's men had made careful reconnaissance. They had identified Lieutenant Talbot by visual observation, and several officers confirmed that he was Winthrop's man, but they saw no sign of the renegade cavalry captain.

It was now Thursday, May 22. Pratt's company remained well hidden by the thick foliage that grew up from the banks of the Mississippi River. Even less comfortable than they'd hoped they'd be due to persistent rain clouds, they still had sufficient provisions to last them another five or six days. They could keep the compound surrounded on three sides without being seen. The bayou stretched out beyond the fourth wall. But with no vegetation growing close enough on their side to sufficiently conceal them, Lieutenant Cutter's men also had to keep back a little extra distance, which would inevitably reduce their tactical effectiveness.

"What is it, Travers?" Pratt asked as his subordinate approached

231

him.

"A lone tracker, Sir. Could be one of Winthrop's scouts returning?"

"Let's find out. Pass the word that Pullman's people are to pick him up – quietly – and then bring him to me."

"Yes, Sir."

Five minutes later, a weathered man of middle-age was marched over to meet Captain Pratt by several privates and a corporal. They kept him covered with their six-shooters, although they now seemed to be in possession of all of his weapons. He was definitely not a soldier.

"Who are you?" Christopher demanded.

"If I may?" The man indicated he intended to reach for something in one of his riding coat's pockets.

Christopher nodded to one of the privates, who reached into the man's pocket and removed a folded piece of paper. He unfolded it and handed it to Pratt.

"I'm Sam Foster. That there is a lawful reward posted for the capture and return of one Daniel Winthrop to the town of Biloxi, Mississippi to stand trial for the murder of Town Marshal Bill Harris. It also specifies that Winthrop is wanted for questioning as the prime suspect with the greatest motive for the killing of one Shawn Haney, also of Biloxi. I'm here to bring him in, and I've also been deputized to serve in this capacity," Foster said, stretching out one arm more so that the brown vest he wore shifted to reveal a previously concealed metal badge pinned to his red shirt.

"You're a bounty hunter?" Christopher asked. He glanced at Travers. "This could work to our advantage. I think we've just found our way in."

Turning back to Foster, he inquired, "Do you know what you're up against? Your outlaw is a Union cavalry commander, and he's got an entire troop holed up in that compound with him."

"I always get my man," Foster retorted. "I haven't got no business with that war of yours. I'm all done fighting mine, but I too earned my command experience. So, you boys Louisiana's local militia? And you're the senior officer?" he asked Pratt.

"I am."

"You're out of uniform, and your posture and position out here suggests that you're not exactly chummy with the men over yonder in that fort, are you?"

"Not exactly," Christopher agreed.

"Well then, would your boys like to do some moonlighting with me and collect a little something extra all the while completing the mission it looks like you already have them on?"

"You want to enlist my men and reward them from your bounty? Did I understand that correctly?"

"Smart folks take advantage of every new opportunity. Nowadays, everyone could use a little more money. You get the idea, Captain. What do you say?"

Christopher drew his gun and shot Foster through the heart at point blank range.

"I'd say revenge is worth more than a pile of Confederate cash that I wouldn't trade any of my men's lives for."

Travers looked dumbfounded for a moment. The rest of the ranks nervously shuffled and peered through spyglasses to try and tell if the sound from the captain's shot carried back to the fort. Winthrop's men didn't react, however.

Meanwhile, Christopher had knelt down beside Foster's cooling body, yanked his badge from his shirt, and wiped off any blood on it. Then he whistled for Gracie who came trotting up to his position. Christopher emptied one of his saddlebags of his military uniform so he'd have nothing in his possession that the Secessionists could use to link him to the Union. He motioned for one of the privates to exchange saddles between Gracie and Foster's horse. This would provide him a mount without the Federal brand. Then he handed his uniform to Travers for safe-keeping, shoved the reward bulletin for Daniel Winthrop into his pocket, and affixed the deputy peace officer's badge to his tunic.

"Sir, I don't know what you've got planned this time, but from where I'm standing this looks crazy," Travers dared to venture.

"It is crazy, Lieutenant. But there are likely civilians inside that compound. I don't think Winthrop would hole up in there if he'd already killed them. My guess is he hasn't found or stolen what he went in there for just yet. He would have moved on with his men if they'd been successful."

"What is he after, Sir?"

"Nothing short of the entire Hutchinson congregation's combined estate. Why else would he track them here and dig in at less than full strength? Hewitt reports Winthrop only has half his troop left. If he hadn't gone into business for himself, he would have reported in to Tithing in Baton Rouge and taken on replacements."

"The same could be said about us after Pea Ridge, Sir," Travers grumbled. "Damned Cherokee."

"I've been thinking about the past, too. Winthrop stole my mail for going on quite a while now. I tried to find a reason for him to correspond with my girl since before they'd even ever met. Or for his men's motivation to accompany the bastard if he wanted another rendezvous with her again. I know that girl's family. There's no way in hell I'd go in there in with a Federal company in or out of uniform unless I was operating some sort of ingenious and probably murderous plan. Unfortunately, I'm developing the ability to think like he does now.

"Those people are still alive, else Winthrop wouldn't still be here. I have to go in and determine if any cavalry is in uniform – which I doubt – and if and how they've separated any civilians. They may be Secessionists, but they *are* civilians and I don't want to risk the innocent lives of women and children." Christopher tried to look away from Travers so his subordinate wouldn't see his worry over Abigail reflected in his eyes. "I think I can make this work to my advantage that these bandits haven't killed all those who aren't loyal to Winthrop yet. If I try serving this warrant, the civilians should let me into their compound."

"They'll likely be taking shots at you before you even get close to that fort, Sir."

"And that's why I'm going in as an armed bounty hunter. I can fire back. It would even be expected of me."

Chapter 63

David Hutchinson returned to join 'Harrison Kent' in church, accompanied by his foreman, Jonathon Davis.

"If you don't mind, we'd like to continue now in private," Mr. Hutchinson said to Jack Talbot, who'd been guarding the prisoner.

"Sure. I'll just be waiting right outside. Call me if you can't handle him," Talbot said.

Hutchinson and Davis exchanged glances. Then the minister proceeded to introduce Johnathon Davis and relate his story. Inwardly, Daniel groaned. These two fools had decided to team up and convert him. He'd have to take something extra from the loot just to compensate himself for suffering through this. For three days Hutchinson had ministered to him and then left him with the Bible to read. He was supposed to find the path to Jesus and build his relationship with God. But at that moment, he really needed to get rid of Jonathon Davis. The Holy Scripture had indeed inspired him, just not in the way Hutchinson had planned.

He listened to Davis describe his misfortunes, the loss of his pregnant wife and his failure to ever finance his own farm.

"Then the War broke out, and we felt compelled to run. It was bad enough that your Yankee capitalists on Wall Street wanted to deprive us of our livelihood, but then they threatened to use the military to actually take away our lives! There was nothing left to fight for – and the way we saw it, certainly nothing to die for. So on through Mississippi we journeyed and I guess *you* would know how that worked out for us," Davis said, his tone accusatory. "And now we wind up here in Louisiana, living no better than niggers."

Daniel then heard how David Hutchinson was always there for Davis, a patient friend, making sure that he had work, a place to call home, and a family. He heard Davis' testimony about how he hadn't started as a true-believer, but he found that the Holy Spirit worked through David Hutchinson and taught him that he too, was worthy of Christ's promise of salvation. The two men definitely professed their own unique interpretation of the Christian religion, which obviously suited their purposes.

Daniel decided to reveal that he had also studied his scripture. "Your story is very moving, and it has compelled me to remember my Bible verses as well."

"That's good," Hutchinson responded. "And what have you recalled?"

"It's from Leviticus," Daniel responded. "I hope I can accurately quote this passage. I'll certainly try." And he began, *"And if one of your brethren who dwells by you becomes poor, and sells himself to you, you shall not compel him to serve as a slave. As a hired servant and a sojourner he shall be with you, and shall serve you until the Year of Jubilee. And then he shall depart from you—he and his children with him—and shall return to his own family. He shall return to the possession of his fathers. For they are My servants, whom I brought out of the land of Egypt; they shall not be sold as slaves. You shall not rule over him with rigor, but you shall fear your God."*

The reason 'Mr. Kent' had chosen that verse was not lost on either man. Jonathon Davis turned red in the face from the suggestion that he was being compared to a slave. He said nothing further, slammed his hand down on one of the pews, and stormed out of the church.

Daniel hoped the gleam in his eyes didn't give away his delight. David Hutchinson just sighed and prepared himself to begin anew with the prisoner. "I can see I still have a lot more of the Lord's work to do with you." Meantime, Winthrop rehearsed in his mind how he would proceed with the minister's own subtle interrogation. How long would it take Daniel to determine the location of the treasure? He could very well be sitting right on top of a fortune.

Chapter 64

Friday, Davis emerged from the plantation's main house where he bunked, stepping out into the rain to see a group from the militia gathered around the compound's fresh water well. As he approached them, he heard some of their conversation. The men stirred restlessly.

"We need to know what's going on," Talbot said. "You can manage here without me for a short time while I go into town to assess the situation. I don't want to be solely reliant on whatever's going to come out of *that* in there." He nodded over his shoulder in the direction of the church.

"I'm not so sure about that plan," Hill volunteered. "Crawford here thinks he heard shots fired somewhere down by the river."

"You think you heard something?" Masterson questioned him.

"I don't know for sure," Crawford admitted. "It could have been a woodpecker at that distance, for all I know."

"You shouldn't be going out there alone, Lieutenant," Hill said.

Talbot angrily waved his subordinate silent. "Just call me 'Talbot' or you could wind up blowing this whole operation!

"But fine, seeing as how the boss is here to keep you three in line, I'll take Masterson into town with me. He's a lot less likely to be recognized than me just in case we can't avoid Tithing's people."

What in the hell is going on with these guys? Davis wondered as he approached the well, acting preoccupied as he drew a fresh bucket of water.

So Talbot and Masterson will be leaving us for a little while? Davis mused. He wondered if any of the other young men – Hill, Crawford, or Ritter – one of which would be left in charge, would have the nerves it would take to stand up to him. Or with Talbot gone, could he employ his own methods to get the truth out of Kent? If that was even his real name, which Davis strongly doubted.

He watched as the other militia-men bade farewell to Talbot and Masterson, who mounted their horses and cantered out of the compound. *If these men were really the militia, it was long past the point where they should actually do something, anyway,* he thought. *There was a war going on.* Fortunately, they had brought their own provisions, but they'd imposed on the Congregation's hospitality and patience for nearly a week. Their presence had gotten old, and Davis wanted them gone.

The weather had seemed to change intermittently from sunny skies to it being cloudy and potentially wet.

Chapter 65

Lieutenant Cutter held his men at the furthest point away from the compound on its north side. Though he was a young soldier, much like Pratt had been only two years ago during the captain's initial mission to Alabama, Cutter was a true veteran now. He'd proven his worth and his instincts at Bentonville, as well as in previous situations. He relied on them now.

When he saw two men exit the Secessionists' base he passed the order down to his men through the noncoms to quietly retreat to a fallback position. The Confederate men, if that's who they actually were, appeared to be heading north towards town. Cutter planned to remain unobserved so he could possibly shadow them. Thus the travelers were given their space and his dismounted platoon went undetected. Everyone held their horses, comforting the animals amongst the tall plants to keep them quiet.

"Sergeant Zwelleger," he said.

A young noncom appeared before him and saluted. "Sir?"

"You're effectively in command."

"Sir?" the very youthful trooper looked confused.

"I'm taking Corporal Gatewood. We're going to follow those two and find out what they're doing. I think one of them is actually Winthrop's lieutenant, but I couldn't be sure at this distance. I doubt they'll report back to Tithing, and we can't afford to let them. They'll paint a distorted picture of the situation and who knows what will happen to our Captain's plans then. We all know Pratt's a good officer. He wants to protect the civilians. If the man I saw is Jack Talbot, that means it's Winthrop we're up against in that compound. He's wanted for murder now, and there are bounty hunters after him. Daniel Winthrop is not the type of man whose intentions I'd trust. Your orders are to hold here and parallel any move made by Travers or Pullman, so as to support them. Don't take any initiative yourself."

"Yes, Sir," Zwelleger replied nervously.

"Corporal Gatewood, mount up and follow me!"

It seemed like only minutes had passed since Zwelleger was left in charge of the Second Platoon when the shooting started.

"What the hell's going on, now?" Jonathon Davis demanded.

Corporal Everts had a wagon pulled up against the compound wall, and he was firing his carbine over it. Private Gamble rushed to join him. The sudden commotion galvanized Crawford, Ritter, and Hill, who broke from their social circle and ran towards Everts and Gamble with their weapons drawn. Davis converged on the group as well.

Everts, not outranked by the other noncoms but not originally from Masterson's platoon – he'd been with Halloway's men before his lieutenant and sergeant died at Mill Springs – felt subordinate to the other corporals. Aware that Masterson's men carried favor with Captain Winthrop, he reported to them immediately as they stepped up onto the wagon, and Private Gamble continued to fire over the compound wall. Meanwhile, men in front of the makeshift fort also engaged. They hadn't hit anything, making the squad leaders wonder why they were unleashing fire-power in the first place.

"Before he left, the Lieutenant ordered that no one be admitted to this compound under any circumstances," Everts explained.

"I was there, remember?" Ritter remarked.

Jonathon Davis took longer to climb up onto the wagon. The conversation he overheard only fueled his suspicions. He motioned to Crawford, indicating that he wanted to use the man's spyglass. Upon focusing it in on a lone man with a small arsenal of weapons and a lawman's badge, Davis exclaimed, "Wait! Hold your fire. He's one of ours!"

Shots still rang out and a man went down out by the trees in front of the compound. The lone visitor appeared both very brave and very handy with his carbine.

"He's what? Who?" Hill demanded.

"He's not your enemy! I know him and I can vouch for him. So hold your god-damned fire!" Davis thundered. He'd recognized Christopher Pratt, though last he'd heard the young man was going to become a blacksmith, not a lawman. But it had been almost two years since Davis had last seen him. Nevertheless, Pratt arrived armed, obviously skilled, and a potential ally at a time when Hutchinson's congregation needed one.

The whole lot of the younger men were quite intimidated by Davis, and Ritter started repeating his orders, shouting so the men outside could hear him. "Hold your fire! Hold your fire!"

Davis jumped down from the wagon, followed by a confused Ritter. "Open the gate!" Davis barked to the men who guarded the main entrance to the compound.

Chapter 66

Christopher Pratt had never imagined the day when he'd be glad to see Jonathon Davis again. But in all likelihood, without Davis' intervention, Christopher would be dead. No sooner than he was in rifle range of the fort-compound, Winthrop's men had begun to take shots at him. Christopher dove for cover, rolling in the dirt as he brought up his carbine and fired back. He downed at least one man before their assault promptly ceased.

And when the men in the fort stopped shooting, so did he.

As Christopher approached the compound and the wary men who looked like militia opened the gates to admit him, he found himself face to face with none other than that same old, distempered plantation foreman he'd known in Georgia. But Christopher had hoped something like this would happen if the Secessionists were still alive. Thus, he continued in his role of a bounty hunter.

"That was pretty stupid of you – and very brave," Davis said by way of a greeting. The two acquaintances shook hands under the watchful gaze of Winthrop's men.

"Thanks I guess," Christopher replied. "It's nice to see you, too."

"What are you doing in Louisiana? You're wearing a badge. If I had to guess, I'd say you're not a blacksmith. On a man-hunt, I presume?"

"Yes. Having once been the victim of crime, I serve by creating justice now. I'm looking for a man named Daniel Winthrop. He's wanted for murder. I intend to bring him back to Biloxi, Mississippi to stand trial for the killing of a town marshal, and he's the prime suspect in at least one other slaying as well."

"Can you identify this man if you saw him?"

Christopher produced the copy of the wanted poster Foster had carried with him. It was a somewhat inaccurate likeness of Daniel Winthrop, but it satisfied Jonathon Davis.

"We have him in custody here. He goes by the name of Harrison

Kent. He was brought here by these militia men, however," Davis lowered his voice, "I've grown suspicious that they aren't who they said they were either."

"Winthrop was a Union soldier who deserted. He may have taken his loyal men with him when he left the Army to go into business for himself, as the rogue leader of a gang of marauding bandits," Christopher said quietly.

"And we're surrounded by them?" Davis asked, still trying to control any alarm that could be revealed in his voice.

"If the worst is true, yes. But I'm here to bring Winthrop in, not fight a war for you."

"You didn't come alone, did you?"

"My posse is out there." Pratt nodded to indicate the area far beyond the compound walls.

"Maybe we can make a deal. I'll help you with your problem, if you help me with mine. It appears we're facing the same situation anyway. Have you any idea how you're going to get Winthrop out of here if these men are actually in league with him?"

"It seems that an alliance would be mutually beneficial," Christopher admitted. "Will your people fight and help us out with this?"

Davis nodded. "For sure. We hate all the Northern tyrants and we value deserters even less – no matter what side they came from. I believe Winthrop and these men came gunning for us from the outset. And that Winthrop fellow had an inappropriate relationship with one of our own. He's up to no good, and he needs to be stopped."

"Do you have any idea what they were after?"

"All the valuables we brought with us from Georgia. It's all we have left. What else could it be?"

"Alright, you'd agree that your men will be fighting to defend themselves, their families, and their properties. When will you be ready?"

"We've always been ready. We've been fighting for our rights for a lot longer than you're actually old enough to remember, boy. Now I can support you, and let you have your man, but not just yet."

"What?" Christopher exclaimed. He thought they just had gotten everything worked out.

"I need Winthrop for as long as it takes."

"As long as it takes for what?"

"As long as it takes to get whatever information he has on the Union occupation and deployments from New Orleans to Baton Rouge. The militia men came here claiming they wanted to bust him up to get that information, but I had doubts about that from the start. However, someone on our side *is* going to want that information and be able to make use of it we can get good intelligence back to Shreveport or wherever the Regulars went. Louisiana's given us a second chance. We have an opportunity to reciprocate. Besides, if I do have to beat the answers out of that little, lying Yankee son of a bitch, I'm certain we will find out just what side these other boys are fighting on, won't we? I'm not going to say whether they'd stand by and let their boss get all messed up, but if they do, it'll be a lot of fun for me," Davis said, rubbing his fist in the palm of his other hand. "And then we'll know for sure who's side everyone else is really on."

As much as Christopher wanted to, he didn't dare ask Mr. Davis about Abigail.

Chapter 67

David Hutchinson felt pretty good about himself that Friday afternoon. He'd just completed the day's Bible Study with Harrison Kent, certain he'd finally made some progress in the redemption of that young man's lost soul. Now, having discovered the plantation's second hidden store of whiskey and spirits, he felt he deserved a hard-earned drink and some time to relax in peace and quiet before he ministered Friday evening services to his congregants.

Now David had known something had happened. No one could not have heard all the gunplay, but he didn't involve himself in the shooting. If the Lord had wanted him present, He'd have made it so. Thus David need not worry about his role in the outcome of events. God's plan always found him.

He sat on the porch of the plantation home sheltered from the light rain, watching the heavens grow darker with the sunset. The sky was probably too cloudy to actually see the sun set, but it was enough to know the sun would set – and tomorrow it would rise again, just like the Holy Spirit would rise up in his people to save them. Perhaps that would also be the case with Harrison Kent.

David spotted Jonathon Davis as he approached, seemingly oblivious to the light rain. His foreman appeared to be deep in thought, so Hutchinson prepared himself for whatever issue Jonathon intended to bring to his attention.

John began without preamble. "We got a new visitor today."

"So I heard," Hutchinson replied.

"A face from the past. Christopher Pratt. That kid who stayed with us in Georgia a couple of years back."

"What's he doing in Louisiana?" asked a surprised Hutchinson.

"Hunting. The kid was hired to lead a posse from out of Mississippi to arrest one Daniel Winthrop, a criminal wanted for murder. And this was definitely the one mixed up in that bad business in Biloxi. So I looked at a picture. Guess who shows a perfect resemblance to him? Your friend at church, Harrison Kent."

"What's Kent doing now? Who's watching him?"

"One of Talbot's men," John answered with a snort of contempt.

"Well, Kent should have been brought his dinner and has made plans to attend our church services this evening," Hutchinson revealed.

John sighed. Hutchinson was a good man, but far too naïve to understand the ways of the world. While David offered him the bottle of whiskey, which he gladly accepted, Jonathon kept to himself his suspicions about Talbot's men. He owed his friend the benefit of the doubt and would give David at least this week to finish his attempt to convert Winthrop. If he failed, John would use his bullwhip, and Pratt could have whatever was left of Winthrop. Davis felt comfortable that the arrival of Pratt and his posse would buy Hutchinson his extra time.

Davis took another drink from the whiskey bottle. He knew he needed to talk with Pratt and come up with a plan to alert his posse. If Talbot and his men were really in cahoots with Winthrop, they'd be facing a very dangerous situation. David didn't need to worry about that right now. Jonathon would take care of it for him.

Davis merely said to his friend, "That's all well and good, but let's keep Pratt's presence here a secret to our prisoner. Use Pratt as a last resort to threaten Kent, Winthrop, or whatever his name is. If he doesn't talk soon, then tell him you're going to turn him over to the bounty hunter, and his posse."

"You've already promised Talbot we'd give him Kent back. Now Pratt thinks he's going to take him, too?"

"Yeah, he does. But you don't have to tell Kent about Pratt right away," John answered him. "I have reason to believe that could be dangerous – for too many of us. So first we'll try to convert our captive your way."

Chapter 68

Major Tithing used his personal quarters to also double as his office in the Pentagon Barracks. The better accommodations had already been usurped by Colonel Cahill upon his arrival. Tithing studied the maps spread across his bunk when his aide-de-camp, Lieutenant Remick, escorted Captain Hunter and a boy, who wore no uniform, but who may have been one of Hunter's subordinates, into the small room.

The men immediately saluted their commanding officer as Remick left. Tithing addressed Hunter, "Captain, report."

"I think you should hear this first hand from my scout, Sir," Hunter responded. "Keller."

The very young man gulped nervously. He obviously hadn't expected to be addressing a Major, but he quickly found his voice. "My captain let my sergeant separate my squad and send us out all over the countryside in every which way, Sir. I followed the river about fifteen miles south of here and found a plantation that looked like it had been fortified. It was manned by militia but it was also surrounded by another militia group that were positioning themselves to attack the first group. It made no sense to me, Sir.

"They didn't see me, so I dismounted and snuck in close. I'm really good at that. The men wore standard issue Union Army boots just like my own, and they had carbines and six-shooters just like we all got issued, Sir."

"Pratt or Winthrop?" Tithing wondered aloud. "Or both?"

The boy continued. "I left fast, got my horse, and rode back to report. Two scouts came out of the fort and headed this way. At first, I feared they were after me. The other troop could have cut me off and boxed me in, but apparently they didn't want to be spotted, Sir. I'm retreating quick when they all fell back so the scouting party from the plantation wouldn't see them. Does any of this make sense to you, Sir?" the boy dared to ask.

Tithing ignored him and the breach of protocol. "Where would you say the scouts are headed?"

"I think they're coming here, Sir," the boy responded.

"Good job. Get back in uniform, Private Keller. Dismissed."

"Yes, Sir." The boy departed, looking rather relieved.

Captain Hunter stood alone with his C.O. who stared past him, the man deep in his own thoughts. So Hunter kept quiet. Just then, Lieutenant Remick returned with a Navy officer in tow. "Sir, this is Lieutenant Mallory, United States Navy, Sir."

The officers exchanged salutes, their conversation casually social for a few minutes.

"I didn't see your boat pull up, Lieutenant," Tithing joked.

"She's got four legs and a tail, Sir," Mallory replied. "I had to borrow a horse to ride up all the way from New Orleans to get here faster. It's hazardous on the river – not just the current, but we've been taking fire from the shore. Louisiana's residents don't like the Navy imposing order here. But they best be warned, the *Hartford* is coming up river. And my ship –" he corrected himself, "Admiral Farragut's ship, she has some guns!

"The Secessts tried to blockade the mouth of the river by the delta, but we went straight through them. We continued even after they started the *Hartford* on fire. She's a proud ship and she won't stop. You can tell these insurgents that she will never sink! They better call it quits now."

"Yes, it was a fine victory at New Orleans and I congratulate your admiral," Tithing said. Then he turned back to business. "So what are your orders?"

"I'm to take measure of the situation here, report back to Commander Palmer on the *Iroqois*, and then wait for further orders from the *Hartford*. We can send a raft down-river at night to report to the admiral."

Tithing glanced at Captain Hunter, realizing he had a very dangerous situation on his hands. The warships were provoking local citizens into open revolt, and he also faced the prospect of some internal conflict in his battalion if Hunter's man had indeed found Winthrop and Pratt taking positions to fight one another. In any event, his remaining force was far from being up to the full strength he needed to successfully deal with any of this.

He'd been ordered by Colonel Cahill to resolve that situation almost a month ago. He'd been unsuccessful, and therefore assumed incompetent, which stained his otherwise exemplary record. But Tithing believed in full disclosure. The Navy needed to be fully briefed, and then he would redeem himself by leading a mission to personally rectify the situation.

But maybe, Tithing thought, *either Pratt or Winthrop sent out their messengers to offer me some help.* Private Keller had reported those men were headed his way. He supposed that he could afford them a day – just one day – to drum up the courage to report in to him. He shouldn't have to wait very long to find out.

Chapter 69

Down the road aways from the Pentagon Barracks, Talbot and Masterson had watched Keller rush back into town to find his captain. Then those two had sought out Major Tithing to make a report.

"This is not looking good. That boy came from our direction. Everyone knows Louisiana's troops are no wheres near here, so there can be only one thing that kid is reporting. Be prepared for me to order you to go back. Someone's got to inform Daniel."

Masterson turned to look at his lieutenant, but he didn't speak. Just then, Tithing's aide-de-camp greeted a Naval officer who'd arrived from the other direction on horseback. The man was immediately escorted to the major's quarters.

Something was afoot.

"If Tithing's next move is to mobilize, I want you to ride south as hard as you can. This could get really ugly, and very fast," Talbot offered as his assessment.

"Yes, Sir," Masterson said in a low voice.

A few minutes later, they saw the Navy officer depart.

"We've got trouble. We should split up. I'll follow this fellow and you stay on Tithing," Talbot ordered.

As the Navy lieutenant departed from Tithing's headquarters, someone suddenly started following him first: Lieutenant Cutter whom Talbot knew from Captain Pratt's troop. If Pratt was in Baton Rouge, Talbot realized with disturbing certainty, there would to be plenty of trouble ahead.

Getting sprinkled on by some light rain as they hunkered down on the opposite side of the Barracks from Talbot and his man, the under cover Lieutenant Cutter and Corporal Gatewood watched the Navy lieutenant leave the headquarters building.

"Now what's going on?" Cutter wondered aloud. "The plan's changed. Could you live with yourself if your lieutenant ordered a completely illegal kidnapping?" Cutter asked the younger man.

Puzzled, Gatewood looked at his superior.

"I'm improvising. Our captain *knows* Tithing won't be of any help. His Army is too rigid in its discipline and thinking. Instead, we could use the Navy's help with our situation – if we reach the right officer."

"What are you going to do, Sir?" the corporal asked.

"I'm going to join the Navy."

Chapter 70

On Saturday, May 24th, Christopher had already grown restless from being cooped up in the slave quarters for only a day with most of the refugees from Georgia. Emma remembered him and had tried to make him more comfortable. But Christopher yearned to be outside scouting out the compound and possibly finding Abigail. She still didn't know that he had survived, unless Emma had somehow gotten word to her. But Emma feared to wander out amongst so many strange, armed white men.

The situation being potentially deadly, he felt it was for the best that Abigail stayed sheltered since the previous day's shooting anyway, and thus she wasn't in the path of any immediate danger. Pratt also reasoned it was better if he stayed away from Winthrop's men, lest someone finally recognize him. Only to keep up their charade, all these criminals that once called themselves Fox Company, had to continue pretending to be with Louisiana's state militia and Davis probably told them that he could control the bounty hunter. It worked to Christopher's advantage that Winthrop remained under lock and key, and his chief lieutenants were either dead already or off on some mission away from the plantation.

Pratt felt relieved when he finally met again with Jonathon Davis and discussed the strategy he'd developed to safeguard the refugees – a strategy he'd spent the morning working out with Mr. Leahy and Mr. Hart.

Pratt had learned that, beneath the workshop that had been transformed into a school, there existed a secondary storage that could double as a storm shelter. Here Hutchinson discovered and consumed more spirits which he shared with the men from his congregation. When Pratt met with Mr. Davis, he suggested using it for the others to find their salvation by hiding down there.

Hutchinson was now through sheltering Harrison Kent – or Daniel Winthrop – whomever he turned out to be.

Whenever David thought he'd made some progress bringing the young man over to his point of view, Kent would throw a different Bible verse back in his face. The young man feigned curiosity, but Hutchinson felt sure he enjoyed being a contrary. He avoided Kent's personal questions. No doubt, Kent had ulterior motives for broaching certain topics – such as the migrants' resources and how they'd endured and survived their journey out of Georgia.

Sick of a week's worth of wasted effort, Hutchinson informed Kent that a bounty hunter had arrived in search of him. "You eat our food, you mock my efforts to save you, and I'm told you may have even committed serious crimes against me and members of my family. I think you should realize there are limits to my patience. If you don't come to God through me with some effort of your own, I'm afraid I'll have to turn you over to the bounty hunter. Please consider that, Mister Kent."

Chapter 71

Lieutenant Mallory, accompanied by two Navy ensigns, addressed the angry crowd which hurled accusing questions and blatant insults at them.

People blamed the Navy for disrupting trade, bringing more occupation forces, and, of course, the loss of lives and the damage done in New Orleans. Admiral Farragut, his forces heavily engaged in Louisiana, as compared to the U.S. Army anyway, wouldn't win any popularity contests with the locals.

However, the people's right to assemble was not denied, only contained. And not even the rain would deter them. After Mallory repeated the proclamation that Farragut would tolerate no insurrection and that any town which harmed United States officers or personnel would be punished by a thorough bombardment to stop the rioting, he felt relief that he'd completed his mission.

He and his men began their trek through town. A barber shop and the local post office beyond caught Mallory's attention. He carried correspondence he wished to send home once the latest mail service's disruption could be resolved.

Several of Baton Rouge's young ladies paid the men admiring attention. Too late, he became aware that the small group of he and the sailors was also being followed by two other young men. They seemed overly interested in Mallory's progression through the town.

Crossing the street outside a tavern, Mallory and his men were jumped from behind before they reached the corner with the barber shop and post office. The brawl in the street, if you could call it that, lasted only briefly. The two junior sailors were sucker-punched to the backs of their heads from behind, and their legs kicked out from under them; they stumbled on the muddy road and were quickly beaten down. Mallory, caught off guard, hesitated to draw his side-arm. His assailants blocked his belated attempt at self-defense as they seized him. The younger of the two grabbed him from behind, holding him, as the other beat him unconscious and then quickly dragged his body inside the barber shop.

Jack Talbot had followed Lieutenant Cutter and his man from a distance. So far, the afternoon had been interesting. The two had anonymously attended an anti-Union demonstration at the Capitol Building in the rain, and now they shadowed a trio of U.S. Navy men.

He was utterly shocked when suddenly Cutter and his subordinate waylaid the Navy officers in the middle of the street and in broad daylight. Leaving the two ensigns unconscious on the street, Cutter and his man dragged the Navy lieutenant into a nearby barber shop and disappeared.

No one had taken notice of Talbot, who maintained his distance.

He kept the barbershop under surveillance, ignoring the rain and pretending to window-shop several closed businesses that had been recently looted. Even prior to the occupation, Baton Rouge had been suffering. Many glass panes were shattered and doors broken in. But Talbot's effort to gather information pertinent to his mission yielded only another mystery when Captain Pratt's two men re-emerged, Cutter now wearing the Navy lieutenant's uniform.

Talbot was probably the only one on the street to this witness this new development, as the two Navy ensigns that had been jumped, had regained consciousness and quickly retreated from the premises. He assumed they intended to return to the Army Barracks, unless they thought they could safely make it back to the rebuilt wharf and their own ranks aboard the *Iroquois*.

This was also where, he concluded, Cutter and his subordinate immediately headed. Hanging back to keep some good distance between them, Jack Talbot followed them.

Some time later, Todd Cutter sat alone in the brig of the *Iroquois*. As far as he was concerned, the situation had become ridiculous. Clad in his new uniform, he'd gotten past the Marines and sailors guarding the ship, but upon reaching Commander Palmer, he'd been summarily arrested. He'd thought to use Mallory as a temporary hostage with which to bargain, but he'd underestimated the Navy command officer's anger. His actual rank and identity in the Union

Army had not impressed the *Iroquois'* captain. Now, he lodged overnight in a cell in the ship's dungeon.

He was awakened in this cell early on Sunday, May 25th as an ensign informed him that Palmer could be expected at any minute and wanted to question him thoroughly. Finally. This had been Cutter's ultimate goal in the first place.

The commander didn't waste any time getting to it. "Where is my officer?"

"He's safe. I didn't harm him. I just needed an audience with you and felt the extreme emergency of the situation demanded extreme actions, Sir. After you hear what I have to say, I believe you'll permit me to assist you moving forward with whatever new action you deem appropriate. Then, I'll also get your man released."

"You delivered him right into the hands of the enemy, Lieutenant!"

"The people I left him with are business owners sympathetic to Louisiana independence. They think I'm part of their underground resistance. When I brought him in, I wasn't in uniform. They were told not to harm Mallory, and I believe they will behave honorably. Otherwise I would never have left him to be confined there, Sir."

"Well I'm never going to release you from confinement here. How about that?" The Commander, with obvious effort, continued, "You risked coming here after attacking a Naval officer. What could be so god-damned important that you'd do such a thing?"

"There's a plantation about fifteen miles south of here," Cutter related. "It was usurped by Secessionist civilians, who were then taken hostage by rogue Union cavalry. We're pretty sure they've deserted and turned into marauding bandits, Sir."

"What the hell? Why haven't you reported this to your battalion commander?"

"We saw that officers from that troop had already beaten us to it, and we're uncertain what tale they've told. We hoped the highest ranking Federal officer in Baton Rouge – you, Sir – could intervene, perhaps even sort it out before the situation gets any further out of hand."

"It's already out of hand!" Palmer thundered. "By taking

Mallory, you've turned what should have been an internal Army matter into what's now my problem as well. Thank you very much." Palmer glared at the young Army officer. "Do you know much about Navy discipline? We take insubordinates like you, tie them to the wheel, and give them a lashing they don't soon forget. That's what's in your future, Cutter!

"Now as if I don't have enough things to manage before the *Hartford* gets here, I suppose you want me to deploy a Marine unit to investigate your unsubstantiated threat to us and our mission to maintain stability here? Well I'd be lying if I said this doesn't have me concerned. And I also took it that if you didn't believe what you were reporting Lieutenant, you wouldn't have risked a whipping to have come here. So while it's not my policy to negotiate with seriously aggravating insubordinates, I agree that we just might have a real situation developing. So I'm going to release you into the custody of two men from my ship, and you're to go and collect Mallory and return here with him. Now," Palmer ordered.

"Then are you going to dispatch a unit to the plantation, Sir?" Cutter inquired.

"No, but I'll take your word for it that we've got trouble. I'm sending a man to contact your regimental commander. Colonel Cahill should have just arrived in town. He'll be the one to settle *this*."

Privately, Commander Palmer was already thinking that he'd have to send a dispatch informing Admiral Farragut about the situation. *Why, when he correctly did his duty, did life always bring him more problems?*

Unarmed and unshackled, Cutter walked through downtown, escorted through the light rain by the two Marines Palmer had assigned to guard him. He still wore a Navy uniform so that the general population sensed nothing amiss with their Union occupiers. Additionally, the Secessionist-sympathizers from the barbershop who'd stashed Mallory would recognize him, even in a Navy uniform, although they knew him as a Rebel operative. He'd introduce the two Marines as other Rebels in disguise and everything would somehow smooth out.

That was Cutter's expectation until the trio was confronted in the street by Jack Talbot.

Cutter's mouth dropped open as Talbot simply strode out into the middle of the street, clad in civilian attire. He squared his shoulders into a soldier's attack posture, his hand straying to his holstered sidearm.

The Marines didn't recognize him. They shouted orders at the wild-haired man to clear off the streets or face arrest as they began to draw their own weapons in response to Talbot's aggressive move. The rogue lieutenant was faster. Shots flew, the crackling sounds echoing off the buildings and making it seem like a pitched battle was underway. The two Marines immediately went down, metal piercing their chests and fountains of blood squirting from each of them. Reacting fast, Cutter dove to the nearest of the fallen men attempting to come up with the dead man's gun. Talbot shot him through his skull, Cutter's body left out in the rain.

Terrified local citizens didn't witness the assault. No sooner than the sound of the first shots rang out, breaking the silence of a previously quiet Sunday afternoon, the streets were cleared and people hurriedly shut doors and windows, hiding in their homes.

Talbot hoped his actions bought Daniel some time. They were going to need it. The lieutenant quickly searched for his own place to lay low before more Marines could arrive.

Chapter 72

Bob Masterson rode his horse at some distance behind the corporal from the enemy troop. On Saturday, Masterson had held his position, and watched the Pentagon Barracks to assess Tithing's next move when Talbot unexpectedly returned on his course following the Navy lieutenant. Or another lieutenant. He didn't seem to look like the same man Talbot had left after earlier. The new man might have even been Lt. Cutter attempting an impersonation. Masterson didn't know or care.

The sergeant received a change of orders to follow Cutter's subordinate, who appeared in a sudden hurry to leave town. If Tithing ever made his big move, Masterson would be far enough ahead of him to spot a large troop deployment anyway.

As he followed Cutter's man, Masterson found himself traveling south, straight back to the plantation. He knew that was their intended destination. The junior trooper stopped and dismounted to rest his steed. Masterson also dismounted and drew a sharp and effective-looking knife. It glistened as the water falling from the sky splashed from it.

Corporal Gatewood sighed as he watched his horse graze in the rain for a minute. All the men were loyal to Captain Pratt, but he wished for some clue as to what they'd gotten themselves involved in. After disobeying their battalion commander's orders to rendezvous in Baton Rouge, they now conducted recon missions on a Southern civilian target, which might or might not be hosting a rogue Union cavalry unit. And the possibility of hostages being held inside the compound existed. To top it off, his lieutenant had him mixed up in attacking United States Navy personnel and impersonating one of their officers.

Things only looked as if they were going to get worse and a lot of men could die real soon. Gatewood felt the increased tension during his urgent travel to return to his unit. He needed to stop momentarily for some time alone to try and wrap his head around it.

A crackling sound in the underbrush, indicative of a large animal or possibly another person's approach, cut through the corporal's thoughts. He drew his six-shooter as his eyes hunted the thick vegetation he moved through. Death was quick for Gatewood when Sergeant Masterson suddenly grabbed him from behind, pinned his arms, and used his knife to easily cut through Gatewood's throat.

Masterson felt somewhat detached as he watched the corporal's blood spill out of the gash he made in the man's neck and spray the nearby plants a new shade of red. But his attention refocused rather quickly on the unmistakable sound of the hammer of a gun being drawn back and locked into the firing position. He turned slowly, letting Gatewood's body drop, only to face Sergeant Zwelleger.

They had known each other in training, but had been assigned to different units. Masterson, already a senior NCO, served with Winthrop, while Zwelleger, apparently promoted later, served under Pratt. In the four years since they'd last seen each other, their assignments had taken them in opposite directions during the course of the war.

Now Zwelleger aimed his gun at Bob Masterson's face. Masterson turned slowly, still gripping his bloody knife. Masterson wondered why Zwelleger didn't immediately shoot him, which is what he would have done were their roles reversed. Masterson preferred not to take the chance that if he threw his knife, Zwelleger's wouldn't fire his gun reflexively and Masterson would find himself shot anyway, or else surrounded by all the rest of the sergeant's squadrons in an instant.

Masterson had never heard Zwelleger's approach and he actually had no idea how many adversaries the underbrush concealed, just waiting to gun him down. So he switched tactics and set upon a different strategy. He'd let the dead corporal finish his mission after all, if it was going to help Masterson save his own life this time.

"Zwelleger, I see someone finally found it fit to promote you. Now I know you just lost your man, and I know how this looks. But he was in my way, and I have to get in there," Masterson said, motioning to the fort.

"I can't let you do that, Bob," Zwelleger said in a nervous voice. "Gatewood was one of mine."

Masterson noted with contempt that Zwelleger now addressed the fellow NCO as an equal, but they weren't equals and never would be. But he *did* know how to appeal to the worries of one in a position of responsibility such as himself. "Then you might want to consider that you're about to lose all the rest of your men."

"Wh-what do you mean?" Zwellegar stammered.

"Tithing's probably on his way here. He's got Hunter with him and they're up to full strength. Our troops might have their differences to settle here, but the major's not going to care one way or the other. With all of us out of uniform, Tithing's going to figure us all for the enemy militia and order Hunter to overrun us both."

"Why are you telling me this?" Zwelleger asked.

"It's what he would have reported had he the chance." Masterson indicated the dead Corporal Gatewood at his feet. "And I understand how you feel about your squadron-mates. We do the same job. But if you get your boys back into uniform, you might keep Hunter from just simply eradicating the whole lot of you."

Zwelleger became more nervous at the thought of engaging Hunter's full force. He postured in an attempt to conceal his fear from Masterson. "Our company has you surrounded, Bob. What good will our survival do for you? You'll have to face our men *and* Hunter's."

Masterson shrugged. He didn't want to mention that Corporal Ritter would gain the cooperation of Jonathon Davis' people once they worked themselves into a frenzy at the sight of Federal uniforms. Combining the Secessionists' fighting men with his own unit, the sergeant might yet have nearly a full company at his command. Winthrop wouldn't be able to give them orders, if he hoped to keep Davis' cooperation through the whole affair. With the troop being almost back to full strength, they'd be defending a fortified position and in Talbot's absence, Masterson would be in command. Tithing still needed to hold Baton Rouge, so he could not send everyone he had. The odds against Winthrop's men weren't too bad. They might succeed with their mission and get out of town with the Hutchinson 'bounty' before Colonel Cahill brought up another battalion, when General Williams arrived with the rest of the brigade.

Things just might work out after all and it would start with Zwelleger being smart enough to survive and deliver his report. The result would play right into Masterson's hands. He answered the other man carefully and appealed to his vanity. "We're peers now, Lawrence. You care about your men just like I care about mine. Now I can't deny I just killed one, but the information I gave you might save the rest of them. I volunteered my report without asking you for anything."

Zwelleger nodded. "That you did."

"Now if you let me go, there's no guarantee I get through the rest of your men. I also can't keep trading this information once you report."

"True."

"So, let me take my chances on my own."

"How do I know you're telling me the truth? You might say anything to save your skin," Zwelleger challenged him.

"That's a fair enough question, but answer me this. Was your man supposed to come back here without his lieutenant? And if they reported to Tithing and got his cooperation, wouldn't they both have been ordered to guide Hunter's men back here? But no. That didn't happen. So I don't think the rest of the battalion's going to be of any help to either one of us."

Zwelleger, too confused now to offer a rebuttal to his logic, thought Masterson's argument sounded reasonable. He lowered his gun, feeling that he was betraying Gatewood, but perhaps saving the others' lives. Besides, Masterson couldn't penetrate Pratt's force's perimeter. Zwelleger decided to leave it up to somebody else to kill Masterson.

Masterson then smiled. "I'll just go and collect my horse."

Chapter 73

Abigail Hutchinson never could sit still and do what she'd been told. Against the protests of Old Man Hart, she left him and the other women and children in the shelter beneath the school, climbed the ladder, and hurried towards the church to find her father. She would protest being corralled in the basement and learn what was actually going on. She caught the eyes of all the militia and the men from her congregation, but none attempted to block her path. Her father or Jonathon Davis could deal with her obvious signs of displeasure.

When she reached the make-shift church, she found one of Talbot's men guarding Daniel. Only it looked like he was taking orders from him. Neither man noticed her entrance. She slid along the wall and then knelt, so if discovered, she could pretend she was in prayer between the second and last row of pews. However, with her small frame, she hoped she would remain unseen.

Now Abigail recognized a member of the militia called Will Ritter. He appeared upset about something, so Abigail kept silent and strained to hear their conversation.

"They're ready to turn you over to the bounty hunter, Boss. I heard them talking, and they've grown sick of your games. Hutchinson's probably spared you from a whipping by Davis, but you've just been going on more and more, aggravating the both of them."

"I've tired of their games myself. What's the status of the Secessionists?"

"They're almost gift-wrapped for us. Ironically, Davis ordered most of the women and children into a redundant storage area beneath the workshop building they'd been using as a school."

"Perfect. Tell the men it's time to put their blue coats back on. We have their women and children right where it will be more than easy to hold them while we demand that all the men surrender. These people know more about prayer than warfare. They won't even put up a fight. Then, I'll interrogate Hutchinson exactly the way Davis wanted to interrogate me. Nothing will stop us short of divine intervention," Daniel said as he smirked.

Abigail's eyes that had widened with surprise as she witnessed the conspirators' conversation, narrowed with her scowl as she reassessed Daniel Winthrop.

A moment later, Abigail's father entered the building from behind her and she shrank down into the shadows. "Did you put his shackles back on?" the reverend asked Ritter who nodded unenthusiastically towards Mr. Hutchinson, glanced at Daniel, and then departed the church.

"Mister Kent," her father began, "Or maybe I should call you Daniel Winthrop? I've decided that in spite of my best efforts, you don't really want to meet God and experience His Love. So you're going to meet His Justice instead. You're going to be introduced to that bounty hunter who's been most patiently waiting to meet you. Let him deal with you. I'm done with this."

Davis entered the church from a side door. He'd steered clear of Daniel for several days now because of his strong distaste for the arrogant interloper. Now, all of his negative feelings for the man returned, registering on his face and in the way he caressed the bullwhip that hung at his side. "Your game is over," he said.

"I guess so," Daniel responded. "But if it's that important to meet God," he turned addressing Hutchinson. "I've decided that I can help you with that after all."

Daniel stood up, his wrist cuffs falling away, having never been locked in the first place. Surprising the other men, his hands held a gun he raised and fired, catching Hutchinson in the upper leg. Abigail's father collapsed. He clutched at the wound, trying to contain the blood spurting out from it. Daniel spun on Davis, ready to fire, but the older man had already drawn his own weapon. He fired, catching Daniel in the arm. Daniel's weapon flew out of his hand. He turned to find it, but Davis' voice commanded, "Don't move, you Yankee scum." Winthrop clutched his bloody arm. "I've been ready for this," Davis told him.

Just then Abigail stepped out from her place of cover and raced to her father. Surprised to see her, no one spoke as she knelt at David

Hutchinson's side. "Pappa! Are you alright?" She threw a furious glance back at Daniel, the truth finally real to her. "You planned this from the start! He's my father, you bastard!"

Outside in the compound, the other congregants heard the gunshots coming from their church. "Did Davis kill that kid?" someone close to Mr. Leahy asked. Leahy dashed across the compound, heading for the church.

The other men still gathered outside watched in amazement as militia allies began to don Federal uniforms stored in their saddlebags and then moved quickly to disarm them. The Union soldiers subdued them without a fight by reminding them that their women and children were taking shelter in the storage cellar that had now become their prison. Uniformed Federal troops now guarded the school building.

Mr. Leahy burst into the church, stopping short when he saw Mr. Davis holding a gun on the wounded Mr. Kent, who gripped his bleeding arm. He then glanced down to see Miss Abigail on the floor, ripping fabric from her dress hem to tie off the blood freely flowing from a leg wound suffered by her father. Reverend Hutchinson, sprawled out on the floor before the Almighty's altar, shook, and his face contorted with pain.

His eyes darting between Davis and Hutchinson, Jim Leahy blurted out, "We were misled. The whole compound's occupied by Union soldiers."

"Call them off!" Mr. Davis ordered Winthrop.

"Why would I want to do that when I've got the upper hand?" Daniel asked. He glanced over at Leahy.

"They have our women and children in the basement under the school. It'd be like shooting fish in a barrel," Leahy gulped. "My wife is being held down there, Jonathon."

"Oh he doesn't worry about wives and children any more," Daniel replied, getting in one more barb.

"You keep pushing me," Davis said threateningly to his prisoner.

"What are we going to do?" Leahy asked, sounding on the verge of panic.

"We'll have to stall while I think of something," Davis said. "Go out there, find whoever's in command, and tell him we have –" He looked at Winthrop. "We have their captain in here. Let's see if that affects their bargaining posture."

"It won't," Daniel laughed. "They're all one murderous bunch of self-absorbed bandits. Hardened thieves and killers. That's all I've got left serving under me. Finish me off and you'll make them mad. But they'll know that then they'll only be richer by what they divide up of my share of your valuables. Nice try, though. Really it was."

"You. Shut up!" Davis thundered. He turned to Mr. Leahy, "Well, go!"

"You were after our wares? That's what all this was about?" Abigail demanded of Daniel. "Well you didn't have to shoot my father! I could have told you where everything was hidden."

"Abigail, don't!" Davis ordered.

Finally addressing him she angrily turned on her father's foreman. "You," she spat, "will never tell me what to do ever again!"

She turned back to Daniel. "Will you help treat him?" she nodded toward father. "And then will you take me with you?" she asked him. Abigail enjoyed the shock her betrayal elicited on Jonathon Davis' face.

Daniel looked shocked, too. Clearly, he hadn't anticipated her request, although he'd become enamored with Abigail enough already to have fantasized about it. He managed to find his voice. "Uh…yeah. If that's what you want."

"Fine. It's exactly what I want. Everything you thought you wanted is in the crypt below us. We haven't been here long enough to use that as a burial chamber. Everything of value was hidden down there. My people could sustain themselves on this farm without having to trade away their heirlooms, prior to now anyway." Abigail thought of Emma, her sisters, and her mother. "If your men get what they came here for, will that satisfy them? They'll follow your order to leave the hostages unharmed?"

"Of course."

"Then now that that's settled…" Abigail turned and drew the pocket Colt she'd kept hidden in her dress and fired the weapon at

Mr. Davis. He never saw that coming either. Four shots followed in quick succession, violently spinning him all the way around and piercing him where he should have had a heart. The man opened his mouth in a look of utter surprise but couldn't say anything as a bubble of blood ejected from between his lips and he fell over, his wounds steaming. Davis was dead before he hit the floor.

"Thank you for Biloxi," Abigail scoffed as she lowered her smoking gun.

Daniel didn't quite know what to say. Events were changing and developing in new directions faster than he could anticipate.

Corporal Ritter ran back inside the church, weapon drawn, and clad in his Federal uniform now. "Boss? Boss?"

"It's alright now. But we've got a man down," Winthrop pointed to Hutchinson, his daughter kneeling at his side. Still bleeding himself, Daniel recovered his discarded gun and moved to acquire Davis' also as he continued speaking. "I made a deal. Hutchinson and his people live."

"It's too late for Papa," Abigail said, tears escaping from her eyes. "He lost too much blood. My father is dead. Thanks a lot, Daniel. I should have killed you!"

Daniel felt emotion come over him, but his avarice chased it away. "The rest of your family is still at my mercy, which was always part of the plan, Abigail," he said softly. "One problem though. I never anticipated falling in love with you."

She stared at him for a long moment, considering that he'd made such a big admission, coming out right in front of his subordinate.

"Sir? What do you want me to do?" Ritter asked, breaking the silence.

"Get some of our men in here, find the way down and under this room, then start moving stuff up to pack in the wagons. The men amongst the settlers ought to be disarmed and contained in the school building with the rest of their families by now. And find that bounty hunter that was going to bring me in. I think I'd enjoy having a word with him."

"Yes, Sir."

267

Hiding behind several wagons, Christopher had listened as Mr. Leahy emerged from the church and surrendered to Corporal Ritter a little while earlier.

"Who's left alive in there right now?" Ritter had asked him.

"David Hutchinson, his daughter, and Mister Davis. They're holding your man Harrison Kent. They want to negotiate."

Ritter laughed. "No negotiations."

Christopher knew two things – there'd be no bargain and he would rescue his dear Abigail.

Suddenly, he heard the sounds from more shooting coming from inside the church.

Chapter 74

Sergeant Masterson had never compromised his loyalty to his captain before. It was true that he never cared for his immediate superior, Jack Talbot, but he respected Daniel Winthrop's daring and effectiveness as a leader – as well as his famous luck. Not to mention he owed Winthrop his life. So it was with a heavy heart that he arrived at his decision to desert his troop.

Christopher Pratt's men completely surrounded the fortified plantation. Sergeant Zwelleger had known how his side's forces were deployed, and he'd probably concluded that Masterson couldn't get back inside to warn Daniel Winthrop. Then Masterson spotted a whole new group of men on horses rapidly approaching from behind him, their movement visible in spite of the cloudy, northern skyline. That could only be the battalion commander, Major Tithing, with Captain Hunter's entire cavalry.

Worse yet, Masterson had gotten close enough to his own unit's position to see that they'd all gotten back into uniform. This would result in the greatest tragedy befalling his men. If mistaken for Secessionists, Tithing might have given them a chance to surrender, thus aiding him in securing the cooperation of other insurgent groups still fighting for Louisiana. But clad in Federal uniform, they'd be judged guilty of desertion and banditry, and Tithing would order them all shot, the standard order for military justice in a time of war. It was the same fate Masterson had hoped he'd tricked Zwelleger into bringing upon Pratt's men. However, armed as they were, and so close to the big payoff, Winthrop would never surrender. It would all end in a bloodbath commencing just as soon as Hunter's men ran into Captain Pratt's deployment, which they would mistake for the Confederate Army and open fire on.

Masterson didn't intend to be caught standing in the middle of it all, in the pouring rain on top of it, just waiting for Tithing to lock him in the stockade forever – if he didn't catch a bullet first. He decided to accept his losses and leave. It would be his last chance.

He guided his horse down to the muddy, swollen Mississippi River, galloping along the water's edge, heading south to find his freedom.

Chapter 75

At the same time, the massive Federal warship *USS Hartford* was headed upriver under full steam. Admiral David Farragut received a most distressed courier in the form of Lieutenant Benjamin Ross. He'd made a frantic journey down the swelling river in the middle of a stormy night aboard only a small raft in order to rendezvous with Farragut. Under orders from Commander Palmer, Ross disclosed a litany of urgent information after a harrowing few minutes while the sailors on the *Hartford* helped to bring him aboard. Ross strained to breathe as he reported.

US Army Major Kenneth Tithing drove his cavalry troops into a confrontation with half of his own battalion just south of Baton Rouge. Several factions had broken off and were operating as a heavily armed gang of outlaws, their aggressive actions rumored to include the taking of civilians hostage at a plantation outside of the city proper. Now at least two units might have allegedly joined forces to loot the compound in defiance of command's authority.

Farragut was furious. His orders had come straight from the Secretary of the Navy and President Lincoln. *Hold the river and maintain order!*

Palmer was being too cautious, Farragut thought. *He doesn't want to take responsibility for the Navy imposing ever harsher actions upon the civilian population. But someone would need to until the rest of the brigade under General Williams arrived and instilled order. The mutiny going on in the Army wasn't helping anything and the whole city was likely to now join in a fight.*

Admiral Farragut had not risen to his rank and record of success by being a timid man. What everyone needed was a strong show of force, and Farragut commanded a beast of a warship that could demonstrate that force. He called his crew to battle stations.

By late afternoon on Monday, May 26, panic had ensued in the streets of Baton Rouge, everyone hurrying to evacuate. The occupying Navy Commander James Palmer didn't relish firing on unarmed women and children. When the body of Lieutenant Cutter was found, still dressed in a Navy uniform, and rumors circulated that two Marines might have also been killed and their bodies dragged elsewhere, Palmer announced his decision to open fire. It was also his choice to give the townspeople fair warning. His men had been attacked, Mallory was also still missing, and he'd just ran out of patience with the insurgency in Baton Rouge. His ship, the *Iroquois*, wouldn't inflict the most damage though. With the *Hartford* due, the rebellious townspeople would experience the full extent of their punishment for defying the United States Navy.

Palmer ordered the announcement, and then allowed history to take its course. The guns were loaded.

Chapter 76

Abigail had two shots left in the chambers. She patiently waited beside her dead father's body. Now it was clear what she had to do. When he'd fallen, she'd been in shock, her only source of clarity grounded in her hatred of Jonathon Davis. But now that she'd had time to review her situation, she realized she could never trust Daniel Winthrop again. She'd acted selfishly in the past. At first, she'd wanted to attain the power to determine her own course for her life, but she'd allowed her desires to dominate her thinking with no regard for any others. At last Abigail admitted to herself that she was responsible for what had happened to her family. The blood was on her hands. She silently swore over her dead father's body that she wouldn't fail again.

Abigail had two bullets left.

Some of the horses were not tethered and wandered through the compound. Without Lieutenant Talbot or Sergeant Masterson around to enforce tighter order and discipline in the ranks, the young and less experienced Corporal Ritter had taken over as Captain Winthrop's right hand man. His style was notably more relaxed and he had figured that the men's horses couldn't actually leave the compound and go anywhere, so the entrance to every structure need not be obstructed by tied-down animals defecating next to the men's new sleeping quarters they'd taken over upon having incarcerated the refugees.

Upon that confinement of Hutchinson's people in the basement of the school house building, Ritter had decided to allow the soldiers to move into the plantation home, bunkhouse, and slave quarters. The men were happy to not have to sleep in the rain. This thinning out of their unit's concentration outdoors, as well as the loose horses, allowed Christopher Pratt to move between the animals and remain unnoticed until he got under the central watchtower that Winthrop had ordered his men to construct for their fort during the week prior.

As he hid beneath the shadow of the watchtower, Pratt hoped he wouldn't be seen making a run for the church.

Abigail Hutchinson had determined the fate of Daniel Winthrop. The man had used her, betrayed her family, and killed her father. *He deserves to meet his end at my hands*, she thought. She heard footsteps approach, then saw a shadow on the wall. She crouched out of sight, drawing back the hammer on her pocket Colt revolver. The shadow became a man silhouetted in the light of the doorway, his hand held just above his gun holster, but Abigail couldn't discern any other details.

"Abigail?" he whispered.

What man now would dare address me by only my first name? Abigail thought. *That damned murderer Winthrop, come looking for me.* His weapon was not drawn. He would not expect her vengeance. Abigail knew his men would come for her once she killed him. Maybe she could take Daniel's weapon once she'd finished with him and make a last stand herself? Maybe her small sacrifice wouldn't make amends for her mistakes, but she couldn't live with herself if she didn't try.

Abigail watched the figure in the doorway. He suddenly spun around, turning his back to her. A new distraction erupted in the compound. Gunfire sounded beyond the church and rapidly moved closer, judging by all the sudden commotion Abigail sensed.

The noise might cover the sound of her own fire, she thought, as she aimed her weapon at the figure in the doorway. She burst up from her crouch and fired twice, hitting him in his back.

Abigail screamed in surprised horror as her victim spun around. She recognized Christopher Pratt in utter agony as he took her shots and fell to the floor clawing at his smoking wounds!

Chapter 77

Captain Hunter agreed with Major Tithing that it would be too time-consuming and dangerous to divide his men and circumnavigate the bayou to the far east of the compound. So they were going straight in – and in full force. They'd run their horses in a direct southern charge, split the troop into platoons to quickly surround the fort on three sides and take out the enemy guards on the potentially accessible borders. A basic siege maneuver.

The opposing force could seriously outnumber them, they discovered when non-uniformed militia blocked their approach to the fort. Going in, Tithing couldn't identify the various armed factions as friends or foes until they turned and opened fire on him. But frightened at the prospect of his first battle, Private Keller had panicked and actually fired the first shots from Tithing's side. The young man, incorrectly thinking that most of the fighting in Louisiana was either over with or would somehow be done by the Marines, didn't plan to die in the South. He would shoot first and not stop until he ran out of ammunition or took his last breath. He spurred his horse forward and leveled his carbine. Everything headed straight to hell from there.

Lieutenant Travers had overall command of Christopher Pratt's force, which surrounded the fort-compound's perimeter. Sergeant Zwelleger had just reported in to him when the shooting started, so there was no opportunity to negotiate a surrender or arrange a meeting with Tithing. Travers was sure their troop looked like they were Rebels to the major, so Tithing must have given the order to open fire. Pratt's company had already started to defend themselves. Who could blame them? His men already stood a great chance of being branded guilty of insubordination at the very least, not to mention probably facing charges of desertion, mutiny, and maybe even treason. They were all as surprised as Travers that they were being attacked from behind their own lines and by their own battalion, but they were forced into defending for their lives now. No one seemed in control of the situation.

The gunfire grew incredibly loud. During a lull in the rain, smoke expanded out and mud was kicked up from horses in full charge while the shots fired from their riders streaked out every which way under obscured visibility. Travers motioned his bugler to his side so he could get out an order, but a stray bullet through the throat suddenly cut down the man. It was clear there'd be no peaceful resolution to this now.

A dusty haze penetrated by flashing fire and the crackling of gunfire lay in Travers' future now. His dismounted men could try to pick off Hunter's people as they rode at them, but they needed to find a way to surrender. They were fighting against their own side!

Upon seeing that the unit laying siege to the fort were returning fire at his own men, Major Tithing assumed that the uniformed force inside the fort were loyal to his command. "Our people are in that compound, and we need to liberate them from this Rebel siege!" Tithing shouted from atop his horse as they charged. "We'll sort out whatever else is going on when victory has been achieved."

With Captain Hunter at his side, the two officers urged their cavalry onward. "Stay the course, men! For our country! For justice! For freedom!"

On the other side, Sergeant Finch couldn't believe his eyes. Their own battalion was attacking them. He signaled to Private Willows, pointing to a good spot in a tree. "Up you go. Pick your shots carefully."

Willows scrambled up a large magnolia while Finch took a similar position in a parallel tree. Both started to fire their carbines.

Sergeant Zwelleger's rifle was left back with his squads as he'd hurried to report to Lieutenant Travers. With only his drawn six-shooter in hand, he hastened to make it back to his men. Tall reeds whipped at him. Bullets whizzed past as he angled northwest until he had to hook east. All the while, he didn't know if he was dodging enemy shots or friendly fire!

Meanwhile, as Lieutenant Pullman had turned his people to reinforce Travers from the south, his men started to take fire from behind them, coming from the fort itself. Caught in a deadly crossfire, Pullman reversed the position of half of his dismounted platoon just to counter the fire from the fort – if they could. His men used their horses as cover. A bad move, the wounded, bucking animals only added to the danger.

Chapter 78

Daniel Winthrop ran back into the church with Corporal Crawford and five other men. All but Daniel ignored Abigail. They hurriedly searched the floorboards and walls of the church.

Daniel approached the young woman who sat on the floor beside a newly fallen body. He frowned as she knelt in a small pool of blood. He looked at her, then glanced at the man sprawled on his stomach on the floor.

Abigail's eyes met his and she said tonelessly, "Under the carpeting, just behind the third row of pews, in between them."

Behind them, a young man let out a cry of excitement. The men clustered nearby set about tearing back the rug. They pulled open a hatch that led to a stairway to a chamber beneath the floor.

"Buckley, bring a lamp!" one man shouted. After detaching a few oil lamps from the walls, they scrambled down the staircase. "We're rich now!" someone yelled gleefully.

Crawford remained with Winthrop.

"Someone had better watch them," Crawford said, nodding at the men in pursuit of their valuable treasure.

"Yeah. You do that, Steve. Keep 'em honest." Daniel said quietly. Approaching Abigail, he drew his gun. He couldn't see both her hands, but he must have sensed she was armed.

Abigail, still near the bleeding body, concealed the now emptied Colt behind her. Her eyes darted to Christopher's still-holstered weapon on his belt, and she wished she'd taken the weapon when she had the chance.

Frightened of Daniel now, Abigail doubted a prayer would save her. The rogue pointed his gun at her.

Daniel heard the slight bump of a heavy, metal object being placed on the floor behind Abigail when she released her grip on the useless Colt. He tensed for a moment as she lifted her hands, but revealed them to be empty. Then she gently turned the body of the fallen man onto his back. Daniel gasped as he recognized Christopher Pratt.

The looks Abigail directed at Daniel sent back so many messages, without any words at all. She stared daggers at him. *Betrayer!* Then her eyes were asking *Why?* Her expression next morphed into a plea for mercy. *Please. Don't.* Finally, resignation showed on her face. Abigail accepted her fate and whispered aloud, "Just end this… now." She closed her spirited blue eyes that Daniel *had* actually fallen in love with. He saw her draw her breath in and hold it, anticipating.

"You thought he was me, didn't you? You wanted to kill me? Didn't you?" Daniel said softly, his gaze shifting between Christopher and the girl. He needed to stall, slow things down. But he knew he couldn't. He was running out of time and all the while dreading what he'd have to do now.

At the end, Abigail thought of the others and the tragedy she'd brought upon her people. She exhaled and spoke calmly. "You and your men have caged up my family in the cellar under the school. Women, children, and old men who cannot fight, and all the others who surrendered to you to protect their loved ones. They've caused you no harm. You promised me that if I helped you to find your treasure, what was and is rightfully theirs, you'd let them live."

"I remember, Abigail. You have my word."

"Then do with me as you wish. Just finish it."

"I'm sorry," he said. Then, Daniel fired. A single bullet pierced Abigail's forehead, above her blue and beautiful but mournful eyes. The sound echoing in Daniel's mind more loudly than that from any shot he'd ever fired before. Abigail fell across Christopher, an expression of peace finally coming over her face.

For a long time, Daniel stood over Abigail's body, reviewing every event that had led up to this moment. He was finally distracted from his thoughts when Corporal Ritter burst into the church to report to his captain.

"Tithing's found us. He's coming in fast with Hunter's men – all of them. They've also engaged some other unit that's out there, Sir, between us and the major. They're out of uniform and look like Secessionists. It will slow Tithing down, although he's moving like he plans to plow straight through them."

Winthrop had heard the exchange of gunfire that continued outside. He knew he needed to focus on unfolding events. "Tell the men to decrease their fire and conserve ammunition as best as they can. Order the men outside to fall back into the compound. Those men who've encircled us a little distance from here are Captain Pratt's people, so let them take care of as many of Tithing's men as they can. With any luck, they'll cut down a lot of them for us."

Ritter protested, "Captain Pratt? Begging your pardon, Sir, but we have Pratt's people in a crossfire right now."

"Which won't do us any good when we're out of bullets, and Tithing's people keep coming. Follow my orders, Corporal!"

"Yes, Sir!"

"And get all the small arms Davis' people had on them. Distribute them to our men with all their available ammunition. Move!"

Captain Winthrop now regretted the way the timing of things had worked out. If he'd known about Tithing, he would have played his hand differently and used Davis' people's help. He realized now that there was no scenario where his self-serving ends would not have inevitably turned Abigail against him. But he could never have afforded – or even survived – disappointing the men he commanded. The entire lot of them had become a murderous band of thieves now – and under Daniel's leadership. That was also too late to change. Nor did Daniel want to change it. But nothing had worked out as he'd figured. Some progress, but many more reversals. Now Winthrop got on with working his mind over how to move wagons filled with bounty out of the compound in the middle of a raging battle. He had to change tactics fast and concentrate on his own survival. A recurring pattern in his life, he realized.

Chapter 79

The *USS Hartford* would soon round the bend in the Mississippi River that led into the port of Baton Rouge. Aboard the *Hartford*, Admiral David Farragut had summoned Lieutenant Ross and ordered that he repeat precisely the exact location of the old San Carlos Plantation.

Night had fallen. The straining ship entered the bend in the swollen, rushing river, and the fort appeared sporadically lit by flashes from gunfire. As the sound of that gunfire echoed through the night, Farragut prepared to seize upon what he viewed as his own opportunity.

Civilians would die. He knew that. But even a ship the size of the *Hartford* couldn't carry enough Marines to engage two cavalry troops, and possibly be misidentified by a third, leading his own men into their crossfire. Stopping Federals engaging each other in battle was not the mission the Navy was sent down here for! But military law dictated that deserting officers and men guilty of piracy be charged, court-martialed, and shot for insurrection. If he used the *Hartford's* cannons to accomplish that, instead of ordering his men to engage in small arms contests, then so be it, if it got the job done quicker.

He could use his ship's battle against the current, which made it difficult to hold her course, in the visibility-hampering darkness, all as reasons for his 'misfires' that hit the fort before he struck Baton Rouge proper, the latter his *officially* intended target. The Admiral might have to sacrifice Tithing and his people, too, but Farragut would not mourn the loss of an ineffective command. Colonel Cahill wouldn't protest, especially with General Williams scheduled to arrive soon with his entire brigade to reinforce him.

Oil lamps were kept burning low so as to not make the *Hartford* stand out as a target in the night. All of the ship's starboard cannons had been cleaned and loaded. The bend in the river was in sight. The rain hammered down. The muddy river rapidly flowed.

Then, the *Hartford's* cannons opened fire.

Chapter 80

Darkness yielded to the pre-dawn light on Tuesday the 27th. It rained hard now – water as well as lead. Though the wind grew increasingly stronger as the storm gathered strength, and blew shots off target, Hunter's people had lost over twenty men with their direct charge and they'd been forced to dismount to face Pratt's troops in the field. Lt. Pullman had redirected his platoon around in order to back up Travers' men as an unexpected cessation of fire from the fort occurred during the night. As darkness had settled in, all of Tithing's men realized they weren't hitting their targets in the brush and were too easily visible astride their horses, even against the black sky. So at Hunter's urging, and because he was under the threat of the lesser ranks mutinying if he didn't, Tithing ordered his men to dismount and scale back their exchange of carbine and small arms fire until the men could once again see who they were aiming at.

Tithing had not intended for his rescue operation to last overnight, but it had happened and there they were. Hunter began to realize that his colleagues had embarrassed the major. Now he was dangerously obsessed with revenge. Hunter could do nothing but follow orders and suggest tactics that would achieve their mission while getting the least number of his men killed. It became eerily quiet for the early part of the night and the men slept fitfully out in the rain. Shots were periodically exchanged, and illumination would occur from intermittent muzzle flashes.

Then the situation became suddenly and decidedly more deadly as everyone came under long range cannon fire. *It had to be the Navy*, Tithing thought. He'd just ran out of time. Admiral Farragut had arrived. The night sky was alight with explosions from thirty-two pound cannon balls coming down harder than the rain with earth-shaking explosions upon impact. The ship had tracked the small arms fire and decided to pummel its source.

Private Keller had never been under such a barrage before. He dropped his carbine and curled up into a ball in the tall grass. He used his arms to pin his legs tight against his sides while he covered his ears with his hands to dim the terrible noise. All his body parts flew in separate directions out of the impact crater that was made as the fire from the *Hartford* found him. Just a red spot and some small patches of flattened grass that were left on fire was all that remained to tell of anything happening there.

The battle went on without Keller.

Unfortunately, the outbound cannon balls also smashed through the retaining walls constructed on both banks of the Mississippi River as the *Hartford* struggled to fight the wild current. The wind shear increased its power to become so strong it could even unpredictably alter the course of heavy ordinance. Flooding occurred on the eastern bank of the river, massive amounts of mud sliding away on the west shore as the water rushed out to cover the newly opened territory. The result: a rapidly decreasing stability of the marshland that approached the plantation-fort.

The desperate men on the battlefield wanted this fight to end quickly. Lieutenant Travers tried to raise a flag of surrender, but Tithing's people assumed they were being mocked with a captured Union flag. They pressed their attack on the major's command. At the same time Travers' own men could not survive against the Navy's continuous bombardment. But it was as the small arms and carbine fire restarted and then intensified twicefold, that Lieutenant Travers was killed in action. He died as he'd lived, trying to fight to see justice for his men.

Out in front of Travers, and with most of his men dead as well, Sergeant Zwelleger led a southbound retreat to link up with Sergeant Hewitt's men when he was shot in the leg. He stayed down in the muddy grass, but water gushed through the undergrowth, covering him with mud, the backflow tugging him towards the river. Masterson's prophesy was about to come true, although Zwelleger never imagined he would die by drowning during a gun fight.

The river actually gave Sergeant Hewitt a crazy idea. He was effectively in command now that his lieutenant was dead. Thanks to Captain Hunter, Major Tithing had the numbers he needed to overrun Hewitt and his men's position. But, if he ordered his soldiers to make a staggered retreat to the shoreline, some might survive if they dove into the Mississippi and managed not to drown. Because if they didn't flee, all of them would surely be shot. It was time for desperate measures. Hewitt decided that the men who couldn't swim would lay down cover-fire for those who could and were willing to brave the river. At least the luckiest ones might get away. No one made it that far. Hunter's people were fast, their weapons deadly.

Up in their sharp-shooters perches, Sergeant Finch and Private Willows weren't capable of becoming mobile quickly enough. Willows watched a cannon ball from the *Hartford* break through Finch's treetop hideaway, disintegrating the entire tree and leaving nothing but burning timber. He swore then that he'd go down fighting. Lining up another shot in his rifle sight, Private Willows fired. The shot pierced the heart of Lt. Remick, who went down as Tithing's frightened horse suddenly jerked hard and away from the falling aide and his stumbling mount. A second later, Willows heard a shrill whistling sound in the air. He tried to dive out of his tree, but it was already too late.

By the time dawn broke over the smoky landscape, Tithing's command had now overrun the western positions along the riverbank to which Hewitt had tried to escape. They began to press east, but the fire from the *Hartford* had softened the land and the rain had soaked it. Lieutenant Nellis, one of Hunter's platoon commanders, was thrown completely out of his saddle as his horse lost its footing in the mud. They were cavalry, thus trained to remount their steeds to press the attack, but that plan hadn't worked out so well. Just the same, Nellis made a startling discovery as he fell over a bloodied body half-buried in the soggy ground. The fallen Rebel was actually Lieutenant Buck Travers! This was no foreign enemy they were fighting, Nellis realized. This was Captain Pratt's missing cavalry company!

But under the curtain of rain, the storm of cannon balls, and the hail of bullets, to whom could he report his discovery? *'Stay the course,'* his battalion commander had ordered. Tragically, that was all he could do.

Meanwhile, Lieutenant Pullman saw that Travers' men were all down, so he doubted that Cutter's platoon had held. His position left him only one recourse: his men would retreat in the direction of the fort. His bugler signaled his command, and the men began to fall back by squads. Then fire from the fort resumed, and they started taking hits from behind, as well as in front of them. Pullman's people were caught in a deadly crossfire between Winthrop's men and Tithing's people, all the while taking incoming fire from the *Hartford*.

In the fort, Corporal Ritter stood atop a wagon that overlooked the southern wall when he saw Pullman's platoon backing towards his position. "Don't let them near here, boys! Pour your fire on them now!"

He joined Private Gamble for the action, and with all the rest of Masterson's former squads, they riddled the rival platoon's ranks with bullets. But as Pullman and his men fell, Hunter's company, led by its captain and Major Tithing, were firing upon Ritter next!

The incoming cannon blasts from the Hartford had tracked up from the river to focus on the fort now. Holes blew open in the buildings. The porch of the plantation home Mr. Hutchinson had been fond of sitting out on to drink his whiskey exploded under long range fire. The rooftops of several of the buildings glowed with sparks trying to ignite during a lull in the rainfall. Corporal Hill ordered his squad to form a fire detail, and they ran with buckets of water hastily drawn from the well to keep from finding themselves burned out before they were blown up. Ritter's men could not help. Their acting commander, using all his people to defend the southern and western walls, had usurped Everts' squad and some of Crawford's people to aid in the defense. Outside, Tithing refused to slow his attack, and the *Hartford* didn't stop shooting.

As Captain Hunter's troop moved up into range of the fort, they immediately drew fire. When Hunter was shot and went down, a flicker of fear crossed Tithing's face. Then, anger replaced it. He swore no sooner than he saw the fort's defending forces were clad in blue uniforms just like his own. *We're here to rescue these fools! Maybe they're too shell-shocked by Farragut's barrage to know any better,* Tithing thought. He wanted to believe anything that would excuse these men – *his* men. But, perhaps they weren't his men. Maybe they never were.

He had one very distasteful option: he could surrender to a subordinate, providing Pratt or Winthrop – whomever was inside – took the chance to prove himself an ally, instead of an enemy, if that was indeed still the case. Or he could continue to shoot it out while the *Hartford* leveled both forces' positions. Tithing didn't believe any man dispatched through all the woods, foliage, and flooding, while under heavy bombardment, would survive and reach Farragut. So his only hope was to pacify the fort and lead an evacuation out from its northern boundaries. The Navy could then level the place for all Tithing cared. Meanwhile, he'd lose no more men trying to circumnavigate the compound under heavy fire.

Visibility constantly obscured by either smoke or the intermittent rain, Tithing couldn't chance it that his flags would not be seen. He called for his bugler and got the message out, but the firing from the plantation-fort continued uninterrupted. *So be it,* Tithing thought to himself. He'd been embarrassed by his company commanders long enough. It was long past the time that he showed them who was really in charge.

Chapter 81

Water flowed in from under the floor in the cellar beneath the school that cramped together more than forty mixed gender refugees who were indignantly being held prisoner down there with no privacy, and in their own excrement. If death by drowning wasn't frightening enough, death from smoke inhalation became the alternative choice as cannon fire from the *Hartford* hit the school building, setting the dry wood in the interior on fire. No longer concerned with gagging from the foul smell, the prisoners now coughed and choked on the smoke that drifted down upon them.

Mr. Leahy and Old Man Hart had had enough. They decided together that Leahy would risk climbing the ladder to determine the location of their guards. As they expected, he reported that all the enemy soldiers were engaged in battling their attackers or the fires. They spared no one to watch the prisoners. Leahy would gather the men who could fight, and they'd make a stand for the sake of their women and children. They had no weapons, but in a charge they might take some. They had nothing to lose by trying now. Margaret Hutchinson wiped the tears from her eyes, hugging her sons Mark and Luke before they followed Leahy. Then she pleaded with Emma, "You go. Get up there and protect Rachael. I'll follow you with Rebecca. We're going to have to run."

Rachael scrambled up the ladder, and Emma followed her out of the water that now lapped against their lower legs. When they were clear, Margaret motioned for the late Mr. Rawling's wife, Anne, to take their baby and go next. The smoke grew thicker, and everyone's coughing worsened. In the greatest distress was the baby, who screamed and cried. She'd made it up half the rungs when a cannon ball tore through the building and exploded at the cellar's entrance hatch. The ladder instantly shattered, and the bodies toppled backwards and into the water. Mrs. Rawlings and her baby disappeared altogether.

Old Man Hart picked himself up out of the water with support of Margaret and another woman. Using ladder fragments, disassembled pieces of his walking crutches, and some cloth torn from the hem of Margaret's dress, he tried to reassemble the ladder.

Rachael Hutchinson appeared above them at the edge of the opening, shaking and bleeding from her close encounter with all the shrapnel from the blast. "Mother! Mother!" she cried above the sharp cracks of gunfire and crashing cannon balls.

"I'm alright, Sweetheart. It's alright. Now listen to me please! Take this! Hurry!"

Rachael climbed down the part of the ladder that remained attached to the cellar hatch. Her mother handed her a small jewelry case that she'd taken with her when Davis had ordered that they ran and immediately hide in the now-flooding shelter. "Now go with Emma. Leave this place. Get away from all the fighting. We'll meet up with you in the city. Find Abigail, Mark, Luke, and your father. You hear me? You tell them we'll meet you in Baton Rouge!"

Chapter 82

Steven Crawford excitedly scrambled up the stairs that led out of the crypt and stumbled back into the church as the ground shook from the impact of dozens of cannon balls. They'd hit upon the mother load of all treasures but the whole place was getting blown to hell. He needed to find his captain and get his orders. They would never get the wagons loaded and make it out alive. For Crawford's part, greed warred with his survival instincts. Now he just wanted someone to give him orders so he wouldn't have to decide what to do next.

As he tripped up the steps to look for Winthrop, he fell across several bodies that had been laid out on the floor of the sanctuary. The handful of ruby gems he'd planned to show his captain spilled, and he scrambled on his knees to recapture every last one of them. With the church's roof ablaze, Crawford began to cough from the smoke. He pulled a bandana over his mouth and nose to lessen its impact, but it still stung his eyes. However, he sensed movement only a few feet away from where he knelt. The body of a young woman shifted and then rolled off the corpse of the man on whom she'd fallen.

Crawford drew his gun as he stood, trying to protect himself and fearing he'd begun to see ghosts amongst the flames. But the girl didn't move again. Instead, the man staggered to his feet, a light stream of blood dripping from his mouth, and one hand clutching at dark holes in his chest, the other feeling for his back. He wore civilian clothing soaked in blood.

Crawford spotted a gun still in its holster at his side, but the fatally wounded man didn't make a move for his sidearm or any other piece to an impressive array of other killing instruments Crawford could now see the man carried on his person. Instead, he looked sad, his eyes glistening as he studied the body of the slain girl at his feet. He seemed about to drop to his knees and cry when he noticed Crawford.

Crawford nodded to the wounded man's weapons belt. "You, lose Sam Colt. Then the rest of that getup. Very slowly." Then he shouted down the stairwell. His voice cracked. "Buckley get up here! On the double!"

The young private scurried up the stairs, dropped the diamond studded necklace he carried, and quickly reached for his revolver when he spotted the nightmarish figure of the bloodied man who stood before his corporal.

"Cover him," Crawford ordered. "I need to find the captain and get our orders. Maybe he'll want to trade hostages for our freedom. It will take some kind of miracle if we can get out of this hell-hole alive."

As if to make his point, a cannon ball exploded just outside the church. Shattered bits of wood and shrapnel penetrated the building, impaling Crawford's flesh in a dozen places. His scream ended in a blood-gurgling moan. He fell before a giant crucifix, his pile of rubies spilling onto the floor once more.

A paralyzed Buckley stared at his fallen squad leader as Christopher Pratt drew his weapon and shot Buckley between the eyes. With a crack of thunder and a blue flash, the private's body tumbled back towards the staircase that descended into the crypt. Then, shaking his head, Christopher knelt down and placed a hand on Abigail's shoulder. His face registered his anguish as he gently closed her eyes. Shaking with rage, immovable resolve settled over him as he rose. Christopher stumbled for the exit of the burning building and into the hail of cannon fire and heavy rain. Mortally wounded, Pratt glanced back over his shoulder at the body of Abigail Hutchinson, and then pressed on.

Chapter 83

If Pratt was surprised that he was still alive, he felt even more surprised when he saw Abigail again. She stood directly in front of him. At first, he thought she'd come back as an angel. He waved at the smoke, wiped away the blood and soot from his eyes, and looked again. No. Not Abigail, after all. He recognized Rachael Hutchinson as she stood in the doorway. Two years older, she looked like a mirror image of her sister at the age when Christopher had first met her.

The girl stopped short when she spotted Pratt, not recognizing him immediately, maybe due to his new goatee, but likely and especially because of the bloody mess he appeared as now.

"Rachael. It's me, Christopher, a friend of your sister's."

"Abigail? Where is she?"

He shook his head. "I'm sorry."

Then Rachael looked beyond him to the bodies that lay on the floor. She stifled a cry as she recognized her sister and her father, both dead. She fearfully backed away from Christopher.

"Hold on now. I didn't kill them." He fumbled in his pockets for the metallic badge he'd carried with him for the past few days. "But I'm going to bring the hand of justice down hard on the man who did.

"Here, I want you to take this," Christopher said as he then removed a small, black keepsake box from his haversack. "One day it might explain some things you may wish to know about your sister. I'm sure Abigail would have wanted you to have it." He extended a bloody hand to Rachael, who grabbed the box and then backed up another step. "I know I won't ever be leaving here," Pratt said, his voice somber and sad.

Emma joined the young girl. When she looked over the blood-covered Christopher Pratt, suspicion and fear registered in her eyes. "Rachael, what are you doing? We thought we lost you, Honey. C'mon. We must be getting."

291

The girl looked back at the bodies of her slain father and sister, before returning her gaze to Pratt.

"You have to go, Rachael. Now," he said softly.

She reluctantly heeded his words. With Emma tugging on her arm, she turned and dutifully followed her out. They made their way back behind the slave quarters to circle around the rear side of the plantation house, finally reaching an exit in the perimeter wall that had been blown open by munitions fire. Unguarded, it led towards the bayou, an area the attacking Union force had elected not to traverse under enemy fire.

Corporal Ritter had all of his forces concentrating on defending the southern wall. Some of those men were laid out dead or dying on the compound's central grounds now, as were some of the men from the congregation who'd tried to take their weapons.

Rachael recognized the body of Mr. Leahy as she ran past.

Chapter 84

Major Tithing lay still where he fell – at least momentarily. Covered in mud from the rapidly deteriorating ground outside the Secessionist compound, he allowed himself some satisfaction for having led his troops this far. Now he had to finish his job and sweep this insurrection away before everyone was swept away by the soggy deluge.

Lieutenant Nellis reached Tithing's position and brought up two squads along with him.

"We can't get the cover or even the footing we need to break down the front door and get inside these walls, Lieutenant. Anyway, not in step with making good time," Tithing said. "But we can go *under* these walls. They won't be expecting that." The plan was inspired by brilliance – or desperation.

Using only their hands, the soldiers clawed their way through the mud and under Hutchinson's fortification of the compound. Against the wall as they were, Ritter's men in the fort couldn't see Tithing's people and didn't know to fire at them.

Soaked in mud from head to toe, Tithing brought half a platoon in behind Ritter's line. The corporal was still firing over the wall when he caught a bullet in his back. He dropped his carbine, clawing for where he felt the pain. One hand recoiled, burned from where the still smoldering gunpowder of Nellis' shot had taken him. And then he tumbled off the open wagon he'd taken for his firing position.

At his side, Private Gamble whirled around, shocked that they were being fired at from behind and horrified they'd just lost the most inspiring young non-com left in the whole company. Instantly, Gamble caught a bullet in his open mouth, and then three more in his chest as Tithing's small force took full advantage of the element of surprise and rushed the wall's defenders. Behind them, the tunnels they'd dug under the fortification walls had begun to fill with flood waters that were steadily growing deeper. The structures on the western perimeter started to sink. Then rain poured down and the fighting continued.

Corporal Everts dropped his rifled weapon, dove off another wagon into calf-high water, fell hard, then rose and sprinted for his life. He hoped to make it to the north wall or, at the very least, find a place to hide. He didn't understand what had happened. Somewhere along the line, he'd followed Masterson and Talbot into this crazy mission, of which he'd made up his mind that his own Lieutenant Holloway would never have joined in on. But the lieutenant was long dead. And now Everts was going to die. And for what?

Chapter 85

Daniel Winthrop risked climbing the watch tower in the center of the fort amidst all the bullets and bombs falling about him. He surveyed the chaos of his own creation. His arm ached where Davis had wounded him. He'd tied on a bandana as a makeshift tourniquet to stave off the bleeding. Other than that, Daniel had not been touched by the maelstrom raging around him. Amazingly, the structure he'd mounted had only been nicked by small arms fire, and it still stood intact on elevated, dry ground. Many buildings exploded or burned bright, like the plantation's big house, while others flooded. The rain kept the fires manageable, as well as Hill's people, who constantly carried buckets of water they refilled from the other buildings they were trying to save from collapsing in the flooding. But more water kept on coming.

While Winthrop only ascended to make a brief surveillance of the situation in order to weigh his dwindling options, his timing allowed him to observe the dark shapes of soldiers actually scrambling into the compound with the water emerging from *beneath* its walls. He thought he saw one fire and Ritter go down. "Will? No!" Angrily, Winthrop fired back, felling a man into the flooding. He dove off of the watchtower as it destabilized in the mud and the answering muzzle-flashes pierced the dense smoke with returning fire to answer Winthrop's shots.

He hit the ground hard, splashing through the puddles, and losing his grip on his pistol. As he reached for it, a booted foot stomped on his outstretched hand.

"When I stoop down low enough to crawl through all this muck, look who I find." Major Tithing's voice was followed by the unmistakable sound of a gun's hammer being locked into firing position, the business end of the weapon leveled directly at Daniel Winthrop's face, along with his superior's contemptuous gaze.

"Winthrop! Don't you dare move or so help me I'll fill you with every round I've got left!" Tithing advanced on his shocked and seemingly cornered prey. Explosions went off all around him and the fires burned, but none so bright as the desire for vengeance that burned in the battalion commander's eyes.

However, Daniel Winthrop offered a bluff. He still had something to bargain with. "Major, Sir! I was about to report for duty, Sir, but I made an error, and my troop went off-course. We ran into these Rebels and engaged them here. I sent a messenger to Baton Rouge for help, but you must not have received the dispatch. My men would have prevailed here and had prisoners for you, Sir." Winthrop nodded to indicate Leahy's body, and several more beyond it. Some only boys. "But we had a revolt, and then we came under this bombardment. But the others we captured are still locked up in another building these insurrectionists use for tactical briefing. You'll find all the rest of them just across this compound, Sir."

"Winthrop, your men are representing my country in uniform, and you were under siege when I found you – by militia armed with Union weapons, no less. As it turns out, Lieutenant Nellis reported the opposing force you engaged was Captain Pratt's! Then when I arrived and my men saw your uniforms, *I* even tried to surrender to *you!* – just so we could sort this all out. But *your* men fired upon *me*. How do you explain that? You can't, can you? You thieving, little bastard!

"As soon as it's safe to do so, you're going to be taken out of this compound, read your formal charges, and then stood up against a wall and shot like the dirty son of a bitch you are!" Tithing already red in the face, glared at Winthrop with rage in his eyes.

The squads with whom he'd entered the fort were now spreading out, ducking behind burning wagons, and maneuvering between panicked horses. Catching Winthrop's people in a crossfire and dodging their bullets, they tried to avoid the cannon fire from the *Hartford* at the same time. Winthrop, guarded by Tithing and Nellis alone, was the only one to spot the dark silhouettes of two new men, stalking the major and his man from behind them.

Winthrop's never-failing confidence fortified him. He grinned. "Your ideas sound like fun, Sir, but I'm sorry I have to ruin your great plan."

Three muzzle flashes from John Hill's gun appeared only seconds before his face became recognizable. He emerged from the smoke, still firing. Tithing and Nellis fell to the earth dead, both shot in the back.

Hill started to smile, as did Winthrop. Daniel's expression quickly tensed to one of alarm. The other figure behind Hill still approached with stealth. Hill, who read the signs in his captain's face, began to turn around, when his whole face blew off from the inside out, in one great burst of mutilated, bloody flesh.

The wreckage that had once been Captain Christopher Pratt stood behind the fallen corporal, who'd toppled over and collapsed in front of Daniel Winthrop, the latter remaining on all fours. Pratt tossed aside a smoking double-barreled shotgun, then drew one of his revolvers.

Winthrop glanced away from Pratt to his own gun. Only a few feet away, the weapon remained where Tithing had kicked it, so far clear of any water. At least it didn't appear as if the powder had gotten wet.

Pratt saw it, too, but his aim never wavered from the face of his enemy. He drew the hammer back. "Go for it, Winthrop. Makes no difference to me."

Fires raged around the two men, revealing Pratt's barely contained rage in splashes of firelight. "But I was there." He nodded, his gesture indicating the direction of the church. "I saw what you did. And I know in a hundred years it could never have been worth it – worth her life – any of their lives. Or the lives of my men back in Georgia two years ago. Yes. I know you were responsible for that, too. At last, I know all about *you*." He sighed, his wounds draining his remaining strength. "There's nothing left to say. It's all too late."

From where he'd been frozen on the ground, Captain Daniel Winthrop only nodded. There *was* nothing left to say, he realized. He simply exhaled his last breath.

"Get up!" Pratt barked.

As Winthrop rose to his feet, his hand drawing out a hidden gun from his boot, a shot rang out in the night. To everyone else, desperately struggling to stay alive, it was but just one more shot. Christopher Pratt drew his other gun and fired off six additional rounds. Then five more from the weapon with which he'd begun

Daniel Winthrop's execution. Every shot hit home, impacting Winthrop an even dozen times. Eleven shots more than were necessary to kill this nihilistic man's twisted dreams. Though for Pratt, these were the last shots he'd ever need to fire.

Throwing his guns aside to fall abandoned upon the hallowed ground, Christopher Pratt staggered away from the compound's watchtower, leaving yet another bullet riddled corpse in one of the many pools of blood beneath it. A fitting monument to Daniel Winthrop's legacy.

Captain Pratt clumsily bent to pick a handful of flowers, planted at some time in the past to make the now besieged fort seem more home-like. A ridiculous thing to do right in the middle of a battle, he realized. But the living would continue to fight. The dead only needed to get on with the business of dying. To that end, Christopher Pratt pushed on, making his way back to the flooded and sinking house of God.

Chapter 86

With no clean air left to breathe and with only smoke above them and water below, the wounded, the infirm, and the innocent died together, victims of the fire and the flooding.

The flow of water gushed in to and out through the storage cellar, the crypt, and the areas beneath the rest of the plantation's various buildings. Between the flooding of the river onto Louisiana's wetlands and the relentless pounding of the *Hartford's* guns, the whole of the plantation-fort began to sink into the water-logged mire. As it was being swallowed, streams and narrow rivers sprang to life, their paths north and east of the Mississippi, shifting the earth and creating small lakes.

Rachael and Emma struggled unsuccessfully to keep from falling into the muddy flow. Men still killed other men all around them. The rain persisted, and anything that wasn't too wet to burn caught on fire. No one seemed to notice the two women as they struggled through the mud and flowing water. They reached the main south gate losing their shoes, the mud sucking at their feet and legs, which made it difficult to move forward to safety. The front wall had been breached, failing to keep the invaders out. But the women were no longer trapped within.

Somehow, they made slow but steady progress away from the fort, but then Rachael stopped abruptly. "Emma, wait! We need to circle around... make our way back through the bayou. Then we can rendezvous with the family in Baton Rouge, just as mother instructed."

"Darlin', there be no way we's making it on foot through the bayou. And there be no way around all dis." She waved her hand in the direction of the ongoing battle. "And it be too dangerous by da river." Emma struggled to breathe as she spoke. "We be making the push for New Orleans. It be our only hope now."

Suddenly her body went rigid, an expression of shock on her face. "Oh no." Then, she pawed at her back before she fell face-first

299

into the mud.

Rachael ran to her side, and dropped to her knees. "Emma? Emma! No!" The darkness prevented her from seeing where Emma had been hit or the extent of her injury.

The older woman moaned as she looked up at Rachael. "Promise me you be heading south now, Honey. Promise me!"

"I will. I swear. Oh, Emma!"

"You be goin' now. Quickly. Emma will just rest here. You be gone, please. Go!"

Rachael staggered to her feet, shocked and frightened at being all alone. Then the fifteen-year-old took off, running for deeper cover in the nearby woods.

Rachael knew not whether she'd been running for only minutes or a full hour, but she'd spent all of her energy and then some. Finally she stumbled, fell, and then tried to catch her breath. Her clothing was damp with sweat and sticking to her, and her muscles ached from running. Rachael didn't know if she could continue without food and water. Knowing she needed at least water to survive, she decided to angle back towards the river once she recovered her strength. She could barely hear the noise from the gunfire now, and no longer smelled smoke from the compound's fires.

Rachael was about to let herself feel relieved when she was startled by a Union soldier, who emerged from the trees behind her. Exhausted, Rachael had no fight left in her, and even less strength to start running again. She figured it was all over for her and she'd wind up being killed here and now – or worse.

But the soldier smiled. "Relax. I'm not going to hurt you. I ran, too. I don't have any more friends back there either. So, it's just the two of us now. So why would I want to hurt you or make you fear me? You're the only company I've got. My name is Bob... Bob Masterson."

"Rachael Hutchinson."

"Have some water from my canteen, Rachael, but drink slowly. Too much, too fast, and you'll get sick. And we can't afford to waste our water," the big man said with a faint smile.

"I must get to New Orleans," the girl said.

"*We* need to get to New Orleans," Masterson said. "I've got this water, a little bit of dried meat. What have you got there?" He indicated the knapsack Rachael carried.

"Money my family gave me so I'd survive," Rachael responded. "Are you going to rob me?"

"No. I won't do that. I'm not a particularly successful thief. But let me see what you've got."

"Why?" she whispered, fear in her large, blue eyes.

"I have some experience with this world, you know. Maybe I can make a suggestion or two you'll find useful if I know what resources you have. If I've learned anything in recent days, it would be something about survival."

Rachael sighed, too tired to stand or to run. Masterson was armed, and he could shoot her if he wanted. So he didn't need to lie to her. He could do anything he wanted to her and she would be unable to stop him.

Rachael took out the small keepsake box given to her by her mother and she opened it. She found no money or jewels. In her haste, her mother must have grabbed the wrong box. Inside, Rachael found a stack of Abigail's correspondence and her journal. Some of the letters were from someone named Daniel Winthrop, the others from Christopher Pratt.

Suddenly, Rachael remembered that Pratt had passed a similar box to her when she'd found him inside the burning church with Abigail's body and that of her father. She'd shoved it in her satchel. A quick look inside and Rachael discovered that it, too, contained letters from her sister, Winthrop, and Pratt.

Masterson, watching her, laughed when he saw the confusion on her face. "It figures. Some treasure," he said shaking his head. "Some treasure."

Chapter 87

Wednesday, 28 May, 1862

Status Update: Subjugation of Louisiana

Following the murder of a Federal officer and the suspicious disappearance of three more, Baton Rouge was subjected to a modest bombardment by the USS Hartford during mid-morning hours.

Intended only to punish insurgents and turn local support against them in the interest of protecting private property from further damage, casualties were kept minimal. Civilians had been warned in advance of the pending bombardment and most have temporarily evacuated.

There is strong concern that the advance force sent by the Army has failed to maintain order on the ground. The US Navy has troops for short siege operations, but not a prolonged occupation.

It is the position of the Navy to demand that US Army Colonel Thomas Cahill receives the further support he has requested by way of another supporting regiment and, to that end, request that Brigadier General Williams comes here with all due haste.

Cahill's regiment, undermanned and having lost one of its leading commanders, now has but one battalion being directed by a Cavalry Captain Jonathon Talbot, who has been effective but still leaves questions lingering about his experience.

To maintain a hold here on the water, the Navy requires strong support on the ground.

I certify the above to be factual:

Admiral David S. Farragut, USN

But the quest for the lost Hutchinson bounty is far from over!

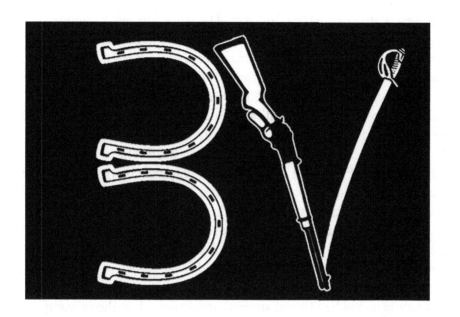

The story continues when in the year 2016, the drug cartel war has exploded into downtown Baton Rouge, Louisiana!

Buried Values: The Library brings back the hunt for a cursed bounty full of valuables-gone-missing since Daniel Winthrop had lost them during the Civil War. The story follows a young lady who is assigned a mission she does not understand. Chosen deliberately because she is inexperienced, the girl is continuously manipulated and lied to while the nation's security is put in danger as rival factions of an organized crime family seek to redefine their relationship with the international drug cartels. Things continue to escalate so far, as to even put the office of the President of the United States at risk. But while this young professional is tasked to infiltrate one of the most influential and entrenched crime families in the South since she appears nearly identical to the Mafia daughter, unexpected results occur as sex, drugs, money and power combine to cause her to stray from the course. Then tragedy leads her to a newfound obsession for revenge her handlers could not have ever foreseen, and a good girl turns very bad.

All hell is unleashed by the storm that follows when the mission also involves an adventurous archaeology professor with his own suspect reasons for seeking the lost treasure. He is caught in the crossfire with his misguided students, who are first told it's all only for a college internship opportunity, but start getting eliminated as the bodies begin to fall. After their popular teacher disappears, six Louisiana State students will bind together to complete his quest to recover a fortune in lost treasure on their own, while the two last honest cops in Baton Rouge attempt to save them as a Class Five Hurricane bears down, and something worse is yet to come.

With the descendants of Bob Masterson, Rachael Hutchinson, and Daniel Winthrop's families back at each other's throats again, a young woman's survival will hinge on a choice: will she fight for justice, or will she fight for only what is best for herself? As she learns the two can never coincide, all will learn what it takes to make a good girl turn really bad.

Told in a blistering action-adventure narrative, Buried Values: The Library digs hard into our true human nature and its regards to sex, love, honor, patriotism, politics, and faith, as well as one's loyalty to family and commitment to public service, versus one's commitment to self. Dare to embark on this dark journey to discover enlightenment.

The Truth has Value. Class is just an Act.

Please enjoy this exclusive excerpt:

Exclusive excerpt from *BURIED VALUES: The Library!*

Tony met Andy Tran on the steps to the library about 10 a.m. the next morning. He wanted to make sure he made up for any lost time the other evenings' many distractions caused his progression with the research. Meanwhile, he held back from telling anyone that he'd lost the letters. He would continue trying to rectify his mistake he made with Naomi on his own. But he had not been able to get in contact with her for two nights already. She didn't answer his calls and successfully dodged him at home. But he'd persistently keep trying later.

So Tony was all ready to get down with new business when he met with his co-collaborator. "Okay, we have fighting, victims, signs of civilians and Union cavalry….. and nothing," Tony reiterated. "Does this make any sense? Who do you think they were fighting?" Tony asked, trying to gauge where Andy's thoughts on this were taking him. Neither of them mentioned the fact that each had come to suspect that Hughes had involved them in a lot more than an archaeological expedition. If Andy was as nervous as Tony about everything that had happened to their little group in the immediate days' past, he too acted as if he only wanted to start moving forward that morning.

Andy stared at Tony hard for a moment while he must have been collecting his thoughts. But he did not put a voice to them. His mouth adjusted and readjusted, but mostly remained clenched tight as the young man apparently wrestled with and then came to a decision. "Sara had a third of the collected letters," Andy said. "Or journal entries," he corrected himself, finishing his cigarette so he could enter the library. "Maybe wherever she went missing, she took the clues we need with her." He flicked the butt onto the ground.

Tony was disappointed in his friend's evasive answer and reflected on the strange disappearances of several members of the team, the ransacking of Professor Hughes' office, and Colin's report of official-looking bureaucrats inserting themselves into their investigation without an invitation – not to mention the strange threatening e-mail and telephone call to his teacher's office. "Sara wouldn't go off on some mission to expose all this without us…" Tony's voice trailed off for a moment as he pondered things further. "We make decisions carefully, and as a group. We all bonded in this endeavor. I don't think any member of this team would go sneaking around individually. Would they? Plus Sara should know that she'd get in plenty of trouble for having the stolen archival materials just like the rest of us would. I've been getting to know her a little as we worked together." Yet Tony's doubt had already been with him. "But what if she's working with someone else?" he asked aloud.

"It's hard to imagine anyone else knowing about this," Andy said. "Doctor Hughes said that he was the very first to receive the letters and handle any and all examinations of this particular collection except for when he passed it to us. Add on to that, and I'm only guessing here, but I think that as soon as the school officially acquired any access to these documents, Hughes pulled them off the 'available-for-study list' for his own personal use. Besides, if work examining these letters had ever been thoroughly enough done before, Hughes would've just consulted the research rather than hired the six of us," Andy reasoned. "He doesn't really have a reason to lie. While I can't say for sure whether we can trust the prof, from where I stand, Colin is actually more suspicious. He disappeared at the same time that both of our other missing colleagues had, but he's the only one who came back."

Maybe my admiration for the leadership of these older boys is blinding me? Tony thought back on his conversation with his professor two days ago at the hospital. 'You mustn't trust anyone,' Professor Hughes had warned him. Tony decided he would consider a little longer whether or not to bring Andy up to date about the phone call to his instructor's office. There wasn't much he could have told Andy anyway. But later he would need to follow up on that and check out the bar and grill or whatever kind of establishment the mysterious phone call to Dr. Hughes' office had originated from. "So why are we working here today?" Tony asked instead, changing the subject as the pair walked into Hill Library's protected government record archives section after their identities

310

were checked against Dr. Hughes' list of personnel he'd provided access for and they'd signed in with the building's security.

"The letters we've been reading started referencing a Captain Daniel Winthrop, right?"

"Yeah," Tony responded, somewhat puzzled.

"Well, it seems Christopher Pratt was also one to go missing and Abigail found someone new. She seems to be the type who loves a man in uniform."

"Alright." Tony thought his voice betrayed him and that he must have sounded bored – because he was, and this was all old news to him by now.

"Well, the promotion and payroll records just might reveal who this Winthrop character was. I mean we know she's not writing to a Confederate officer to come rescue her from her father's merry flock as they flee Georgia, right? They'd all be looked down upon for having not stayed and defended their new country and the State of Georgia. So it seems that our girl can't stay on the South's side."

"You think she was a traitor? Or a spy?"

"Nuh-uh. I don't."

"Then you suspect what I do, don't you? Winthrop was the traitor and led forces who were at least wearing the Federal uniform when they met their end, and against another fellow officer's unit who they engaged? Pratt's most likely." From what Tony had been reading, the story could have continued to evolve in that direction. This was as good of theory as any.

"That theory's supported by Colin and Jim seeing no signs of the Confederates ever fighting in Old Town," Andy said. "The military action that's popularly known of took place several miles north of here. And besides Doctor Hughes, our two classmates are presumably the most experienced explorers who have been down there to date, right? Davina and I didn't pick up on anything contrary to that either. There were no Southern-style sabers, no engraved weapons, rank insignias, or uniform tatters reported on the human bodies or even on the horse saddle remains – nothing of the sort. Now a lot could be buried by repeated flooding. So we'll start the dig to discover anything further on that front.

"But if Confederate soldiers were already in position to defend the civilians, they'd be laid out with the bodies of the non-combatants we already found. Since the dead civilians weren't looked after, Southern soldiers wouldn't have been either. If they followed Union forces in, then they'd have the element of surprise, but the Federal troops seemed to have had the benefit of cover and a chance to entrench. It would follow that there'd have been some Confederate casualties found in some of the flanking buildings, right? Those results might have also occurred even if it had been a rout. And there'd be no where to take cover from a cavalry charge once they vacated the fort, perhaps to join up with other units assigned to the Barracks. And even a one-sided Southern victory like Fredericksburg was hardly bloodless for the Army of Virginia. Some of Louisiana's Confederates would have died in the fort and be left with the civilian dead who weren't buried either. So any scenario I can imagine happening here was part of a disorganized melee. Both sides should have lost lives, but it looked like the South never fought down here. Instead, we have evidence of death for only Federal troops and mostly unarmed Secessia civilians. It had to be an insurrection inside the forces fighting with the Union."

"Well, maybe it was the Indians?" Tony offered with a half-turned up smile.

Andy showed a second of amusement with his friend's remark, but then reminded him, "That still doesn't tell us what Daniel Winthrop was really up to. Let's crack open some very old records and see if we can't find out."

For the next few hours, time seemed to be slipping away from them as they combed through officer rosters, death records, and official correspondence until their vision grew blurry and the realization that it was nearly four o'clock and they hadn't eaten dawned on them.

Andy was startled by the time for another reason. "Darn it! I totally forgot about my Tuesday-Thursday class!" Then he stumbled upon what he was looking for. "Wait. Here it is!"

Captain Daniel Winthrop was a Union Cavalry officer in command of a scouting company under Major Kenneth Tithing's mounted battalion. He'd even served with Christopher Pratt, though the two officers were assigned to different companies. But the two men would have definitely known each another.

The reinforcement of those facts thrust a lot of possibilities into Tony's mind – some of them rather heroic and some others rather distasteful where it concerned whatever finally went down in Old Town. Maybe Winthrop went to rescue Pratt's old girlfriend? But maybe he instead went there to eliminate the refugees, using Abigail's correspondence to help him locate where her father resettled his followers. But why?

Of course! They took a bounty-full of valuables. They must have when they fled Georgia as they knew they might not ever be able to come back. Tony didn't think Andy had realized this, but whoever had been strong-arming his professor must have. Hughes wasn't performing for an archaeological autopsy. He was preparing for a grave robbery!

In the meanwhile, Daniel Winthrop was probably the first to try, but Tony now thought for certain that the conspiring captain wouldn't be the last.

Just then a scream pierced the stillness of the library, followed by a few more screams belonging to several different voices. Curious, Tony and Andy closed their books and rushed downstairs to see what all the commotion was about. A door was open to the staff-only rooms and a young employee was backing away, pointing at a new materials transportation bin, shaking with fear and panic in her eyes.

Tony couldn't help himself and he ran right through the open door and jumped right over a counter that partitioned off the staff-only area, Andy closely following him. Packed in amongst all the newest books in a large, rolling container tub was Jim Dent's body dressed only in his undershorts, a bullet hole in his stomach and another in his chest above where his heart had been. He was laid out on top of the blood-stained corpse of Gunther Krupp who was just one huge, red mess.

Both boys could not believe what they were seeing. Library employees had begun crying.

Until one gathered herself together. "I'm sorry, but you boys will have to step away now and wait for the police to arrive from the front lobby area. This library is being locked down immediately and we've been instructed to let no one leave," came the choked-back instructions from a regular staff librarian in her upper-middle ages. "Law enforcement will want to question everyone who is in the library today."

SPECIAL THANKS
&
ACKNOWLEDGEMENTS

There were so many friends and professionals who have helped bring Buried Values to life and whom I'd really like to thank for the contributions they have made along the way in this journey of mine to becoming a newly published author that I cannot easily name everyone here, all at once.

Please look to my acknowledgements feature on BuriedValues. com and let me know if you feel I've mistakenly forgotten you. I will also do my best to personally thank everyone. The acknowledgement page will be continuously updated and new aspiring writers may also find useful links to many industry professionals who might help them publish their own works as well. Online you will find links to these professional services that have helped tremendously towards bringing Buried Values to you.

ABOUT THE AUTHOR

Joshua Adam Weiselberg has grown sicker and angrier with humanity over every passing year. Buried Values came to be written as the author's weapon of choice for going to war.*

The alleged love affair with romance falters time after time next to raw sexuality. Or the romance's establishment is founded in so much deceit, so one or both partners can use each other to their own selfish advantage. There is little love with Buried Values.

Claims of religious faith should be discredited immediately as there is almost always no honesty accompanying them, hypocritically breaking their defenders' commandments for the sake of their most treasured Buried Values. It only takes opportunity to break the pretense of morality. Don't proselytize. Shut up!

Government and the dedicated service to its institutions were established as a necessary conduit for the altruism that builds and maintains civilization. But that defines it as a tool and there is no guarantee any tool will only be used for altruism. The author has seen enough and "had enough" of this tool being applied more often than not by those corrupted by their own Buried Values.

Reality is vulgar. The writing for this series is meant to demonstrate that and not be subtle at all in how it achieves this. Illustrated fiction can be escapist, fun, but examples of the actual facts *are* offensive. Buried Values are vulgar and offensive. This information does not require an apology.

*The Truth has Value. Class is just an Act.

Josh Weiselberg appears here in his role as a Western Re-enactor somewhat resembling Christopher Pratt in Louisiana after *he's* had enough and chosen to now only serve *his true Buried Values.*

Made in the USA
Middletown, DE
26 February 2022